S11? FOR

'If anyone's looking for the next big courtroom drama… look no
further. Murphy is your man'
– **Paul Magrath,** *The Incorporated Council
of Law Reporting Blog*

'Peter ... to

Also by Peter Murphy
Removal (2012)
Test of Resolve (2014)

The Ben Schroeder series
A Higher Duty (2013)
A Matter for the Jury (2014)

AND IS THERE HONEY STILL FOR TEA?

A BEN SCHROEDER NOVEL

PETER MURPHY

NO EXIT PRESS

First published in 2015 by No Exit Press,
an imprint of Oldcastle Books Ltd,
PO Box 394,
Harpenden, Herts,
AL5 1XJ
noexit.co.uk
© Peter Murphy 2015

ISBN
978-1-84344-401-5 (print)
978-1-84344-402-2 (epub)
978-1-84344-403-9 (kindle)
978-1-84344-404-6 (pdf)

2 4 6 8 10 9 7 5 3 1

Typeset in Garamond MT and Franklin Gothic Book
by Avocet Typeset, Somerton, Somerset TA11 6RT
Printed in Great Britain by Clays Ltd, St Ives plc

For more about Crime Fiction go to www.crimetime.co.uk / @crimetimeuk

Say, is there Beauty yet to find?
And Certainty? And Quiet kind?
Deep meadows yet, for to forget
The lies, and truths, and pain?... oh! yet
Stands the Church clock at ten to three?
And is there honey still for tea?

Rupert Brooke,
The Old Vicarage, Grantchester

1

Sir James Digby

OF THE DAYS OF my earliest childhood, before I started school, I remember little. I remember bright autumn days when the garden was covered with brown leaves fallen from the oak and sycamore trees which bounded the garden, which Sykes had not yet swept away. On breezy days, I watched as the leaves were swept up off the ground, and glided across the lawns haphazardly in the swirling eddies of the breeze. I imagined the leaves in a race, and traced a finishing line near the house with my shoe, and appointed myself judge of the winners. When the breeze was not strong enough for them to race without assistance, I would take Sykes's broom, which he always left propped up against the same corner of the garden shed, and furiously brush the leaves along the path towards the finishing line. I remember rainy days in winter, when I was not allowed in the garden, when I would sit in the living room on the sofa and watch the patterns made by the rain drops as they traced their paths down the window pane, and tried to guess which drop would be the first to disappear into the general dampness as it reached the wood of the window frame. I remember light summer evenings when it was difficult to go to sleep because it was not yet dark; hearing the voices of my parents, and their friends and the older children of their friends, in the garden below my window, the sound floating dreamily up to where I lay restless in bed. I remember that, before I did go to sleep on such evenings, I would hold my breath for some time – how long I do not know – allowing the sounds to pass through my head until they merged and lost all meaning; and that by this means I had the power to go in my mind to another place, in which there was no sound, a place which was still and had no limits at all. And I remember standing with my parents and with Roger on the dark platforms of the great railway stations of Manchester and Crewe when we went away for holidays, watching with awe as the huge steam locomotives puffed their way slowly to a stop, making more noise than should have been possible in the world, as they pushed their steam out and upwards towards the soot-coated glass of the roof high above.

I knew from an early age that my family was different. My father was always known as 'Sir Alfred'. All my friends' fathers were addressed as 'Mr' except for the one or two who were doctors. I knew that our house, an early eighteenth-century manor house in the countryside outside Clitheroe in the heart of the Ribble Valley, was far bigger than the houses most people lived in. I knew that we were unusual in having a household staff, though under my father's careful stewardship of our small estate it had dwindled to four: Mr Bevan, who helped my father to manage the business side of the estate, keeping accounts and dealing with the leases of our two or three tenant farmers; Sykes, who took care of the garden; Mrs Penfold, who cooked when we had visitors and took care of the inside of the house; and her husband, Mr Penfold, who took care of the outside of the house, and did odd jobs, and sometimes drove my father when he went to catch the train for London, or my mother when she had a lot of shopping to do and, without ever telling my mother, placed the odd bet for my father on the Cup Final or the Grand National. I learned that we were proud Lancastrians. Our coat of arms featured the red rose; we had seats at Old Trafford during the cricket season; and at dinner, when my father proposed the loyal toast, we claimed the privilege of toasting 'The King, the Duke of Lancaster'.

My parents explained to me that the Baronetcy was the family's reward for having backed the right side more than once in the various royal succession questions that kept recurring for more than a century after the Civil War. Generations later, we were still on good terms with the Royal Family. My parents knew the King and Queen and were their guests at garden parties and dinners. When we were old enough, Roger and I were introduced to them too, and I found them very charming. All this seemed normal to us. My father would talk about the King in much the same way as any man would talk about his friend. His title, 'Sir Alfred', was as much a part of him as the light gabardine raincoat and hat which he insisted on wearing everywhere and from which my mother could never part him. In any case, while I was proud of the Baronetcy, it was of no direct interest to me. I was born on 2nd November 1913. At that time, my brother Roger was almost four years old. It was always made clear to me that, as the older brother, he would inherit the title and with it, the responsibility of running the manor house and the estate. As the younger son I would enter a profession – the Army, the Church or the Bar – perhaps spending some time in one of the colonies.

I cannot remember ever resenting Roger for being my older brother. Indeed, I can truthfully say that the title never came between us once. We were extraordinarily close. When I was eight, he was sent away to his boarding school. But before that, we were constant companions. We roamed the estate together, fighting wars as Saxons, Crusaders, or Cavaliers against invisible Normans, Infidels, or Roundheads; batting for England, making centuries in the face of the most hostile Australian bowling. We spent many a long summer day down by the stream at the far end of the estate – which we called the river – lying on its banks tasting blades of grass; conducting expeditions to find the site of Toad Hall, wondering how Toad would have got from the river to the road to find a car to drive, and where the Rat lived, and where he kept the boat he would have used to make his way along the river, and where lay the entrance to the great forest where the more frightening animals had their lairs. How many days we spent together in this way I cannot say; just that it felt, at the time, like a whole lifetime of days. We had a language of our own – a mad combination of English without verbs, supplemented by a variety of human or animal noises picked up during our wanderings around the estate – which mystified our parents and, I am sure, must have caused them to suspect that their progeny were not quite right in the head. But if they did suspect such an affliction, they never said so. Even today I can remember some of the language, and I can have a conversation with Roger in my mind, one into which no living person can intrude.

After Roger went off to school, we carried on during school holidays for a few years as if nothing had ever interrupted us. My parents had decided that we would always go to different schools, and when my turn came to go, while the closeness remained, it necessarily changed. We had our own circles of friends, but we still spent some holidays together and we were regulars at Old Trafford during the cricket season. We shared a love of reading and I followed the trail of literature he left me: Sir Walter Scott and Daniel Defoe in childhood; and in adolescence Dickens and Edgar Allan Poe. I took on his love of poetry: he left me the Sonnets, of course, and Alexander Pope, Alfred Lord Tennyson, and Elizabeth Barrett Browning. Finally, as he left for his final year of school he led me to Boswell's *Life of Johnson*. He had loved it from the moment he picked it up, and I came to love it just as much. We practised talking to each other in Boswell's wonderful formal eighteenth-century English; ever afterwards I played Boswell to his Johnson, and we wrote our letters to each other in their style.

He wrote to me as he left for a month in France before going up to Cambridge.

London,
14 August 1927

Sir,
I am sensible of the great kindness with which you have favoured me since my arrival in Lancashire to prepare for my journey. I cannot allow that France is in any way superior to Lancashire, or its people in any way comparable to ours. But I shall endeavour to make a record of my travels which I undertake to submit to your perusal on my return, and it may be that I shall allow Mr Davies to publish it if sufficient terms can be agreed. I know not whether tea will be available to me there. A gentleman with whom I dined lately, and to whom I put the question, replied thus: 'Sir, I doubt that a leaf of tea is anywhere to be found in France'. 'Then Sir,' I remarked, 'it cannot be right to trust the inhabitants of that country, for no people ignorant of tea can be truly civilised.' A gentleman who had much travelled in France protested and insisted on the gentility of the French people. 'Nay, Sir,' I replied, 'I shall report to you about that matter on my return.' I doubt that I shall find myself in agreement with him.

I trust, my dear Sir, that I shall find you in good health on my return, and remain your humble and devoted servant,

Sam Johnson

I replied.

Digby Manor
20 August 1927

Sir,
Nothing could be more welcome to me than to receive your letter of the 14th instant with its habitual protestations of your high regard for

me, which I assure you, are fully reciprocated. I have reported to your friends at the Club the anxiety you entertain as to the conditions you may expect to find in France. The proposition that tea will be hard to find and, if found, likely to be of inferior quality, is universally allowed. But certain gentlemen inform me that there are wines whose virtues may provide some limited compensation for the sense of deprivation you will certainly encounter. I look forward with keen anticipation to your report of your travels, which I apprehend any publisher would gratefully adopt for public subscription. I expect you may find France somewhat different from the Hebrides, but I trust you will find the people just as civil. I await the pleasure of taking tea with you and dining at the Mitre on your return.

I remain, my dear Sir, your humble and respectful servant,

Jas. Boswell.

I idolised and adored Roger. He was my captain when we fought the Normans and when we made our centuries against Australia, and I followed his lead without question in everything we did. He was, throughout those early years, the rock on which my life was built.

2

1965
Wednesday, 3 March

PROFESSOR FRANCIS R HOLLANDER had not arranged for anyone to meet him at the airport. Apart from his solicitor Julia Cathermole, the Secretary of his Club, and the one or two colleagues who had to know, he had kept his plans to himself. It was not a social trip, and he was doing his best not to attract attention. If it were not for the interest he had recently aroused in the press, that would not have been a problem. Indeed, he might reasonably have assumed that his presence on board BOAC flight 247 from Washington DC to London Heathrow would pass entirely unnoticed. But as things were, he knew that the press might very well be lying in wait for him somewhere. In his mind he had created the spectre of a confrontation with reporters demanding a statement even before he boarded his flight in Washington. Mercifully, he had been spared that; there had been no obvious press presence there. But he had no way of knowing what awaited him when he touched down in London. It was not that he wanted to avoid the press; on the contrary, some carefully-planned publicity was exactly what he wanted and needed. But the operative words were 'carefully planned'. He had no desire to be jostled by a throng of reporters at the airport while he was tired and groggy. He preferred to meet them on his own terms – in central London, at a properly convened press conference, when he felt refreshed and awake.

Hollander was in his mid-thirties, tall and thin, with pale skin and thinning light brown hair brushed carefully back to reveal a prominent forehead. His habitually thoughtful look had resulted in a perpetually wrinkled brow. He had travelled, with no concession to the discomfort of the long flight, in his customary light brown suit, pale blue shirt with blue and yellow polka-dot bow tie, spectacles with light brown frames, and meticulously polished brown lace-up shoes – all of which he regarded as his trademark academic uniform. He had braced himself for an unwelcome reception, and had rehearsed a set speech a hundred times during the flight but, to his relief, when he emerged from Customs with his luggage into a cold, misty London morning, he was not aware of anyone paying particular attention to him. He closed his eyes and took a deep breath with a silent prayer of gratitude. But even so, when the man approached as he stood, shivering slightly, in the queue at the taxi rank, Hollander was not particularly surprised.

'Welcome to London, Professor Hollander,' the man said. 'I'm sure you don't want to spend all morning standing in this queue. Why don't you let me give you a lift?'

Hollander was about to offer his prepared speech, but stopped himself almost at once as he realised his error. He knew almost instantly that he was not dealing with the press. Hollander was not exactly an expert in such matters, but he had made several trips behind the Iron Curtain, certainly enough to know when he had a minder. The man who had approached him was of average height, well short of Hollander's own six feet three, but he was well built and carried no extra weight. He was dressed in a light grey raincoat, the belt tied tightly around his waist, and a slightly darker grey trilby hat with a black band around the rim. Hollander put his age at late forties or early fifties. He had both his hands stuffed into the pockets of the coat. Even through his irritation Hollander could not resist a momentary smile at the blatant stereotype of the hat and coat. His instincts were awake now, and the glance over his shoulder to his left, his blind side, was automatic. Sure enough, the stereotype was complete. An almost identically dressed second man stood a few feet away, apparently uninterested, doing his best to blend in with the groups of passengers leaving and arriving at the terminal. It doesn't matter where you are, he reflected; some things never change. He knew the drill. He had a minder – whether he wanted one or not.

'That's very kind of you,' Hollander replied, picking up his suitcase.

'My pleasure. Allow me.' The man relieved him deftly of the suitcase, leaving Hollander to carry only his brown patent leather briefcase. Hollander was soon grateful for the gesture as the man led the way at a fast pace across the access road, through a number of bleak open concrete spaces, and into the covered car park. As they approached the black Humber Hawk, the driver climbed smartly out of his seat. He was a small man, dressed in a dark blue suit and tie. Without a word, he took the suitcase from the minder and consigned it to the boot. The minder ushered Hollander into the back of the car on the driver's side before walking around the back of the car to take his own seat beside him on the passenger's side. The second man had disappeared somewhere along the route.

'My name is Baxter,' the man said, extending his hand, once the driver had left the car park and was threading his way towards the main trunk road leading into central London. Hollander nodded. He doubted the name was genuine, but everyone had to use some name or other, and it was of no consequence. He took Baxter's hand without enthusiasm.

'Where are you staying?'

'At my club – the Reform Club in Pall Mall.'

Baxter glanced up towards the driver, who indicated by a slight nod of the head that he had heard.

'Very nice. We will get you there as soon as we can. Let's hope the traffic's not too bad.'

They drove on in silence for some time. Hollander followed the road signs, noting that the driver was indeed taking the shortest route to the city centre. He tried to sit back and relax, but he was unsettled. The press would have been unwelcome, but at least he would have known exactly what they wanted. He could have answered a few questions, promised more in a few days' time, and fought his way through to a taxi. But with Baxter, he was in uncharted territory. Why were they taking such an interest in him? It could be good or bad; but it was certainly not simply neutral. Baxter had not brought a car to meet him at Heathrow for the pleasure of his company.

'Look, Baxter, I appreciate the ride into town, but ...'

Baxter turned towards him.

'Please don't be concerned, Professor,' he said. 'I am here to help you – together with those I work for, of course.'

'Help in what way? What interest do you have in helping me?'

Baxter smiled.

'I think you know that without my telling you,' he replied. 'But if I have to spell it out for you, we have a common interest in the outcome of the forthcoming legal action to be brought against you by Sir James Masefield Digby QC.'

Hollander turned his head away again to look straight ahead. Of course. He suddenly felt very stupid. How could they not take an interest? But the question was: what was their agenda? Whose side were they on? This was Digby's territory, after all. He felt any slight sense of security he had slipping away. The car's heater was beginning to have some effect and the windows were steaming up. With a gentle circular motion of the back of his right hand, he created a small area of clear vision on the side window to his right. But there was nothing worth seeing unless he kept looking straight ahead, past the driver, through the front windscreen. Traffic was light and they were making good progress towards town.

'Naturally, we have read and analysed your article with some care,' Baxter was saying. 'It seems obvious that you have information, and perhaps sources of information, which would be of interest to us.'

Hollander had no idea how to respond. Nothing very coherent came to mind.

'I realise that Digby may well take legal action, of course,' he replied. 'I and everyone involved with the Journal knew that there was a risk before we ever published...'

Baxter laughed out loud.

'A risk? Professor, with all due respect, you know as well as I do that Digby has only one possible response to your article. He has no choice at all. In the eyes of anyone reading your article, anyone taking it seriously, his reputation is in pieces. You have destroyed the man. Of course he is going to sue.'

Hollander looked down at his feet.

'This is not mere conjecture,' Baxter continued. 'If you read the papers here, you would know that Digby has already made his intentions known quite clearly in the British press, and he has already retained solicitors and counsel. So it's no longer a question of risk; it is about to become a reality. To put it bluntly, he is going to sue you for everything you are worth. The action will be extremely expensive to defend, and should you lose, it will be ruinous.'

Hollander remained silent for some time. Baxter showed no inclination to press him further until he was ready.

'All right,' he said eventually. 'Let's assume you are right. What exactly is your interest in the matter?'

'I should have thought that also was fairly obvious,' Baxter replied. 'You have written an article in which you claim that Sir James Digby QC, a pillar of the community, leading barrister, Queen's Counsel, and all-round good chap, has been spying for the Russians for a number of years, giving away our secrets behind our backs.'

'I am quite sure you knew that before you read my article,' Hollander rejoined.

'A conclusion that you reach,' Baxter said, ignoring the comment, 'without any actual evidence, as far as we can see: which means that Digby is going to have you for breakfast in court – unless, of course, you do in fact have some evidence. If you do, we would like to know about it for our own purposes. That, in a nutshell, is our interest in the case, Professor.'

Hollander smiled. 'Yet, earlier, you said that we had a common interest ...'

'We do,' Baxter replied, 'in certain circumstances. If what you wrote in your article proved to be a pack of lies, then we could not care less. We would happily sit back and watch while Digby gives you the thrashing you richly deserve. On the other hand, if there is substance in it, that is a matter in which we have a very serious interest, and we are prepared to offer you certain assistance in defending yourself against Digby's action – in our interests, of course, as well as yours.'

'What kind of assistance?' Hollander asked cautiously.

'The answer to that question is rather technical,' Baxter replied. 'I would need to discuss it with Julia. But it would be designed, obviously, to make it worth your while to share with us any information, or sources, you may have which are not credited in the article.'

Hollander's jaw dropped. There were only four people, of whom he and Julia were two, who knew that he had retained Julia Cathermole as his solicitor. They had exchanged correspondence and a phone call, but ...

'How in God's name do you know about Julia?' he spluttered. 'I have only just ...'

Baxter laughed again. 'Julia Cathermole's father was family,' he replied. 'Nigel was a colleague for many years, and we have kept a benign eye on Julia's progress ever since she became a solicitor, and particularly since she started her firm. We have only had contact with her very occasionally. But we had an interest in one of the first big cases she handled, a few years ago. We haven't spoken to her about your case, but it wasn't too hard to find out that you were interested in having her represent you, and in our view you couldn't have made a better choice.'

Hollander shook his head and returned his attention to the small area of vision on his side window.

'Our only reservation,' Baxter continued, 'is that we are not sure you understand fully what your defence is going to involve. It is going to be a long and complicated case, and it is going to be very expensive. Cathermole & Bridger is not a cheap firm of solicitors. Have you thought about that?'

Hollander had, in fact, thought a great deal about that, without arriving at any real conclusion. He had some resources, or rather, potential resources which had been promised before the article was published, and he had reason to hope that sympathy for his stance would attract further support. But thus far, there was very little actual money in the bank. It was something he would have to raise with Julia immediately. He was suddenly quite sure that Baxter knew all that already.

'We want to make sure that you don't have to worry,' Baxter said. 'We will make certain arrangements. Tell Julia what I have said when you see her. She will know what to do. All you have to do today is to check into the Reform, have a nice quiet day, enjoy a good dinner, and get a good night's sleep.'

'But ...'

'That's all you have to do.'

Hollander peered uselessly through his area of vision, which was now steaming up as fast as he could clear it.

'I still don't really understand,' he said. 'You are going to considerable lengths here.'

Baxter shrugged. 'There's no great mystery, Professor,' he replied. 'My superiors believe, rightly or wrongly, that they can't afford to have you lose this case, any more than you can afford to lose it.'

They passed the remainder of the trip in silence.

'What is it about the Reform Club?' Baxter asked, as the car pulled up alongside number 104 Pall Mall.

'What?'

'There must be something about the place that attracts people like you.'

Hollander stared at him blankly for several seconds before opening the door.

'People like me?' he asked.

'People who are lost without a bit of intrigue in their lives,' Baxter explained.

'They do a very nice dinner,' Hollander replied tartly, pushing himself out of the car on to the pavement, 'and they have comfortable rooms. Perhaps you should find someone to propose you for membership.'

The driver deposited his suitcase on the kerb next to him with a friendly salute and climbed back behind the wheel.

'Perhaps I should,' Baxter smiled.

Hollander closed the door, none too gently. Almost at once the driver pulled the car smoothly away from the kerb.

3

Ben Schroeder knocked on the door and waited for Bernard Wesley's familiar shout of 'Come!' before entering. Ben had been a member of Chambers for two years, and had adapted to the general practice of putting one's head around the door of any room which was not displaying a 'Conference' sign without knocking. But the general practice did not apply to Bernard Wesley's room. Wesley was a Silk, and the Head of Chambers, and although he was capable of a great personal warmth and charm, he had never quite relaxed the formality he had learned as part of his own training at the Bar. The room reflected Wesley's temperament exactly. The inlaid top of his antique desk was a dark green, which complemented the lighter green leather of his sofa and armchairs to perfection. Much of the wall space was devoted to huge, deep bookcases, laden with handsome leather-bound volumes of the law reports. The remaining spaces were adorned by a number of original eighteenth-century racing prints. Wesley was standing by the window behind his desk, one of a pair of enormous sash windows which offered a panoramic view over the Middle Temple gardens. He turned towards Ben and moved back towards his desk.

'Ben, come in. Have a seat.'

Ben lowered himself into the armchair to the left of the desk. He was a handsome young man of twenty-seven, almost six feet in height with a thin, lithe build. His hair was black, and his eyes a deep brown, set rather deep in his face because of strikingly prominent cheek bones, allowing him to fix a witness with a disconcertingly intense stare when he cross-examined. He wore an immaculately tailored three-piece suit, dark grey with the lightest of white pin-stripes, a thin gold pocket watch attached to a gold chain threaded through the middle button hole of his waistcoat, and a fluted white handkerchief in the top pocket of his jacket. As a young Jewish man from the East End of London, his pathway into the most conservative of professions had not been smooth, but a number of striking successes in the courtroom had made his place in Chambers secure, and had already brought him wider recognition at the Bar. If his place in the profession had ever been in doubt – and Ben's temperament had often led him to doubt it – he had every reason now to believe that the time for doubt had passed. The fact that he was to be Bernard Wesley's junior in this case was ample proof.

Ben laid his papers and notebook on the corner of Wesley's desk. The papers were wrapped in a backsheet which bore the name and address of the prestigious West End firm of Harper Sutton & Harper.

'We don't have much from Herbert, do we?' he asked, 'apart from the article itself.'

Wesley seated himself behind his desk.

'No,' he agreed. 'He won't have had much of a chance to go into it yet. It's all blown up too quickly, hasn't it? In any case, I strongly suspect that Herbert wants our advice before he digs too deeply into this particular hornets' nest. For one thing, Herbert is a strictly civil man, needless to say, and this may well have criminal implications. Merlin said he had referred Herbert to a criminal solicitor who can help out with that side of things, if needed. Is he going to be with us today?'

'Yes, Barratt Davis, of Bourne & Davis. They send quite a lot of work to the more junior tenants in chambers.'

Wesley nodded. 'I've heard Merlin mention them. Crime really isn't my field, as you know. Are they dependable? In a case like this ...'

'They are very good. They prepare a case well and they stay with it. I've done a fair bit of work for them, including that capital murder I did with Martin Hardcastle last year.'

'Ah, yes,' Wesley said. 'I remember that, of course.'

He paused.

'Has that memory receded to some extent?'

'To some extent,' Ben replied.

Wesley nodded his understanding. 'That's a hard case to lose. But to those of us not involved, it did appear that the prosecution had an overwhelming case. And you came out of it very well in the Court of Criminal Appeal – as opposed to Martin Hardcastle. Has he been heard of since?'

Ben closed his eyes. A hard case to lose. Yes, a case which ended with your client being hanged certainly qualified as a hard case to lose; especially when your leader turned out to be an alcoholic who missed the most important day of the trial and then advised the defendant that there was no need for him to give evidence in support of his alibi. Ben had spoken out against Hardcastle's advice, but in vain; the QC had the client's trust. Predictably, Hardcastle's advice failed to prevent the verdict of guilty, but his professional failings attracted no sympathy in the Court of Criminal Appeal. Hardcastle's career lay in ruins, but Billy Cottage had been hanged, notwithstanding.

'I believe he has retired from practice,' Ben replied, opening his eyes.

There was a silence.

'Do you know Digby well?' Ben asked, anxious to change the subject. 'I am sure you must.'

'I know him,' Wesley replied. 'But not well. He is a Chancery man, one of that rare breed who understands things like land law and trusts. He ventures out into the real world occasionally for a probate action or the odd defended divorce. I had one of those against him a year or two ago. He was called in 1935, I think, took Silk in the mid-1950s. Not the most exciting advocate, but a very sharp mind.'

'That sounds very much like the Chancery Division,' Ben said, smiling. 'But he doesn't sound like the sort of man who would get caught up in espionage, does he?'

Wesley looked up briefly at the ceiling.

'What kind of man does get caught up in espionage?' he asked. 'I've never seen the attraction myself, I must say. But I suppose a sharp mind would come in useful. He is one of the country's leading chess players. Did you know that?'

Ben shook his head. 'No. Not something I follow, I'm afraid.'

'Neither do I,' Wesley said. 'I just about remember how the pieces move. But apparently, he is a very strong player. And I seem to remember hearing that he worked for the Security Services during the War.'

'Really?' Ben asked. 'Doing what?'

'Interrogating suspected German spies, and the like. There were a number of members of the Bar who remained in practice and were called in when needed. Helenus Milmo was certainly very involved, and I think Digby was one of them also.'

'And he has a title.'

Wesley nodded. 'Yes. He is *Sir* James Masefield Digby, a baronet. It's a hereditary title. The family is from Lancashire, if I remember rightly, and the title goes back a couple of hundred years. The family has close ties to the Royal Family. Digby had an older brother who was first in line to inherit the title, but he died young. So when Digby's father died, the Baronetcy fell to him and he became *Sir* James.'

Ben nodded. He removed the ribbon from his papers, selected the document on top of the stack, and skimmed through it.

'Well, I don't think Herbert needs our advice on whether or not the allegations Hollander makes are libellous,' he observed. 'I would say that was a given, wouldn't you?'

Wesley thought for a moment or two.

'Assuming them to be false,' he replied. 'On that assumption, yes, I would agree.'

4

The Ivy League Political Remembrancer

1965, Volume 1, February

*Perfidious Albion: Why the United States can no longer
Afford to Trust Great Britain*

Francis R Hollander,
Associate Professor of Political Science, Yale University

*When, if ever, will the United States, and particularly the CIA, wake up and
realize that Great Britain is no longer a reliable ally, and that we can no longer
afford to trust her with our nation's secrets? The steady drain of the most sensitive
secret materials and information to the Soviet Union via a succession of highly-
placed spies has made a joke of the much-vaunted British Special Intelligence
Service, SIS, otherwise known as MI6. But it is a joke which is no laughing
matter for America, because too many of the secrets which have found their way
to Moscow are ours. Consider the recent history alone. On May 25, 1951, two
British men, Guy Burgess and Donald Maclean, disappeared and later surfaced
in Moscow, apparently residing contentedly in that city as distinguished guests of
the Soviet government. What do we know of these men?*

*Guy Burgess is known to have visited the Soviet Union in 1934. By 1938
he was working for MI6. Later, after spending some time with the British
Broadcasting Corporation, he returned to intelligence work via the Foreign
Office, and in 1950 he was appointed Second Secretary at the British Embassy
in Washington DC, remaining in this post until his disappearance the following
year.*

*Donald Maclean, a linguist by training, had a distinguished career in the
Foreign Office. In 1935, he was Third Secretary in London, but in 1938 he was
posted to Paris, and in 1940 was promoted to Second Secretary after playing a*

heroic role in the evacuation of the personnel of the British Embassy there in the face of the advancing German forces. In 1944, he was posted to the Embassy in Washington as acting First Secretary, and in 1947 he was appointed secretary to the British Delegation to the Combined Policy Committee, a role which would have given him first-hand access to almost all of our military intelligence and secrets, including information related to our nuclear weapons program. Between 1948 and 1951 he seems to have had serious personal problems. He was posted first to Cairo and then to London, from where he vanished with Burgess in May 1951.

Burgess and Maclean were both professional and personal associates of a third man, H.A.R. 'Kim' Philby. Philby joined MI6 in 1940, and remained with the Service until 1951. That date, with its implied link to Burgess and Maclean, is no coincidence. In his first post in MI6 he reported to Guy Burgess. During the War, he had important responsibilities, first for the supposedly neutral states of Spain and Portugal, later for North Africa and Italy. In 1944, however, he was appointed head of a new Section of MI6 concerned with the Soviet Union and the beginnings of the Western resistance to communism. In 1946 he became Head of Station in Turkey, the historic bridge between East and West and, therefore, a key area for intelligence in what was to become the Cold War. Then, in 1949, he was appointed MI6's representative in Washington, a post in which he would no doubt have remained indefinitely. But when Burgess and Maclean disappeared, suspicion fell on Philby as being the so-called Third Man: that is to say, a spy who had worked for many years with Burgess and Maclean to pass some of our most sensitive secrets — not to mention those of his own country — to the Soviet Union. He was forced to resign from MI6 but, remarkably, he was exonerated after a number of inquiries. He later re-emerged as a freelance journalist working for a number of respected titles, including **The Economist.** *He was last seen in Beirut in 1963, from where he disappeared, like his friends Burgess and Maclean, no doubt to a hero's welcome in Moscow.*

I obtained some of the information for this article from sources who cannot be named for fear of compromising their professional standing and, indeed, their personal safety. But much information is now in the public domain as a result of more recent well-publicized scandals in Great Britain, which frustrated the natural inclination of the British government to cover up the failings of its security services. In 1961, a Russian-born intelligence officer, Gordon Lonsdale, was unmasked as a spy, arrested and prosecuted. In 1962, George Blake, an officer of MI6, was convicted of spying for the Soviets since the early 1950s. In the same year, John Vassall was likewise arrested and convicted of passing Admiralty secrets. In 1963, the British Minister for War, John Profumo, was compelled to resign after the revelation of his relationship with a call-girl by the name of Christine Keeler, whose services he was sharing with a naval attaché at the Soviet Embassy in London – an affair in which many believe MI6 was implicated.

Certain questions must be asked. What do these British spies have in common? Is there anything which explains the reluctance of the British government to reveal their activities frankly and openly, if not publicly, at least to its most important ally, the United States? Are there others linked to the known spies, still at large and in positions of influence, who continue to betray their country and ours to the Soviets? If so, who are they?

First, what do they have in common? Guy Burgess, Donald Maclean, and Kim Philby are all graduates of Trinity College or Trinity Hall in the University of Cambridge and began their studies there in the period 1929 – 1931. All are known to have had communist sympathies during their time in Cambridge. Maclean and Philby were members of the Cambridge University Socialist Society. Burgess had also been a member of the Apostles, a secretive debating society based in Trinity College which has left-wing, anti-establishment tendencies. The three men continued to associate after their time at Cambridge and worked their way into the heart of the British establishment where they were seemingly immune from suspicion and where they had ample opportunity to pass secrets. They did this by posing as loyal patriots who had repudiated their early sympathies with communism. In 1937 Philby went to Spain to cover the civil war as a journalist from the Franco side, and received an award – the Red Cross of Military Merit – from the General personally for his efforts. Burgess and Maclean also took steps to hide their left-wing leanings. All three are known to drink heavily. Burgess is a known homosexual – the practice of which is a criminal offence in England. All three have been implicated by Soviet defectors in the business of espionage. And Burgess and Philby had a long, close personal and professional relationship with James Jesus Angleton, now the doyen of the CIA, a man educated in England and inured in English ways, and who learned his trade as a spy at the feet of Kim Philby.

Are there likely to be others? There have been whispers of a 'fourth man'. But in truth it would not be surprising if there were a fifth, sixth, or even a hundredth man. It seems plain that there was at least one first-rate talent-spotter at Cambridge in the early 1930s. Some have whispered about Anthony Blunt who was, during the relevant period, a research student and later Fellow of Trinity, and an Apostle. But Blunt is a respected art historian, Surveyor of the Queen's Pictures, and evidently quite above reproach. As, apparently, is anyone in Great Britain who has been to the right school and college, wears the right tie, and is part of the Establishment. The belief that a gentleman would never betray his country appears to be just as strong now as it was during the Victorian era.

The early and mid-1930s was a period when left-wing causes, including communism, had considerable appeal to young intellectuals. The rise of fascism and the Spanish Civil War, and the apparent unwillingness of western governments to lift a finger to stop it, was repugnant to many. To many, it seemed that the Soviet Union offered the only hope of resistance. The young students of Trinity were fruit ripe for the plucking by any Soviet agent. Before and during the World War there may have been every reason to see the Soviet Union as an ally – the temporary pact between Hitler and Stalin notwithstanding. After the War, the Soviet Union suddenly became the enemy. But by that time, it may be that some had been ensnared into spying for Moscow and were in too deep to get out.

Consider the case of Sir James Masefield Digby QC. Sir James – the title comes from his position as a baronet, a minor branch of nobility – entered Cambridge University in 1931, the same year as Donald Maclean, a year after Guy Burgess, and two years after Kim Philby. Like Maclean and Philby he was a member of the University Socialist Society. Like Burgess, he was an Apostle. Like all three, he made his way into a respected professional way of life, in which he could have considerable influence. But in Digby's case that profession is the law. After completing his degree at Trinity, he was called to the Bar by Lincoln's Inn in 1934 and went on to practice as a barrister in London. He took Silk – became a Queen's Counsel, a mark of distinction which opens the way for practice in more important cases – in 1955. Nothing overt to suggest espionage so far. But Digby has another talent.

Digby is a strong chess player, one of the strongest in Great Britain. I also play chess to a respectable level and, in 1962, I was invited to accompany the United States chess team to Varna, Bulgaria, where it was to compete in the Olympiad, an international team tournament held every two years. Sadly, I am not good enough to play for a team which can boast the likes of Bobby Fischer, but I have worked closely with the Fédération Internationale des Echecs – FIDE – the world-governing body for the game. Chess is a very political game, largely because the Soviets view their success in it as an advertisement for communism. As the son of a Russian mother who fled Soviet Russia as a child, I am fluent in the language and I am able to negotiate for the team in that atmosphere, perhaps more effectively than others might.

While in Varna, I was approached by a Soviet grandmaster by the name of Viktor Stepanov. I had already met Stepanov a number of times because he had often represented the Soviet Union at meetings of FIDE. I liked him more than other Soviet players I had met. Once you got past the usual Soviet paranoia, Stepanov could be a charming and interesting conversationalist. His English was good and he seemed to be a man of broad education. But he was not in a conversational mood on this occasion. He insisted on taking me to drink vodka in a doubtful-looking bar some distance from the tournament hall. I remember that we seemed to take a very roundabout route to get there, which I took to be his way of losing his minder – rightly or wrongly I always assume that Soviet grandmasters have KGB connections. They certainly have minders.

After three or four vodkas, Stepanov told me that he was desperately unhappy and wished to defect to the United States. It took me several minutes to recover from the shock. I was astounded, not only to learn that he wished to defect, but also that he should have offered such dangerous information to a man he did not know well. I began to protest that I was not the right person to ask, but he interrupted me. He said he knew that I am a professor of political science and assumed that I must have connections with the CIA – which, for the record, I do not. Before I could stop him, he insisted on telling me that he had valuable information to pass to the CIA, information which could prevent the loss of many secrets and the deaths of western agents behind the Iron Curtain. It would probably have been safer, both for Stepanov and myself, if I had stopped him from going further, but I did not.

Stepanov told me that in 1948 he had been instructed to attempt to recruit an English spy, a chess player. His instructions came from Moscow, but he was led to believe that the arrangement had been instigated by an agent in London. The man in question was James Masefield Digby, and the occasion was the World Chess Championship tournament. Stepanov was told that although Digby worked as a lawyer, he had worked for MI6 during the War and retained links with the Service.

It had not been possible to hold a world title tournament during the War, and in 1946 the title had become vacant because of the death of the holder, Alexander Alekhin. The five players judged to be the strongest in the world were selected to contest the title, and if I were to tell you about even a fraction of the diplomacy required within FIDE to bring that about, I would need to write another article. It is enough to note that the tournament was split into two parts. The first began in The Hague on March 1, 1948, and the second was held in Moscow, beginning on April 11 of that year. Stepanov was told that Digby would be covering the tournament as a journalist on behalf of various newspapers and chess magazines, and that he was vulnerable because of his left-wing leanings and his frustration about the lack of respect for chess in the West compared to the Soviet Union. He said that, following his instructions, he approached Digby in The Hague, but only to build a relationship. The serious work was to be done later in Moscow, where it was far safer. I think everyone assumed that various intelligence services would be taking some interest in the tournament. He told me that Digby confirmed that he retained links with MI6 and agreed to work with the Soviets. Every year since 1948, Digby had been invited to Russia to attend the prestigious Soviet Chess Championship, sometimes under cover of working as a chess journalist, but sometimes simply as a guest, invited to play in a minor tournament or give a simultaneous exhibition to students.

Needless to say, I pressed Stepanov for details, but he refused to tell me any more until I had approached the CIA about his defection and received a favorable answer. We agreed to meet at a tournament in Belgrade, in which he had been given permission to compete, early in 1963. On my return to the United States from Varna, I used a contact to obtain an interview with a senior officer of the CIA. I told this officer what had happened, and asked him to take the matter further. I offered to act as a go-between for Stepanov, as he had chosen me to confide in. The officer thanked me profusely, and promised to see what could be done and to keep me fully informed. But no decision was made, and early in 1963 I saw Stepanov's obituary in the Soviet chess magazine **Sixty-Four**. It said that he was a middle-ranking grandmaster, who had won a few relatively minor tournaments and had made a relatively minor contribution to opening theory in the Sicilian Defense. His body had been found in his flat in Moscow. He had apparently died of a heart attack. Well, that's what they always say, isn't it?

There is no way of knowing how many secrets Digby and those like him have passed to the Soviets, or how important those secrets were, or how many agents of ours behind the Iron Curtain have died as a result. I feel partly responsible for the death of Viktor Stepanov, though in truth I do not feel that I could have dissuaded him from trying to seek freedom in the West. In a gesture of atonement, and because it is a subject on which the light urgently needs to shine, I publish this article. I hope that, as a result, both our Government and that of Great Britain will find it less easy to ignore the extent of this tragic history of espionage and the damage it has caused.

5

Bernard Wesley tossed Francis Hollander's article on to his desk, removed his reading glasses and placed them beside the article.

'I have not read out the whole article, of course,' he said. 'It goes on at some length. I left out the more arcane points of political theory which Hollander presumably intended to lend it an air of academic respectability. But I think the parts I have read are enough for our purposes today.'

He looked around his room. Ben Schroeder sat to his left at the side of his desk, notebook open, pen in hand.

In front of the desk on his left, Sir James Masefield Digby QC sat slumped in his chair. Digby was a tall man, thin and willowy in build, wearing a dark grey three-piece suit and a blue and white spotted tie. His hair was still mainly dark, but there were flecks of grey, with more prominent grey in his sideburns. His face was a handsome one, and used to wearing a confident smile. But today there was no air of confidence about him. Today, his face was lined with stress, and dark marks around the eyes suggested a prolonged lack of sleep. His shoulders sagged. He had kept his head lowered while Wesley had been reading from Hollander's article.

Sitting beside Digby, in front of the desk to Wesley's right, was Herbert Harper, senior partner of Harper Sutton & Harper, one of London's leading firms of solicitors, a firm of choice for the rich and influential in divorce and important civil cases. Harper was also dressed in a dark grey suit, but two-piece, and with a rich purple tie over his white shirt. He had been in practice for more than 40 years and was now over 67 years of age, but there had never once been so much as a rumour of impending retirement. He still had an energy which many men half his age might have envied, and he relished his work. Harper's relationship with Bernard Wesley went back many years. They knew each other well, and Harper sent much of his firm's work in the courts to Wesley's chambers. Harper's experience had accustomed him to most of the vagaries of litigation, but this was a case which disturbed him. It had implications which went far beyond the realms of any work he had done before.

Barratt Davis sat farthest from the desk on the sofa by the wall. He felt a little overawed. His work was in the criminal courts and it was a rare experience for him to mix with solicitors of Harper's eminence. On the other hand, he had the confidence which came from knowing that he might hold a key piece of the puzzle faced by the others in the room. He was aware that his expertise was one which everyone present would prefer to avoid – if it could be avoided – and he was more than content to bide his time and wait to be asked for his opinion if it became relevant. Davis was also a non-conformist in one respect and, even in this company, he was determined not to abandon his customary sartorial rebellion. His suit was a professional black, but he wore a dramatic yellow and blue tie over a dark blue shirt, and he had been gratified to see Harper's eyes open wide as they were introduced. By his side sat his assistant, Jess Farrar, dressed in a light grey two-piece suit, her hair tied back in a neat bun.

'James would like your advice about how to proceed in this situation, Bernard,' Harper began. 'At present he takes the view that he has no real choice in the matter. But I have advised him that we need to examine the options very carefully before committing ourselves. To begin with, I have one or two technical questions. Firstly, do our courts have jurisdiction? Secondly, if so, is Hollander judgment-proof?'

Wesley nodded. 'I think Ben has looked at the question of jurisdiction.'

'I have,' Ben replied. He smiled inwardly at the invitation to participate so early in the consultation. His previous experience with a Silk, Martin Hardcastle, during the Cottage murder trial, might have suggested that as junior counsel he would be allowed to open his mouth in the presence of a Silk rarely, and only when strictly necessary. Bernard Wesley's approach made a welcome change.

'Hollander has published the article in England entirely independently of the original publication in the United States. That's quite apart from allowing the press to reproduce extracts from it. The newspapers have covered themselves by making sure to attribute every word to Hollander, but Hollander has re-issued the article here himself. I don't see any reason why the English High Court could not take jurisdiction and, if we get judgment, we can ask an American court to enforce it, if necessary. Service of process might have been a slight problem, but Hollander seems to have made that easy for us. He has gone out of his way over the weekend to advertise his arrival in England and the fact that he is staying at the Reform Club. So, service will not be a problem.'

'I saw that in the *Sunday Times*,' Wesley said. 'Apparently he gave a press conference on Friday evening. It is almost as though he is daring us to come and get him. I think we ought to take some note of that.'

'As to Hollander being judgment-proof …' Ben continued.

'This is not about money,' Digby interrupted. 'It is about repairing the damage to my reputation.'

'Yes, James,' Harper said, sounding a little impatient, 'but we have been through this before. Bringing proceedings for libel in the High Court is an expensive business. It is not just a question of damages. There are the costs to consider.'

'*The Ivy League Political Remembrancer* is an independent journal,' Ben continued. 'As far as I can see, it is Hollander's own creation and he is in charge of it. He is described on the inside cover as the Managing Editor and Editor-in-Chief. There are one or two assistant editors, but there is no indication that they have any voice in how it is run. And it does not seem to be connected directly to Yale University.'

'So it may be something of a pyrrhic victory,' Wesley observed. 'We may win a judgment and an award of damages, but if Hollander has no assets to speak of, we may recover very little and be stuck with our own costs – not to mention that we might well incur further costs in trying to enforce the judgment in America.'

Wesley looked at Digby, who raised his shoulders and spread his hands out wide in a gesture of resignation.

'I am aware of the risks,' he said. 'But what choice do I have? If I don't sue Hollander for libel immediately, people will assume that what he says is true. They are bound to. I will have no future at the Bar, or in Society. I will be an outcast. Both I and my family will be ruined. The Queen may even take away the Baronetcy, for God's sake.'

'On the other hand,' Harper said, 'if you do sue him, you will be at the mercy of a jury, and you will have your whole life dissected in public. Whether you sue or not, they may still try to prosecute you in the criminal courts. And as Bernard says, even if we win, we may not even be able to cover our costs, let alone collect the damages.'

'I am not short of cash, Herbert,' Digby said. 'I will pay your costs, if I have to. Any damages I am awarded will go to charity in any event. This is about clearing my name.'

There was a silence for some time.

'Barratt, I would welcome your input on the possibility of criminal prosecution,' Wesley said. 'I am particularly concerned about whether it is likely even if James does not sue for libel.'

Barratt had allowed himself to sprawl slightly in the comfort of the sofa. He now quickly sat up straight.

'The Attorney-General moves in mysterious ways,' he replied. 'We have had cases recently in which you would think a prosecution is quite inevitable, but nothing is done. On the other hand, there are cases where action is taken against someone and you ask yourself why on earth they are bothering. In this particular case, I think they will prosecute if they think they have the evidence.'

'Because …?' Wesley asked.

'They need to reassure the public that they are doing something,' Davis replied. 'Before Burgess and Maclean there had been no real evidence to suggest the need for prosecutions for espionage since the War. Burgess and Maclean got away. They would have gone after Philby if they thought they had the evidence, but clearly, they didn't, and they eventually lost him. But they went after Lonsdale, they went after Blake, and they went after Vassall, and they are still not sure they have cleaned the stables. They even went after the wretched Stephen Ward, poor fellow. Many people don't view the Profumo scandal as an espionage case, but I think that is naïve. The press is still talking about a fourth man. People still don't think the Security Services are secure. The Government is still under pressure. Unfortunately, James has a high profile. They will probably feel they cannot ignore him. But the good news is that they can't prosecute him without evidence.'

Wesley nodded. 'And that's the key to it,' he said.

'Either way,' Digby insisted, 'I have no choice.'

'There are always choices,' Wesley replied.

'For God's sake, Bernard. I have already told the newspapers I intend to sue.'

'That does not tie your hands. You can always find a reason.'

'Not in this case. The man is accusing me of treason, of betraying my country.'

'Yes,' Wesley agreed. 'But on what basis? On the basis of a conversation he claims he had with some Russian chess player who has rather conveniently died, and who in any case did not provide Hollander with one single fact to corroborate what he allegedly told him. What else does he have? The fact that you went up to Trinity at about the same time as Burgess, about the same time as Philby? So did a couple of hundred other men. The fact that you may have held some left-wing views during your time as a student? My God, James, if everyone who held left-wing views at University were to be suspected of treason, we would have to spend the next hundred years prosecuting them all. Hollander himself says that it was fashionable to be left-wing at the time, because of the Spanish war and so on. I am having some difficulty in seeing why anyone would take this article seriously.'

'People *are* taking it seriously,' Digby insisted.

'But if that's all he has, any jury would laugh him out of court – after ordering him to pay you an enormous sum in damages.'

He turned towards Ben.

'Would a judge even leave the question to a jury in a criminal case?'

Ben shook his head firmly. 'Not a chance,' he replied firmly.

Wesley nodded. 'What's your feeling, Herbert?'

'I understand how James sees it,' Harper replied. 'But there are always choices. Suing for libel is a natural instinctive reaction in this kind of situation, but with libel, you always have to question whether it is the right thing to do. You have to think of the cost, for one thing, as I have said. And libel is always a double-edged sword. I must admit, I am not sure what to do in this case, but I think it must be considered very carefully. We are in no danger from the statute of limitations. We need to take our time and think about it.'

Digby brought a hand down on Wesley's desk.

'That's all very well, Herbert, but this article is out there, making the rounds here at home, as well as in America. With every day that goes by, if I do nothing, my reputation suffers more and more damage.'

'Yes,' Wesley said. 'I do understand your concern.'

'Do you?' Digby stood and reached down for his briefcase, which he had placed on the floor, leaning against the leg of his chair. He put a hand inside and took out a collection of newspapers. 'Have you seen this? *The Sunday Times*, "Leading QC may have spied for Soviets". *The Daily Mail*, "Has this Baronet betrayed his Country?". *The Daily Express*, "Is this the face of the Fourth Man?". Do you want more – do you remember what *The Daily Mirror* called me?'

Wesley stood and leaned against his desk.

'I have read every word of those articles, James, all of them. And I do understand how you feel. But allow me to tell you what is troubling me. Herbert is right about libel. It is a double-edged sword. If you win you are vindicated. On the other hand, if you lose, your reputation is damaged beyond repair, and if evidence has emerged a criminal prosecution may follow. As Barratt says, they can't prosecute without evidence, and on the basis of the materials I have been shown, I do not see any evidence.'

He paused for some seconds.

'And that is what concerns me.'

'I don't follow, Bernard,' Harper said.

'I am wondering why Hollander has taken the step of publishing such a serious libel without any evidence to back it up,' Wesley replied. 'He must have known that he was exposing himself to a potentially ruinous lawsuit; one to which Ben and I both fail to see he has any defence – unless he were able to show that what he has said is true. And if he compounds the libel by trying to justify it, the damages would generally be even greater. Not only that, he is now parading around London, virtually daring us to sue him. It doesn't make sense to me. What does he have to gain?'

'Taking a charitable view,' Harper said, 'it is possible that he sees himself, however misguidedly, as acting in the public interest.'

Wesley nodded. 'Possibly. James, can you shed any light on this? What do you know about Hollander? Have you met him?'

'I have met him several times, at this or that chess tournament,' Digby replied. 'I have spoken to him. I have never done anything to offend him, as far as I am aware. I can't claim to know him well, but my sense of Hollander is that he is a frustrated man. He is an average chess player, who would like to be a grandmaster but knows enough to realise that he never will. So he hangs around the fringes. He speaks some Russian – because of a family connection, I believe – so he can make himself useful to American players and teams travelling abroad for tournaments, and to the American delegations to FIDE. It gives him a sense of importance that he will never have as a player.'

'He is also an academic at a respected university,' Wesley pointed out.

'He is an associate professor. I have no doubt that a little notoriety will do him no harm at Yale,' Digby retorted. 'He is obviously a shameless self-publicist, and apparently merely starting his own journal was not enough to satisfy his ambition.'

Wesley seemed on the point of replying, but checked himself. 'Well, it may not matter,' he said. 'I was curious, that's all. His motives may become obvious as we go along.'

He paused again.

'May I suggest that we all take time to think about this for a day or so in the light of what we have discussed? If, James, you then wish to proceed, Ben will draft the pleadings quickly, Herbert will serve them, and we will get the case under way.'

'I don't need any more time to discuss the matter,' Digby said. 'What I need is to start restoring my reputation. My instructions are to sue Hollander for libel without delay.'

Wesley nodded. 'Your instructions are that this article is wholly false?'

Digby drew himself up in his chair.

'Bernard, do you think for one moment that I would be here if …?'

'I have an obligation to ask,' Wesley replied. 'Think carefully, James. Is there anything in your past that could give rise to suspicion, even if it were unfounded? Anything to explain why Hollander may have got the wrong idea about you, put two and two together and made five?'

'No,' Digby said. 'And it is not a matter of getting the wrong idea. He is lying about me. We need to proceed with the action without delay.'

'Very well,' Wesley replied. 'But perhaps you would indulge me for a moment?'

'Of course.'

Wesley walked to the bookcase to the right of his desk and took a volume from a shelf.

'This is an anecdote of Chief Justice Holt in an old case called *Johnson v Browning* in 1704,' he said. 'The Chief Justice said he remembered: *"another case very lately where a fellow brought an action for saying of him that he was a highwayman; and it appearing upon the evidence that he was so, he was taken in court, committed to prison, and convicted and hanged at the next sessions of gaol delivery. So that people ought to be well advised before they bring such actions."*

Wesley closed the book.

'Just some food for thought,' he said.

6

Bernard Wesley had resumed his seat behind his desk. The consultation had ended, and everyone except Ben Schroeder and Jess Farrar had gone.

'I've asked the two of you to stay,' he said, 'because I think we need to make some further inquiries. I want to know more about Professor Francis R Hollander. I want to know who he is: his background, personal and academic; where he studied, what degrees he obtained; what his political affiliations are; and what he has written, apart from the present piece. If there is anything odd about him at all, I want to know. There is something not quite right about this case.'

'You mean, because he is making himself too available?' Ben asked. 'Acting as if he can't wait to be sued?'

'That's part of it, certainly,' Wesley replied. 'But I also want to know what his personal agenda is, and I want to know if there are people supporting him, people we can't see at present. He claims to have had no contact with the CIA before he went to them with the Stepanov story. Is that true? Is there anything in his background which suggests otherwise?'

'I suppose it's possible,' Ben suggested, 'that the American Government, or the CIA in particular, feels that it is not getting anywhere with our Government – too many people defecting and no one being held responsible – and they decided that it might be a good idea to bring it all out in public. If so, they might have put Hollander up to it.'

'Yes,' Wesley agreed. 'Then, the question becomes: have they done it speculatively, waiting to see what evidence might come out of the woodwork; or do they know something we don't? We may not be able to find the answers to all these questions without some help from James. But he is in too emotional a state to help us very much at the moment, so I want to make a start without him.'

'I will start a trawl of the libraries tomorrow,' Jess volunteered. 'I will start digging and see what I can find.'

'Good,' Wesley replied.

'I thought I might take a look at Stepanov,' Ben added. 'According to Hollander, he is the man who recruited James. I am not sure how much information there will be, but it may be worth taking a look.'

'I agree,' Wesley said. 'And give Jess whatever help you can.'

'Of course.'

* * *

Ben and Jess rose to leave, but Wesley gestured them to stay in their seats.

'There was something else I wanted to mention,' he said. 'There is no really delicate way to put this, but I think I am right in saying that you two are seeing each other. Is that the right expression? I'm not very *au fait* with how people express these things nowadays.'

Ben and Jess exchanged smiles.

'Yes, we are,' he replied. 'And seeing each other is a good way to say it.'

Wesley smiled thinly.

'Yes. The thing is that Jess works for Bourne & Davis.'

'Yes.'

'And Bourne & Davis send you instructions, brief you for their cases in the courts.'

'Yes.'

'Ben, you understand the implications, don't you?'

Ben's smile suddenly vanished.

'Bernard, if you're asking whether I know it's frowned on for a barrister to socialise with solicitors who instruct him ...'

'Or even solicitors who *might* instruct him, or their employees ...'

'Yes. I am well aware of that.'

'Jess, I don't mean to exclude you from the conversation,' Wesley said. 'But I've had a communication from the Middle Temple, the Inn of Court to which Ben and I both belong. They are concerned about what is called touting for work. It is a disciplinary offence for a barrister to use his social connections with a solicitor to tout for work. Obviously, a romantic involvement may count as socialising.'

Ben shook his head in frustration.

'There is no reason for them to frown on anything,' he insisted. 'Not in our case.'

Wesley looked him directly in the eye. He stood and walked around his desk to lean against the front.

'Ben, it goes a bit further than being frowned on. The Inn has set up a committee to look into any cases of apparent touting which come to its attention. Apparently, they feel that the rules are being disregarded, that it's becoming more prevalent to have social contact between barristers and solicitors. They are afraid it is getting away from them. It's not a trivial matter. Technically, you could get disbarred for it.'

Jess looked at Ben in horror.

'For God's sake,' Ben protested. 'It *is* the second half of the twentieth century, Bernard.'

Wesley held his hands up hopelessly.

'I agree with you,' he replied. 'But as you well know, the Bar doesn't live in the second half of the twentieth century. Some would say it is only now dragging itself rather reluctantly into the second half of the nineteenth. Don't shoot the messenger, Ben. The Inn has raised the matter with me, about your particular situation and, as your Head of Chambers, I have a duty to bring it to your attention.'

He paused.

'Look, I don't mean to pry. But do you mind my asking? How serious is your relationship?'

Ben closed his eyes. He was silent for some time. He looked at Jess, then back at Wesley.

'It is very serious,' he replied quietly. 'Jess kept me sane during the Cottage case. What with the verdict and the trip to the Court of Criminal Appeal, it was a very emotional time for me. And then, when Cottage was hanged ... I know barristers are supposed to be objective and not get emotionally involved, but ...'

'You can't help it,' Wesley replied. 'You have to put your feelings on one side to make a good job of the case, but that doesn't mean the feelings aren't there.'

Ben nodded. 'I was able to deal with it most of the time, certainly while I was in court,' he said. 'But Jess's support kept me going. She drove me to London to see my grandfather when he had his heart attack during the trial. After that, we gradually fell in love. I ...'

Wesley pushed himself up off the table.

'That's all admirable,' he said. 'I'm not judging you, please believe me. In fact, I am all in favour. The only problem is how to get the Middle Temple off our backs.'

'*Our* backs?' Ben asked pointedly.

'Yes. It comes back to me as Head of Chambers, as well as you.'

'My God,' Jess said quietly.

'Look, don't despair, either of you,' Wesley said. 'I'm not saying that we can't find a way to deal with this. I am sure we can. But we can't ignore it. What I am suggesting is that you allow me to undertake a little diplomacy on your behalf.'

Ben looked up questioningly.

'I am a Bencher of the Inn, Ben. I am a member of the ruling body. I know how they think. I can talk to them in a way they will understand, and I have the seniority to be a bit more candid with them than you could be. Look, why don't the two of you come up to Hampstead for dinner? I was telling Amélie about you and, of course, she now insists on meeting you and Jess. She is an incurable romantic, I'm afraid. I should have invited you long before. How would a Saturday be?'

Ben looked at Jess. They both nodded.

'A Saturday would be fine. Thank you, Bernard.'

'Don't let it get you down. It may take a while, but I think we can get around it. So don't do anything drastic. Just be discreet. In particular, no public displays of affection. Understood?'

'Understood,' Ben replied.

7

Julia Cathermole walked carefully up the short flight of stairs leading from Pall Mall to the double doors which marked the main entrance to the Reform Club. Her heels were higher than she was accustomed to. Indeed, she had dressed for the day with unusual formality. The senior partner of Cathermole & Bridger, a small firm of solicitors with a rapidly-growing reputation, she preferred to impress through her work rather than her appearance. She had a natural sense of style which enabled her to look good in clothes of any kind, and she relished her sometimes unconventional approach to business dress. But there were occasions when she reverted to the more typical lawyer's black suit; occasions when she wanted to make a particular kind of impression on a client. Today was such an occasion, though she had been unable to resist a jaunty black-and-white silk scarf worn over her jacket and she had tied her hair back with a matching bow.

She looked around her. Straight ahead, a further three or four steps led to another set of double doors, which marked the entrance to the saloon. To her right was the porter's lobby. She approached the window and inquired for Professor Francis Hollander. The porter walked quickly around to the front of his desk.

'This way, Madam, please.'

He more or less sprinted up the steps, opened the right-hand door, and held it open, waiting for her to catch up with him. He pointed to her right.

'Through there in the morning room, Madam. The gentleman in the bow tie,' he said.

'Thank you.'

'Enjoy your luncheon, Madam.'

She would have identified him even without the porter's

assistance. It was partly that his was by far the lightest-coloured suit in the room. Most of the members dressed in dark grey or black. But she thought there was something unmistakably American about his clothes and hair, about the look of his spectacles. He was sitting at a corner table to her right, by one of the two enormous windows which looked out over Pall Mall. Except for the windows, the morning room was enclosed by huge oak bookcases which held part of the Club's extensive library. The room was a place for members to take coffee, or something stronger, while catching up on the news from a wide range of newspapers. A cheering fire was burning in the central fireplace, casting a glow over the warm red leather chairs and sofas. A handful of members and their guests were engrossed in drinks and subdued conversation. He saw her as she entered the room and stood immediately, his hand outstretched.

'Miss Cathermole?'

'Professor Hollander.'

They shook hands.

He pulled back one of the two chairs at his table, and held it out for her as she took her seat.

'What may I get you? The barman here mixes a mean dry martini. I can't resist them myself.'

She smiled.

'I prefer gin and tonic, thank you.'

Hollander raised an arm, and a white-jacketed waiter instantly made his way from the bar on the other side of the room to take his order.

'How was your flight?' she asked.

'No complaints. It was long, of course, but comfortable enough. No complaints at all. I've had the weekend to get over it.'

'I've been reading about your activities over the weekend,' she said pointedly.

'Ah, yes,' he smiled. He had, of course, no good reason for not having consulted her before holding his press conference. It would have been the proper thing to do, the sensible thing to do, and appropriate, given her position as his prospective solicitor. Her implied reprimand was fully justified. But he had wanted to make sure that she did not talk him out of it. He had intended to throw down the gauntlet to Digby through the press, and he had done so in no uncertain terms. Digby had nowhere to hide now.

'It's obviously not your first time in London,' she said, once it had become clear that he was not going to explain or apologise.

He smiled again. 'No, I've been privileged to spend quite a bit of time here. I usually come over for the Hastings Chess Tournament during the Christmas and New Year period. I also spent a semester in Cambridge while I was working on my doctoral thesis, and I still have a number of friends there, and here in London. I'm getting quite used to it. As you see, I have even joined a Club to bolster my British credentials.'

The waiter brought her gin and tonic and a small bowl of salted peanuts. They raised their glasses in silence. She replaced her glass on the table.

'As I explained when we spoke yesterday evening,' she said, 'we have an appointment at the chambers of Miles Overton QC at 4 o'clock, so that we can get counsel involved immediately. Some solicitors like to delay involving counsel until the last minute, but I've always found that to be counter-productive. Counsel need to be involved from the beginning so that they can help to formulate our strategy. There are some matters we have to discuss first, but it's only a matter of five minutes by taxi, so we have plenty of time to talk over lunch.'

She took a sip of her drink and nodded her approval.

'Let me start with the obvious. I'm flattered that you want to retain Cathermole & Bridger. May I ask how you found out about us, what made you decide we were the right firm to represent you?'

He looked down for some time. She had the impression that he was hesitating, calculating his reply. It worried her. She had asked him a routine question, and his reply ought to have been straightforward.

'I was given your name by Donald Tate, who is on the faculty of our Law School,' he replied. 'He said you would remember him from... what was it, a conference on private international law?'

She nodded. 'Amsterdam, two years ago,' she said, 'of course. How is Donald?'

'He is fine. He is in line for promotion from associate to full professor, so it's a busy year for him. But he is fine. He remembered meeting you at the conference, he was impressed, and he had heard very good things about your firm.'

She looked at him keenly, disguising the scrutiny behind her smile. He had given her a plausible answer, but not a convincing one, given what was involved in the case he wanted her to defend. She remembered meeting Donald Tate and exchanging ideas with him – and several others – in a break-out session during the conference in Amsterdam. But that was hardly likely to have produced a very profound impression on him. She sensed that he was following her thoughts.

'Well, I appreciate his recommendation,' she said.

'Actually, that's not the whole story,' Hollander admitted.

'Go on.'

'Donald has a friend, an attaché at your Embassy in Washington, who knew your name.' He paused. 'He said you had connections within … a branch of the Government Service.'

Julia nodded slowly, as she began to understand.

'I see.'

'I'm sorry,' he continued. 'I assumed you knew. I thought you were responsible for the welcome at the airport when I arrived, even though he said he had not spoken to you.'

She looked at him blankly.

'I have no idea what you're talking about.'

Hollander sat up in his chair.

'When I arrived on Wednesday I was met at the airport by a man calling himself Baxter,' he said, 'who gave me to understand that he is with MI6. He had a car with a driver. He gave me a ride into town, brought me all the way to the Club, as a matter of fact.'

'And that was a complete surprise to you? You were not expecting to be met?'

'Not at all.'

'Did this man Baxter give you any explanation for meeting you in this way?'

Hollander hesitated. 'I'm not sure "explanation" is the right word. He seemed to know that you were representing me. That's why I thought you must have …'

'No, I have not had any contact with them about you …'

'… or perhaps he guessed, or perhaps he heard something from the Embassy. In any case, his message was that MI6 and I had common cause.'

'Meaning Sir James Digby?'

'Yes. He said that the Service shared my interest in the outcome of any lawsuit Digby might bring against me.'

He paused again.

'And he offered help.'

Julia looked up sharply.

'What kind of help?'

'He was less than specific,' Hollander replied quietly. He seemed embarrassed. 'He said it was a technical matter, and that he would have to speak to you about it. But unless I misunderstood him, I think part of it was some contribution towards my legal costs.'

Julia's jaw dropped. It took her some seconds to recover.

'MI6 wants to pay for your defence of the case?'

'Well, as I say, he wasn't too specific. But he referred to the financial implications of the litigation a number of times. That's something we would have had to discuss today. You had sent me your letter of engagement, which explained the arrangements about fees and costs very clearly. I came over here in a position to give you a cheque for the retainer today, and I was making arrangements to meet the monthly bills and any expenses, as your letter indicated. But now, it seems, MI6 may want to help. I'm not sure how that would work, whether Baxter intends to pay your firm directly, or through me.'

'Through you, I would think,' Julia replied thoughtfully. 'I wonder if Baxter knows how much this is going to cost: a defended libel action with leading and junior counsel, and potential exposure for the other side's costs. I wonder if someone over there has done the arithmetic?'

'He seemed to be aware that it could be expensive,' Hollander replied. 'I assumed he had done his homework.'

'Well, if we accept their offer, we will have to make it clear to them,' Julia said.

'*If* we accept their offer?'

Julia nodded. 'I need to understand what I would be committing you to – and what I would be committing my firm to. I want to know what the conditions are. I want to know more about what's going on.'

'I got the impression that the money is not their main concern,' Hollander added. 'They are more interested in something else.'

'Are they indeed?' she asked. 'Well, let's get to the point, then. What do they want in return?'

Hollander did not reply immediately.

'They must want something,' Julia pointed out. 'Even assuming that the Service has some interest in seeing you prevail, they are really pushing the boat out, aren't they? All right, they will recoup their costs if you win, but it's still a considerable risk. So, what do they want in return?'

'They want information,' Hollander replied. 'They want to know everything I can tell them about Digby.'

'Is there more information?' she asked. 'Things you didn't put in your article?'

He nodded. 'Yes. I held back a lot of information. I didn't want to give away everything I know, at least not immediately.'

'If it's information you want to use in court, you will have to disclose it eventually,' Julia said. 'So I see no reason why you shouldn't tell the Service, too. But I want to know everything you know, whether we use it in court or not. Understood?'

'Understood,' he replied. 'But I think they know about Digby already.'

Julia nodded.

'Perhaps,' she replied, 'but it would be good to know that, one way or the other, wouldn't it?'

* * *

'My father was with the Service for many years,' Julia said. 'I have never worked for them, but I have had some contact through one or two cases my firm has been involved in. That probably explains why Donald's friend made the connection.'

They had taken their seats in the restaurant, always referred to in the Club as the coffee room, where Hollander had reserved a corner table at the far end of the room, away from the windows overlooking Pall Mall, but with a view over the lawn at the rear of the Club. A waiter had taken their orders for vegetable soup and baked halibut, accompanied by a bottle of the Club's White Burgundy. The room was relatively quiet, and they were undisturbed, except for the waiter approaching to offer bread and a carafe of water.

'Does that mean you grew up abroad?' he asked.

'Yes, to some extent. But my parents sent me back home to boarding school as soon as I was old enough. I went out to wherever they were at the time for school holidays, of course, so I got used to a lot of travel. But it wasn't until I left University and began my legal studies that I eventually began to lead a more settled life.'

'I'm sure your father has long since retired?'

'Oh, yes. Actually, he died about five years ago.'

'I'm sorry.'

'Thank you. My mother is still alive. We have this old, rambling house in Norfolk, and she still lives there with a lot of help from a cleaner, a nurse and a gardener. Fortunately, my parents were not short of money. Professor Hollander ...'

'Francis, please ...'

The waiter arrived with the soup. A second waiter brought their wine and opened it quickly, cradling the bottle in his arms, without setting it down on the table. He offered Hollander enough to taste, and it was pronounced excellent. The waiter filled two glasses. She waited until he had retreated.

'Of course, and please call me Julia. Francis, when we go to see Miles Overton this afternoon, I would like you to take my lead as far as mentioning the Service is concerned. I don't want to tell him about Baxter and the offer he has made until I've had the chance to think about it more. I will have to talk to Baxter myself before we commit to anything. I don't want Miles worrying about information that may, or may not, be forthcoming. And I certainly don't want him worrying about where his fees are coming from. That's all done through his clerk, anyway, and my firm is responsible for his fees, whatever the source.'

'Fair enough,' he replied. 'I'll take your lead on that. What are we expecting to cover this afternoon?'

'The law,' she replied. 'It is important to understand the claim Digby is going to make against you, and what defences you may have. Barristers are procedural experts too, so we will look to him to adopt a strategy for the case as a whole.'

'You said in your letter that you have worked with Mr Overton before,' Hollander said, 'so you must have great confidence in him.'

'Miles is one of the best,' Julia replied, without hesitation. 'I should warn you that he is not the easiest of men to get on with. He can be rather brusque and direct. He's not what you would call a natural diplomat. But he is very effective in court, and he is well respected by the judges. He is just the man for this case.'

'What about his junior?'

'I don't know her personally yet,' Julia replied. 'But I do know her by reputation. Her name is Virginia Castle. She has only been at the Bar for a few years, but she is making a name for herself. Her job will be mainly to do the legal research and help Miles to prepare, but she is more than capable of holding her own in court if we need her to.'

'That sounds very encouraging,' Hollander said, finishing his soup and setting his spoon inside the bowl. 'It is good to have the best.'

'We will need the best,' Julia responded forcefully. 'We are up against some of the best on the other side. Digby's solicitor is Herbert Harper, the senior partner of one of the most highly-regarded firms in London. Herbert has been doing this for a long time, and he doesn't miss a trick. And as for barristers, as a QC himself, Digby would probably have had his choice of QCs to represent him. He has chosen Bernard Wesley, who is every bit as good as Miles. He would probably have been my second choice if Digby had not collared him first. His junior is a young man called Schroeder; again, I don't know him, but I understand he is also making a name for himself.'

The waiter came to remove the soup dishes.

'It sounds as though we will have a good fight on our hands, then,' Hollander said.

'Francis,' Julia replied, 'in Sir James Masefield Digby, you are taking on the British Establishment. The Establishment never gives up without a good fight. Even with whatever help the Service can offer, we are going to have our hands full.'

8

Miles Overton QC stood as Julia Cathermole and her client were shown into his room in chambers.

'Julia, welcome. Do you know our junior, Virginia Castle?'

'By reputation only, until today,' Julia replied, taking Miles's hand and kissing him lightly on the cheek.

She turned to Virginia, who had made her way across from her seat by the side of Overton's chair, her hand outstretched. 'But I am pleased to have the chance to instruct you at last. Your reputation precedes you.'

'As does yours, Miss Cathermole,' she smiled.

Julia laughed. 'So people are forever telling me. And it's Julia, please.'

'Ginny,' she replied. 'Only Miles insists on Virginia.'

They shook hands warmly, understanding and liking each other instantly. Ginny was seen as a rising star in Miles Overton's chambers. As a woman of decidedly left-wing views, the product of a girls' grammar school in Newcastle-upon-Tyne and the London School of Economics, she might well have expected to find it hard going in one of the more conservative sets of chambers in London. But Ginny had simply refused to expect – or accept – any such restrictions. She had a formidable legal mind which was envied by most of the men in chambers; she was known as a resourceful advocate, and a calm but tenacious fighter in court. She also had a charm and an engaging wit, with which she had learned to disarm even those who were least disposed to like her. She was popular in chambers as well as successful.

Julia Cathermole admired those qualities, because they closely mirrored her own. At thirty-nine, Julia was six years older than Virginia Castle. In little more than a decade after being admitted to practice as a solicitor, she had built her firm, Cathermole & Bridger, into a force to be reckoned with on the London legal scene. The two partners and six associates were becoming accustomed to dealing with high-profile cases almost as a matter of routine. Julia had a gift, which she loved to exploit, of causing opponents to underestimate her. Her record at Roedean and Girton – where she had taken a starred First in law and played a hard game of hockey – spoke for itself. But it was surprising how often that record was overlooked. She had a cheery, outgoing manner which suggested that she might be just as much at home with horses at a country show as representing clients in difficult court cases in London. Opponents frequently misread her, to their cost. At some point they inevitably discovered that the breezy solicitor with the wild hair had a photographic memory, a gift for reducing complex cases to an understandable, manageable simplicity, and a steely determination to win for her clients. Often her opponents recognised these qualities only when it was too late.

'This is Professor Francis Hollander,' Julia said. With a nod, Hollander shook hands with Miles and Ginny. Miles seated Hollander and Julia in chairs in front of his desk and took his own seat.

'I hope Vernon offered you a cup of tea or coffee,' he said.

'We are fine. We had coffee after lunch, thank you,' Julia replied.

Overton nodded and was silent for some moments before beginning.

'Well, Julia, even by your standards, this is – how to put it… a challenging one.'

Julia smiled. 'That's why I am here, Miles. I need the best. Not only is it a challenging case, but against us we have Harper Sutton & Harper and Bernard Wesley.'

'So I understand,' Overton replied. 'That, of course, only makes our task even more difficult. Not only does Professor Hollander make an extremely serious charge against a distinguished member of the Bar, a Queen's Counsel, but he does so, as far as I can see, without any real evidence to support the charge. You must forgive me, Professor Hollander, but there is no point in beating about the bush. I hope you will forgive me if I speak bluntly.'

'I would prefer it.'

'Good. Then I must tell you that, as the case stands now, neither Miss Castle nor I see any way to defend you against liability for libel. Our best course would be to offer an immediate apology and retraction, and mitigate the damage to Digby's reputation as much as possible. I can talk to Bernard Wesley. I doubt that Digby is interested primarily in money. His family is wealthy, and he has a good practice at the Bar. He is interested mainly in his reputation, and it may well be that there is still time to salvage it.'

Hollander shook his head.

'That is not what this is about, Mr Overton. I went into this with my eyes open. It was not my intention to smear a man's reputation unjustly. Digby has betrayed his country. I know it.'

'What you think you know is neither here nor there,' Overton replied.

'But …'

'Let us assume for a moment that you are correct: that James Digby has been passing secrets to the Russians for some years. God knows how, and God knows why, but let's assume he did. Who knows about it? Who can prove it in court? On your account of the matter, it may be that Viktor Stepanov knew it, but unfortunately Viktor Stepanov is no longer with us, and even if he were, we don't know how credible he would be. Virginia, I believe you have looked into the possibility of getting any statements he may have made into evidence?'

'Yes,' Ginny replied. 'A judge has some power to allow some hearsay under the Evidence Act 1938, but the Act was not intended to take the place of oral evidence, and I can't see any judge letting in such important evidence when the other side would have no means of challenging it.'

'If Digby sues,' Hollander said, 'it will all come out.'

'Oh? And how exactly will that happen?'

'Quite naturally,' Hollander replied. 'Do you recall the case of Oscar Wilde?'

For some moments Overton stared at him blankly before he burst out laughing.

'Oscar Wilde?'

'Wilde brought everything on himself in the end, didn't he?' Hollander said. 'If he had not had Queensberry prosecuted for libel originally, the truth would not have emerged. If the truth had not emerged he himself would not have been prosecuted. The authorities would never have disturbed him. His position in Society would have protected him. He was one of their own. It is the same with Digby. He is part of the Establishment. They would never go after him on their own initiative, left to their own devices. It goes too much against the grain. But I believe that he will not be able to resist suing me and, once he does, the truth will come out. That will leave the authorities with no choice.'

'So you see yourself in the role of the Marquess of Queensberry, Professor, do you?' Overton asked. 'Not a particularly worthy role model, I should have thought.'

'Even a Marquess of Queensberry may have a good cause, Miles,' Julia suggested.

Overton shook his head.

'I know you relish a good fight, Julia, but it's not like you to point an unloaded weapon at Harper Sutton & Harper and ask them to put their hands up. What am I missing?'

She smiled. 'I don't give up just because a case is a challenge, Miles, you know that. I understand your reaction to this article. My reaction was exactly the same when I first read it. But even having known Francis for as short a time as I have, I think I can shed some light on what led him to publish it.'

'I would be delighted to hear it,' Overton replied.

She nodded. 'My experience of academics is that there are essentially two kinds,' she said. 'The first kind is the ivory tower brigade, who shut themselves away and pursue esoteric subjects and write abstract treatises which are of little use to mankind, and which very few people outside their own specialism even bother to read. Why they do that I have never personally understood, but they seem to derive some satisfaction from it. The second kind is the crusader brigade, who think that their research and teaching should serve a useful purpose in the real world. Francis falls into the second group. He needs to feel that his work makes a difference.'

'That's all very well,' Overton protested. 'But the only difference he is making here is that he is going to bring a ruinous lawsuit down on his own head, and that of his University. I am not sure what useful purpose is served by that.'

'The University is not involved in this,' Hollander pointed out. 'The Journal is entirely independent of the University. I founded it with two friends just over three years ago, and we run it on a shoestring. We have no assets. They can sue all they want, but there is no money for them there.'

'That does not give you a licence to publish libel,' Overton said.

'I don't believe my article is libellous,' Hollander retorted.

'A jury will almost certainly find otherwise, unless you can produce some evidence. What did you expect to gain from this?'

'I have already told you. I am trying to expose truths that need to be exposed.'

'Think about it for a moment, Miles,' Julia persisted. 'Francis is a patriotic American. The concerns he raises are real concerns, which affect both his country and ours. You know what's been going on these last few years. Our security services are out of control. Even now, after Burgess and Maclean, after Philby, after Blake and the others who have been convicted, our Government either doesn't know, or is refusing to tell us, how much damage has been done, what advantage we have handed to the Soviets through their treachery and our sheer incompetence. It is time someone stood up and said so. If we remain silent, we have only ourselves to blame when Russia starts pushing its empire even further in our direction.'

Overton pulled himself up in his chair, and placed his hands in front of him on his desk.

'I understand that, Julia,' he said, 'and I am the first to agree that something must be done about the incompetence of the Security Services. If you had written about Burgess and Maclean, if you had written about Philby, if you had demanded a public inquiry – not that you would have been the first to do that – no one could have any possible complaint. But ...'

'It's not just about the incompetence of the Security Services,' Hollander interrupted, his voice animated. 'It's not even about the fact that your Government covers everything up, that it instinctively protects everyone who wears the old school tie, or comes from the right kind of family – bad as all that is. The fact is, Mr Overton, that this treachery has cost lives. How many, I don't know. But when agents are betrayed behind the Iron Curtain, they are tortured, and then either killed or sent to the Gulags. We don't even know how many Digby betrayed every time he went to Moscow.'

Overton did not reply immediately. As a Silk, he was unused to being interrupted during a consultation. Moreover, he had no doubt about what he had already said – the case was legally indefensible, and Hollander's stance was almost suicidal in terms of legal strategy. But Overton found it impossible to ignore the sincerity of his manner. Hollander deserved to be heard, as well as told what was best for him. He decided to try another approach.

'Leaving Stepanov aside,' he asked of the room in general, 'what do we have?'

Ginny spoke up. 'Digby did make a lot of trips to the Soviet Union,' she pointed out, 'and I imagine they would be easy enough to document?'

'Absolutely,' Hollander replied. 'For one thing, he would have needed a visa to visit the Soviet Union. And he did in fact send back articles to the newspapers and chess magazines. No, he was there. There is no doubt about that.'

'Can we put him together with Stepanov?' Ginny asked.

'I am sure we can. They were together at many tournaments, including the 1948 World Championship. Stepanov wasn't a great player, but he was one of the Soviets' fixers. He was one of the people they relied on to smooth things over with FIDE and tournament organisers.'

'Smooth things over in what way?'

'The Soviets like to think they dominate world chess,' Hollander replied. 'In fairness, they do, in terms of playing strength. They have almost all the strongest grandmasters. But they try to dominate in other ways also. There have been persistent rumours that they fix tournaments – I mean, they order some of their players to lose to or draw with others to achieve a particular result, or to promote a particular grandmaster popular with the Government. Chess is a highly political issue in the Soviet Union because they like to hail their successes as proof that the Marxist-Leninist system works. They have a record of non-cooperation with the International Federation. But however dominant they are over the board, they have problems in terms of the world game. They need a few diplomats like Stepanov, men who speak other languages and know how to talk to foreigners in a civilised way, to sort things out for them. So Stepanov was a regular at international tournaments, as well as the Soviet championship. There is no doubt that we can put him with Digby – on many occasions. There are probably photographs.'

'That's something,' Ginny said. 'But we would still need a connection ...'

'That may be possible,' Julia said. She hesitated. 'I can't say any more at present, but I believe it is possible that we may soon have access to some evidence to support Professor Hollander's article.'

Every eye in the room was on her. Hollander, in particular, seemed taken aback.

'Are you going to tell us what this evidence consists of?' Overton asked quietly.

'I don't know,' she replied candidly. 'But I will know within a few days, and I will make it available to you as soon as I can.'

Overton considered for some time.

'Well, I suppose there is no need to do anything at this precise moment. The ball is in Digby's court. But I fully expect that Harper Sutton & Harper will issue a Writ and serve a Statement of Claim for libel within a matter of a few days. You should tell Herbert Harper that you will accept service on Professor Hollander's behalf. But then, once that happens, we will have to make a very serious decision. Virginia…?'

'The only possible defence we see to this claim is one of justification,' Ginny said.

'In other words, we have to prove that the allegations made in Francis's article are true,' Julia said.

'Wholly or substantially true. We gave some thought to a defence of fair comment on a matter of public interest, but there is no real sense in which this article is comment. It is putting forward new facts rather than commenting on existing facts.'

'You must understand, Professor Hollander,' Overton resumed, 'that once you set out to justify what you have written, you are in effect repeating the libel in court and attacking Digby's reputation for a second time. That will increase the level of damages if you lose. There is a potential for enormous damages if you fail to substantiate your claims against Digby. Once they serve their Statement of Claim, we will have fourteen days to file our Defence, so we must decide what we are going to do. If you would like me to approach Bernard Wesley and try to find a solution to this case, this would be the time to do so. If we delay, it will probably be too late.'

'We will justify the claims,' Hollander said.

'I cannot advise that without some evidence,' Overton insisted. 'James Digby is not Oscar Wilde. If we are going to justify, we need some evidence.'

'The evidence will be there,' Hollander replied.

9

Saturday, 13 March

Baxter would have preferred to meet Julia Cathermole somewhere less conspicuous than St Ermin's Hotel. For one thing, the choice of venue there was limited. The Caxton Bar, with its dark interior and low ceilings was claustrophobic, and there was nowhere you could sit that afforded a view of all the tables. Besides, Baxter had a personal distaste for the metal-topped bar. The alternative was the lobby balcony, the hotel's trademark meeting place, accessed from the entrance hall by means of steep, narrow stairs which give a shockingly sudden sense of height, of climbing so far over such a short distance; and which can induce vertigo when you turn around at their summit and find yourself confronted with what appears to be a precipice, an abrupt drop back down to the entrance hall. Once you get over the vertigo, the lobby balcony, presided over by a central, faintly ridiculous pulpit-like edifice, is open and airy, defined only by its sinuous balustrades curving seductively back on themselves around its perimeter, the low ornate ceiling providing the only sense of intimacy. It offers complete visibility, but is correspondingly more public. Julia had specified the lobby, the corner to the left of the main entrance. At least her choice of table was sound. Well, with her background, Baxter thought, she ought to have some sense of how things should be done, some knowledge of basic tradecraft.

Baxter's other objection to the hotel was that it was too obvious in itself, almost a cliché, really. The Special Intelligence Service's association with St Ermin's was one of the worst-kept secrets in London. The Service had taken over a floor of the hotel during the War. Churchill had used it for the meeting which created the Special Operations Executive, the special section of the Service designed to play havoc with the enemy in Europe. But C had told him that Julia had a sentimental attachment to St Ermin's because it had been a favourite haunt of her father's, and at present Baxter needed Julia's full and willing cooperation. He consoled himself with the thought that if anyone was watching, they could probably have followed him wherever he went, and they could certainly follow Julia. It had become too easy to be inconspicuous in London – unless, of course, you were an MI6 watcher wearing the regulation raincoat and trilby.

They shook hands. She already had a coffee in front of her. He sat, and ordered one for himself as soon as the waiter approached.

'Thank you for giving Professor Hollander a lift from the airport,' she began.

'My pleasure,' Baxter replied. 'I hope he is comfortable at the Reform.'

'He seems to be,' she said. 'I know you must be busy, Mr Baxter, as am I, so may I come straight to the point?'

'Please do.'

'I would like to confirm, if I can, the details of the conversation you had with Professor Hollander during the drive. First of all, I understand that you told him that the Service has an interest in the outcome of the action which Sir James Digby is about to bring against him. Is that correct?'

'It is.'

'The Service is prepared to take sides against an Establishment figure, a baronet and leading Queen's Counsel, on behalf of an unknown American academic apparently bent on stirring things up?'

'I would prefer to say that the Service is interested in discovering the truth, regardless of who may be implicated. We are very interested in whatever information Professor Hollander may have to give us, and we may have something of value to offer him in return. Professor Hollander is not the first person to delve into Sir James Digby's history. We would like to know what he has.'

'And if Sir James is implicated …?'

'We will deal with that if and when it happens. Look, Miss Cathermole, the Service has come in for a lot of criticism over the last few years, most of it fully justified. We have been betrayed by men we trusted, men who were our colleagues, men who were our friends. We have been made to look stupid and, worse than stupid, negligent in looking after the security of our country. C is determined that this chapter in our history has to be brought to an end. It is now my job, and that of every officer of the Service, to make sure that this happens. If that involves challenging a few Establishment figures – believe me, whatever may have happened in the past, I fully intend to do it.'

'Fair enough,' she replied.

He shifted uncomfortably in his seat.

'Our distinct preference,' he continued, 'would be to see Professor Hollander defend himself successfully in the action.'

'That might solve a number of problems for you,' she replied. 'I see that.'

'Look, let me ask you bluntly. Does Hollander have any evidence against Digby?'

She thought for some time.

'He has information,' Julia replied. 'Whether he has evidence is another matter.'

'Explain, please.'

'He has information which seems to me to be reliable, on the face of it,' Julia explained. 'But legally, it is hearsay, and I cannot see any judge allowing it to be admitted in court. So it is of limited, if any value, to Professor Hollander in defending the action.' She paused. 'On the other hand, it may well be of considerable value to the Service. You don't have to concern yourselves with the Rule against Hearsay.'

'Quite true,' Baxter smiled. 'In fact, we thrive on hearsay. In some ways, it is our stock in trade.'

'Then I think you will find his information interesting.' She paused again. 'Now I want to ask you something.'

'Please.'

'You must understand that I am reading between the lines here. If I am barking up the wrong tree, I want you to let me know. Hollander is quite convinced that the Service already had its own suspicions about Digby before he published his article. That may just be the conclusion he draws from the information he has. I am not asking you to confirm or deny it in so many words. Even if you do have something, I assume it doesn't go beyond suspicion, given that no action has been taken against him.'

Baxter was showing no sign of responding.

'All right. What I want to ask is: whether you have anything you might be prepared to put on the table in exchange for the information he has to offer you? Something we might actually be able to use in court, even if it is not conclusive in itself? If so, it might make a real difference to Hollander's prospects of success.'

'Possibly,' Baxter replied. 'We might have something of that kind to offer.'

Julia felt her heart start to beat a little more quickly. She made a conscious effort not to betray any excitement in her voice or her body language.

'I am not asking for details, but would this material be information only, or potential evidence?'

'It would be potential evidence,' Baxter replied at once. 'But I must be clear about one or two things.'

'Very well.'

'You must understand that the material in question is of the highest sensitivity.'

'I assumed as much,' Julia said.

'Yes, but you may not understand exactly what that means in this context. My superiors would prefer not to release it if Professor Hollander can win his case without it. At this stage, we have no way of knowing exactly what evidence he has. If the action can be won on the basis of evidence already available to him, we would prefer that you take that course. On the other hand if, as we suspect, Professor Hollander has insufficient evidence, we would prefer to release the material than to see him lose his case. I will have to ask you to speak with my superiors before a final decision is made.'

'That's not a problem,' Julia replied, 'as long as it does not involve any delay. If Hollander can produce no evidence, it won't be long before Digby's lawyers are applying to strike out Hollander's Defence, and once that happens, it's all over.'

Baxter nodded.

'Understood. I will leave it to you to contact us when you are ready. The second thing is that we will need you to persuade the judge that the proceedings must be held *in camera* and without a jury. And anyone to whom the materials are disclosed will have to sign an Official Secrets Act form.'

Julia stared at Baxter for some time.

'When I said the materials were sensitive, Miss Cathermole,' he continued, 'what I meant was, that any disclosure could be dangerous to national security, and could put lives at risk. We cannot take the chance of a leak.'

'I will have to consult with counsel about those conditions,' she replied, after some time. 'Do you have any objection to my telling him in confidence what is going on?'

'No objection,' Baxter replied. 'He will need to know in order to make the application. But I'm afraid these conditions are non-negotiable.'

'I'm not sure a judge will be very happy about them,' she said.

'As I said, they are non-negotiable.'

She nodded.

'Very well. Lastly …'

Baxter smiled.

'Professor Hollander's legal costs. I was wondering when you would get around to that. I can confirm that the Service is prepared to meet them. We will reimburse Hollander covertly. I will make sure that the necessary paperwork is sent to your office.'

She returned the smile.

'Look, I have to ask. Have you considered…?'

'The potential cost? Yes. We have counsel to advise us. We are aware of what we may be letting ourselves in for. But, to look at it another way, it gives us an even greater incentive to make sure Professor Hollander comes out on top.'

Julia sat up in her chair.

'There is just one other thing. I am Professor Hollander's solicitor. The fact that the Service is paying my firm's fees does not mean that I act for the Service. I act for Francis Hollander, and my sole duty is to uphold his interests. If his interests should lie in reaching a settlement, or taking some other necessary action, I will take that action, and I will not consult with the Service about it first. I have to know that you understand that.'

'I understand,' Baxter replied. 'As I say, we have our own counsel.'

She stood.

'Then, thank you,' she said. 'I will be in touch very soon about arranging a further meeting.'

He stood and extended his hand.

'Good,' he said. 'It has been nice meeting you.'

She took his hand. 'Again,' she said.

He looked at her in surprise.

'I'm sorry?'

'Nice to meet you *again*. You came to our house to visit my father in Vienna in the summer of 1938. I was at home for the summer. You were a very young officer then, and you were using the name Moore.'

He stared for some time, and then laughed aloud.

'I am impressed,' he said. 'You have a remarkable memory, Miss Cathermole.'

'Yes,' she replied. 'I do.'

10

Baxter left St Ermin's Hotel a deliberate five minutes after his meeting with Julia ended. It was a fine, though chilly, Saturday morning, the air fresh and invigorating. He walked briskly, though without hurrying, the short distance from the hotel in Caxton Street to number 54 Broadway, which since 1924 had served as the headquarters of the Special Intelligence Service, MI6. Almost mechanically he performed his habitual piece of street-craft, walking past the entrance, crossing Broadway by St James's Park tube station, and walking along Tothill Street some distance towards Parliament Square, just to check, before doubling back along his route.

As he had anticipated, C was waiting for him. By tradition, the head of the Service was referred to simply by that letter of the alphabet. His identity was, in theory, a secret withheld from the public. But anyone with a serious interest in military or intelligence affairs knew, or could discover without undue difficulty, that the current C was Dick White, a former police officer who had previously served as chief of the domestic intelligence service MI5. Relations between the two services had come under considerable strain since the defections of Burgess and Maclean, largely because of MI5's perception that MI6 preferred to rely on breeding and pedigree, and the old boy network, than on objective personal assessments in recruiting its officers and deciding how far to trust them. White's appointment in 1956 had been designed partly to ensure that the two services could work efficiently together, and he had achieved some success. White was regarded by some of Baxter's colleagues as too much of a boy scout, insufficiently innovative and too risk-averse to be an effective leader of a traditionally swashbuckling service, which understood that it could not provide real intelligence without breaking a few rules. But his masters in Whitehall, who had by now become wary of breaking rules, saw him as a safe pair of hands and welcomed his caution. His predecessor, John Sinclair, had resigned over the officially unexplained death of the diver 'Buster' Crabb, almost certainly during an operation to inspect the hull of a Soviet warship moored in Portsmouth harbour as the guest of the British Government, an operation which had been specifically forbidden by the relevant Minister. Whitehall looked to White to clamp down on that particular kind of swashbuckling in future.

White had come in on this Saturday morning especially to meet Baxter, even though Professor Francis R Hollander did not exactly constitute a national emergency. The defections of Burgess and Maclean and, more recently, Kim Philby, had left an indelible imprint on the psyche of the Service and, despite its recent successes in arresting and prosecuting spies and dismantling several Soviet networks, any hint of internal sabotage was taken very seriously. White knew things about the departed spies, and about others such as Anthony Blunt, which were not yet known even to his political masters, and which would turn their hair white if they were to be told. The case of James Digby had a similar potential, but it was at risk of being played out on a very public stage. White was determined to prevent that from happening. He needed to know exactly what was going on, and to take any steps necessary to prevent yet another blow to his Service.

Baxter declined coffee. He had already drunk enough for the day at St Ermin's. C had dressed down for the occasion in a dark brown sports jacket, grey slacks and a green and yellow tie over a darker green shirt. He was seated in the armchair behind his desk, a copy of the *Daily Telegraph*, carefully folded, on the desk in front of him. The building was deathly quiet. One or two officers, including the duty officer, one or two secretaries, and the duty librarian, were finding themselves something useful to do in various corners, but otherwise the place was deserted. Baxter hated it like this. It gave him the creeps. He thrived on the bustle and energy which permeated the building during the working week. At weekends it had an aura of decay about it.

'Julia thinks Hollander has no evidence against Digby that would stand up in court,' Baxter began. 'She didn't say it in quite so many words, but that was the effect of it.'

'Really?' White asked. He turned his swivel chair halfway round towards his window, then back again. 'Then he has behaved rather rashly, hasn't he?'

'Yes. I am sure counsel will have left Hollander in no doubt that he is likely to go down in flames if it goes to court, and that if he tries to defend his article as being true, the only result will be that the damages will be even greater than they would be otherwise.'

'What does Hollander think about that?'

'He isn't interested in settling, apparently. His attitude seems to be: let Digby sue and be damned.'

White nodded and thought for a while.

'Well, I don't know what your reaction is, but it seems to me that Hollander has made some kind of calculation about this, and we don't know all the factors he has put into the equation.'

'I agree, sir,' Baxter replied. 'But apparently he has convinced himself that Digby is stuffed whatever he does. If he fails to sue, the press and public will draw their own conclusions. If he does sue, the truth about Digby will come out one way or the other.'

'Which means one of two things,' White said. 'Either Hollander believes that we will provide him with evidence of some kind, in which case he thinks he would win; or someone at the CIA has been talking out of school and promised to back him behind the scenes, presumably because they share Hollander's suspicions of Digby and think that this is a way of neutralising him, regardless of whether Hollander wins or loses in court.'

'Or perhaps the CIA has its own evidence against Digby,' Baxter suggested. 'It would hardly be surprising. The Americans would have agents watching the chess scene, just as we have.'

'Yes,' White replied, 'though if the CIA had its own evidence, one would have hoped that they would share it with us; but then again, perhaps not, given recent events.'

He was silent for some time.

'You realise that we may have to do our best to help him?'

'Yes, sir.'

'We need to monitor this case very carefully. How are your arrangements going?'

'They are going well, sir. Hollander was easy. We have a contact at the Reform Club where he is staying, so we already have a device in his room and we can gather the data on a daily basis. We did Digby's home during the week, while he and his wife were at work and the housekeeper had finished for the day. We are doing the chambers – Overton's, Wesley's and Digby's – this afternoon, while it's quieter in the Temple. We have the listening team for the chambers set up in a room in a residential chamber in Inner Temple. The usual occupant is a judge who did some work with us during the War while he was a barrister.'

'What about Julia?'

'My judgment is, it would be unnecessary and too much of a risk. Julia will keep us fully up to date.'

White nodded. 'Good. Keep me informed, please.'

'Of course, sir.'

* * *

Bernard Wesley's chambers occupied the second and third floors of number 2 Wessex Buildings, an ornate building which forms part of the magnificent arch at the bottom of Middle Temple Lane, where the lane leads out of the Temple on to the Embankment. Baxter knew that the outside door of the building would be open, and he had a key which would open the door to chambers. He had chosen a Saturday afternoon, rather than Sunday, because the Middle Temple would not be entirely deserted. A few barristers would be at their desks, labouring on urgent briefs. That, of course, involved the risk that there might be someone hard at work in Wesley's chambers who would not be expecting visitors. Baxter was ready for that. The forgers had provided him with a note on what appeared to be the letterhead of the Middle Temple Estate Office, introducing him and his companion as employees of the Inn of Court who had come to investigate a rodent infestation in the basement and check whether it had spread into chambers. His companion was called Whitehead. He wore a dark blue workman's uniform with the Middle Temple emblem, the *Agnus Dei*, emblazoned in bright red on the breast pocket. He carried a large tool box which contained nothing that would be of the slightest use for eradicating rodents. He also had a rather large folding ladder, again not obviously relevant to a search for rodent activity. It was out of place, but Baxter was not concerned about it. In Baxter's experience, people did not ask technical questions about equipment once you had established your credentials. In any case, the ceilings in the Temple were high, and the ladder was needed to reach the chandeliers.

Baxter opened the door of chambers quietly, and then shouted as loudly as he could.

'Hello? Anyone in? I'm from the Middle Temple. I just have to make an inspection. Won't be very long.'

There was no reply. He nodded to Whitehead.

'Wesley's room is the second on the left. Schroeder is across the corridor. I'll just go and see if there's anyone in there.'

'Right you are,' Whitehead replied.

Just under twenty minutes later, the chandeliers in Wesley's room and Schroeder's, and both their telephones, had been fitted with listening devices. Baxter was not a technical man, but he believed Whitehead when he said that these devices were incredibly sensitive, beyond anything that even the spy fiction writers could imagine, and Whitehead read that kind of stuff for fun in his spare time, when he was not dealing with the real thing.

'Got anything interesting planned for the weekend?' Baxter inquired, as they made their way downstairs, having carefully locked the door of chambers. Their nondescript van was parked nearby, in Temple Place, just outside the Inn, where it would attract no attention.

'Not really,' Whitehead replied. 'I'm taking the missus out for a bite to eat this evening. They've opened one of those new steak houses in the High Street. They say it's quite good. She's been on to me to try it for a while. How about you?'

'Oh, just the usual,' Baxter said.

Whitehead had worked with Baxter on and off for a number of years as occasion required, and he had never discovered what 'the usual' was. He had never asked, and he was not going to ask now.

11

Sir James Digby

I went to school at the age of eleven. It has become fashionable now to hate one's boarding school; to talk (and in some cases write) endlessly about its snobbishness and prejudice, its petty jealousies and ingrained brutalities, its unquestioning conformity to the ideals of King and Country, its toleration of bullying and privileged cliques, its promotion of sports above intellectual pursuits, and all its other failings. All of that is true, and much more besides. But I did not hate Baxendale. Its setting in rural Derbyshire was pretty enough and the masters, for the most part, were competent teachers and interested in the boys. There was fagging; there was corporal punishment, applied rather too often and with too much enthusiasm, often by the prefects or other more senior boys; there were house rivalries; there was rugby and cross-country running in freezing cold weather; there were toilets and showers with no doors; the food was variable; and there was no toleration of missing home and family, so it could be a lonely place.

But I did well enough at Baxendale to earn my place at Trinity without extending myself too greatly. The small primary school my brother and I both attended in Clitheroe, where we wrote sentences and simple sums in chalk on slate boards, took its duties seriously. Our teacher, Mrs Chamberlain, a stout lady in her late fifties, was kind and patient. But, even before our first day at school, both Roger and I were tutored by our mother in reading, writing, basic arithmetic, and telling the time, which she believed could not be taught too early, and which she did not wholly trust Mrs Chamberlain to teach as they should be taught. As a result, we both had the blessing and the curse of being considered advanced for our age. By the time I reached Baxendale I had no trouble keeping myself towards the top of the class in most subjects. This might have marked me out for a certain amount of harassment from the sporting fraternity, except for the fact that I was a passable outside half, and I did not mind turning out for my house, and later the school. I was not particularly big or particularly fast, but I believe I was one of the few boys who saw rugby as a game of strategy, rather than simply an excuse to fight each other and get covered with mud without being punished. I began to see how the game could unfold. I saw how I could control the game from the number 10 position; and how I could mislead the opposing defence as to the direction of play; and how, by showing the ball to a defender – preferably a heavy, immobile prop forward – I could create a gap for a break, or open up a pathway for my inside centre to run on to the ball. I was not strong in defence, but that weakness is charitably overlooked in outside halves who have attacking ability, and my wing forwards always covered for me when we were defending our own line against a heavy onslaught by the opposition. Our rugby master, who had played for his native Yorkshire, and had been mentioned as a possible candidate for international honours, encouraged me to take up the game more seriously with a view to getting my 'Blue' at Cambridge. But the game did not appeal to me quite that much, and I see now, with hindsight, that my ability to read a game of rugby was my chess brain working before I had discovered my flair for chess. It was chess that was to become my passion.

I had learned how to move the pieces from my father, but he had little interest in the game, and ranked it together with draughts or, for that matter, whist or snakes and ladders. But my house master, Mr Armitage, a good club and county level player, ran a chess club for the boys before prep on Tuesday evenings. For whatever reason, I decided to go almost as soon as I arrived at school. From the first moment I took one of the carved pieces in my hand and moved it from one square to another, I knew that my life had somehow changed. I did not know why or how, just that it had. Mr Armitage's subject was chemistry, but I always sensed that chess meant far more to him, and that if there had been a way for him to make a living by playing or teaching chess, he would have left Baxendale behind him years before. Mr Armitage was not content – at least in my case – to allow boys to throw the pieces around the board without instruction, in the hope that they would eventually learn. He had realised that most boys would abandon the game out of boredom long before they learned anything worthwhile. So he taught us to read chess notation so that we could read and play through published games. He kept a good selection of chess books in his rooms, and any boy was free to borrow a book as long as he signed for it. I was one of the few who did. Once I got used to it, I found it easy to set up the board and follow the moves the players had made, and I began to see why one player had won and the other had lost the game. In most of the books, the games were accompanied by commentary from a master or grandmaster, which made it easier to understand what had happened. I began to see patterns in combinations of moves which recurred in different games, and why certain positions were strong or weak. I learned that there were standard opening moves, both for White and Black – the Ruy Lopez, the Queen's Gambit, the French Defence.

After some time Mr Armitage started to invite me to come to his rooms for an hour. He would sometimes play games against me himself, making suggestions as to what moves I might play as we went along. Sometimes he would set me problems: White to play and win in four moves, Black to play and force a draw. Sometimes he would select a book and work through a game with me, asking me why such and such a move had been played, why White had refused the offer of a pawn, how Black could have improved his defence. Through those games, I began to learn about the great masters of the past – Anderssen, Steinitz, and Morphy – and the more modern players, particularly Capablanca. I began to see how their styles of play differed from each other. It was quite obvious to me that Mr Armitage saw more in these games than simple technical proficiency. When Morphy won a game with a dazzling sacrifice of a piece, it was, to him, a thing of beauty, a work of art capable of producing feelings comparable to those evoked by van Gogh's paintings or Mozart's music. He never once explained himself to me in those terms, but as I listened to him speak about the games, I understood clearly the effect they had on him.

Nonetheless, when I experienced such a feeling myself, it took me utterly by surprise.

'I want to show you a game,' he said one evening, 'which I think you will like. It was played not very long before you were born. It has a remarkably pretty ending.'

He lit his pipe as I set up the board, and he showed me Edward Lasker v Sir George Thomas, a game played in London in 1912. I remember to this day the effect the game produced on me. When it ended on the 18th move with Lasker forcing checkmate, I suddenly started to cry. I could find no words. My hands were trembling. I felt my mind departing, without any conscious action on my part, for that silent limitless place I had learned to visit as a child. Now, it felt as if I were fainting away, and

I dug the nails of one hand into the palm of the other to bring myself back. Mr Armitage said nothing. He respected my privacy by turning towards the window, and continued to smoke his pipe.

What was it about this game? I have thought about that question many times since, and all I can say is that it is truly astonishing. It starts out with a routine queen's pawn opening, a variation of the Dutch Defence. After ten moves White has some spatial advantage, but that is nothing unusual – White has the advantage of the first move – and after ten moves Thomas must have felt that he had a rather defensive, but quite playable game. Then: devastation, lightning from a clear sky. On his 11th move Lasker sacrifices his queen – his most powerful piece – on h7. It is a move so unexpected, so apparently suicidal, that it is utterly shocking. Thomas has no option but to accept the sacrifice, taking the queen with his king, because the king is in check and has nowhere else to go. Of course, Lasker had foreseen each of the next seven moves, and calculated that Thomas had no defence against the unrelenting assault on his king that followed. But it is the way in which the checkmate is forced that is so beautiful. First White's two knights perform a ballet, a graceful, but deadly *pas de deux*, circling each other, forcing the black king first to h6, then to g5, away from his place of safety. Then the remaining pieces take over, dancing together in a perfectly choreographed sequence. Two pawns stab at the king in turn, brutally direct where the knights were so subtle, giving one stab each, driving the king down the board as far as f3, into the heart of White's territory. A bishop and rook join the chase, giving one check each, pushing the king to g1. He has travelled the full length of the board, seven squares from where he stood, unsuspecting, when Lasker began the combination with the queen sacrifice. He is completely encircled and cut off from the friendly forces that might have defended him. Finally, a casual move of the white king to d2 exposes the black king to White's other rook, which checkmates the king without even moving from its square. The king has no more moves left. The game was an impressive piece of calculation by Lasker. But the beauty of the game lies not just in the calculation, but also in the sheer elegance of the solution; the delicate dance of the white pieces combining against the king with perfect efficiency, each of them playing an essential role in the victory; the pathetic final image of the black king, stranded helplessly so far from home. This is high drama. It is beauty in the sense that theatre is beautiful. But it is also beautiful in the sense that pure mathematics is beautiful, when a profound logic is reduced to a simplicity of breath-taking elegance.

I know now, with a greater experience of life, that I fell in love that evening. I am sure Mr Armitage knew that, but he did not say so. He was wise enough to let me come to terms with it myself. He allowed me to recover my composure, and we played a couple of casual games at 10 seconds a move before I went to prep. I have been moved by great art since, by van Gogh and Mozart, and by the Sonnets when I came to reread them as an adult. I have been moved romantically, as I was for the first time a few years later when I first saw Bridget on our lawn at the manor house, wearing her thin summer dress, barefoot, during an unexpected warm summer downpour, laughing delightedly at the rain, with no thought of seeking shelter. But I have not been moved by anything in my life as I was moved that evening by Lasker v Thomas, London 1912.

I decided that evening that I would devote my life to chess, as far as it was possible. I wrote to Roger about it. He replied.

School
3rd December 1924

Sir,
I have your letter of the 26th ult., the receipt of which affords me great satisfaction, but from which I apprehend that you may have become engaged in a most hazardous endeavour. I do not doubt but that your most excellent intellect and disposition equip you abundantly for success in this most gallant of games. Yet, sir, I know of at least one gentleman, possessed of the most admirable qualities of spirit and mind, who in the pursuit of that occupation so neglected his business, his religious duty, his family and his estate that he permitted himself to fall into ruination. This man, sir, might have aspired to the highest offices of the Church or the Law, but he ruined himself to such a degree that he was compelled to seek his fortune in some uncivilised corner of the world. Out of the natural affection I bear you, my dear sir, I implore you to take heed of his example.

I dined pleasantly last evening at the house master's residence, where I found Carstairs, Malcolm, and others, together with a divine of the Scottish church, the Rev McHenry of Glasgow, a guest of the house master. Carstairs (to the said divine): 'Sir, is it not true that there is

little merit to be found in the city in which you minister?' The minister
would have spoken, but I intervened in his defence. 'Nay, sir,' I replied to
Carstairs, 'for when a man is tired of Glasgow, he is tired of life.' Work
presses much upon me, masters clamour for my pages, but I remain
otherwise unharmed, and your most humble and devoted servant,

Sam Johnson

Mr Armitage arranged for me to begin to play in tournaments
for my age group, though there were only a few available, organised
occasionally by the local chess clubs. By now I was making progress
on an exponential level, because I had seen into the inner workings
of the game and I was approaching an intimate understanding of its
governing first principles – a stage which I truly believe eludes the vast
majority of players. It is the most creative stage of any pursuit to see
and understand its *prima materia*. It unlocks every door in the mind. Mr
Armitage and I progressed into a study of basic endgames. I learned
to checkmate the lone king with king and queen, then with king and
rook, then with king and two bishops, and finally the fiendishly difficult
ending with king, bishop and knight. We went on to basic pawn and
rook and pawn endings. I have always believed that an affinity for the
endgame, the most pure form of chess, marks out the greatest players.
Anyone can learn a repertoire of sound openings, but each endgame is
different, and the ability to force the win or salvage a draw in the often
complex reaches of the endgame is crucial to success in serious play. I
was beating Mr Armitage in equal combat fairly consistently by the end
of my first year, and he wrote to my father asking if he might take me
to compete in the County under-15 Championship during the summer.

12

My father kept the trophy from that first tournament on the mantelpiece in his study for the rest of his life. There were to be others during those years at school, the County Championship, the British Boys Championship, and more. I had joined the chess club in the town, and I was in the process of building my own chess library. Armed with suggestions from Mr Armitage, I asked any relatives interested in buying me presents to give chess books. Everyone knew what I wanted for Christmas or my birthday. All they had to do was to ask me for a title. Some aunts and uncles gave up asking and simply sent book tokens twice a year. It was not long before a useful library began to take shape.

My decision to devote my life to chess was, of course, less successful. I had judged it best to say nothing of my plans until I was within sight of going up to Trinity. It was inevitable that in my final year of school, I would give some thought to what subject I would read once I reached Cambridge. Looking back now, I see how remarkable it was that I did not once doubt that I would get a place there to read whatever I chose to read. I was working hard, and the school had good connections with Trinity. But my parents worried that I was playing too much chess, devoting too much time to studying the game. They warned me that my academic results would suffer. They never did. It is difficult to explain to someone who has never experienced it that, when you understand the governing first principles of a discipline, it costs little mental energy to pursue it. You can carry on with your other activities with no loss of energy as long as you budget your time carefully. I duly got top marks in my higher examination in English, French, and German, and was offered a place to go up to Trinity in October 1931.

When I came home from school for the last time in June, I had the inevitable discussion with my father. I remember the evening well, warm and balmy, the French windows of the study open to the lawn of the manor house, as I took a glass of brandy with him after dinner. I knew that much had changed since Roger had stood in that same place for his interview four years earlier. He had embarked on a trip through France; there had seemed to be little sense of urgency about his future plans. At Trinity, he had read classics and philosophy, subjects which had nothing very much to do with his future as a baronet running an estate in rural Lancashire. But even then, there had been signs that things were changing.

The General Strike had unnerved the country. Even my father's friends in London, who thought of themselves as remote from the heartland of the British working classes, were affected by the human misery which was all too obviously on display. We were a northern family. My father felt a sense of obligation to the people of the North, towards whom the Government often seemed to act so contemptuously. Our family was unusual in having a car, a large Austin saloon. As we drove around Lancashire and sometimes into Yorkshire, Roger and I all too often saw boys of our own age, in very different circumstances to ours. We saw ragged, barefoot children chewing on crusts. We saw the faces of their fathers and mothers and, even at our young age, we learned to recognise the look of hopelessness and despair. My father would sometimes stop the car to talk to people he saw in the street in some dying textile or mill town, and I am still haunted by the memory of children pressing their noses up against the windows of the car, gazing intently on the intimate details of a life they had no hope of sharing. In 1929 there was the Wall Street Crash and the Great Depression, and the feeling that the British way of life was truly under threat. The estate suffered greatly from the Depression. How much it had been depleted my father never confided in me, though I know that my mother fully expected to lose the Manor and spent nights on end crying over it. By 1931, socialist societies were springing up in every city and in every university, but the Labour Party suffered a disastrous defeat in the general election.

'Roger will take over the Baronetcy and the running of the estate, of course,' he began, as we settled ourselves into armchairs turned to face out into the shadows which were just beginning to fall over the darkening grass and trees. 'I had hoped that the estate might provide you with some income, so that you could at least have something while you were setting yourself up. But I am afraid that seems unlikely at present. Still, that's all three years away. Things may have picked up again by the time you graduate.'

It was said without conviction.

'Have you given some consideration to what you will read?'

'Not really.'

'I don't see you as the clerical type,' he smiled.

'I have no real religious convictions, I'm afraid.'

He drained his glass and stood to pour us both a re-fill.

'I'm not sure that's an insuperable barrier in the Church of England.'

We shared a laugh. We were both very fond of our vicar, Norman Jarrett, an amiable man who always seemed very flexible on any question of doctrine. We turned up at church on the major feast days, and Remembrance Sunday. He and his wife, Ada, were frequent guests at the Manor. But he had never inspired me in religious terms.

'I have no doubt that you could get your commission in the Regiment. But the way things are going in Europe ...'

He left the rest of the sentence unspoken, but I knew exactly what he meant. Already there were many who predicted the rise of fascism and a conflict with socialism, many who could feel the first tremors from the dormant social fault-lines beneath the surface of politics in Spain and Germany.

'I had thought of going to the Bar,' I said. It was true. I felt no great enthusiasm for the law. I was not afraid of public speaking, but neither did I find it a powerful attraction. The great advantage of the Bar, as I saw it, would be that I would be self-employed and free to devote time to chess whenever practice permitted. My father had a lot of connections, and I was sure that he would speak to a few solicitors about sending some work my way.

He took a thoughtful drink from his glass.

'Well, you could do a lot worse. It can be difficult in the early days, I believe, but I am sure we can sort something out about that. Yes, I think that might be very good for you. Would you practice in London or up here? I am told that you can have a good practice in Liverpool or Manchester these days.'

'I am not sure,' I replied. 'I must make some inquiries. I will have to join an Inn of Court and eat some dinners, and I am sure I will meet people who can advise me there.'

He nodded. 'I know two or three High Court judges,' he said, 'all members of Lincoln's Inn, if I remember rightly. I will make arrangements for you to be introduced to them.'

He stood and walked to the French windows. It was almost

completely dark now and he quietly pulled them shut and locked the bolt.

'It will be a load off my mind, and off Roger's too, I'm sure, if you have a solid profession to fall back on. I suspect the Bar is one which will thrive in almost any economic circumstances. I don't think it matters much what you read at Trinity, does it? You will do your legal studies at the Inns of Court, and take the Bar exams, when you come down, won't you?'

And so it was settled. As it did not matter much, I decided to read modern languages, with an emphasis on German, a language I had mastered with ease at school. My French was also fairly good, and would serve as my second language. I never told my father that the only profession I truly wanted was the profession of a chess player. I had intended to tell him. I had rehearsed the scene many times during the preceding five years. But with the decline of the economy, the beginnings of social unrest here and in Europe; with the sense of unease that underlay the outwardly confident society in which my family moved; with the difficult times I knew the family and the estate faced, I could not bring myself to tell him that I had fallen in love with a profession which was no profession, which could offer no means of support. I knew by then that in England, in the West, that was the truth about chess. It was an amusing, harmless, respectable pastime engaged in by amateurs who made their money by their pursuits in the real world. It was not an art form which could move people, much less one which offered a living, however meagre.

I knew others who had made their mark in the chess world, of course. I had sat across the board from Hugh Alexander, Harry Golombek, and Stuart Milner-Barry, all strong players with grandmaster potential. Hugh and Roger had been up at Cambridge together; Hugh had taken a First in mathematics at Kings. Their lives and mine would intertwine both on and off the chess board in the years to come. We had never spoken much about playing professionally because the option did not exist. We knew that it was different in the Soviet Union. Even then, though the great age of Soviet chess still lay some years in the future, the Soviets had adopted chess as a symbol of the success of Marxist-Leninist thought. Their success was a matter of national pride. They set up schools to train promising young talent, held many state-sponsored tournaments, and provided a modest state income to some of their most gifted players. It all came at a price, of course. It was a form of propaganda. We knew that. We were not naïve. But it was hard not to let a part of your mind drift enviously towards the East.

I had read a great deal about chess history by then. I knew how indifferent every western culture had been towards the game: even in England during the days of Howard Staunton and Henry Bird, who could have mounted a respectable challenge to any player in the world. Any player with grandmaster potential ever since had been an amateur, perhaps eking out some travel money by means of journalism or writing books, but otherwise dependent on his job in the bank or the civil service or, like Mr Armitage, the school. There were issues of class, too. No man of proper breeding could be seen to be a chess player, any more than he could take to the stage or accept money for playing cricket.

For reasons which will be all too obvious, I was profoundly affected by the story of Paul Morphy, 'the Pride and Sorrow of Chess' and undoubtedly one of the greatest geniuses the game has ever produced. Morphy came from a well-to-do Creole family in New Orleans, a family which regarded it as utterly unacceptable, socially speaking, for one of its sons to play chess, except perhaps occasionally for pleasure, while sipping a mint julep on the porch during a lazy, humid, Louisiana afternoon. Morphy did what was expected of him and practised as an attorney, though apparently without enthusiasm and with little distinction. He fought against the social chains for long enough to be acclaimed as the unofficial champion of the world, having made a triumphant visit to Europe during which he demolished all the strongest players of his day. He was recognised for the genius he was in the chess world, and by some intellectuals outside it – Longfellow and Oliver Wendell Holmes spoke at a dinner in his honour in Boston after his return from Europe. But in the end, the chains regained their hold on him. The demands of his social situation, which he had already hopelessly compromised, prevented the continuation of what could only have been the most brilliant career. His mind began to decline. He eventually went completely mad, gave up chess, and shut himself up in his house, leaving only to visit the Café du Monde or the Court of the Two Sisters, walking hurriedly through the streets, talking incomprehensibly to himself, until his death at the age of 47. Years later, I visited his house. It is still there for anyone to see, in the Rue des Ursulines. I stood outside for a long time, and found myself weeping.

Roger wrote to me not long before I went up to Trinity.

London
3 July 1931

Sir,
Nothing could afford me greater delight than the prospect of your
impending admission as an undergraduate at the College. I own freely
that I owe much to the divines and fellows of that most excellent
institution for the development of my own faculties, to which pursuit,
perceived by many to be utterly futile, they most selflessly devoted
themselves for some three long years. I am greatly in their debt, more
so than I can repay. But have every hope, my dear sir, that your skill
in the elegant German language will in some measure compensate for
my own lamentable deficiencies in the realm of more ancient tongues,
and so restore to some degree the fame of our house. I entreat you,
sir, not to fail to make the acquaintance of a gentleman I esteem most
highly, who after the most illustrious successes as an undergraduate,
which compare most favourably with my own poor efforts, has remained
at the University, pursuing higher studies in the field of art. I shall
address a letter of introduction to him on your behalf before your arrival
at Cambridge, and I have no doubt that he will entertain you most
hospitably. The gentleman's name is Mr Anthony Blunt, and I have hopes
that he will, with your consent, introduce you to a certain society of
gentlemen in the University with which I believe you will be well pleased
and find worthy of your attendance. You will be pleased, sir, to greet him
on your arrival and present to him the compliments of your most humble
and devoted servant,

Sam Johnson

13

'According to the map, it's just ahead on the left,' Jess Farrar said. 'So let's begin to slow down. Change down into third.'

Ben Schroeder checked his mirror and selected third gear. His clutch control was not yet very fluent, and the Hillman Minx shuddered slightly as he came up on it rather too quickly.

'Good,' Jess said. 'About 75 yards ahead on the left. So signal, "I am slowing down and intend to stop". There are no parked cars to worry about, so start pulling slowly in towards the kerb. Slower, Ben, down into second – clutch! clutch! – all right, good. And brake. You're getting too close to the kerb. Straighten up. Good. Now, clutch in, gear lever to neutral – neutral, Ben. Handbrake on. Release clutch. Switch off ignition.'

She breathed out heavily and nodded.

'Good, you are making good progress. We will make a driver of you yet.'

Ben laughed. 'I am sure I frightened you to death.'

She reached across and kissed him on the cheek.

'There was the odd scare, but nothing serious,' she grinned. 'This was good tonight, Ben. You drove all the way from Islington to Hampstead, in the dark and through some rain. This is the kind of practice you need. However many lessons you have, you still need time behind the wheel, so that when it comes time for your test, it all feels automatic.'

'It doesn't feel at all automatic yet,' Ben protested. 'I feel I have very limited control over the car.'

'It will come,' she replied. 'Give it time. I will drive back, so don't worry about that.'

Jess had taken the job with Barratt Davis while she worked out what she wanted to do with her history degree from Bristol University, but she was enjoying it enough to be thinking of making a career of her own as a solicitor. She was an inch or two shorter than Ben's five feet ten, and her figure was fuller than his almost austere slimness. Her eyes were hazel, and her hair, which she usually held at the back with a silver pin, a slightly darker shade of brown. When not dressed for work she wore autumnal browns, oranges, and yellows. Tonight, a pretty orange dress just below the knee.

Jess and Ben had met the previous year, when Barratt had instructed Ben in two very difficult cases in Huntingdon, one involving a vicar accused of molesting one of his choir boys, the other involving a man who was to be one of the last in England to be charged with and hanged for capital murder. The cases had been fraught with difficulty, tense, and traumatic. The vicar, the Reverend Ignatius Little, had been acquitted, but had later committed suicide in a police cell after being arrested for a similar offence. William Cottage had been hanged in August for the murder of Frank Gilliam, whom he had killed in a frenzied rage before raping and attempting to murder Frank's girlfriend, Jennifer Doyce. The difficulty of the case had been compounded by the fact that Ben's leader, Martin Hardcastle QC, was an alcoholic who decided not to call Cottage as a witness, even though Cottage claimed to have an alibi for the time of the killing. A verdict of guilty followed. Ben had argued in the Court of Criminal Appeal that the verdict should be overturned, but to no avail. The Home Secretary had refused a reprieve.

Ben and Jess had grown gradually closer during these exhausting trials. When Ben's beloved grandfather suffered a heart attack during the Cottage trial, she drove him to London, went with him to the hospital, and drove him back to Huntingdon the next morning. It was this episode which had led Jess to talk Ben into driving lessons. Ben had been born and raised in the East End of London, had attended school and university in London, and had spent his whole life travelling on public transport. But if he was to practise outside London, driving could be a necessary skill. Jess arranged lessons for him, and put L-plates on her car so that he could practise between lessons. Despite his pessimism, she felt that he was getting the hang of it.

Cottage's execution had left Ben feeling lost and hopeless, utterly defeated, devastated, not knowing where to turn. So on that very morning, she took him to Sussex, to the house of her aunt and uncle who were staying in France for the summer. She stayed with him, sat with him in the garden in silence for hours on end, walked into the village to shop or visit the King's Arms, shared a simple supper with wine with him before an early night. On the second night they made love for the first time, and Ben's right mind began to be restored. By the time they returned to London a week later they were in love.

Ben knew the rule about seeing solicitors or those who worked for them. This was seen in the profession as a form of 'touting for work'; but the rule made no sense to him, and in any case he was too much in love to care. They were discreet, spending evenings at his flat in Canonbury or at hers in Covent Garden. Their relationship was no secret to Barratt Davis, who approved unreservedly and felt nothing but disdain for the pretension of the Bar in laying down such archaic rules of conduct. It was now no secret to Bernard Wesley, who also approved, but who, as Head of Chambers, felt he had a duty to counsel Ben and to try to guide him through this professional minefield. An invitation to dinner at the Wesley house was a promising sign, but one which gave both Ben and Jess some anxiety. Sometimes, late at night, as they were falling asleep, they would talk about their predicament, imagining solutions as radical as starting a new life together in Australia. But then the morning would come, and their families were still there, and there was work to do, and a new day to be lived.

Ben locked the car. Jess carried flowers, which they had bought for their hostess. They walked together in the lightest of rain to the front door, which was enclosed by a white stucco porch and lit by an enormous carriage house lamp. The house was a massive one which backed on to Hampstead Heath, and there was a freshness in the still evening air.

'Ben, Jess, welcome,' Bernard Wesley said. He looked over his shoulder, and called out. 'Amélie, they are here.' He took the flowers from Jess and kissed her on the cheek. 'Thank you. Do come in.'

He placed a hand on Ben's shoulder. Ben had been told that dress was casual, but his pupil-master and mentor, Gareth Morgan-Davies, who was second in seniority in chambers, and who had known Bernard Wesley for many years, warned him that 'casual dress' meant something different to Bernard Wesley than it might to most others. It signified mainly that there was no need to wear a tie, and Gareth had advised a smart jacket with an open collar. Ben was relieved to find that Gareth's advice was exactly right.

The house was warm and inviting. They were ushered into a spacious living room with a high ceiling, tastefully furnished in contemporary style. Amélie was a petite, vivacious woman, with dark hair and mischievous eyes, who seemed to glide rather than walk into and out of rooms. Her informality contrasted immediately with her husband and yet, strangely, complemented it. She wore a striking red and black kaftan with black sandals which, whenever she was seated, spent far more time off than on her bare feet. Both wrists and her left ankle boasted thin bracelets. She greeted both Ben and Jess with a warm kiss as Bernard introduced them. Amélie was an academic, a specialist in modern French history, and although her lightly-accented English was flawless after many years of life in England, she floated effortlessly between English and French, which she also read and wrote every day of her working life. Bernard was opening a bottle of Chablis which had been waiting in ice in a pewter cooler on a side table.

'I have sherry if you prefer, or I could probably even mix a martini, if anyone would like one.'

'That looks fine,' Ben said.

'Just a small glass for me, please,' Jess said. 'I have to drive home. We gave the chauffeur the night off.'

'You can't get the help these days, can you?' Wesley replied with a smile.

Amélie took a glass of Chablis and excused herself to return to the kitchen.

'*Malheureusement*, we have also given the night off to the chef,' she smiled. 'So I must take his place for a few minutes. Please excuse me. *Dix minutes*, Bernard.'

'*D'accord, chérie.*'

Wesley waved Ben and Jess into comfortable armchairs, and asked Jess about her family and work. Being used to Bernard Wesley only as his formal Head of Chambers, Ben was surprised at his ability to put Jess at ease with a relaxed and casual line of chatter, bringing Ben into the conversation too, at intervals. Exactly at the end of the predicted ten minutes Amélie appeared, pushing open the sliding doors at the far end of the room, which led into the adjacent dining room. The room was lit only by two small wall lamps and two large candles held in exquisite silver candlesticks. From somewhere outside, not loud enough to intrude, the soft strains of *Eine Kleine Nachtmusik* drifted around the table. A rough country pâté awaited them, with a basket containing two baguettes and glasses of a white Burgundy.

'Help yourselves to bread,' Bernard said. 'Just tear a piece off.'

'The pâté is delicious, Mrs Wesley,' Jess said.

'It is Amélie,' she insisted, then paused.

'Bernard tells me that you are conducting, how shall I say, the forbidden *affaire, n'est-ce pas?* How exciting! I must know everything about it!'

Ben was momentarily thrown off balance. Was she mocking them? But her eyes were sparkling and she was smiling warmly; she was an ally.

'Amélie likes to get straight to the point,' Bernard said apologetically.

Jess laughed. 'We don't mind,' she said.

'Quite the contrary,' Ben added. 'We are only too glad of all the advice we can get.'

'The powers that be,' Bernard explained, 'take the view that a barrister who has any kind of social relationship with a solicitor, or someone who works for a solicitor, must be touting for work, which is strictly forbidden under the code of practice.'

'But you told me that the solicitor already sends Ben work,' Amélie protested.

'That is true,' Bernard agreed. 'But to some people, it makes no difference. These people believe it is wrong under any circumstances for the Bar to fraternise with solicitors.'

'Fraternise?' Jess repeated. 'What a terrible word! Is that what we are doing? Fraternising?'

'I know,' Bernard said sympathetically. 'The Bar does like to keep a safe hundred years or so behind the times.'

'*Ce sont des imbéciles,*' Amélie said. 'Bernard, there must be something you can do about it.'

'I am certainly going to try,' he replied. 'The benchers can give their approval if they are convinced that it is a serious relationship. The point is supposed to be that a barrister should not use his social contacts to persuade a solicitor to send him work that might otherwise go to another barrister who doesn't have the same contacts. Work should go to the most deserving, not to those who can exploit their social contacts. That is obviously the real purpose of the rule, and it has nothing to do with your case.'

'The Bar can be very reactionary,' Ben said quietly. 'It has always seemed to me that they cling to obsolete rules for their own sake.'

'They have that tendency, certainly,' Bernard agreed. 'But they have to move with the times to some extent. They should be getting worried that they may be vulnerable in law if anyone took them to court over it. You see, they may not be able to justify the rule except in a genuine case of touting. So the rule is far too wide. There was a member of the Bar some years ago – I forget his name – who had a daughter who was an actress. The daughter became engaged to marry a solicitor, and the Bar threatened to disbar this poor chap if he went to the wedding.'

'Mon Dieu,' Amélie said, horrified. 'What did he do?'

'He told them to get stuffed and went to the wedding,' Bernard smiled, 'and fraternised with his son-in-law regularly thereafter. Of course, the Bar did nothing. It just made them look stupid. They know the rule needs to be changed, and we are going to encourage them to change it now before they look even more stupid.'

Amélie touched Jess's hand.

'Don't be discouraged,' she said.

'I'm not,' Jess said. 'I sometimes get angry about it, but I am determined to stay calm and see it through.'

'Good for you,' Amélie said.

Jess turned to Bernard. 'Thank you,' she said.

'You are very welcome.'

Amélie laughed. 'It is a cause dear to Bernard's heart,' she said.

'Oh?'

'But of course. It is not known generally in the chambers, I think, but Bernard is himself the incurable romantic.'

Ben smiled. 'Really?'

'She exaggerates,' Bernard insisted.

'Non, pas du tout.' She leaned over towards Jess confidentially. 'I met Bernard in Paris many years ago. I was finishing my studies at the Sorbonne, and he came to see the city before he started his practice.'

'I had just finished my pupillage with Duncan Furnival,' Bernard said.

'Oui, c'est ça. As a student I did not have much money, so I had a tiny flat in a building on the Quai aux Fleurs.'

'The whole place was not much bigger than our living room and dining room here,' Bernard said.

'Yes, and it was on the sixth floor.'

'And no lift.'

She laughed. 'But every day after we had met, Bernard would call on me and bring some flowers, and if we could afford it we would go to the *bistrot* and eat a *croque monsieur* and drink a glass of *vin ordinaire*. He was very proper, but also very gallant, the complete gentleman *tout à fait comme il faut*. And he was as romantic as can be. And now, every year, we find a *bistrot* for our anniversary, either in London or in Paris.'

Bernard was smiling but he had turned slightly red. She took his hand.

'I am sorry, *chéri*, I embarrass you. I didn't mean to.'

'There is no need at all to be embarrassed,' Ben smiled. 'Not with us.'

'I think that is very charming,' Jess said.

Bernard stood. 'Why don't I help you clear away so that we can get to the next course?'

* * *

The remainder of the dinner had been superb, a classic country *boeuf aux carottes*, followed by a light lemon mousse. Jess volunteered to help Amélie clear away before she made coffee. Bernard steered Ben into the conservatory at the back of the house, which looked over Hampstead Heath, though tonight the darkness and the rain obscured any view. A tray with glasses and a decanter of Armagnac stood on an unfinished light wood sideboard. The chairs and tables were wicker, there were brightly-coloured red and green Indian rugs on the floor, and some vivid modernist paintings on the walls. The room felt intimate and cosy.

'I really appreciate this, Bernard,' Ben said. 'We have been worried about it.'

'Of course, you must have been,' he replied, pouring each of them a glass of Armagnac. 'But I meant what I said earlier. I am quite optimistic. They should be looking for a way out, it seems to me.'

He paused to swirl his Armagnac in his glass and take an appreciative sniff.

'If you don't mind talking shop for a minute in the absence of the ladies…?'

'No, of course not.'

'Good. Tell me… what is your impression of Digby?'

Ben shook his head. 'I'm not entirely sure,' he replied. 'On the face of it, he is the innocent victim of a wicked libel and it's not hard to understand why he wants to do whatever he can to restore his reputation.'

'On the face of it?'

Ben sipped his Armagnac. 'He plays the part to perfection. But… there is something missing.'

Bernard nodded. 'Yes. I have that impression too,' he agreed. 'I'm not sure why.'

'Perhaps he is not angry enough?' Ben suggested.

'Perhaps. He got rather indignant when I tried to suggest that suing Hollander might have its own problems and there might be another way of dealing with the situation.'

'Indignant, but not angry,' Ben insisted.

'Yes,' Bernard said. He paused. 'Well, perhaps that's just Digby's personality, or the way he was brought up. Perhaps that's all there is to it. He does practise in the Chancery Division, after all. They are all so damned civilised over there.'

Ben smiled. 'Well, we may be imagining things.'

'There is something else, though,' Bernard said. 'I am still worried that Hollander has published such a serious libel without any evidence that we can see. I'm not satisfied with Digby's theory that he is just a publicity-seeking American academic who doesn't care how ruinous the proceedings are as long as he creates a sensation.'

'No,' Ben agreed. 'There must be easier ways to make a name for himself than this. So, what do you think he has up his sleeve?'

'I'm not sure,' Bernard replied. 'But he has something, Ben, I know it. Every instinct I have tells me so. How is Jess getting on with her research?'

'It's going well. She is waiting for some written materials. She wants to read every word Hollander has ever written in any journal, anywhere in the world. That may help, but I have a nasty feeling that whatever real evidence Hollander has may not be easy to find.'

He sipped from his glass again.

'Until it's too late,' he added.

14

Amélie and Jess joined them, bringing the coffee and cups, with a small silver tray laden with dark chocolates.

They sat down around the wicker coffee table, enjoying the quiet darkness of the Heath against the subdued lighting of the conservatory.

'Jess has a question for you, Bernard,' Amélie said. 'She is hesitant to ask you herself, although I told her not to be concerned.'

'You must ask whatever you like, Jess,' Bernard reassured her. 'Don't be shy about it.'

Jess was holding her hands in her lap, one gripping the other.

'I am sure I am just worrying too much,' she said. 'But I am not sure how this works exactly. You said you would talk to the other benchers of the Middle Temple and try to convince them that Ben and I have a serious relationship. But where would this happen? Can Ben and I be present? Can we say something, talk to them ourselves, so that we can explain the situation?'

Bernard sipped his Armagnac thoughtfully.

'They have convened a committee,' he replied, after some time, 'which means that they want to handle the situation relatively formally. I will arrange for Ben to appear in front of them – with me as his advocate, of course. I would imagine that will take some time to arrange, but that is a good sign. I am not going to press them. I don't think we should send the signal that we are anxious about it, or regard it as anything urgent. And the more time they have to think about it, the more opportunity they have to reflect on what they are doing and come to their senses.'

Amélie and Jess exchanged glances.

'But Jess will also be there, at the hearing, of course?' Amélie asked uncertainly.

Bernard seemed uncomfortable. 'No, I don't think so,' he replied.

'Technically, this will be a disciplinary hearing against Ben. Jess is not a member of the Inn, and so they cannot accuse her of doing anything wrong. Technically, it doesn't concern her.'

'But this affects Jess also,' Amélie protested. 'It affects her future, and the future of the man she loves. Of course it concerns her.'

'I said "technically",' Bernard replied. 'Of course it concerns Jess, and if the committee want to hear from her, they will let us know. But I don't think they will. I would prefer to keep this as simple as possible. I would like both Ben and Jess to prepare a short written statement, just to set out the history of the relationship: how they met; the fact that Barratt was already sending Ben work before they met; their plans for the future, and so on. Ben will be there to answer any questions.'

Ben looked at Jess. She seemed pale and was looking down. He glanced at his watch.

'Amélie, it has been a delightful evening,' he said. 'Dinner was wonderful. But we have to drive back to Islington. We should really be going.'

'Of course,' Amélie replied, getting to her feet. 'I am so glad you could come.'

She walked over to Jess and put her arms gently around her. At first she sensed Jess pulling away, but she held her in the hug for some moments and eventually felt her relax into it, and then felt a tear on her shoulder. She kissed Jess on the cheek, not a quick social kiss but a lingering, fond one, with understanding.

'*Ne t'inquiète pas*,' she said, '*ça va se passer bien*. It will be all right.'

Jess nodded. Stepping back, she opened her handbag, took out a white lace handkerchief and dried her eyes.

'I am here,' Amélie said, 'any time you want to talk.'

'Thank you,' Jess replied.

* * *

They drove back to Canonbury in silence. As ever, she drove skilfully and navigated her way effortlessly through the rain, past the dim street lamps and the faint black-and-white directional signs. But there was a hint of anger in her driving: in her acceleration away from traffic lights the instant they changed to green; in her unusually aggressive overtaking; and in the sharpness of her turns. Ben sat passively in the passenger seat, waiting for an opening to break the silence in a meaningful way. It never came.

She pulled up in front of his flat, put the car in neutral and engaged the hand brake, but did not switch off the ignition. She allowed her head to sink onto her hands in the middle of the steering wheel. Eventually, she raised her head, and turned to look at him.

'I am going back my place tonight,' she said.

The words filled him with terror. Losing her was a nightmare that sometimes haunted his dreams. Never in these dreams had he been able to imagine how he would cope without her. He loved her completely. But he felt her withdrawing from him, and he felt powerless to prevent it.

'Jess, please,' he began, 'I know you're angry, but ...'

'Angry? Why should I be angry? Just because you and Bernard Wesley are going to huddle together in private with those old men in the Middle Temple and then tell me whether I am allowed to be in love with a member of your secret society?'

'It won't be like that.'

'Oh? That's what I heard Bernard say, Ben. I won't be there while my future is decided. It's a technical matter. You are the only one involved. You will let me know what happened after it is all over.'

'Jess, if you would listen to me for a moment. It's all right.'

'No, Ben,' she replied firmly. 'It is not all right. It is not all right that I can't say a word in my own defence. It is not all right that they treat me like someone who doesn't even matter.'

She felt tears welling up again and grabbed the handkerchief from her handbag.

'It is not all right, and I don't know what to do about it.'

He tried to put his arm around her shoulders, but she shrugged it off.

'No,' she said. 'You didn't say a word about it.'

'What could I say?'

'You could have ... oh, I don't know ... something, anything; something to show me that you at least care.'

He exhaled heavily.

'Jess, look, we are both very tired. Switch the engine off and come upstairs. We will talk tomorrow, and I promise I will find a way to make this right.'

She shook her head.

'I need some time,' she replied. 'I am going back to Covent Garden tonight.'

Reluctantly, he opened the car door and began to get out, then he turned back.

'Well, can I at least call you?'

She threw her hands in the air. 'Yes, call me.'

'When?'

'I don't know, Ben. I need some time to be by myself and think this through.'

His heart was cold with fear as he closed the door. He watched until she turned the corner and was out of sight.

15

It was almost 10 o'clock when Ben set out at a brisk pace to walk the short distance from the station along New Street to the magnificent Victorian Burlington Hotel. The journey to Birmingham had involved an early train from Euston, but he had timed it well, and was a few minutes early for his meeting. It had not been an easy appointment to arrange. B H Wood, the founder and editor of *Chess*, a popular and successful magazine, was a busy man. But the name of Sir James Digby had engaged his attention, and he had eventually agreed to meet Ben for an hour to offer some insight into the world of chess, and Ben's client in particular.

Ben was not feeling at his best. He had not had a great deal of sleep over the last week. After Jess's abrupt departure for Covent Garden on the Saturday night, now some nine days ago, he had felt alone and abandoned. He had spent much of that night lying wide awake on top of his bed, until he fell into an uneasy shallow slumber as dawn was approaching. Sunday was a little better, but not much. He felt listless, and tried calling her number repeatedly, but she did not answer. He felt that he was doing everything he could to resolve the suspicion of touting. What did she expect of him? The possibility that he might have lost her through some, God only knew what, careless word, preyed on his mind. He tried to concentrate on books he had borrowed from Islington public library, one dealing with the history of chess and one offering a basic introduction to the rules and strategy of the game, illustrated by a few games played by the great masters. There were also copies of articles written by Professor Francis R Hollander, which Jess had left after her latest research expedition to the libraries at LSE and King's College, and which he had hoped to read before the next conference with Sir James Digby.

But his mind was wandering, and he found himself unable to focus for more than one or two minutes at a time. In mid-afternoon he gave up and walked aimlessly around his flat, snacking on instant coffee and biscuits, until he collapsed into bed shortly before midnight and finally managed a few hours of sleep. It was a pattern which was to repeat itself during the week. Each morning, the shrill ring of his alarm clock roused him in time to get ready for court. But he could find little enthusiasm for the work. Mercifully, Merlin had found him some simple enough cases in the county court, which did not tax his brain to any real extent, but they had nonetheless proved to be as much as he could focus on. After court, he declined drinks with members of chambers, and made his way back to his flat. This morning and the night that preceded it had passed just like the others – with Ben snatching at sleep until the alarm warned that it was time to get up and prepare for his excursion to Birmingham.

Wood was waiting for him at a corner table in the hotel's fine lobby. He stood as Ben approached, and they shook hands. Wood was tall and well built, dressed in a brown sports jacket and slacks, with a green and white chequered open-necked shirt. His dark hair was beginning to thin, but he had a ready smile, and there was a definite twinkle in his eyes.

'I hope you haven't been waiting too long, Mr Wood,' Ben said.

'Not at all. I've just arrived.'

'Good. It was kind of you to meet me here, so close to the station.'

'I am based in Sutton Coldfield,' Wood replied with a smile. 'But no one ever knows where Sutton Coldfield is. Everyone seems to get hopelessly lost trying to find me. It is easier to meet in the city centre.'

'Well, I appreciate it. How long have you been producing *Chess*?'

A waiter approached, and they ordered coffee.

'I started the magazine in 1935,' Wood replied, 'so it's been about thirty years now.'

'That must have been quite an undertaking.'

Wood laughed. "Yes, you could say that. It was a gamble at the time. There was no way to predict whether it would be successful or not. I have been fortunate, but I suppose I give chess players what they want – some good games to play through, and a way of keeping up with the news.'

'What led you to do it?'

'It was a way of making a living from chess. This is a dilemma which haunts every strong British chess player. I know I have the ability to play at the top level, but I can only realise that ambition if I can devote enough time to the game – which means becoming a professional.'

'But there is no way to make a living just by playing?' Ben asked.

'Exactly. In the West, professional chess players spend more time writing books and articles, acting as referees and arbiters, perhaps teaching occasionally, than they do playing. It is necessary, to make a living. But it means that they don't have the experience of playing in the big international tournaments. Harry Golombek and Leonard Barden are good examples, as am I, except that I found my own individual way of doing things. Most of our stronger players do their best to combine chess with a career, fitting in the odd tournament here and there when they can, and having relatively little time to study the game – which you have to do constantly to compete at the highest levels. Hugh Alexander is a good example of that. So is Jonathan Penrose, who is probably the most naturally gifted player Britain has produced so far. But I don't think he will ever take chess up full time as a professional. You have one or two men – Peter Clarke, and Bob Wade, a New Zealander – who are giving it a go, but it is a hard life, with no guarantee of making enough money to live.'

The waiter brought their coffee, set it down, and walked quietly away.

'You said "in the West",' Ben observed.

'Yes. The Soviets do things very differently. Chess is a national obsession in Russia, for one thing, so there is a much bigger market. But it's not just that. The Government has adopted chess as a national project. They set out to dominate the game, and they have. But, of course, they have done it by sponsoring promising young players, bringing them on from an early age, giving them the opportunity to study chess as a discipline in its own right, teaching it in schools alongside history and physics. They allow the best players to compete regularly in tournaments, both in Russia and abroad.'

'That must be an expensive project,' Ben said.

'It is. But they don't care about the expense. It is a form of propaganda for the communist way of life. Success comes from following the Marxist-Leninist path, which offers a combination of discipline and creativity. The State sponsors the art of chess as a statement about what communism can achieve.'

'And, as a result, they have a lock on chess at the highest level?'

'Indeed.'

'Is there any chance of a western player competing with the Russians, perhaps being a realistic contender for the world championship?'

Wood shrugged. 'There are those who think Bobby Fischer has the ability. But the question is whether he will get enough support to overcome the Soviet machine.'

He took a long drink of his coffee.

'But you haven't come to Birmingham to listen to me going on and on about the Soviet domination of chess.'

He paused.

'I am sorry about this business with James,' he said. 'How is he holding up?'

'Quite well, in the circumstances,' Ben replied.

'Good. I have been following it in the papers, of course,' Wood said. 'From what I have read, he seems to be quite insistent about suing Hollander.'

'He is,' Ben replied. 'It's a very serious libel. He can't let it pass unchallenged.'

'No, of course.' Wood looked away, across the lobby to the main entrance, and back again. 'Don't answer this if you don't think you should, for any reason, but does he have a strong case, would you say?'

'Very strong, as far as we can see,' Ben replied. 'So far, Hollander has not produced a shred of evidence to support his claim that James was working for the Soviets and, as far as we know, James has never been under suspicion.' He smiled. 'I hope you are not about to disillusion me.'

Wood laughed. 'No, I don't think so. I certainly hope not.'

He reached down by his side and picked up a worn brown leather briefcase, from which he took four sheets of paper with handwritten notes, and a black hard-backed book. He scanned the notes.

'When we spoke on the phone, you mentioned three names to me, including James,' he said. 'First, Professor Francis Hollander. I'm afraid I know very little about him. You probably know more than I do, certainly about his academic record. As a chess player, there is very little to say, really. He is a reasonably strong player as an amateur, but nowhere near the standard of the American élite, Bobby Fischer, Sammy Reshevsky, Reuben Fine, Arnold Denker, and the rest. I understand he speaks fluent Russian; in any case, he accompanies their teams and players to certain events to act as interpreter and generally lend a hand with arrangements on the ground. That's about all I can say.'

Ben nodded. 'What about Viktor Stepanov?'

Wood handed Ben the hard-backed book.

'You will find a short biographical note in here, together with one or two of his games,' he said. 'You are welcome to keep it. I have several copies lying around the office, and if I ever want more, all I have to do is ask. This is an excellent example of chess as propaganda, as you will find if you delve into it.'

'Thank you,' Ben replied. He looked at the cover. '*A Survey of Soviet Chess.*'

Wood laughed. 'Yes. Foreign Languages Publishing House, Moscow, which in itself tells you what to expect. It is actually quite an informative book, and it does provide access to quite a number of published games which you might not find very easily anywhere else. But it really is the most shameless piece of propaganda. The biographical note on Stepanov is not terribly detailed, and this was published in 1955, several years before his death, but you may find something of interest in it.'

Wood drained his coffee cup.

'My impression of Stepanov is about the same as the impression you are likely to get from the book,' he continued. 'Moderate strength grandmaster, very useful player, capable of beating anyone on his day, but not destined to scale the heights of the world championship. His main claim to fame is that he represented the human face of Soviet chess.'

'Meaning …?'

'The Soviets tend to think that because they dominate the game in terms of playing strength, they can throw their weight around and order people about when it comes to organising international tournaments and laying down the ground rules for the world championship. Needless, to say, that attitude tends to alienate everyone else. Eventually, they seemed to realise that a little cooperation would go a long way, and they brought in Stepanov as a kind of diplomat. He spoke excellent English, and two or three other languages, and for a Russian he was very charming. He reminded me of Andrei Gromyko, their ambassador in London, in that respect. Stepanov poured oil on troubled waters, and he was very good at it. I met him a number of times, and I have to say he was very impressive.'

Ben nodded. 'Is it likely that he had connections with the KGB?'

Wood laughed loudly. 'That's a bit like asking whether Cardinal Angelini has connections with the Vatican,' he replied.

Ben joined in the laughter. 'I'm sure it is a very naïve question,' he admitted.

'The real question,' Wood said, 'is what you mean by "connections". No Soviet chess player would be given permission to leave the country to play in a chess tournament without convincing the authorities that he is a loyal member of the Party. If there is one thing the Soviets fear even more than losing the world championship to Bobby Fischer, it is the spectre of grandmasters defecting to the West. That would really put a dent in the image of Soviet chess. So you have to conform, or at least appear to conform. There are some, like Botvinnik, who are genuine Party men through and through. But most of them are not too interested in politics. They just want to play chess. And some, especially the grandmasters from the Baltic Republics, like Paul Keres, have no reason to feel any affection for Moscow. For them, any loyalty to the Party is no more than skin deep. Be that as it may, the KGB is a part of their lives. Every Soviet team or group of players going abroad for a tournament has a complement of minders, who keep them on a tight leash.'

He looked up at the ceiling, then down again.

'I am quite sure that there are those the KGB can call on for particular purposes,' he added, 'and I think Stepanov would have been ideally qualified for the job, with his diplomatic skills and his gift for languages. But whether he actually had that kind of connection with the KGB is anyone's guess.'

He paused.

'The third name you gave me was Sir James Digby.'

* * *

'I've known James for a very long time, of course,' Wood said. 'We have crossed swords many times over the years, most recently just last year. I won a tournament at Whitby and I beat James in the second round. He was off form. He seemed rather preoccupied with other things, and didn't place very high.'

'What can you tell me about him generally?' Ben asked.

Wood reflected on the question for some time.

'That's a hard question to answer,' he replied. 'I would not say we are close, exactly. You don't get close to people you play against in chess tournaments. You tend to be too focused on chess. But I did spend a couple of weeks in his company once, years ago.'

'Oh?'

'We were both members of the British team at the 1939 Chess Olympiad in Buenos Aires, with Hugh Alexander, Harry Golombek and Stuart Milner-Barry. The tournament was cut short on the outbreak of War. The Government ordered us back immediately. They wanted some of us – Hugh mostly – for secret work, code-breaking and the like.'

Ben nodded. 'James was involved in interrogating suspected spies,' he said.

'Yes, that's right,' Wood said. 'I remember that now. But I lost touch with him during the War. It was during our stay in Buenos Aires that I got to know James, really. We all talked a great deal, especially during the voyages to and from Argentina, and we came to know each other quite well at that time.'

'What was your impression of James?'

'Very favourable, I would say. He struck me as a very modest man. There was no suggestion of superiority because of his title or his family, or even about being a barrister. He was there as a chess player, he was very approachable, and he treated everyone he met in the same way, courteously and fairly. He was quite happy, for example, to take the reserve spot on the team. He had no airs and graces at all. But he did believe in himself. By that I mean that he had enormous confidence in himself as a player. And ...'

'And ...?'

Wood hesitated. 'I'm not sure this has any relevance,' he said, 'but James did have something of a chip on his shoulder about the plight of the western chess player. We all do, of course. It's something we all live with. But James seemed a bit obsessive about it sometimes. He could go on and on about the injustice of it all, and how the Soviets had set an example of how things should be – you know, chess as an art form and art being a contract between the State and the artist, the State supporting the artist and the artist putting his art at the service of the State, and so on. I remember he cross-examined Harry and myself about how we proposed to support ourselves as chess players. He was particularly interested in what I was doing. But I had only just got *Chess* underway at the time, and none of us could give him any satisfactory answer about how we were going to do it. I remember thinking it was rather odd in a way, because he was a barrister, and presumably he was going to do well for himself. But it seemed to me that he wanted someone to wave a magic wand and magically make it possible for him to become a professional chess player. It was almost as if talking about it would somehow make it happen.'

'Was he good enough at that time,' Ben asked, 'to play professionally, I mean?'

'If he had been supported and nurtured, Soviet-style, from a young age? He would undoubtedly have been grandmaster material,' Wood replied, without hesitation. 'A number of us would. But that wasn't the world we lived in. It might have been a world we sometimes dreamed of. But it wasn't real.'

'And yet James did quite a lot of work as a chess journalist, didn't he?'

Wood looked at Ben as if unsure how to respond.

'Yes, he did,' he replied eventually. 'And that was something else which was a bit odd.'

'In what way?'

Wood shook his head. 'It's difficult to define. James didn't generally cover tournaments for the main newspapers. Hugh, Harry and I have done quite a bit of that for the *Sunday Times*, the *Telegraph*, and so on. So has Leonard Barden, for the *Guardian*. But James seemed to cover chess mainly for publications which didn't have serious chess columns. All right, he would place the occasional piece with a mainstream paper or a chess magazine; and his material was good – I ran several pieces he sent me over the years, as did the *British Chess Magazine*. But...'

'But why is that odd?' Ben asked.

Wood thought for some time.

'He did a lot of travelling for a reporter on that level,' he replied. 'Chess journalism is not exactly highly paid. You have to be careful about your expenses. If you are writing a standard chess column, you can get reports of the games from any given chess tournament – especially something as big as the Soviet championship – quite easily, from any number of sources. There is no need to travel to all of them, and it wouldn't be economic to travel to all of them – not for what he would be paid for the kind of reporting he did. All of us have to be careful about that. We have to ration ourselves.'

'Perhaps, as a barrister, he had the money and just liked to travel to chess tournaments?' Ben suggested. 'Perhaps it made up for not being a player?'

Wood shook his head. 'No,' he replied emphatically. 'Nothing made up for not being a player. Not for James.'

16

Ben waited anxiously for Barratt and Jess to arrive for the consultation with Bernard Wesley and Sir James Digby. When he had returned to chambers from Birmingham the previous day, he had had every intention of tracking her down, even going to Barratt's office on some pretext, if he had to. That would have been a gross breach of professional etiquette – any such contact should be made through his clerk – but she was still not returning his calls, and he was feeling desperate. But Merlin had whisked him away to the Marylebone Magistrates' Court in the late afternoon, to represent a sales representative who was in danger of being disqualified from driving for repeated offences of speeding and ignoring automatic traffic signals. The situation had remained unchanged overnight: he was unable to contact her. Barratt and Jess proved to be the last to arrive, minutes before the consultation was due to begin, and she avoided his eyes. If Bernard Wesley sensed that anything was wrong, he gave no indication of it.

'Now that we are all here,' he began briskly, 'let me remind everyone of where we are. We issued a Writ for libel and served our Statement of Claim on the 15th March. We received a Defence from Hollander's solicitors dated the 29th March, which contains only one defence, namely justification. You all know what that means. Hollander proposes to prove that what he said in his article is not libellous because it is wholly or substantially true. If he were to succeed in that defence, our claim would fail and we would be ordered to pay his costs.'

'If he were to succeed in that defence,' Digby said, 'my life would be over.'

'Yes,' Wesley agreed. 'So, the question becomes where we go

from here. Herbert, I understand that we have still not received any indication from the other side that Hollander has any evidence to support his defence.'

'No indication at all,' Harper confirmed. 'The concern, of course, is that they have something they are not telling us about.'

Wesley nodded. 'We cannot allow the situation to remain as it is, for obvious reasons. We must avoid being ambushed at, or just before, trial by evidence we have not seen.'

'Well,' Digby said, 'in the Chancery Division we would ask for further and better particulars of the Defence. We are entitled to notice of the facts he intends to rely on. Then, if those particulars are not forthcoming, we would apply to strike out the Defence; and if the judge won't do that, we would object to the defendant adducing evidence at trial to prove facts which should have been disclosed.'

Wesley smiled. 'We are every bit as sophisticated in the Queen's Bench Division, James, I assure you,' he replied. 'That is exactly what we are going to do. Ben is in charge of that.'

'I will be sending the Request to Herbert for service on the other side very soon,' Ben confirmed.

'Good,' Wesley said. 'But obviously, we have not just been sitting back waiting for Hollander to show his hand. We have also been making certain inquiries of our own. Jess, I recall that we had delegated Professor Hollander to you. What can you tell us?'

This invitation to report gave Ben a legitimate reason to look directly at Jess, something he had carefully avoided up to this point. Jess returned his look briefly, and gave him what might have been the suggestion of a smile. Ben was momentarily heartened, but she looked away quickly and seemed unusually subdued as she produced her notes and began to speak.

'Professor Francis R Hollander was born on the 11th June 1933, in Savannah, Georgia. After high school in Savannah, he attended the University of Georgia, where he received his Bachelor's degree, majoring in politics with a minor in American history. He went on to Yale to do his Master's degree and stayed on for his Doctorate, both in political science. He joined the Yale faculty almost immediately afterwards and is currently an associate professor. He is a keen chess player, as we know. Sir James knows about him in the context of chess, so I didn't delve into that. But I did look into his academic interests and writings. I must thank Mr Harper for opening some doors for me and getting me into the libraries of two London University colleges, King's and LSE. I'm not sure where I would have found some of the materials in this country without his help.'

Harper nodded and smiled. 'My pleasure. I'm glad some of the money I have given my *alma mater* over the years has finally produced some benefit.'

'Most of Hollander's work,' Jess continued, 'seems pretty uncontroversial, at least for our purposes. He is very interested in the relationship between the States and the Federal Government, how power is shared under the Constitution, how far the Federal Government can influence State legislation, that kind of thing. He has written two or three pieces jointly with an associate professor at Yale Law School, Donald Tate, and several more on his own. We have copies of it all – Ben and I have copies.'

'I have gone through them quickly,' Ben added. 'I agree with Jess. There is nothing of great interest to us.'

'Not so far,' Jess continued. 'He did write a short piece about political responsibility for the Security Services about two years ago, but it was very technical – nothing rhetorical at all.'

'Which makes his attack on James even stranger,' Wesley mused.

'Yes,' Jess replied, 'but now we come to more recent developments. About 18 months ago, he founded his journal, the *Ivy League Political Remembrancer*. When we first saw the article about Sir James, it seemed clear that the *Remembrancer* was Hollander's project. We noted then that he is the general editor as well as managing editor, which indicates that the publication is essentially his sole responsibility. There are one or two other names, but they seem to be support staff. Since then I have tracked down the earlier issues – there are only three or four – and there is a marked difference in the tone and content of the work when compared to Hollander's earlier pieces in other publications. In the journal, we have rhetorical pieces actively criticising the Government, particularly in the field of foreign policy. Again, we have copies. The tone is conservative and isolationist, for example a revisionist analysis of the Marshall Plan, condemning it as a waste of American resources, and a piece highly critical of every administration since Truman for giving away too many secrets about the American atomic and nuclear programmes.'

'Now we are getting closer to it,' Harper said.

'Except for the fact that the earlier pieces in the *Remembrancer* were not written by Hollander,' Jess replied. 'The only piece under his name is the article about Sir James in the February 1965 issue. The others are all invited contributions.'

'So,' Wesley said slowly, 'he was creating a forum for other academics to express their views: views that might not be acceptable to a more mainstream journal.'

'Exactly,' Jess said, 'but then, apparently, he decided to make use of that forum to speak his own mind. And that leads us to yet another strange thing about Hollander.'

'Go on,' Wesley said.

'Well, he is on track for promotion to full professor and tenure. I don't know much about the American academic system, but my father has a distant cousin who is a professor at the University of Virginia. I was able to speak to him by phone. He is a mathematician, but he tells me that the career path is essentially the same, regardless of subject. There is a career path, typically about seven years, from assistant, to associate, to full professor. Promotion to full professor usually brings with it a grant of tenure. That means that it becomes very hard to dismiss the professor. It is designed to protect academic freedom. You can't get rid of a tenured professor for expressing his academic opinions, however controversial they may be. You can only dismiss a tenured professor for certain kinds of misconduct.'

She paused for a moment.

'So the conventional wisdom is that, if you want tenure, you don't make waves before you get it. You establish your reputation with safe, uncontroversial articles. Then, once you have tenure, you can chance your arm a bit more if you want to.'

There was silence for some time.

'How long does Hollander have to go before he would be awarded tenure?' Wesley asked.

'A year or two,' Jess replied.

'Then it would seem that his recent forays into the realm of the sensational, including his attack on James, are unwise,' Wesley said, 'at least according to conventional wisdom.'

'The professor I spoke to at Virginia said he must have an academic death wish,' Jess replied.

17

'Yesterday morning, I had a meeting with B H Wood, the editor of *Chess*,' Ben began. 'He sends his best wishes, James. He will act as a character witness, if we need him.'

Digby smiled. 'Baruch is a nice man,' he replied, 'and a strong player. He wiped the floor with me at Whitby a year or so ago.'

'So he told me,' Ben returned the smile. 'He asked me to tell you how distressed he is by all this. He said you spent some time together in Argentina at a chess Olympiad and got to know each other quite well.'

'Buenos Aires, 1939,' Digby confirmed. 'He had just started *Chess* three or four years before that. He has done very well for himself. It is very well produced.'

'He found a way to turn his passion into a career,' Ben observed.

Digby did not reply for some time.

'He would prefer to be playing,' he said eventually. 'He does play, of course. But whenever he plays he is also reporting the tournament for *Chess*, and so he has to spend much of his time on that rather than on preparation.'

'He said that was a burden that all the best British players have to bear,' Ben said, 'the need to make a living, I mean.'

'That is quite true,' Digby replied quietly.

'He had very little to say about Hollander,' Ben continued, 'nothing we didn't already know, really. But we did discuss Stepanov. He gave me this book. It has a short piece about Stepanov and gives one or two of his games.'

Ben held up the *Survey of Soviet Chess*.

Digby laughed. 'Of course, the dear old *Survey*. It's been a year or two since I delved into that, but I am sure that one of the games they give is his splendid win over Keres in the Championship, in the early 1950s, I would think?'

'Yes,' Ben replied.

'His best game ever, a real masterpiece,' Digby said.

'The biographical note is fascinating,' Ben said. 'If I read you one or two paragraphs, I think you will get the picture.

Viktor Stepanov was born in Leningrad in 1914. His parents fully supported the Revolution of 1917 and the principles taught by Marx and Lenin. Recognising that the young Viktor had a great talent for chess, they did not divert him into other fields of study as would have happened in a decadent Western culture, but encouraged him to pursue his love for the game. He became a Young Pioneer, and joined the Pioneers' chess club. Before long, he was winning tournaments because of his creative and original approach to chess. His parents then sent Viktor to Moscow where he was enrolled at the Chess Academy, and received instruction from senior Soviet masters and grandmasters. With the benefit of their teaching and advice, Viktor Stepanov quickly rose through the ranks and attained the rank of master at the young age of 22. Like many others, his career in chess was cut short by the Great Patriotic War, in which he served with distinction.

After the War, Viktor Stepanov quickly resumed his playing career, winning a number of tournaments, placing well in the Soviet championship in several years, and attaining the title of grandmaster. Unfortunately, for some time, Viktor Stepanov fell prey to the bourgeois temptation to play safely, in the hope of resting on his laurels, and ceased his constant exploration for creative and original work in chess. This had the result that his tournament results became less satisfactory. But he received advice from more experienced grandmasters, and on their advice, Viktor Stepanov engaged in a long period of self-criticism in accordance with the principles of Marxism-Leninism, with the result that he re-discovered his creative flair, and won many fine games. He has made some important contributions to opening theory in the Sicilian Defence. He also serves as a teacher at the Moscow Academy where he passes on his skill and wisdom to the next generation of Soviet grandmasters.

'Grandmaster Stepanov is also a fine linguist, being fluent in English and German, among other languages. At some cost to his playing career, he selflessly placed his linguistic talents at the service of the State whenever they were required. He acted as an interpreter for the Soviet prosecutor in the trial of the Major Axis War Criminals at Nuremberg at the end of the Great Patriotic War, and in later years he played a leading role in negotiations on behalf of the Soviet Chess Federation with respect to the organisation of international chess tournaments, and the participation of Soviet players in tournaments abroad.'

Ben closed the book with a smile. 'This was published in 1955. It doesn't say what Grandmaster Stepanov got up to after that. We know that he died, apparently of natural causes, in Moscow in 1963. We have his obituary from the Soviet chess magazine *Sixty-Four*. There were also brief mentions in *Pravda* and *Izvestia*.'

'It would be interesting to know what he did during the Great Patriotic War,' Wesley said. 'Is there any light you can shed on that, James? You must have known him.'

'Yes,' Digby replied, after a moment's hesitation. 'I knew him reasonably well, I suppose. The first time I met him was at Nuremberg. I was an interpreter for the British prosecutors and he was with the Russian team, so we saw each other professionally and at parties given, usually, by the Americans, who had more money to spend on such things than we did. He wore a military uniform at Nuremberg, and he had the rank of captain, if I remember rightly. I met him many times in Moscow subsequently. But then we were talking about chess. I don't recall that he ever told me what he had done during the War. It would not surprise me in the least if he was in intelligence work of some kind. The Russians would have needed German speakers, just as we did, and linguists of Stepanov's quality would have been rare.'

Wesley thought for some time.

'Was he the kind to be a solid Party man, would you say? Hollander's article suggests that by 1962 he was desperate to defect to the West.'

'That was relatively recently,' Digby pointed out.

'Yes, but if that is true, it must have been building for some time. Did you ever form any impression of him? By that I mean, did he seem to be a loyal servant of the Soviet Union, as the *Survey* suggests, or were there signs of restlessness, of his turning his eyes towards the West, perhaps? Did he ever say anything about that to you? After all you had known him for many years. It would have been much more logical to appeal to you than to Hollander, wouldn't it?'

'Perhaps,' Digby replied. 'But I don't know what was going on in his life. Perhaps he had some particular reason for approaching the Americans rather than the British.'

'Did he know what work you had done during the War?' Ben asked. 'Would he have known that you had connections with the Security Services at that time?'

'I may have said something about it at some point. I couldn't go into any detail, of course, even then. I was still bound by the Official Secrets Act. He may well have guessed. So many of us in the chess world did that kind of work during the War; and we were both linguists.'

There was a silence for some time.

'Mr Wood explained to me that all the Soviet grandmasters have some contact with the KGB, whether they want it or not,' Ben said. 'He told me that they are only permitted to travel outside the Soviet Union for tournaments if the authorities are satisfied that they are loyal to the State, and are not likely to defect. He also said that their movements are closely monitored while they are abroad.'

'That is quite correct,' Digby replied. 'There is a very obvious presence at whatever tournament they compete in. You can't help but notice it. It is almost comical at times; they are so obvious. I am sure it is no fun at all for the Soviet players. They are discouraged from socialising with the rest of us. We have found ways, of course. When I went as a journalist, I was allowed to interview them. And there were some social events, opening and closing ceremonies and receptions and the like, when we could talk to them less formally. But Hollander was right about that. It would not be easy for a player to find a way to approach someone from the West and ask to defect; and it never happened to me.'

'Did Wood have any insight into Stepanov?' Wesley asked.

'Not really,' Ben replied. 'He said you can't always tell whether a particular grandmaster is a genuinely loyal Party man or not.'

'You can in certain cases, especially the ones from the outer reaches of the Empire,' Digby insisted. 'They have no natural allegiance to Moscow, and Stalin made a lot of enemies in the outer reaches of the Empire. Sometimes they can't hide the resentment, and they make comments when they think no one is listening. But not Stepanov. He was always the diplomat, always very controlled. Besides, he hailed from Leningrad. Whatever his real thoughts may have been, he knew how to keep them to himself.'

'Yes, I see,' Wesley said. 'Anything else, Ben?'

'To change the subject slightly,' Ben said, 'who would pay your fees and expenses as a journalist when you went abroad to cover tournaments?'

The abrupt change of direction appeared to take Digby aback.

'Oh, whatever newspapers and journals were interested in my reports,' he answered. 'I should add that I did not always charge very much. I had money from my practice at the Bar. I went to the tournaments because of my love of the game. Why do you ask?'

'Mr Wood mentioned that he found it surprising that you were taking so much time away from your practice,' Ben replied.

Digby laughed. 'Yes, so did my clerk, and he never let me forget it.'

* * *

As the consultation ended, Ben was the last to leave Wesley's room.

'Ben,' Wesley said, as he was about to walk out, 'that last question you put to James, about his travel expenses and so on, seemed rather pointed. Did Wood suggest that you raise the subject?'

'Not exactly,' Ben replied. 'But he made it clear that he was puzzled. James went abroad a great deal, many times to Russia to cover the Soviet championship. But he wasn't reporting for the leading newspapers or magazines on a regular basis. It was more the general interest magazines which would not usually have had much to do with chess. Wood seemed to think he could have done that kind of reporting just as effectively without leaving London. It seemed odd to him, and it seems a bit odd to me.'

Wesley shrugged. 'It could have been his love of chess tournaments, couldn't it? He might have gone to soak up the atmosphere, and I daresay whatever reporting he was doing would have benefited from that. After all, one of the advantages of the Bar, once you get established, is supposed to be a certain degree of financial reward. There is nothing wrong with indulging one's interests now and then.'

'No, I suppose not,' Ben admitted.

'Does Wood have doubts about James, do you think?'

Ben thought for a few moments.

'No, I don't think so. At least, he said nothing directly.'

'Do you?'

Ben looked directly at his Head of Chambers.

'To be honest, I'm not sure. But it has crossed my mind. Hasn't it crossed yours?'

Wesley smiled. 'I think I will wait for Hollander's response to our Request for further and better particulars,' he replied. 'With any luck, that will clear it up, one way or the other.'

* * *

She was waiting for him outside the clerks' room.

'I'm sorry.' They said the words together at exactly the same moment, and then laughed, nervously, tentatively.

'Come to my room,' Ben said, putting an arm around her shoulders. 'I don't think Harriet is back from court yet; she had to go to Oxford. Do you have time? Does Barratt need you?'

'No. I told him I would be back at the office in a few minutes.'

Ben closed the door, and they stood close together for some time before he offered his outstretched arms and she allowed him to pull her gently into an embrace. She raised her head from his shoulder to look into his eyes.

'I was angry,' she said simply. 'I was angry at the thought that a meeting is going to take place, at which I am not even entitled to be present; I am angry that a group of old men, men I don't even know, think they are entitled to decide the fate of my love life without even consulting me.'

He nodded.

'I understand,' he said, 'and I am sorry I didn't offer you more reassurance.'

She shook her head.

'I can deal with being angry,' she replied. 'I'm not really angry at you; it just came out that way because I can't shout at the old men. So I made myself angry at you, and I made both of us endure a few miserable days. I'm sorry.'

She reached out a hand and stroked his hair.

'Ben, the important thing for me is to know where I stand in your life. I wouldn't blame you if you tell me that your practice has to come first. I would understand that. I just need to know.'

He kissed her on the forehead.

'Jess, I love you,' he said. 'I will not allow anything to come between us.'

'But if you had to give up the Bar, you would hate me, it would never work ...'

'It's not going to come to that,' he replied.

'But what if it did ...?'

'There is still Australia.'

'No, come on ...'

'Jess,' he said, 'do you love me too?'

'Yes,' she replied simply.

'Then trust me, please. I will not allow this to separate us. There will be a way, and we will find it. Together.'

18

Sir James Digby

I went up to Trinity to read modern languages in October 1931, and began to learn to know the city which was to play such a huge role, if not in my life as it actually was, then certainly in how I saw my life in my mind. Cambridge – the people I met and the experiences I had as an undergraduate – took on a deep symbolism which seemed to touch and underlie everything that happened to me after my time there. Like many students, I found that a great deal of my time and energy was expended on people and activities outside my formal studies. But I would like to believe that it was not frittered away, as it was with friends who found religion, or alcohol, or some other diversion, during their first lonely weeks as young boys away from home for the first time. As it happened, the academic work necessary for me to take a good degree required relatively little of my time and effort. Languages always came naturally to me. My main language was German, with French a respectable second. The Cambridge degree course was very much geared to literature rather than the mechanics of language. I had been reading Goethe, Schiller, and Thomas Mann at school, and at Cambridge I simply continued where I had left off.

I find it difficult to describe my relationship with the German language. It embarrasses me because it is a relationship I do not understand, even though I have now lived with it for many years; and when I speak of it I am conscious of falling off an intellectual cliff into deep and unfathomable waters. But I have set out to speak truthfully, and because German has had some importance in my life I must do my best. I remember seeing German at home, as a young child. My father was a man of great intellectual curiosity, who read widely. His study contained books on many subjects, some of them scientific, and some of those in German. I think it was the physical attributes of the language which first made it so fascinating to look at, long before I could read a word of it. It was partly the curious Gothic script in which older German books were printed. It was partly the use of the *Umlaut* – my first experience of written accents, which somehow define the structure of a language so well, and which are so sadly lacking in English. It was partly that interesting character which looks like a giant capital B and is used to represent the double S. It was not long before I got hold of a dictionary and started to learn a few words. But it was when the opportunity came to learn German at school that I discovered something which unnerved me then, at the age of twelve, and still unnerves me today when I think about it. My experience of German was not of learning the language, but of *remembering* it. German is a language which becomes easier as you go along. It is difficult at first – for most people – because its word order and its counter-intuitive use of prepositions are very different from English. If you don't grow up speaking the language you have to learn these things. But I already knew about the word order and the prepositions before my teacher taught them, and when I wrote or translated into German I got the grammar right from the very beginning. It was always that way for me. My German is intuitive and ingrained. I can pick it up again to have a conversation or read a newspaper after years of ignoring it, and German phrases often pass through my mind. Some people I try to explain this to say that it is simply a result of being good at languages; or perhaps I read ahead of the lesson in my grammar book. As an explanation of my relationship with German this does not satisfy me. My French is quite good. But I had to *learn* French, and now, when I return to France, it takes two or three days before I hear it properly and return to some degree of fluency.

Once I had settled into my room in the Great Court at Trinity and found my way to Heffers, where I would buy my books, and the modern language block, where I would attend my lectures, I took advantage of some gloriously warm early autumn weather to walk around the city; exploring the other colleges and the backs of the river; feeling the depth of history in the ancient buildings. I drank in the heady atmosphere of the early Michaelmas Term; the incessant frenetic activity of a new academic year; the new, smartly-painted bicycles whizzing past me on the streets with a cheerful ring of the bell; the sense of excitement and promise hanging almost tangibly in the clear autumnal air; the new faces in new undergraduate gowns, standing in groups outside their colleges, talking about themselves far too loudly, to prove to anyone passing by that they had arrived, that they, too, were now of the University, and stood on the brink of dazzling academic careers.

I had been to Cambridge before, of course. I had visited Roger once or twice a year while he was up at Trinity. So I was not seeing the city for the first time. But you see Cambridge in one way when you are a visitor, and in another way when you become a part of it yourself. I was seeing it in this new way for the first time. I was seeing Cambridge, as I would always remember it best: a place where everything was possible; a place where everything that was best about England was deeply rooted and flourished; and a place as yet, for a short time, unaware that its tranquility was soon to be questioned so rudely and so deeply.

During Freshers' Week at the start of term, the various University Clubs and Societies – the ones that were open to general membership without special invitation – set out their stalls in different colleges and trawled for members. The Union, the political societies, the Christian Union, and a host of sporting societies, from rowing and rugby to cricket and golf, were much in evidence. But I had already decided how my time should be spent when I was not immersed in German literature. Actually, it was more or less decided for me. I had by now acquired a national reputation as a junior chess player. I had won the British boys' championship twice just before leaving school and, by dint of winning my county championship, qualified once for the senior British championship; though I had an unaccustomed attack of nerves in my first appearance in that lofty arena, played too aggressively, and did not fare as well as I had hoped. Nonetheless, I had made a good start as a chess player, and I had crossed swords with the likes of Hugh Alexander, who represented the cream of British chess at that time. As it happened, I saw Hugh briefly at the chess club stall in St Catharine's when I went to sign up. As the child of an Anglo-Irish union, Hugh is a man of enormous charm with a perennial twinkle in his eyes. He is also a brilliant mathematician and had just graduated from King's as I came up to Trinity. He had known Roger socially, and they had obviously got on well. He was staying on to do research for another year. We chatted for a few moments as I signed up to play chess for the University.

* * *

I had not intended to join any other clubs, but the recent political events changed that. I have mentioned that, as a northern family, we had seen the ravages of the previous several years at first hand. The country had never fully recovered from the Great War. We owed a war debt to America of almost a billion pounds, which was already overdue; our foreign investment had been wiped out; our coal and cotton export markets had disappeared; our international trade was atrophying; the sympathetic markets of the great Dominions were less inviting as their governments took more and more control of their home affairs. It seemed to matter little what party was in power. Stanley Baldwin and Ramsay MacDonald seemed equally inadequate to the task, and perhaps in truth it was a task too demanding for any politician. The North was the heartland of the industrial economy, and it was all but in ruins. Looking back, I think that, but for the Second War, it might never have recovered. All the families we were close to on the estate and in the surrounding county had suffered from the worsening economic conditions. The Government seemed oblivious to the effects of poverty and hunger, and seemed to be governing in the interests of the capitalists. As a family, we felt embarrassed and distressed. We were landowners and employers. People thought of us as naturally allied to the Conservative capitalist machine. But my father had no sympathy with the Government's policies; with its obstinate refusal to see that the economy could never recover until the people who created the wealth by means of their labour were lifted out of their misery, and had some reason to feel positively towards their country. My father's views were well known locally and we never felt threatened, even during times of unrest. While the people of the North were rightly angry, they were never unjust. They knew where the blame lay. But my parents felt these things deeply, and their feelings naturally rubbed off on Roger and on me.

There were periods of hope. For ten days in May 1926, the General Strike offered the Government the opportunity to acknowledge the suffering caused by its policy of cutting wages and devaluing the pound, in the hope of jolting the export trade back to life. But Baldwin's administration chose to ignore the opportunity, and chose instead to grind the miners into submission by force, inflicting a disastrous defeat on the Trade Union movement. By 1928, all women over the age of 21 were eligible to vote, which gave the Labour Party a renewed impetus, and the Party returned to power in 1929. But in the same year came the Great Wall Street crash, and here, the Great Depression. As I was preparing to go up to Trinity, our international trade had declined by 50 per cent; our industrial input by over 30 per cent. Unemployment was fast approaching three million, and there were areas in the North where it reached 70 per cent. A general election was to be held on the 27th October 1931, just three weeks or so after I arrived in Cambridge. It was a disaster.

Since 1929, Ramsay MacDonald had presided over a Labour Party split by his conviction that it was necessary to curb wages and public spending – seen by most Labour voters as the natural policy of Baldwin's Conservative Party and the source of their troubles. Paralysed by the rift, the Government became increasingly dysfunctional. MacDonald broke away and purported to found a 'National Labour' party, which operated in coalition with the Conservative and Liberal Parties as a Government of National Unity, an uneasy alliance claimed to be necessary to restoring the economy in the interests of national survival. But he was regarded within his own party as a traitor. As one of the founding fathers of the Labour Party, he had betrayed his followers. Only two of his Labour ministerial colleagues agreed to participate in the coalition government. MacDonald himself was expelled from the Labour Party but, at the election, the National Government was returned to power with a huge majority, winning 470 seats in the House of Commons. The Labour Party, of which Arthur Henderson had hurriedly assumed command, was in total disarray and was all but wiped out. It lost 80 per cent of its seats and seemed spent as a force in government. The Liberal Party, similarly, had been overwhelmed by the Conservatives.

A day or two after joining the chess club I joined the Cambridge University Socialist Society which, even then, was considerably to the left of the Labour Party. Some of its members were openly Marxist. I did not mind that. Something needed to be done. Apart from the election, there were already whispered fears about certain political trends in Europe, about the eventual rise of what the Society's activists were calling Fascism. At the first meeting I attended I had my first long conversation with another linguist in my year, from Trinity Hall. We had nodded and said 'hello' in hall and in lectures from time to time, but had not really spoken until our first CUSS meeting. I liked him immediately. We went for a couple of pints after the meeting, and found we had much in common. Like me, he came from a well-to-do family and had a father who was no stranger to the corridors of power. Indeed, his father had been Deputy Speaker of the House of Commons and leader of the Independent Liberals after the 1918 election. But he seemed unaffected by his family background, except perhaps for a natural self-deprecation and some lack of self-confidence. He was modest and unassuming and had a friendly face. Like me, he felt for the victims of the economic crisis and believed that changes must be made. His name was Donald Maclean.

19

Within a short time I settled into a routine, one which will always represent the quintessential Cambridge day I remember. Getting up early, rushing through the communal baths and back to one's room to get dressed – sports jacket and slacks, shirt and tie; off to breakfast in hall; back to the room, grab the gown, books and notebooks, and off to lectures. Lectures were public events attended by large audiences, and provided little opportunity to ask questions or explore the subject in detail. But in the afternoons, after lunch in hall, there would be less formal supervisions in college, at which we would meet with a Fellow in small groups of three or four. I loved supervisions because you could challenge what the Fellow said, put forward your own ideas, have an exchange of views. Looking back now, I am sure the Fellows must have been constantly amused, if not irritated, by our pretentiousness and unjustified self-importance; our intellectual musings as yet unaffected by any emotional depth, any real contact with life.

After supervisions, there was tea, and then study, until it was time for a drink in the Junior Common Room. The day ended with dinner in hall wearing jackets, ties and gowns, followed by a walk or a pint or two in a nearby hostelry. Sometimes, the pint or two had an exciting ending. The beer sometimes gave rise to a certain lack of discipline in the wearing of gowns, as all undergraduates were obliged to do after dark when out of college. The Proctor, whose job it was to enforce the University's many arcane regulations, employed 'Bulldogs', disconcertingly fit young men dressed in the style of college porters, with formal dark jackets, striped trousers and bowler hats, who had been known to outrun members of the University's athletics team. If caught gownless before you reached the safety of college, you were liable to a fine of three shillings and fourpence. I confess that I had to pay up a number of times during my time at Trinity.

At weekends we were expected to do a certain amount of work, but there was no shortage of ways to enjoy one's leisure time. On Saturday afternoons in the Michaelmas Term, which grew progressively colder as the term progressed, some of us would make our way to Grange Road to watch the University rugby team play matches in the build-up to the Varsity Match at Twickenham in December. I had not quite lost my interest in the strategic aspects of rugby, though I had no intention of playing again, and Roger and I were regulars at Twickenham for the big game throughout his time at Cambridge and mine. There were long walks out to Grantchester, and at least one excursion by train to Ely to marvel at its glorious cathedral. Whenever Roger was in London, and had time to spare, I would go in by train to meet him for an early dinner, rushing back hoping to return to college, if possible, before the porters closed the college gates for the night and it became necessary to find some less orthodox way of gaining access to one's room.

In many ways, the informal talks with friends, either in the pubs, or in one's room – often late into the night – were as much a part of one's education as lectures or supervisions. Making friends from different backgrounds exposed me to many aspects of life I would never have dreamed of otherwise, and I heard views expressed which would never even have occurred to me. I spent a number of such late nights with Donald. Although in some ways a shy young man who did not speak a great deal in supervisions, he had vast depths of understanding and feeling, particularly when the conversation turned to socialism, as it usually did before too long. It was Donald who persuaded me to embark with him on the lengthy and laborious task of reading *Das Kapital* in the original. We justified this to our supervisor, Dr Munday, as an exercise in tackling a difficult technical work in German. Dr Munday was far too conservative to approve of Marx, and in any case scorned his German as prosaic and devoid of interest. But Marx's use of the language was not our main concern. We read it with fascination. Donald was completely captivated. There was much in it that I very much wanted to believe in. There was a vacuum somewhere inside me; I had been conscious of it ever since the day when, at a very young age, I had decided – with some regret, because I genuinely liked the man – that the Rev Mr Norman Jarrett had failed to persuade me that the Church of England held the keys to the secrets of life. The inevitable march of history, the inevitable victory of the proletariat in the inevitable class struggle, held a strong attraction for me. They struck a chord because of what I had seen, and what my father had taught me, earlier in my life.

On account of this inspiring prediction of the ultimate triumph of social justice, I could forgive Marx many things, including his obvious naïveté, his flawed economics, and even his prosaic German. Like the Bible, I concluded, it did no good to examine *Das Kapital* in great depth. You found too many absurdities, too many inconsistencies. What mattered was what it stood for. It was a symbol rather than a book. And a symbol was something I needed in my life.

20

In mid-November, I returned to my room after lectures on a Wednesday afternoon to find that someone had pushed an invitation card under my door. The card had the Trinity coat of arms printed at the top, but the content was handwritten in black ink and in a sharp elegant hand. The writer informed me that Mr Anthony Blunt, Research Student of the College, would be at home in his rooms in Bishop's Hostel for sherry during the early evening on Saturday, and requested the pleasure of my company. The name rang a bell immediately; I remembered Roger's letter, and I recalled his mentioning Blunt several times when I had visited the year before. But I could not remember anything particular he had said about the man and, with two supervisions looming, I made no inquiry of him. I left the invitation leaning against the clock on my mantelpiece, and on Saturday afternoon I duly put on a suit and tie and made my way across college for six o'clock as bidden.

Anthony Blunt was a striking figure, tall and angular. He welcomed me with a show of enthusiasm, but when he looked at me it was with the art critic's detachment, a coldly aloof stare as if I were a canvas being critically examined rather than a human being simply looked at; as if, in his eyes, I had the burden of proof of my own existence and worth. But it was only when I came to know him much better that I made that connection. At the time, it simply made me flinch a little. We shook hands, and he handed me a glass of dry sherry which had already been poured, and which had stood, next to the bottle from which it came, on a side table to the right of the door as I entered. He looked me up and down, again an appraisal, but more cursory than the look into my face. Then he picked up his own glass from the table.

'So,' he said, 'you are Roger's brother, are you?'

I am sure my surprise showed.

'Yes,' I replied. 'You must forgive me. I remember Roger mentioning your name, but I didn't realise you knew him well.'

He took a sip of sherry, smiling.

'Not as well as I should have liked, I must confess,' he replied.

I heard a loud guffaw coming from a sofa, which stood behind me and in front of the fireplace. It was startling. I had not realised that anyone else was present, and I had been so absorbed by Anthony that I had hardly taken in any detail of the room. As I turned towards the sofa, the voice continued.

'And you can take that any way you like,' it said.

Anthony shook his head sadly, took my arm, and walked me towards the sofa.

'This wretched creature,' he said, 'is Guy Burgess. Historian, a year ahead of you. He has no idea how to behave in civilised society. God knows why I continue to invite him to my rooms. Guy, this is James Digby. Say hello nicely.'

'Hello, nicely,' Guy said, with a giggle. He extended a hand without making any effort to get up. I took the hand as briefly as I decently could.

'Whatever he may tell you, Anthony continues to invite me to his rooms because I am so amusing. I make all his friends laugh, something he can't do himself. But he's a terrible host. Always the same cheap sherry, and never enough to get you seriously sloshed. My glass has been empty for ages, dear boy. You are such a bore. Are you going to get me a re-fill or do I have to get up and get it myself?'

To my surprise, Anthony took the glass without the least show of irritation, and returned it to Guy, filled to the brim. Guy took it without any acknowledgement whatsoever. He stared at me for some time, giving me the opportunity to do likewise. I had not recognised him at first, but now I remembered seeing his face in and around Trinity. We had never spoken. It was difficult to judge his exact height because he was sprawled untidily across the sofa, but he was fairly tall, with handsome dark features. His jacket and trousers looked as though they had been expertly tailored, but were as wrinkled and creased as if he had slept in them – which, as I got to know him better, I realised might well have been the case. His tie had some kind of food stain on it. I got used to his appearance eventually, as I suppose everyone who knew him did. It never really changed. A general dishevelment and a degree of disregard for personal hygiene were something of a trademark with Guy, but none of this seemed to bother him or slow him down at all. In all the time I knew him, while I often saw him better turned out than on the first day I met him, I never saw him completely tidy; and I never saw him completely sober.

Anthony waved me into an armchair to the left of the sofa, and sat in another opposite me. He had left the remains of the bottle of sherry on the coffee table in front of Guy. Guy had by now finished his inspection of me.

'You won't get anywhere with this one, Anthony,' he remarked, 'any more than you did with his brother. Another one lost to the girls, I fear. I don't know what the world is coming to. What is going on in our schools?' He turned to me. 'Where did you go to school?'

Before I could reply, Anthony held up a hand.

'Oh, do behave yourself, Guy. You're not out chasing your street boys now. James is the brother of a friend of mine, and he is my guest. If you can't treat him civilly, you can leave.'

Guy was grinning, looking up to the ceiling as if asking Heaven what he could possibly have done wrong. But he said nothing, and eventually allowed his body to sink into an obvious sulk. I was sipping my sherry nervously.

'Roger is an excellent fellow,' Anthony said. 'How is he?'

'He is very well. Thank you.'

'Good. If I remember rightly, he was going home to run the family estate when he went down from college. Somewhere in Lancashire, isn't it?'

'Yes, in the Ribble Valley, just outside Clitheroe.'

'Ah, yes. Not a part of the country I know, I'm afraid.'

'Roger is in London at the moment,' I continued. 'My father wants him to go on one or two management courses, and then he is thinking of going abroad for a year or so before he commits to the estate.'

'You must make sure to give him my warmest regards. And tell him that if he sets foot in Cambridge without visiting me I shall be mortally offended.'

I smiled. 'I will, of course.'

'A risk no one should even consider taking,' Guy said, without rising from his slumped position. His words were now slightly slurred. We ignored him. In response, he drained his glass, then poured in the remains of the bottle, half filling it. He held the empty bottle aloft for Anthony to see. Without a word, Anthony stood and made his way to a bookcase to the right of the fireplace. The lower part of the bookcase was a cabinet, from which he took another bottle of the same sherry.

He placed the bottle before Guy who, as before, did not acknowledge it.

Anthony resumed his seat. He extracted a silver cigarette case from an inside pocket of his jacket, removed a cigarette and placed it in a black holder. 'Would you care for one?'

'No. I don't smoke. Thank you.'

'Notice that he doesn't ask me whether I would care for one,' Guy complained, emerging briefly from his sulk. 'They are going to make him a Fellow in a year or so, you know. Aren't they, Anthony? Ever so grand.'

Anthony again ignored him. Suddenly, Guy stood and smartly adjusted his tie as if suddenly experiencing a new burst of energy.

'I'm bored,' he complained. 'I thought you were going to invite some boys for me to meet. I suppose I shall have to go and find my own somewhere else.'

'Yes, well, if you must, I suppose you must,' Anthony replied.

'Very pleased to meet you, James,' Guy said, with a mock bow, 'even if you are one for the girls. I am sure we will run into each other in hall. You can tell me where you went to school and I will have a word with the headmaster.'

'Goodbye, Guy,' Anthony said.

Guy left a little unsteadily, without another word.

* * *

Anthony lit the cigarette. 'I am sorry about Guy,' he said. 'He seems a bit off form today. He had already had a bit to drink before he arrived. He can be that way sometimes. He can also be a quite delightful boy. Believe it or not, he can be quite good company when he is in the mood.'

I did not reply. Anthony saw that my glass was empty and refilled it without asking.

'Roger told me you are a chess player,' he said. I was grateful for the change of subject.

'Yes.'

'Good?'

'Yes, fairly good, I suppose. I've won tournaments at the junior level, and I am hoping to do better in the senior events from now on.'

'You will get your Half Blue then, I expect?'

'I hope so. The Oxford match is next term, so I have some time to prove myself.'

'I'm sure you won't have the least difficulty in doing that,' he said. There was a silence for some time as he smoked his cigarette.

'I see you have joined the Socialists also,' he said. 'Would you care to explain why?'

He saw at once that the question had startled me. He took a drink of sherry, laughing.

'I am so sorry, dear boy. I didn't mean to play the Grand Inquisitor. Let me put your mind at ease. I am a fellow traveller, I assure you. I am surprised Roger didn't tell you that.'

I sipped my sherry.

'Well, it doesn't matter, and it is no secret. I have a particular interest, you see, in prising art away from the corrupting influence of the establishment in this country and, for that matter, the West in general. Art is my chosen field. It is my passion. I believe art should serve the interests of Society, of the People, rather than serving the complacent tastes of a degenerate Bourgeoisie which has lost any ability to appreciate its value, as opposed to its price. I want to encourage writers and artists to express such views and create art in that tradition and, of course, Cambridge is the perfect place to do that.'

He stubbed out the cigarette.

'What's your excuse?'

I laughed at the question, but then I thought about it. And then, for some minutes I unburdened my mind to Anthony about the social injustices I saw all around me, the families we knew who were suffering, the evils of unrestrained capitalism and the need to do something to change the system. He listened without once interrupting. I felt that he did not believe me, and called him on it.

'No, no,' he replied at once. 'I believe you completely. I've seen the same things and drawn the same conclusions as you have. Social justice is impossible in the capitalist world order, and can only be achieved after some revolutionary change. And you are right in thinking that no such change is imminent in Western Europe. In fact, things are moving in quite the opposite direction. I understand all that. What surprises me is that you have not yet moved beyond that into the more positive aspects of socialist society – what it can create, rather than merely what it can replace.'

'In what respect?'

'James, I love art. That is my passion. What is yours? I am not speaking about your undergraduate studies, or even your future career. What do you care about more than anything else?'

I bowed my head.

'Chess,' I replied.

'Describe your feelings about chess.'

I took a deep breath and told him, in no particular order, about chess; about its history; about the depth of its theory; its affinity to pure mathematics; about its symbolism; about Edward Lasker v Sir George Thomas, London 1912; about Paul Morphy going mad and wandering the streets of New Orleans muttering incomprehensibly to himself; about the lack of interest and support for chess in the West, and about ...

'...the lack of any understanding within the Establishment that chess is not just a game, but an art form in its own right?' he suggested. 'An activity to which one might justifiably devote one's talents, not just for personal gratification, but as a means of improving society?'

I sighed deeply. He was the first person who had ever articulated back to me the thoughts which had been playing in my mind for so long. I nodded.

'Of course,' he continued. 'And am I not correct in thinking that despite the general lack of interest in the West, the Soviet Union has a flourishing chess culture?'

'The Soviet Union is the undisputed world leader,' I replied at once. 'But they do it because ...'

The words died in my mouth, but Anthony heard them anyway.

'As a form of propaganda for the benefits of Marxist thought? Yes, undoubtedly. Every system of government loves to boast about its achievements. It is simply a form of advertising. But James, when you see the propaganda for what it is, and put it to one side, what do you have left? What is there of substance? You have a society in which chess, and chess players, are valued and rewarded for pursuing their art. I am sure it is a competitive business. There must be many who fall by the wayside. But that is true of every field of human endeavour, is it not? How many attics could you explore in England or America and find discarded canvases done by some country yokel who fancied himself to be the new van Gogh or the new Monet or, in deference to your part of the world, let's say even the next L S Lowry? The important point is surely, not whether an individual succeeds or fails, but whether he is allowed to try.'

He smiled at me while lighting another cigarette.

'Are you saying that you never considered that as a valid reason for interesting yourself in socialism? Well, that's very altruistic of you, I must say. Quite different from my case. Oh, I believe in the working class, of course, and I believe that we must strip away all this nonsense about the class system and hereditary power, and so on. But it's what socialism can do for art, and what art can do for socialism, that interests me, James. And I suspect that, when you are a bit older, when you have created more beautiful games of chess, and when you find that no one cares very much, you may well come around to my way of thinking.'

* * *

'You won't forget to remember me to Roger, will you?' he repeated, as I left, over an hour later. I wrote to Roger that same evening, posted the letter on Monday morning, and received his reply before the end of the week.

London
18 November 1931

Sir,
As I trust you will readily appreciate, words almost fail me to express the most profound satisfaction and pleasure afforded to me by the reflection that so great an adornment of our College should have deigned to speak so fondly of me, and should have conveyed to me by way of your most welcome letter such delicate feelings of affection for me. You are, sir, without fail, on your next meeting with Mr Blunt, to communicate to him most urgently my reciprocal feelings of warmth and intimacy, and my intention to visit him as soon as my labours permit me to come to Cambridge. I hope that I may do so before long, so that I may gratify my keen desire to see your goodself as well as Mr Blunt, and perhaps to accompany you on your journey to Lancashire upon the conclusion of your first year of study. In any case, there are few men alive I esteem so highly as Mr Blunt, who, I daresay, will within a few years achieve such fame among artists as no man in England has been enabled to boast of in recent times. Your harmonious intercourse with such a man can bring you nothing but benefit in your studies and in the good opinion in which you will yourself be held in college.

As for my own studies, they progress well. During my sojourn in London, I have been gratified to learn from two gentlemen of my acquaintance that, upon their recommendation, the gentlemen of the Reform Club have seen fit to elect me a member. I dined in the company of several such gentlemen last evening to celebrate my election, and found the food and wine and the company to provide the greatest satisfaction. As I know you, sir, to be a man of a liberal disposition, nay sir, I have heard it said, a man of even more radical opinion than the merely liberal, I may perhaps be so presumptuous as to suggest that you yourself may find that Club to be a satisfactory haven for you when you have occasion to visit London. If this suggestion meets with your approval, I will urgently importune certain well-disposed gentlemen on your behalf.

I remain, sir, your most humble and obedient servant,

Sam Johnson

Folded inside was a note from Roger himself, as it were.

Dear James,

I am sure it is unnecessary for me to point this out, but for the avoidance of doubt, my use of the word 'intercourse' in the accompanying letter is to be interpreted in its 18th century sense of general social contact, the sense in which Johnson used it, as opposed to the more specific meaning it tends to be given today.

Fondly,
Roger

21

In the spring term I devoted myself mostly to my studies and to chess. I was selected to represent the University for my Half Blue, and played alongside Hugh Alexander against Oxford. I just failed to qualify for the British Championship, but it was to be my last failure to do so for many years. I went with Donald to meetings of CUSS, which seemed to become ever more radical as the year wore on. I saw Anthony several times in college, and we spoke cordially enough. He confided in me that his appointment to a Fellowship now seemed to be assured, and he always asked after Roger. I often thought back to our first conversation, but as the spectre of examinations approached, I immersed myself in my books, with the welcome result that my name appeared in the First Class Honours list. I was awarded a scholarship for my second year which entitled me to remain in my college room rather than move to digs outside college.

* * *

I spent most of the summer at home, leaving only for a week to play in a chess tournament, which I won with some ease. On my return I found that my parents had organised a garden party on the lawns of the Manor, and invited friends from far and wide. Roger was about to leave for his year abroad; he was leaning towards South America. I was expecting to spend most of my time in Germany and France during the next two summers, to work on my linguistic skills, and I am sure my parents felt there was no way of knowing when they might have the two of us together again for long enough to plan a party of this kind.

The party took place on a Sunday afternoon in late August. It was a blazing hot day, with a threat of thunderstorms. The men wore white jackets and cravats; the women wore brightly-coloured cocktail dresses and hats, high heels without stockings, and strings of pearls. The staff had set up a makeshift bar on a long trestle table, to the left of the French windows as you went out on to the lawn, partially covering the former site of the finishing line for the leaf races. There, they made Pimms cocktails and dry martinis, and uncorked bottles of champagne. Three further tables had been erected farther into the garden, on which every form of food capable of being eaten on a stick was piled high on huge white plates, and at various points across the lawns there were smaller wooden tables and chairs rented for the day. It was all very last-days-of-the-Raj, and I could not help sensing an unspoken anticipation of the end of an era.

We had new near neighbours, a Doctor and Mrs Williamson. Doctor Williamson had recently opened his practice in Clitheroe, and my parents had heard good reports of him. The Williamsons brought with them their daughter Bridget. She was eighteen; she had light brown hair and a freckled face, and mischievous eyes. She wore the prettiest yellow dress with matching hat and shoes. I couldn't take my eyes off her.

At about 5.30, when the party was in full swing, the heavens opened without warning. The air was still and humid. Then suddenly, from nowhere, a lone black cloud appeared and hovered over our lawn, showing no sign of moving on. The staff made frantic efforts to rescue some of the food, but there was thunder now, and lightning, and my father ordered everyone indoors in the interests of safety. The guests had in any case bolted for the house as the first drops fell, laughing as though the storm had been ordered up specially for them, as part of the entertainment. All except Bridget.

As I dashed through the doors out of the rain, I turned back towards the garden for no real reason, and to my astonishment saw her; she was almost at the end of the first lawn, just as it narrows and leads through a pair of short privet hedges to the second lawn. She had cast off her hat and shoes, and she was walking slowly in a circle, her face and arms uplifted to the sky. No one else seemed to have noticed her. Turning up the collar of my coat, I ran through the torrential rain, calling her name.

'Bridget! Come in! There's lightning around. It's dangerous so near the trees.'

She smiled and stopped in her tracks. She waited for me to reach her, then she took my hands in hers and, without a word, she began to run away from the house to the far end of the garden, pulling me after her. The storm had made it so dark now that the house was barely visible – only the lights in the dining room indicated where it was. The lawns were in complete darkness. We stopped just before the line of poplar trees which marked the end of the garden and the beginning of the grounds of the estate. She raised my hands to join her own, saluting the sky and the elements, and we stood together, silent in the rain, being one with the storm and with each other.

'I've always wanted to do that,' she confessed quietly after some time. 'Wasn't it incredible, to look into the face of nature like that? I've ruined my dress, haven't I? Mother will kill me, but it's been worth it.'

'I was worried about you,' I replied, not knowing what else to say.

'I'm sorry,' she said. 'I didn't want anyone to be worried. I knew I would be all right.'

After some time, the black cloud began to move away over the roof of the house, and the sky grew a little lighter.

'I suppose we should go back,' she said. 'But would you please kiss me first?'

I nodded. My senses were overwhelmed. Her face was astonishingly beautiful in the grey and yellow light that followed the storm. Her perfume mingled with the scent of the rain, and of the newly-cut, drenched grass, and of the electricity left over in the air after the departure of the thunder, and of her wet body and hair. As I held her I was aware of her strength and her fragility, of the suppleness of her body to which the dress now clung like a rag pulled from the sea, revealing the shape of her small breasts and slender thighs. And I saw the water and blades of grass which had half covered her beautiful bare feet.

We kissed long and intensely, a first time for me, and I sensed for her also. She touched me briefly, very intimately, as she ended the kiss and we walked in silence back to the house, holding hands until we were almost at the French windows.

'I'm sure you think I'm a bit strange,' she said. 'Actually, you must think I'm completely mad.'

Actually, I didn't know what to think. All I knew was that I was hopelessly in love with her.

'I am quite normal, really,' she added. 'I'm going to study anthropology next year, at Bristol.'

Oddly, no one even seemed to realise that we had been gone. The staff had rescued the bar, if not the food, and the party was still in full flow. Only Roger gave me a knowing look as Bridget gave my hand a final squeeze before making her way to the kitchen to ask my mother if she could borrow a towel and something to wear until it was time to go home. I went to my room, to change, and to try to regain my equilibrium. Just then, the world felt shaky. It was another moment after which my life was not the same but, as with all such moments, I would not fully understand that until much later.

22

Almost as soon as I had returned to Cambridge for my second year, I received another of Anthony's invitations. Stiff white card, printed college coat of arms, precise small handwriting in black ink. Sherry in his rooms, at six. Anthony had by now been elected to his Fellowship and was a familiar figure in Trinity, but despite his connection with Roger I had not really expected to see a great deal of him, except in the impersonal setting of dinner in hall.

I had expected to spend my extra-curricular time on chess and the Socialist Society. Donald and I helped to man the CUSS stall for Freshers' Week that year, and we were surprised at the strong level of interest, not only from the new crop of undergraduates, but also from second- and third-year men. We signed up a good batch of new members. The feeling was growing that socialism represented the way forward, both to tackle social injustice at home, and to prepare a response to the ominous rumblings of fascism in Europe. There was also a feeling that, if the Labour Party continued to be ineffectual, a new approach to socialism might be necessary. There were already some who were turning their eyes towards the Soviet Union to provide a model.

The Treasurer of CUSS for that year was a Trinity economist, H A R Philby, known to everyone as Kim. Kim was a gregarious man with an infectious sense of humour and a taste for the good life. He was extraordinarily charming, and when I spoke to him, I somehow had the feeling that I not only had his full attention, but was the only person important to him at that moment. He was also one of those men with apparently limitless energy who seemed to move seamlessly from work to party and back to work, without drawing breath or pausing to re-charge his batteries. In some ways he was an unlikely socialist, but I took that simply as an indication of how widely socialism was being embraced across the university spectrum. I had met him several times during my first year, and had liked him immediately. This year, I would see much more of him. He asked me to give him a hand with the Society's books, claiming that economists usually made terrible accountants, and were not to be relied on to keep a sound set of accounts. I had an – admittedly rudimentary – understanding of book-keeping from conversations at home with my father and Mr Bevan about the estate, and Kim easily charmed me into giving him an hour or two every week. He provided the drinks and would never accept a penny for them from me.

I met Guy as I was walking up the staircase to Anthony's rooms.

'Oh God, has he invited you as well?' he began. 'I might have known. I find these sherry evenings a bit of a bore myself. It would be nice to have something a bit stronger, wouldn't it?'

'You look as though you've had something a bit stronger already,' I commented.

He giggled.

'Well, I see there's no pulling the wool over your eyes, is there, my dear? But come on, let's be honest, a glass or two of the real stuff is the only way to fortify yourself for an evening with Anthony.'

I must have raised my eyebrows, or given some other sign of dissent, because he went on hurriedly.

'Don't get me wrong, my dear. I love Anthony madly, desperately, as we all do. But he's not exactly the life and soul of the party, is he? I see you're not convinced. Anyway, James, it is good to see you again, especially on such a special occasion.'

I knocked on the door.

'What's special about it?' I asked. 'I didn't see mention of anything particular on the invitation.'

He tapped the side of his nose with his finger.

'You'll see,' he replied enigmatically.

Anthony welcomed us with the familiar warm sherry, which drew a knowing grin from Guy as we seated ourselves in front of the fireplace. On the hearth were a tea pot, two tea cups, two small plates, and a discoloured old toasting fork lying beside the gas ring. Several circles of crumbs provided evidence of the recent consumption of crumpets. We drank for a while, Guy taking two glasses of sherry to my one, as Anthony went through the formalities of asking about Roger, about my accomplishments in chess, and about my studies. Guy seemed content to drink in silence and slip gradually ever further down the sofa. Eventually, Anthony refilled our glasses and came to the point.

'I have asked you here today,' he announced, 'because it is my intention to propose both of you for membership of a certain Society. I have mentioned it to Guy already, James, but I haven't had the chance to talk to you for any length of time, so I am afraid I am rather springing it on you. But I only have limited time for the nominations. The Society I refer to is usually known as the Apostles.'

I am sure that my surprise was quite obvious to him. I had heard of the Apostles from Roger, who had given me the distinct impression that he had kept his distance from it during his time at Cambridge. He had painted it as a rather effete group of men from privileged backgrounds who liked to spend their Saturday nights in pretentious philosophical debates on subjects about which no one in the real world cared.

'The Society was created in 1820,' Anthony continued. 'Membership is in theory open to men from any college, though in practice the membership has generally been drawn from Trinity and King's. It started as a debating society much like any other, and indeed was originally called the *Conversazione* Society. But before too long, it acquired a rather radical reputation.'

'They questioned the authority of the Church of England, no less,' Guy interrupted, rather drunkenly from the sofa. 'Imagine the balls on those men. I do imagine that sometimes, actually.'

Anthony was clearly displeased by the interruption, but he was in a serious mood now, and did not intend to be deflected.

'They did eventually reach that position,' he agreed. 'But they were far more radical than that. At that time, of course, all Fellows were required to be Church men, and to subscribe to the Thirty-Nine Articles. But the Society created a space in which everything could be questioned – not only the Thirty-Nine Articles, but every religious tenet, even the very existence of God. The rule was that each man was entitled, and indeed expected, to speak with complete candour, holding nothing back, even his most intimate feelings.'

'I'll sign up for that,' Guy said, holding up a hand. 'Bring me the form.'

'I need hardly say,' Anthony continued, 'that in those days that was an extremely radical agenda. Any man who was interested in a Fellowship was taking his academic life in his hands merely by participating in such a debate. If the debates provided evidence of other personal proclivities, it might have spelled the end for any of the members. So a tradition arose of secrecy. Members were not permitted to discuss the Society's proceedings with anyone outside the Society. At times, the rule was that the very existence of the Society should be kept secret, though that was, of course, impracticable, since everyone already knew that it existed.'

'By "personal proclivities",' Guy said. 'Anthony means being queer. He's not telling you that because he doesn't want to put you off. But it's a requirement for membership. Women are unapostolic, phenomenal, as they say in the Society. They have a rule that any member seen in intimate embrace with a woman is to be ritually castrated in the presence of the entire membership. Quite right too.'

'Guy, for God's sake, shut up,' Anthony said. The harsh tone of his voice took both of us aback. Anthony was usually well able to ignore Guy's snide interventions during casual conversation, but there was a time and place, and he had had enough for one night. The message was not lost on Guy. With a quick raising of the eyebrows in mock horror, he lowered himself into a position in which he was almost lying on the sofa, his left leg protruding awkwardly sideways, hanging in the air. But I could not help smiling inwardly. That was the other thing Roger had hinted at about the Apostles, though, of course, without Guy's absurd exaggeration.

'The Society still insists on discretion,' Anthony continued. 'There is no longer a threat from the Church, but that does not mean that there is no threat. Completely free debate is still too often seen as a danger to well-structured social order. It is vital that it should continue and, if it is to continue, it is vital that the members have confidence that their candour will not be exposed or abused. For similar reasons, membership is by unanimous election. Any University man may be proposed as a member, but any member may blackball him, and even a single blackball is fatal to his application.'

'When do the Society's meetings take place?' I asked, because I felt the need to ask something.

'Every Saturday evening, in the room of one of the members,' he replied. 'The meetings always follow more or less the same pattern. One member, called the Moderator for the week, prepares an essay on a subject of his choice, or one assigned to him by the other members, and he is called to the Hearthrug, as we say, to read his essay, which is then debated. A vote is taken, whereby the proposition is agreed to, or not agreed to. The traditional sustenance is "whales" – sardines on toast – with whatever a member may care to drink.'

He paused to refill our glasses, opening a new bottle.

'Members have an obligation to attend every meeting unless physically absent from Cambridge.'

He paused to take a long drink.

'But, in due course, if after a number of years that obligation becomes too onerous, a member may become an Angel, or take wings, as we say. He still remains a member and may attend meetings whenever he wishes, but is no longer subject to the obligation. There is also an excellent annual dinner in London, by the way, open to both members and angels. That is why I am proposing you both now. I have decided to take my wings quite soon.'

This revelation brought Guy back to life. He sat up quickly and stared at Anthony.

'But my dear chap, you can't do that,' he protested. 'You are the quintessential Apostle. The Society will fall apart without you.'

Anthony smiled thinly.

'That's very flattering, Guy, but completely untrue. Many more distinguished men than I have taken their wings without doing any harm to the Society. Besides, I plan to attend meetings whenever I can. But I am beginning to see that my academic interests are bound to take me away from Cambridge more and more. Art is a worldwide study and I must be out in the world to study it. Before that happens, I would like to leave my mark on the Society by having one or two new members of my choice elected. I think both of you would be admirable additions to the Brethren.'

I looked at Anthony blankly.

'I'm not sure why you think so in my case,' I said. 'I am a linguist and a chess player. I'm not really philosophically inclined.'

'It's not a question of one's area of study,' he replied. 'Apostles come from all fields of study. We have had some very distinguished scientific members, as well as economists, historians, and so on. It's more to do with your personal qualities. To be elected you must be *apostolic*; in other words, you must have the qualities of candour, discretion, and intellectual inquiry necessary to the Society's work. I think you have those qualities. They have already propelled you from being a scion of an aristocratic family to being a leading member of the Socialist Society. Your views on chess have progressed from its being a mere game, fit only for entertainment, to a radical art form in its own right – an art form of benefit to Society, even perhaps with the potential to change Society. I must confess that I do not yet entirely understand that concept. But on any view, you have already made a considerable intellectual journey, and I am quite sure that it has a long way further to go. I, therefore, wish to become your *Father*; I want you to become my *Embryo*, and allow me to guide you to your *Birth*. I am speaking the language of the Society, you understand.'

At that moment I simply put whatever reservations I had about the Apostles aside. I felt flattered that someone of Anthony's eminence, as I saw it then, should go out of his way to want me as a member of a Society which was clearly of great importance to him. What if some of the subjects they debated were of little practical use? If elected, I might have some influence in choosing subjects which mattered more.

'Thank you,' I said.

'Why, on the other hand, I am putting Guy forward, I cannot begin to explain.'

Guy smiled broadly and raised his glass in a toast.

'It's because my boyish charm is so irresistible,' he said.

Anthony returned the smile.

'That must be the reason,' he replied.

* * *

I have no idea what electioneering went on behind the scenes; what promises were made or inducements offered; what horse-trading was done; what compromises arrived at late at night. I was later to learn that elections could be prolonged affairs, involving a good deal of antagonism, spite, and rancour. The Society's records, held in the *Ark* – a trunk kept in a member's room – told that in years gone by, the process had often dragged on for months and done considerable damage to relationships between members. A blackball is a source of enormous, though transient, power; many members must have yielded to the temptation to use it, or threaten to use it, to gain some personal advantage or to advance some agenda of their own. In addition, like all university societies, and despite its pretensions, the Apostles were a group of emotionally immature young men, often still trapped in a schoolboy mentality and given to fits of moodiness, sulking, grudges, and irrational jealousies. But by 1932 some degree of discipline and order had been imposed, and it was understood that it was bad form to use a blackball unless a candidate seemed clearly unapostolic, or there was a serious reason to exclude him. Anthony never seemed to be in doubt that both Guy and I would be elected, and so we were. How much we owed to his personal standing in the Apostles, which was very high, and how much to his political dealings, I have never known and have never cared to know.

Guy and I were received into membership in November. The most striking feature of the evening was that we were solemnly advised of our obligations and took a solemn oath to honour them. The admonition that we were to attend meetings until we took wings was presented in a way that struck me as more than faintly ridiculous. It consisted the reading of the *Curse of Roby* – a ritualistic curse placed on Henry John Roby who, in 1855, had the effrontery to resign after a year of membership on the grounds that he found the Society's proceedings boring and had better things to do on Saturday evenings. The only specific sanction imposed on Roby was that from the time of his resignation, his name was to be stripped of capital letters and written only in small characters – henry john roby. Apparently, the curse did not have much practical effect on Roby, who went on to enjoy a distinguished career and lived to a ripe old age. But he was never invited to rejoin the Society, even though others who resigned over the years because of personal circumstances were often welcomed back into the fold when those circumstances changed. Whether Roby cared one way or the other about that, I do not know.

The admonition to keep the Society's affairs secret, on the other hand, was far more dramatic and really quite disturbing. This consisted of a terrible oath binding me to pray for the eternal damnation of my own soul if I should as much as breathe a word to the unapostolic – anyone outside the Society – about its proceedings. Guy seemed to find this just as amusing as the *Curse of Roby*, but I must confess that I found it intimidating. I mentioned it quietly to Anthony as he was introducing me to the pleasure of *whales* later in the evening. He smiled.

'Yes, it all sounds rather formidable, and terrifying, doesn't it?' he said. 'But at the same time, it's all rather silly. You know, the Society rejected the idea of eternal damnation some time in the nineteenth century, so I've never quite understood why they ask us to pray for something we are not supposed to believe in. It's about time someone devised a more secular curse of some kind. Perhaps it's a contribution you might make?'

He took me aside.

'The real point, James, is the importance of personal loyalty to your

Brethren,' he said. 'There is no threat of eternal damnation, but it is what is expected of you. It is a question of the values we have, the principles by which we live our lives. It is no more, but no less, than that. We expect your loyalty – for a lifetime.'

That night, when I returned to my room, I picked up my pen and tried to compose a letter to Roger. He was now travelling in South America for his sabbatical year. I missed him a great deal. He had written to me several times, but for me, keeping up any regular correspondence was difficult, as he changed his address with some frequency and I was never sure that my letters would be delivered. In any case, the words for the letter I had intended to write that night would not come. I suppose I was anxious about his reaction to my becoming an Apostle. I desperately wanted to avoid anything which might incur his displeasure or ridicule. I decided to wait and to tell him about my election in person when he was back in England.

I never tried my hand at writing the secular curse.

23

At the end of my second year, Downing College held a May Ball. Several colleges held balls every year, and some had a better reputation than others. Despite the name, May Balls were held in June, after examinations had been completed, and they represented a way to let one's hair down and prepare for the summer break. The May Ball was a grand occasion. The men wore white tie; the women wore formal ball gowns. Large tents were erected in college, and Downing had the great advantage of having a large expanse of lawn between the hall and the Master's lodge, which avoided any sense of crowding. There would be a tent for dancing, in which a series of bands played throughout the night; tents for food; tents for drinks, and the entire college was open for strolling and conversation. It had been a busy year for me. I had represented the University at chess again, and played successfully in a county championship which qualified me for the British Championship in the summer. I was active in CUSS with Kim and Donald, and attended meetings of the Apostles faithfully every Saturday evening. At the same time, I was still on track for a First in my exams. I felt I was entitled to a special evening.

I had been exchanging weekly letters with Bridget. Hers were full and informative. She had a chatty style of writing, and told me almost every detail of her life in Bristol, her anthropological studies, and the people she met, the lecturers and students. I had the impression that she had the happy gift of writing whatever came into her head, without self-censorship. I am sure my letters must have seemed very different to her. I had seen her only once or twice since the fateful night of the storm; I was still sure that I was in love with her, and she seemed to feel the same way. But I never wrote to her entirely openly. I was most open about my college work and chess activities, perhaps because they were things I thought she would understand readily enough. I was more cautious in writing about my work with CUSS, and especially the

Apostles, which I referred to only occasionally, and without revealing the name, as a college debating society. What I was afraid of, I really do not know. Nothing I was doing was unusual for a Cambridge man at that time. I had no real reason to be secretive about it. Bridget was never in the least critical. She sometimes asked questions about my work, but always in a matter-of-fact way, without comment. Nonetheless, sometimes I felt a fear of offending her, of antagonising her in some way; and at other times I had a nagging fear that word of something I was doing would leak back to my parents through some unguarded remark she might make to hers. This led me to censor myself and present her with a carefully constructed image of myself which, even at the time, struck me as ridiculous. We ended each letter with a declaration of love, and I can truthfully say that we never questioned our love, or our intention to be together, despite our youth, our immaturity, our total lack of experience of personal intimacy, and our abysmal ignorance about the true nature of long-term relationships. Not once did we ask ourselves whether we ought to be meeting other people, perhaps people who were available in the places where we lived, before committing ourselves to a lifetime together. I envy the young people of today their knowledge and sophistication about sex and relationships, their calmness and lack of haste in selecting partners, their more balanced and less desperate approach to life; and I congratulate them on consigning so much of the hypocrisy which affected my generation to the history books.

I naturally asked Bridget to be my partner at the May Ball. She replied at once, accepting, and then bombarded me with letters twice or three times a week, describing the gowns she had looked at, and advice from her mother for staying awake all night, and all kinds of details which made clear how excited she was about it. There was no question of risking having her found in my room at Trinity, which would have resulted in my being sent down on suspicion of nameless indecencies. I booked her a room in lodgings in Lensfield Road, close to Downing. She came to Cambridge a day early. I wanted to show her around the city, and hoped that we could become accustomed to each other's company again, so that we could start learning how to act in public as a couple, before the big occasion where there would be so many people to talk to.

The ball was spectacular. We feasted on salmon and salad, followed by strawberries and cream, and drank a good deal of champagne and wine. Many of my friends were there, and I felt a real pride and pleasure in introducing Bridget to them. She seemed totally at ease, whether talking with my fellow students and their girlfriends, or with the Fellows and their wives. She proved to be an excellent dancer too, which made up for my well-known deficiencies in that area. Between about 1 and 3 o'clock in the morning, we had a low period, when we were exhausted after so much dancing and general revelry. We were both tempted to call it a night, and I offered to walk her back to her room. But the tradition of the May Ball demanded that we see it through until dawn broke, and our pride would not allow us to quit, so we took some coffee and walked to the far side of the college, by the chapel. It was a beautiful night, mild, the sky full of stars, and we lay on the edge of the lawn gazing up at them until the coffee took effect and we returned for the rousing finale in the dance tent as the eastern sky began to offer the first hint of the coming daylight.

Even as the Ball was ending, its traditions continued. Those with sufficient energy would walk to Scudamore's boatyard on Magdalene Bridge, which remained open for May Balls, and would rent a punt to progress slowly along the river to Grantchester for breakfast. We had discussed this with several other couples during the Ball, with a view to getting a group together. They had seemed enthusiastic at the time, but weariness must have overtaken them, because when we were ready to leave, they were nowhere to be found. I asked Bridget whether she wanted to go anyway, just the two of us. She did.

As we left the city behind and moved into the open countryside, it was partly light, the rising sun still no more than a warming orange glow to the east. At that point the river is bordered by leafy green banks, which creates the impression of punting through forest glades, and you have to be careful to keep the punting pole clear of overhanging branches. The river and the morning were still, the tranquility disturbed only by the occasional flap of wings and a light splash as a heron dived elegantly in pursuit of some prey. We arrived at Grantchester and I lifted the pole out of the water, allowing the punt to drift slowly into the bank before tying it up securely. I stood and offered her my hands to help her out on to the bank. I was about to turn to the path which led to the village, where breakfast awaited. She shook her head.

'Later,' she said quietly.

She took my hands again and pulled me down to lie beside her on the dewy grass. I took off my jacket. She released the knot of my tie and undid the top button of my shirt. She had not worn stockings, and she had abandoned her formal heels on the walk from Downing. I was speechless, and I could only watch as she unbuttoned the front of my dress trousers and slowly pulled them down. We kissed passionately. I ran my hand up to the top of her leg and we stroked each other lovingly for what seemed an eternity. Eventually she guided me inside her and we gave ourselves to each other with complete abandon.

It was not just romantic convention that detained us in that moment. We genuinely wished we could stay there, on the bank of the river, forever. It was only much later, back in her room, when we had changed out of our formal wear, and the punt was gone, and the Ball was over, and there was nothing left to protect us from the reality of the new day, that we began to think about the implications of what had happened between us. We had been reckless, and there might be consequences.

'I don't regret it at all,' she said, defiantly. 'It was really beautiful.'

'Neither do I,' I insisted. 'If you are pregnant, I would like to marry you and make a home for you and our child. I'm not entirely sure how we will manage, but I know there will be a way.'

She looked at me curiously.

'What if I'm not pregnant?' she asked. 'Would you still want to marry me then?'

'Yes, of course,' I replied.

She kissed me.

'Good,' she said. 'Then I will marry you, as long as that is what you really want.'

Two weeks later, her period arrived, exactly on time. She wrote to tell me, and I felt a huge wave of relief flood over me. On the evening of the day her letter arrived I played a chess match for Trinity against Queen's. I dispatched my opponent ruthlessly in less than thirty moves, then went out and downed several pints in quick succession. I wrote back to Bridget in a light style, something about our luck holding, being lucky together as a couple, perhaps we had a future as professional gamblers, and we made jokes about it, back and forth, for quite some time. But neither of us questioned the decision to marry, even though it had been made at a moment of such crisis. From that time on, it was accepted between us as something which would eventually happen. I did not think much about what we had done after the shock and anxiety had worn off, beyond thinking that we had got away with it, that our luck had been good and, when looking back in a romantic mood, that the fates had rewarded us for fearlessly indulging our spontaneous passion for each other. It never dawned on me that it might have any more significance than that, until much later.

24

Julia Cathermole had given a great deal of thought to how she would signal her acceptance of the Service's offer to provide evidence to Professor Hollander, and to how she would arrange what she knew the Service wanted in return. One option had been to contact Baxter and meet him at St Ermin's Hotel or, if he insisted, in the more secure environment of his Headquarters in Broadway. But after long consideration, she had decided to bypass Baxter if she could. Julia was not sure how many doors her father's memory would open, but she saw no harm in finding out – as long as she did not let the grass grow. The High Court had given the parties in the case of *Digby v Hollander* a provisional trial date in October, but it was by no means certain that Hollander would make it as far as trial. The inevitable Request for further and better particulars of the Defence had arrived from the offices of Harper Sutton & Harper, and the threat of an application to strike out the Defence – to plunge a dagger into the heart of Hollander's case of justification – was looming. She needed the evidence, and she needed it soon. She had to act without delay. She concluded that her best chance of getting what she wanted was to go to the top, and to invite the man at the top to come to her, instead of going to him.

Julia's dinner parties were a legend among the young smart set in Kensington and Chelsea. She had a wide acquaintanceship in cultural circles, and those who accepted invitations to dinner at her town house on Eaton Square might find themselves sitting next to the conductor of a major symphony orchestra, a best-selling author, an up-and-coming painter, or even the occasional notorious rock musician. Many influential lawyers and politicians, and even cabinet ministers, proved susceptible to the prospect of a fascinating evening *chez* Julia. She hoped that such an invitation – and her father's memory – would be enough to lure C out for the evening, and to her immense relief, it worked. As soon as he accepted, she made a number of calls and attracted an eclectic gathering of luminaries from the musical world and a famous poet from Spain – but no one from the world of politics, or from the law, with the single exception of Miles Overton QC.

As ever, she spared no expense on the catering, and personally supervised the menu and selection of wines. She meditated at length over the seating plan. She sat Dick White next to a celebrated oboist and Miles Overton next to the Spanish poet, and well away from each other. She wanted them to meet later in the evening, and not before. Later in the evening was another of Julia's specialties. It was understood that an invitation to remain behind late for brandy was additional to the dinner invitation and was not extended to all guests. Moreover, Julia had a mischievous disposition, and usually ensured that at least one very beautiful young woman remained as her personal guest, giving rise to a beguiling mystery about her personal life, and to outrageous gossip on the same subject, all of which amused her greatly. But on this occasion, just after eleven o'clock, she graciously bade farewell to all her guests except Dick White and Miles Overton, and conducted them upstairs to her personal study, leaving the catering staff to clean up and restore the dining and living room to some semblance of order. The club-style green leather chairs were comfortable. The brandy was old and distinguished.

'Dick, I've asked you and Miles to stay because I want to talk about something which is important, and rather urgent. You know, of course, that Miles is representing Francis Hollander?'

Dick nodded. He had a considerable store of information available to him about the case of *Digby v Hollander*, and he had fully expected the conversation to turn to the case at some point during the evening.

'Yes,' he agreed.

'I think we can talk in complete secrecy here,' she smiled. 'Or at least, Dick, if that is not the case, I am sure you would know.'

He returned the smile.

'I am sure we are perfectly safe,' he replied.

'As you know,' she continued, 'your man Baxter met Francis at Heathrow when he arrived in London, and indicated the Service's interest in assisting him to some extent in defending himself against the action brought against him by Digby. When Francis told me this, I had a meeting with Baxter myself and he confirmed that the Service has a strong interest in ensuring that Digby does not prevail, and was prepared to support Hollander in various ways, including funding and information.'

She noticed that Miles's eyes had opened wide, and turned to him. 'Miles, I have not told you about this because it has not been necessary until now. The financial arrangements were put in place immediately, but you don't deal with that, of course. As far as your clerk Vernon knows, Hollander is paying privately for his legal services, and that is all he needs to know.'

Miles smiled and held his hands up. 'I don't need to know any more, either,' he said.

'As far as any supply of information is concerned, the arrangement I made with Baxter was that we would approach the Service if it became necessary.'

'If Hollander had no answer to Digby's case, and couldn't contest it on his own?' Dick asked.

'Yes, and no,' Julia replied. 'Francis has information about Digby – again, Miles, I'm sorry, but this is very sensitive, and I couldn't go into it before I knew there was no other way. He has information, but he doesn't have evidence.'

Dick nodded. 'Baxter told me that there was information you couldn't use in court, for technical reasons.'

'Technically, it's hearsay,' Julia replied, 'and I know Miles and his junior, Ginny Castle, both feel there is virtually no chance of a judge admitting it at the trial.'

She turned to Miles, silently inviting him to elaborate.

'There is limited provision for some hearsay to be admitted,' he replied, 'but if it is evidence on which the case virtually depends, we can't see any judge allowing it. The problem is that you can't test hearsay by means of cross-examination. In this case, the source of Professor Hollander's information is deceased, so cross-examination is impossible anyway.'

'But Baxter led me to believe,' Julia continued, 'that even if not admissible as evidence in court, the information might be of value to the Service. You don't have to concern yourselves with technicalities such as the Rule against Hearsay.'

'That is true,' Dick confirmed.

'He also led me to believe there is information the Service could put at our disposal which might be admissible in court.'

She stood and refilled the glasses. From below there were muted sounds of items of furniture being restored to their proper places, and china being put away to the accompaniment of laughter and snatches of conversation in French.

'That is also true,' Dick replied, 'and we are prepared to help in principle, as long as certain conditions are in place. But I should say that I don't know how much weight the court would give to the evidence we have. It is what I believe you would call circumstantial evidence. It enables us, within the Service, when taken together with other material, to draw conclusions to a degree of probability which is acceptable for some purposes – some, but not all, purposes of intelligence work – but I can't guarantee that a court would be prepared to draw the same conclusions for the purposes of your case.'

'That is a risk we will have to take,' Julia replied. 'At this point, the weight of the evidence is almost a secondary consideration. We have no admissible evidence, and the other side are about to apply to strike out our Defence, at which point Hollander goes down in flames.'

'Any evidence is better than none,' Dick smiled. 'Yes, I see that, of course.'

He paused.

'Baxter was instructed to make it clear that our release of this evidence depends on certain conditions being put in place.'

Julia nodded. 'Yes.'

'The reasons for the conditions should be obvious enough when you see and understand the evidence. In the case of any leak, not only could our national security be affected, but the lives of certain people working in our national interest would be endangered.'

'See and *understand* the evidence?' Miles asked.

'The most significant parts are encrypted,' Dick explained. 'You will need the help of an officer who can decrypt it. Baxter can do that for you.'

'What are the conditions?' Miles asked.

'First, everyone who sees the evidence must sign the form for the purposes of the Official Secrets Act, confirming that they understand that they can be prosecuted for any unauthorised disclosure.'

'I would have expected that, of course,' Miles said.

'It goes without saying that there will be no disclosure except to the parties and essential members of their legal teams. We can talk about what we mean by essential members. We will make Baxter available to both sides, separately.'

'Understood,' Miles said.

'Finally, the judge must be asked to order that the trial be held *in camera*, so that the public and press are excluded, and the trial must be before the judge sitting alone, without a jury.'

Miles and Julia exchanged glances.

'I know' she said. 'I told Baxter I wasn't sure about that.'

'Is that a problem?' Dick asked.

'It might be,' Miles replied. 'It will probably be easy enough to persuade the judge to sit *in camera* while this evidence is dealt with. That is common enough in cases involving sensitive intelligence or diplomatic information. But if you are suggesting that the entire case should be tried *in camera*, that is a different matter. All proceedings in our courts are open to the public and the press, unless there is a very good reason to exclude them. It is a fundamental principle of the administration of justice in this country, especially in a case of libel.'

'I understand that, Miles,' Dick said, 'and my Service supports that principle in general, because we are here to serve an open, democratic society. But unfortunately there are cases in which too much openness places our democratic society at risk, and this is one of them.'

Miles took a long sip of brandy and thought for some time.

'To have any chance at all, I would need a certificate from the responsible Minister, explaining to the court why this rather drastic step is needed,' he said eventually.

'That will be no problem,' Dick replied.

'As for the idea of the action being tried without a jury,' Miles continued, 'that is even more difficult, I'm afraid.'

'Surely that would be for the judge to decide?' White asked.

'Unfortunately not,' Miles replied. 'It's not just a matter of practice. There is a statutory right to trial by jury in libel cases. I won't bother quoting you chapter and verse, but take it from me, that is the case. Parliament decided that someone whose reputation has been attacked publicly should have the right to ask a jury of his peers to decide whether the attack is justified, and whether he is entitled to have his reputation vindicated.'

'Then, that presents a serious problem,' Dick said.

'Jurors can be made to sign Official Secrets Act forms,' Miles pointed out. 'It has been done before.'

'I am sure my predecessors have allowed that on a case-by-case basis in the past,' Dick agreed. 'But I would be very reluctant to do so in this case.'

'I don't see why not,' Miles said. 'The jurors are not allowed to take information away with them from court.'

'Except in their heads.'

'Yes, but we are talking about evidence which has to be decrypted before they can even make sense of it,' Miles insisted. 'There would be very little risk of a leak. And you could have your people vet the jury panel before the jury is selected.'

Julia laughed. Miles smiled reluctantly.

'Well, yes, I know you're not supposed to, but we all know it has happened.'

He sat up in his chair.

'Frankly, Dick, I'm not optimistic. Even if we succeeded in persuading the trial judge, the other side would not let it rest there. Bernard Wesley would take it to the Court of Appeal, possibly even the House of Lords, before the case even comes to trial.'

'Well,' Dick replied slowly. 'We might disclose the evidence to the parties before the judge decides on the mode of trial. Who knows, it may have some effect before you get near the courtroom.'

'That would be the ideal solution, of course,' Miles agreed.

'But if that doesn't happen, we will have to confront the question eventually,' Julia said. 'Look, God knows, late evening after a dinner party is not the ideal time to be discussing the law. But, Miles, isn't there an exception to the right to jury trial? Something to do with evidence that would be too difficult for a jury to understand?'

Miles nodded.

'Yes, I think you are right,' he replied. 'I can't remember exactly what the Act says now – as you say, Julia, not the ideal time to be doing our legal analysis – but Virginia and I will look into it next week and see what we can come up with. But I don't want to get anyone's hopes up. There is an obvious and easy argument for having a jury in this case, and Bernard Wesley will be screaming bloody murder about it, if I know him.'

'Then, Miles,' Dick said, 'you will have to scream even louder, won't you?'

25

Sir James Digby

I graduated from Cambridge with a First Class degree in modern languages in June, 1934. My passion was still chess, and in an ideal world I would gladly have devoted myself to the game, but it was obvious to me that the only way to eke out some kind of living as a chess player was to become a journalist, and even then it would have been a sparse, hand-to-mouth existence, and other part-time work would have been needed to make ends meet. I could have chanced it. I often wonder why I did not, what I thought I had to lose by giving it a go, at least for a year or two. I would still have been young enough to change direction if it hadn't worked out. Perhaps it was a preoccupation with worldly comforts. Perhaps it was a feeling of obligation to Bridget, now that she had accepted my proposal of marriage. Perhaps it was a feeling that being a professional chess player would be looked down on, certainly by my family – not the done thing, not for the Digbys of Lancashire. Perhaps it was all of those things. In the end, I don't really know why I abandoned my passion without any real fight. It might have been that my enthusiasm for chess was not all I thought it was. Or it might have been a simple case of moral cowardice.

Whatever the reason, or reasons, I decided to pursue my original plan of a career at the Bar. My father had a good friend, Lester Carville, who was a Silk at the Chancery Bar and a Bencher of Lincoln's Inn. I went to London to see him in July. It was the legal vacation, and he had time to spare. He met me in his chambers in the Inn, took me to lunch, and encouraged me to join Lincoln's and to consider Chancery work as a career. I took his advice, submitted my papers to become a student member of the Inn that afternoon, and made arrangements to start on the twenty-four dinners in hall which every aspiring barrister must attend before being called to the Bar. There was also the question of two terms of intensive legal education at the Inns of Court School of Law, followed by the Bar examinations. The course was to start in September. It was tempting to take some time off before plunging into this new world, but I wanted to get started as soon as possible, and Lester had hinted that there might be a pupillage available in his chambers if I passed my exams by the following July.

I found a small flat to rent in Holland Park, and returned to spend what was left of the summer at home. Roger had returned from South America just before Christmas, and was now spending most of his time on the estate, working with my father. Consequently, I had not seen much of him, and it was good to talk to him again for hours on end as we used to; walking around the estate, going into the village; spending an hour or two in the King's Arms; sometimes picking up fish and chips to eat from a newspaper during the walk home, as dusk was falling along the quiet country lanes. He looked fit and tanned, and had an endless fund of stories about his travels in South America, during which he had encountered everything from revolutionary priests to homicidally inclined llamas – he professed himself unable to decide which was the more dangerous animal – and he had learned to speak and read Spanish well. He had come to regard South America as a likely breeding ground for socialism because the people had been oppressed for so long – living in so much poverty, denied any proper education, indoctrinated by a Church, at the service of the State, to accept a life lived under almost feudal conditions – yet he felt they still had an unbroken, resilient spirit. He spoke of going back one day to help them in their struggle for freedom and dignity. He had obviously been deeply moved by the people he had met. I was surprised by his depth of feeling, and it was the first time I knew for certain that we shared a belief in an active socialism as an antidote to fascism and oppression.

Bridget was home from Bristol, too. Both families understood now that we were informally engaged, and both seemed to be genuinely pleased about it. Of course, as the younger son, my romantic life was scrutinised with far less anxiety than Roger's. I am sure that my parents were concerned for my happiness, but it was Roger's duty, not mine, to produce an heir to perpetuate the Digby line and inherit the Baronetcy in due course. Perhaps, for that reason, Roger was always shy and skittish about the subject when it came to his own love interests, and deftly avoided our parents' gentle questioning over dinner. He was never very specific about his love life, even with me, though when I got him alone late one evening, he did drop a hint that there was a certain young lady in London who had come to his notice. Relieved of that kind of pressure, Bridget and I spent a lot of time in each others' houses, and were able to sneak away to hideaways for more intimate purposes from time to time. We were very careful.

***

In September, Bridget returned to Bristol and I went down to London to begin my legal studies. I knew within a matter of days that my decision to try for the Chancery Bar was right. Chancery barristers spend a good deal less time in court than those in other areas of law. Much of their practice is advisory. This, I calculated, would give me a better chance of making time to play in enough chess tournaments to do myself justice. I felt it was also better suited to my talents. I had no illusions about having any great abilities as an orator, thundering away at a jury, but I was quite confident about my ability to absorb the kind of law I would encounter in Chancery practice, and to explain a case to a judge with the same background. Many of my contemporaries had a pathological dread of land law, wills, and trusts. The Rule against Perpetuities alone induced panic attacks in some of my friends who were destined for the criminal or personal injury Bars. But I knew exactly what I was dealing with from the first day, and it made perfect sense to me once I made one fundamental discovery. This was that the law dealing with land, wills, and trusts was the product of a centuries-long game of chess, the object of which was, not to checkmate the King, but to avoid paying tax to the King to the maximum extent possible without provoking the King to order your client to be beheaded or abjure the Realm. Medieval lawyers had pondered tax-avoidance schemes for hundreds of years, hunched over candles in cold, draughty chambers, exactly as lawyers do today in warm, comfortable offices with electric lighting. All the arcane kinds of interests in land, formulations of complicated trusts, and obscure testamentary provisions, which students find incomprehensible as abstract rules of law divorced from the real world, yield up their secrets with little resistance when you ask yourself the simple question of how they helped to reduce the client's tax bill, or that of his heirs and assigns. And you could not help but marvel at the ingenuity of those lawyers so long ago. Legal acumen is not a modern invention, however superior we may like to think ourselves to be today.

The work was demanding. I knew I would have to put chess in any form on hold for the year. But I managed to enjoy a limited social life – quite apart from the regular dinners in Lincoln's Inn hall. Roger was as good as his word, and solicited a number of friends to propose me for membership of the Reform Club, to which I was elected in November. I ran into Guy at the Club once or twice, and Anthony quite frequently. He had decided to take a sabbatical year from his Fellowship; he was lecturing at the Courtauld Institute and had become the art critic for *The Spectator*. I told him of a letter I had received from Donald, which I had found rather odd. In it, he said that he was seriously considering a career in the Foreign Office. Of course his background in languages would be a great asset, but I was surprised that he would opt to go in that direction given his active involvement in socialism at Cambridge. That was how naïve I was then. Anthony smiled, and for a moment seemed poised to respond to what I had said, but then changed the subject with such ease and charm that I forgot about it until we had parted company at the end of the evening. I even found time to return to Cambridge once or twice for Apostolic meetings. And twice, once each term, Bridget came from Bristol covertly to spend the weekend with me. I passed my Bar exams, and was called to the Bar in February, 1935. Lester Carville offered me a pupillage in his chambers, to begin in late April, which I accepted immediately.

* * *

On the surface, things were working out well for me. But it was impossible to close my eyes to what was going on around me. It seemed that all the pessimistic predictions Donald and I had made over our pints of bitter after CUSS meetings were coming true, one after another. Italy remained in the grip of fascism under Mussolini. In Germany Hitler was systematically eradicating the last vestiges of democracy as he transformed the country from the Weimar Republic into the Third Reich. Portugal was drifting ever deeper into the grip of a dictatorship. And in Spain, the writing was already on the wall.

26

I daresay anyone who has lived for any length of time has, at various points, longed for the ability to put the clock back; for the ability to erase a certain moment from history; to start over again from a particular point in time; to make a story end more happily. For me, that moment was the year 1936.

The King died on the 20th January, and was succeeded by Edward VIII. It was a heavy blow to my father, who had enjoyed the King's personal friendship, in addition to respecting him as a monarch. He and my mother attended the funeral, and had a private meeting with the Queen, but my father never approved of the new King's cavalier attitude to convention and apparent indifference to his constitutional responsibilities. As the year wore on, and the question of the new King's relationship with Wallis Simpson threatened to destroy the monarchy and bring down Stanley Baldwin's government, my father grew bitter and disillusioned. He seemed to lose interest in everything except the estate and his family, and Roger wrote to tell me that he spent long periods of time alone in his study, where he preferred not to be disturbed. That was not at all like my father, and I wondered whether his disapproval of the new King was the whole story.

The war in Spain finally erupted in July. Before long, it became clear that Franco's Nationalists were better equipped and enjoyed a huge military advantage over the Republican militias. Their newer, faster German and Italian fighters gave them superiority in the air, and they were able to carry out punishing air strikes almost with impunity. The Army of Africa had devastating heavy artillery and efficient modern rifles. The Republican militias were relatively poorly trained and lightly armed; the rifles they had were not always compatible with the types of ammunition available to them. The Nationalists were rapidly gaining ground, and at times it seemed that their victory would be a formality. Quite early in the war Madrid was threatened. Franco had declared it to be a priority to take the city, and he was spurred on by his German and Italian allies, who regarded it as a vital step and who never ceased to remind him how much he was in their debt for the personnel and supplies they had put at his disposal in the interests of creating a European fascist axis. The newspapers were reporting that Madrid was already experiencing siege conditions, and was likely to suffer shortages of food and medical supplies. I took an active interest in the news from Spain, partly because I also had a certain amount of inside information available to me.

Donald, to my continuing surprise, had been appointed Third Secretary at the Foreign Office in London the previous year. I didn't see a lot of him – we were both very busy – but we would meet for a pint from time to time, and he had grown very pessimistic about Spain, especially as it was becoming clear that our government had absolutely no intention of intervening. By September it seemed that the fall of Madrid was only a matter of time, and a short time at that. In the first week of that month I received a terse note from Roger – from him to me, not Johnson to Boswell. It told me only that he was arriving in London in two days' time, that he would be staying at the Reform, that he wanted me to meet him there for dinner, and that I was not to discuss anything with our parents before we had the chance to talk.

I arrived at the Reform on that Wednesday evening intrigued by what Roger had written, but I was also preoccupied with the first heavy case I had received as a barrister. I had been accepted as a tenant in Lester's chambers at the end of my pupillage, and my first months of practice had been meagre in both quality and quantity. But now I had been asked to advise two brothers who had been disinherited by their father in favour of an animal welfare charity not long before his death. There were suspicions that the father might not have been of entirely sound mind by the time he came to change his will, and the estate was a substantial one. It seemed that litigation was inevitable. I had promised the solicitors an opinion by the end of the week, and it had been absorbing most of my time and energy.

Roger was waiting for me in the dining room when I arrived. He had selected a secluded corner table. It was a bit on the early side for dinner, and the dining room was empty apart from the two of us. A glass of dry sherry, his favourite pre-dinner drink, was in front of him on the table, but he had hardly touched it. I also could not help noticing that he was wearing a rather shabby old suit and a threadbare tie, almost as if getting dressed up to go to dinner in his club were something in which he had lost interest. Roger had always been a stickler for being properly dressed for all occasions, something he had learned from my father. After a brief embrace I sat opposite him and asked a waiter to bring me a whisky and soda. I watched Roger closely. He seemed anxious, almost skittish, looking down at the table, playing with the end of his tie.

'Have you spoken to Father?' he asked.

'Not recently,' I assured him. 'I did as you asked.'

He nodded.

'Thank you,' he said. He seemed unsure, reluctant to begin. 'We have never talked about this very much,' he continued eventually, 'but from what you told me about your time at Cambridge, I gather that you and I have probably taken a very similar path in terms of our political beliefs.'

I nodded, but did not immediately reply.

'Given our family background,' he said, 'it would have been natural for both of us to turn out to be dyed-in-the-wool conservatives, men who embraced the hunting-shooting-fishing classes.'

I smiled. 'Not something I have ever found very attractive,' I replied.

He returned the smile. 'Nor I, though I suppose a certain amount of that must have rubbed off on me, and once I became Sir Roger in the fullness of time, I might have found it impossible to resist.'

I shook my head, still smiling. 'Not you.'

'Well, perhaps,' he replied. 'In any case, it's something I have been thinking about quite deeply over the last year or two. I haven't said much to anyone else about it, but ... the fact is that I now regard myself as a committed socialist.'

Having finally said it, Roger lifted his eyes up from the table and allowed his hands to release their hold on his tie.

'You almost told me as much when I was home last summer,' I pointed out. 'It was obvious from what you said about your trip to South America.'

'Yes,' he agreed, 'and I meant every word I said. I felt for those people, and there is no doubt that I had become an intellectual socialist by then. But South America is so far away, and information about what is really going on is hard to come by. I was spending almost all my time on the estate, learning how to run the place, meeting all kinds of important people Father felt I ought to know. I couldn't even get down to London very often any more. And I suddenly realised that if

I went on like this for another couple of years, I was going to forget every principle I had ever learned; I was going to become a country conservative, a loyal son of King and Empire.'

I smiled and shook my head.

The waiter returned with menus, and we took a few minutes to order dinner.

'You are right,' I said, after returning the menus to the waiter. 'I found myself drawn to socialism almost as soon as I went up to Trinity. But that is nothing unusual at Cambridge. Many men saw what was going on in the country; we saw how the Labour Party was powerless to prevent the poverty and the inequality and the injustice, and we wanted to do something about it. It didn't make you stand out particularly. I am sure it must have been the same in your day?'

'It was moving in that direction,' Roger agreed. 'But I think it speeded up considerably in the years you were up.'

The waiter had returned with our bottle of the Club claret. He asked whether Roger wished to taste it, but Roger signalled him to pour. It was something Roger had taught me when I was elected. The waiter was duty bound to ask, but the Club claret was an institution not to be challenged, and was to be poured without the demeaning demand that it be tasted. In all my years as a member I have never drunk a glass which did not fully justify our trust in it. Roger nodded his thanks to the waiter as he retreated.

'Besides,' he said, 'there is more to it than just combating the poverty and the inequality, isn't there?' He paused.

'Go on,' I replied quietly.

'James, I am talking about fascism. Germany and Italy have already been taken over. And now Spain is about to fall. Our government obviously has no intention of lifting a finger to stop it.'

'I am not sure there is much they could do,' I said, 'apart from a military intervention, and I am not sure how we could do that without support.'

Roger leaned forward towards me across the table.

'James, we are going to have to fight them eventually,' he replied firmly. 'If we don't do it in Spain we will have to do it closer to home – certainly in France, and very possibly in this country too.'

I sat back in my chair.

'There is no real support for fascism in this country,' I said. 'Unthinking and unquestioning conservatism, yes. But even the Conservatives believe in democracy. There will always be political parties here.'

Roger banged his claret glass down on the table.

'No, you are missing the point,' he insisted. 'Do you really think that men like Hitler and Mussolini are going to stop because there is no local support for fascism in a country they have set their sights on? They will march in anyway. Look at the way the German arms industry is churning out weapons – tanks, aircraft, warships. They are rearming at a frightening rate. Do you know how much weaponry they have been able to put at Franco's disposal in Spain? Do you know how many military advisers they have on the ground there?'

Actually, I did. Donald had given me the essential statistics of the German and Italian support for the Nationalists according to information gathered by our Security Services, and even the Security Services admitted privately that they probably did not know the full extent of it.

'This is the test case,' Roger was saying. 'This is how Hitler assesses how much resistance he is likely to encounter when he pursues his own territorial ambitions in Europe. If there is a precedent for non-intervention in Spain, it will embolden him to think he can occupy territory for the fascist cause elsewhere in Europe without even being opposed. It will give him confidence.'

The waiter returned with our first course, a cold Vichyssoise soup. He offered bread rolls and refilled our wine glasses before retreating. We enjoyed it in silence for some time.

'Roger, if the Government won't act,' I said, as the waiter cleared away the soup bowls, 'there is not much we can do about Spain. All we can do is try to elect a government that sees the dangers and makes plans to stop the fascists from threatening our borders. It's a matter of practicality.'

He shook his head. 'I don't agree. There are things we can do.'

'Such as?' As I asked the question, for no reason I could account for – it was a warm evening – I suddenly felt a chill inside me. It took Roger some time to respond and, as he was about to speak, the waiter in charge of the trolley bearing the daily roast stopped at our table to serve our main course, roast beef with Yorkshire pudding and vegetables. After the trolley had departed, Roger looked around the dining room. A few more diners were in evidence now, but our conversation at the corner table remained secure.

'The Republicans are recruiting what they call international brigades,' he replied eventually, 'brigades of volunteers from different countries to fight under the command of the local militias. And there are some arms shipments making their way to Spain from certain sources.'

I put down my knife and fork. I had heard from Donald that efforts were being made to bolster the Republican resistance, but he had said that most of the information filtering back to the Foreign Office was extremely vague; much of it hardly rose above the level of rumour.

'How do you know?' I asked.

'I asked some people I know.'

There was a silence. He was obviously not about to elaborate.

'Well, who is organising all this?'

'I can only tell you what they told me. I believe the Comintern is putting a lot of money and other resources into it.'

'The Soviets?'

'Yes,' he replied. 'Well, why not? They obviously see the dangers even if we don't. They see how important it is to stop fascism in its tracks, and if we can stop Franco now, it would be a huge blow to the Axis. Even if Franco can't be stopped, if we can make them fight an extended war in Spain it would use up resources they might otherwise turn on us.'

I made no move to pick up my knife and fork. The roast beef was delicious, but I had lost interest in it.

'We?' I asked quietly.

He looked me directly in the eye across the table.

'I am going to volunteer,' he said.

I looked at him for what seemed like an eternity. Out of the corner of my eye I saw the waiter hove into view, no doubt concerned that our dinners were for the moment lying untouched. I waved him away.

'Volunteer to fight?'

'Yes.'

The terseness of Roger's letter suddenly made sense.

'This is why you didn't want me to speak to Father?'

'Yes,' Roger said. His face took on a sad expression. 'I told him and Mother three nights ago at dinner. The time had come for me to pack to leave. I admit I had been avoiding it, but I couldn't keep silent any longer. To say that he didn't understand would be something of an understatement. We had a terrible row. He stormed out of the dining room to his study, and stayed there for most of the next two days. He wouldn't even say goodbye when Penfold drove me to the station.'

'How did Mother take it?' I asked.

'She didn't say anything at dinner,' Roger replied. 'She cried quietly to herself while we were at the table. But she helped me pack my things and hugged me as I left. If anything could have stopped me going, it would have been that hug, not anything the Old Man said.'

I leaned forward, put both elbows on the table and clasped my hands together.

'I am sure one of the things Father put to you is that you are his heir,' I said. I managed a grim smile. 'And, in fairness, it is the traditional role of the younger son to be the soldier. The older brother is supposed to stay at home to continue the dynasty. If anyone is to go to Spain it should be me.'

'I can't absolve myself of my responsibility just because of that,' he replied. 'But – and this is one of the reasons I wanted to speak to you tonight – I want you to promise that you won't try to follow me. One of us going is enough. It's not fair to our parents. Someone must be here to take care of them. If England were facing invasion, then everyone would take up arms, of course. But at present this is still a foreign war, thank God.'

'I don't see how I can possibly make such a promise,' I said, although in truth, the thought of going to Spain had never crossed my mind for a moment.

'You must,' Roger insisted gently. 'You are not going to talk me out of this, even if you are a barrister now. If Father couldn't, you can't, and I would be grateful if you didn't try. I don't want there to be bad blood between us, and I am counting on receiving letters from Boswell while I am in Spain – assuming that letters are still being delivered in Spain.'

Roger refilled our wine glasses and I took a long drink.

'You do know that …?'

'That it is illegal to fight for a foreign army as an irregular? Yes, James, I do know that. All the volunteers have to hope that there are so many of us that the Government will be too embarrassed to prosecute us for doing what the Government should have done itself, using our regular forces.'

'I am not at all sure they will take that view,' I said.

He nodded. 'I know. That is a chance I am just going to have to take.'

The waiter reappeared, looking disapprovingly at so much untouched food. I told him rather abruptly to clear the plates away, discouraging the question he was preparing to ask about why we had not enjoyed it. Roger ordered us a bottle of whisky and a soda syphon. I knew that

I would never dissuade him from what he proposed to do, although everything in me wanted to scream and shout and rage at him until the very walls of the Reform Club collapsed under the onslaught. I am sure my father had had the same reaction. For both of us, the possibility of losing Roger was so dreadful, the risk so unthinkable, that we could never accept it. I also felt ashamed that I had never considered doing what Roger was about to do. I hated fascism as much as he did, and I recognised the threat it posed, but I had never once done more than debate the question with my fellow socialists. Roger was going to do something about it, or die trying; and that, of course, was the horror of it. Our whisky arrived. I had one, weak, argument left, one which I knew troubled Donald, as it did me. It was worth trying on Roger.

'It's not as though the Soviets are angels,' I said. 'Look at what Stalin is doing to his own people, even loyal Party members.'

Roger nodded, pouring a large whisky for us both.

'I agree,' he said. 'The Revolution is one thing in theory and something quite different in practice.'

He took a long drink of his whisky.

'But unlike the fascists, the Revolution does at least point in the right direction. It is possible to see Stalin as an aberration that will disappear as socialism becomes more mature. In any case, at the moment, the Soviet Union is the only real hope we have of containing fascism and preventing it expanding any further. I believe they are sending equipment and advisers to Spain to do for the Republicans what Germany and Italy have done for the Nationalists.'

We drank in silence for some time as the dining room filled up.

'When will you leave?' I asked.

'The day after tomorrow,' he replied. He lowered his voice and leaned forward confidentially. 'I will tell you this so that you have some idea what is going on, but I must ask you not to tell anyone the details, certainly not anyone at home.'

I nodded my agreement.

'I am taking the night ferry to Dieppe in the guise of a tourist. From there I take the train to Paris. When I arrive at Gare du Nord, there will be a taxi waiting. There is a safe house of some kind in the city where all the volunteers meet to receive a briefing. Then we take a train for the south west. There are two clandestine routes into Spain. One involves stowing away on board a ship out of Marseilles, either to Barcelona or Valencia. The second is a hike overnight in the darkness from Perpignan across the Pyrenees into Spain. I won't know which route I will be taking, or which unit I will be assigned to, until I get there. I will send a letter to you here, care of the Club, as soon as I can, but I have absolutely no idea when that may be, or whether it will arrive. I am going to rely on you to contact Mother and tell her as much as you think she would want to hear.'

We embraced on the steps of the Club as I left to return to Holland Park. My heart was breaking and I could find no words to say goodbye. Roger sensed it.

'I must insist, Sir,' he said, as we parted, 'that I hold you in greater esteem than any gentleman now living.'

'Sir,' I replied through my tears, 'I am sensible of your affection, and hold you in just as great an esteem.'

After I had walked a hundred yards or so along Pall Mall I stopped and turned to look back towards the Reform. Roger was still standing on the steps, leaning against the wall, staring after me. We exchanged waves.

27

In the week which began on Monday 9th November, the case involving the two brothers and the father of unsound mind settled. The solicitors for the estate accepted that our evidence of mental incapacity would very likely be overwhelming at trial, and agreed that the will should be set aside in my clients' favour. A short hearing was held before a judge of the Chancery Division for that purpose. The solicitors were delighted, and I had received a substantial fee. I took Bridget out to dinner to celebrate. She was living close to me in Holland Park now, and had taken a temporary secretarial job while she worked out what she wanted to do with her degree in anthropology. I had not heard from Roger, apart from one short, cryptic note in early October which confirmed that he had arrived safely in Spain and was awaiting instructions for his deployment, but gave no further detail. She knew I was fretting about it and, in the hope of cheering me up, she suggested that I go up to Cambridge for the weekend, attend a meeting of the Apostles – my debating club, as we still called it – have a few drinks and relax for a day or two. It sounded like a good idea, and I was grateful to her. I took a train up to Cambridge on the late afternoon of Friday the 13th.

To my surprise, on Saturday the 14th, I found Anthony in residence, and we attended the Apostles debate together. He invited me to his rooms for a drink after the meeting ended, some time after midnight, and asked after my practice and after Bridget. We talked with a chuckle or two about Guy, who had somehow landed a job producing programmes with a political edge for the BBC, another career move which still surprised me, in my state of naïveté. Anthony told me that he had visited Spain in March, before the outbreak of war, with Louis MacNeice, and he talked to me at some length about finding the country so obviously on the point of conflict. He had also visited the Soviet Union with his brother Wilfrid the year before, and had been very impressed by what he saw, although he was alert enough to recognise that what they saw was being strictly controlled by the inevitable minder who accompanied tourists everywhere, to make sure they did not see too much of the reality of life under the Revolution. He was particularly positive about the Soviet attitude to art, and told me that he was developing a theory about the role of art in a socialist society, and would like to discuss with me how chess might fit into that picture, once his ideas on the subject were more concrete.

At about 1.30, as I was thinking of finding my way back to my own room, there was a knock on the door. When Anthony answered it, a black-suited college porter wearing a bowler hat offered him what looked like a letter. There was a whispered conversation, which I could not hear from my seat in front of the fireplace. The door closed again and there was a silence. I sensed that something was badly amiss. I stood, turned, and saw Anthony standing by the door, the letter in his hand, his face white, unable to speak. I took one or two faltering steps towards him. He handed me the envelope. I saw that it contained a telegram, accompanied by a hand-written letter from the Secretary of the Reform Club, who said he had found out my whereabouts from Bridget and, considering it to be a matter of urgency, had taken the liberty of forwarding it to me at Trinity by messenger.

The telegram was addressed to me, as next of kin, from a consular officer at the British Embassy in Madrid, who was regretfully obliged to inform me that my brother, the Hon Roger Digby, was reliably believed to have been killed in action in a suburb of the city on Sunday the 8th of November, while engaged in defending the city on behalf of irregular Republican forces against a Nationalist attack. The Embassy was making every effort to confirm the information, and to arrange for recovery of Mr Digby's body, but I should understand that conditions in the city were extremely difficult, and no assurance could be given about when inquiries might be complete. The family was advised to keep in contact with the Embassy for the purpose of effecting the repatriation of the body, if desired. The officer assured me of the Ambassador's personal condolences.

I do not remember much more until some time after I had woken up, in Anthony's bed, late the following afternoon. Bridget was sitting on the bed, holding my hand. I felt heavily sedated and, for some time, completely disorientated. As the events of the previous morning slowly came back to me I remembered screaming hysterically, throwing myself to the floor, and rolling around out of control, colliding with the furniture; I remembered Anthony grabbing me to make sure I didn't injure myself, and sitting beside me on the floor and holding me firmly in his arms for what seemed a very long time. He told me later that he had eventually seized an opportunity to slip me a powerful sleeping pill and put me to bed. I think, in fact, that he must have slipped me something more powerful than a sleeping pill, because I must have gone from uncontrolled hysteria to complete unconsciousness in a matter of minutes; but I have never asked him about it, and whatever he gave me I am profoundly grateful for. He spent a fitful few hours on the sofa, and as soon as it was light he contacted Bridget and asked her to come to Cambridge by train as quickly as she could. They were acts of kindness I shall never forget.

* * *

It is difficult to believe that a man could die in a modern capital city like Madrid in 1936 and that his body should disappear without a trace. But that is what happened. Our family solicitors in London were in constant contact with the Embassy, and we understood at once the conditions under which they were operating. The city was under siege. Its normal life was grinding to a halt. Supplies of food and medicines were running low. Refugees, including shepherds with their sheep and farmers with their livestock, were crowding into Madrid from every direction. The Nationalists' Heinkel and Fiat fighters were carrying out punishing air attacks against the Republican militias, and the sound of artillery pounding the suburbs could be heard in the city centre. Madrid was a dangerous place to be, and there was no way for the Embassy to maintain anything like normal consular services. It was a miracle that they could communicate with us at all. I was the point of contact for our solicitors, and I called my parents every evening. But I never had anything more than the merest glimmer of hope to offer, and even that was far-fetched. As I called I could hear the life fading from my father's voice day by day.

When we finally received confirmation of our worst fears it came, not from the Embassy, but from a man called George Watson, who called at the Manor unexpectedly one day in March 1937. Watson hailed from Gateshead, and he had been one of many ordinary British men who had travelled to Spain on their own initiative to fight for the Republican cause. I am ashamed to say that I had long had the impression that the Englishmen who went to Spain were almost all university graduates, left-leaning officer-class intellectuals, such as Roger and my fellow Apostle, Julian Bell, who also died there. In fact there were many men like Watson, honourable working men who had been forced into long-term unemployment by the economic disasters of the previous decade, and the Government's apparent indifference to their plight; who believed in socialism, but no longer so much in the Labour Party; and who also saw Spain as a vital line of defence against fascism. These men enlisted as foot-soldiers in their hundreds and offered their lives on that line of defence.

Watson had been wounded in action and had lost the use of his left arm. He got himself repatriated, basically by going back the way he had come, via Marseilles and Paris. While making his way home, he came to the Manor and gave my parents Roger's identity card. It was a difficult moment. Like any parents, until Roger's body was accounted for, they harboured a belief, or at least a hope, that one day he would walk through the front door, alive and unharmed, the victim of nothing worse than poor war-time communications; and that life at the Manor would resume exactly as it had been before he went away. Now, that belief, or hope, was as dead as Roger himself.

Watson had been standing not far from Roger when he was killed. His account of the circumstances was lucid and detailed. On the morning of Sunday the 8th November, Varela's Nationalist forces had launched a ferocious three-pronged attack on the western perimeter of the city. The main thrust of the attack was the Casa de Campo, a large wooded area, the site of a historic royal hunting ground running down to the Manzanares River. There were no rows of suburban streets to protect the city, or slow the invading forces down, in that sector. If the Casa de Campo fell to Varela, he would be free to advance unhindered into the very heart of the city. The Republican militias deployed almost all their available personnel to defend the Casa de Campo sector. The militias were lightly and badly armed, and many of their recruits, including Watson himself, had learned to load, fire, and clear their rifles only the night before. But they had numbers and, by some miracle, were able to hold Varela's forces at the perimeter. That same evening, the first of the organised international brigades arrived in the city with Soviet military advisers, and evidence of further Soviet support, in the form of Ilyushin 15 biplane fighters, appeared in the skies above

Madrid to counter the threat from the Heinkels. Varela's chance to take the city quickly and without significant resistance had come and gone. The defence of Madrid on November 8th was a major success for the Republican forces.

Roger, in effect, had the rank of a First Lieutenant in a militia brigade, and Watson was a member of his company. At the height of the fighting Roger was ordered to lead his company in an effort to take down three heavy artillery emplacements which were partly camouflaged by the trees on the north-western edge of the Casa de Campo, and which were causing havoc among the militias trying to defend one of the main roads into the city. Using the trees to provide cover of their own, Roger's company successfully disabled two of the emplacements. But the officer commanding the third had placed snipers in defensive positions a short distance away and, as Roger led the company from the front, one of the snipers shot him through the heart, killing him instantly. Watson and some others tried to drag his body away, only to be driven back by remorseless fire. But Watson did manage to seize his service revolver and his identity card.

Watson said that the men of his company liked and respected Roger, and regarded him as a natural officer, even though he had received as little training as they had. He was courageous and imaginative, and led from the front, Watson said. Although he had gone some distance out of his way, Watson refused to accept anything from my parents for his visit to the Manor except a cup of tea and a sandwich – not even his train fare back to Gateshead.

* * *

We held a memorial service for Roger at the village church in April, with our old friend Norman Jarrett presiding. Friends came from far and wide; friends from the estate, from Clitheroe and the neighbouring towns and villages; local worthies from all over Lancashire; and friends from the Reform and elsewhere in London; friends from Cambridge. There was a letter from the Palace, and a wreath from Anthony. I was expected to deliver a eulogy but, as the day approached and I had already torn up several notebooks full of notes which utterly failed even to scratch the surface of the feelings I wanted to express about Roger and about his death, I finally gave up, and in place of a eulogy I read aloud the letter I would have sent him. I didn't try to explain it, and I am sure all those present thought I must have taken leave of my senses, deranged with grief; perhaps I was. But I didn't care. I was not speaking to them; I was speaking to Roger.

Digby Manor
21 April 1937

Sir,
Lacking the intimacy you now have with the immortal and the eternal,
I cannot tell whether you are sensible of the depth of grief and despair
into which your untimely death has plunged all who hold you dear. That
grief and that despair grow stronger, not weaker, with time, and present
no prospect of relief. Yet for all their awful reality, I cannot summon
up the words to describe them. Nor, sir, do I believe that even Mr
Garrick, at the height of his powers, could have demonstrated the utter
devastation of them on the stage. I am unable to credit that I shall never
more take tea with you in your rooms in the Temple, never more dine
with you at the Mitre or the Club.
*   It is, sir, I am sure you will allow, entirely natural for me to be angry*
with you for deserting me in favour of foreign adventures, with no more
than a day or two of forewarning, and no opportunity to enjoy your
company before your departure. You will also allow my feelings of guilt
that I permitted you to usurp a role which ought to have been mine, of
which you so graciously and unselfishly relieved me, it being the duty of
the younger son to become a soldier and travel to fight on foreign soil.
Yet I know, and I am assured in the strongest terms by every gentleman
of our acquaintance, that you did so, not in pursuit of any personal fame
or glory, but in pursuit of a cause whose nobility is allowed by all. All
of these gentlemen beg leave to pay their respects through me, and in
particular, sir, Mr Blunt, whose praise I know you will esteem highly as
you esteem the gentleman himself.
*   I could not stand beside you in your battles in Spain. But you will*
recall, sir, how often in earlier years we took up arms together against
Normans, Infidels, and Roundheads, nay, sir, how often we won brilliant
victories over them, and this without ever leaving these shores or
suffering any loss or casualty. How innocent we were then of the realities
of war, and of life. You have played your part, as you were determined to
do, in stemming the tide of evil and I am confident that your sacrifice will
not have been in vain. Yet I know not how I, and the many who love you,

will ever be able to bear the loss of your voice, of your strength, of your infinitely benign presence.

I shall, of course, do my utmost to discharge faithfully the duties which fall upon me by virtue of your death, including the duty appurtenant to the title which I shall in due course assume. But I wish to assure you, sir, that there is no title or other thing whatsoever, which I would not immediately and joyfully abandon and renounce, if I could but receive news that the reports of your death were the product of some terrible error, understandably made in the chaos and confusion of the conflict.

Yet I fear it is not so, and I must accept that you will be an eternal loss and source of grief to all of us, and in particular, to your most humble and obedient servant and devoted brother,

Jas Boswell

I left the church feeling cold and alone, with a void in my heart which could never again be filled. Much later, after the reception, when the friends had dispersed, and my parents were resting, I walked in the garden, and said a more personal goodbye to Roger, in the far left-hand corner of the second lawn, the site of one of our greatest victories against the Roundheads. I am sure he would have enjoyed the irony.

28

'I see we have company,' Ben Schroeder said confidentially to Bernard Wesley, as they arrived in front of Mr Justice Melrose's courtroom in the Royal Courts of Justice at 10.20.

The gothic qualities of the building, with its high vaulted ceilings, arched pillars and heavy stone floors, made many of the corridors veritable whispering galleries, and those barristers and solicitors who appeared there regularly had learned to keep their voices down outside the courtrooms. Ben had indicated the 'company' by a slight nod of the head. They had expected to find Miles Overton and Virginia Castle, with Julia Cathermole and Professor Hollander, and indeed they were huddled together a few yards away. They did not expect to find another member of the Bar standing outside court. But there he was, giving every appearance of readying himself to appear before Mr Justice Melrose, and accompanied by three men wearing dark grey suits and carrying soft leather briefcases bearing the Royal coat of arms. The list on the courtroom door suggested that *Digby v Hollander* was the only case scheduled to come before the judge before lunch. Wesley had gestured to Herbert Harper and Sir James Digby to take seats on the bench against the wall of the corridor.

'I don't know him,' Ben said. 'Do you?'

'Evan Roberts, Civil Treasury Counsel,' Wesley replied. 'Unless I am very much mistaken, that means that the Government is starting to take an active interest in the case.'

'How can they do that?' Ben asked. 'The Government is not a party to the action.'

'They can ask to intervene,' Wesley replied, 'if they think there are matters to be discussed which will affect the national interest.'

'But surely they can't just show up unannounced,' Ben protested. 'We haven't been given notice of an intention to intervene.'

Wesley nodded. 'We will complain to Melrose about that for the record, but it won't do any good. The relevant minister is always entitled to intervene if he can show that he has a legitimate interest. The only thing we can do today is listen, and gather as much information as we can. Melrose will give us time if we need to respond. He knows we have been taken by surprise. So we will have a good grumble about it and see where the land lies. It's Miles's application today. I have a nasty feeling that the Government may be supporting him. Let's go and have a word with Roberts.'

They walked towards the dark-suited men with briefcases who were whispering animatedly to Evan Roberts, but before they could say anything they were interrupted by a black-gowned usher, who threw open the double doors of the court with a dramatic flourish.

'All parties in *Digby v Hollander*, please make your way into court,' he announced loudly.

Ben turned towards Herbert Harper. But Harper and Digby had already jumped to their feet and were heading towards the doors of the courtroom. Ben made his way into court and took his seat behind Bernard Wesley. Harper and Digby slid quickly into the row behind Ben. To Ben's immediate right, Evan Roberts was arranging his papers. Beyond Roberts, Ginny Castle was leaning forward, talking to Miles Overton in the Silks' row in front of her. There was a sharp rap on the door leading on to the bench. The judge's associate, who sat in front of the bench, stood.

'All rise,' he said.

As those in court stood, Mr Justice Melrose entered and took his seat on the bench. Today, he wore the bright red robes of a judge of the Queen's Bench Division. Ben, however, had a vivid recollection of the judge looking rather different, wearing the black robe of a judge in the Court of Criminal Appeal. Mr Justice Melrose had been a member of the court which had dismissed the appeal of his client Billy Cottage, with the consequence that Cottage had been executed not long afterwards – one of the last men to suffer that fate before the abolition of the death penalty and before the decision had been made that any further outstanding death sentences would be commuted. It had been a matter of time, so little time. The hearing had been a traumatic one for Ben. The pronouncement of the death sentence at the Huntingdon Assize had been bad enough. The dismissal of the appeal had felt like a second, and final, death sentence, as it had indeed turned out to be. All three members of the court had thrown questions at him constantly as he argued the appeal, but those asked by Mr Justice Melrose had been the most pointed, and most clearly conveyed a sense of foreboding about the outcome. It was a dark cloud which had a silver lining. His romance with Jess had blossomed when she took him away to her aunt's home in rural Sussex to recover, as soon as they had listened to the announcement of Cottage's death on the BBC's radio news. That had helped a great deal. But there were still nights when he woke in the small hours, with the words of the death sentence ringing in his ears. He found himself staring at the judge, and dug the nails of his right hand into the palm of his left to make himself concentrate on the case at hand.

'May it please your Lordship,' Miles Overton was saying, 'I appear for the Defendant, Professor Francis R Hollander, with my learned friend Miss Castle. My learned friends Mr Wesley and Mr Schroeder appear for the Plaintiff, Sir James Digby QC. My learned friend Mr Roberts appears for the Intervener, the Home Secretary.'

Bernard Wesley jumped to his feet.

'I am sorry to have to interrupt my learned friend,' he said. 'We have had no notice of an intervention. I submit that the proper procedure would be for the Home Secretary to give notice of his intention to intervene, and to serve a pleading indicating the grounds of the proposed intervention and the specific issues with which the Home Secretary is said to be concerned. This is a private lawsuit in which the Home Secretary has thus far demonstrated no such interest as would entitle him to intervene.'

The judge looked inquiringly at Evan Roberts. Roberts was a tall, thin man, who looked down on the world over a pair of gold pince-nez spectacles, which he wore around his neck on the thinnest of gold chains, and lifted on to his nose when reading from a document. His face was friendly and bore a very faint, though permanent, suggestion of a smile. His manner was very calm, and he gave no indication of being either surprised or thrown off balance by Wesley's interruption.

'My Lord, I do concede that we could have been quicker off the mark in applying to intervene,' he said. 'I am quite willing to undertake to serve the proper pleadings within twenty-four hours.

But I would ask your Lordship's leave to be heard today in connection with the application to be made by my learned friend Mr Overton. It is the Home Secretary's view that there are matters here in which the Government has a strong interest. I believe that will become clear once my learned friend has begun to explain the matter to your Lordship.'

Mr Justice Melrose nodded.

'There is one more thing, my Lord,' Roberts continued. 'I think my learned friend was going to begin by making this application to your Lordship. But, as I am on my feet, I will do so. The application is that your Lordship should sit *in camera* to hear this application.'

Wesley sprang to his feet once more.

'My Lord, this is outrageous,' he protested. 'If I understand correctly, the very reason we are before your Lordship today is because my learned friend Mr Overton wishes to apply for all further proceedings in this case to be held *in camera*. To have that application itself heard *in camera* would mean that no part of this case is to be heard in open court. This Defendant has libelled the Plaintiff in the most public of ways, and yet he wishes to hide from the public when called to account for his actions. My Lord, the Plaintiff has been libelled in public and he is entitled to seek redress and the restoration of his good name in public. It is especially objectionable that the Home Secretary should try to assist the Defendant in his goal of secrecy before he has even justified his position to your Lordship.'

The judge smiled.

'I hear what you say, Mr Wesley,' he replied. 'But it is important that all parties should be able to address me freely. I must do the Home Secretary the courtesy of assuming that he would not seek to intervene without having some proper reason. I think the wisest course, out of an abundance of caution, is to accede to Mr Roberts's suggestion for now. However, if it later transpires that there is no need to remain *in camera*, I will resume sitting in open court at that time.'

Wesley inclined his head briefly.

'As your Lordship pleases.' He sat down.

The judge's associate stood.

'The court will sit *in camera* until further notice. All members of the public, and all those not involved in the case, please leave the court.'

The only person affected by this pronouncement was a formally-dressed elderly journalist who had intended to report the proceedings on behalf of *The Times*. He seemed disgruntled, but made no protest as the usher shepherded him out of court before affixing to the door a notice that the court was closed.

Miles Overton stood again.

'My Lord, the Defendant's application is that the trial of this action should take place *in camera*, and that the action should be heard by your Lordship sitting without a jury.'

Bernard Wesley turned around briefly to exchange glances with Ben Schroeder.

'I recognise that this application seeks to depart from the general principle that trials should take place in public and in open court,' Overton continued, 'and from the general principle that proceedings for defamation are to be tried by a jury. But we submit that both general principles may be departed from when there are circumstances which justify that course. I submit that there are such circumstances in this case. May I say at once that we do not seek to prevent the Plaintiff from attempting to restore his good name, and I anticipate that if he were to prevail in due course, your Lordship would give judgment in open court, referring to as much of the evidence as might be proper to deal with in open court.'

Overton paused for a sip of water.

'That brings me to the ground of the application. Your Lordship will have seen from the pleadings a rather obvious connection between Professor Hollander's article and the subject of espionage. To put it bluntly, he has accused Sir James Digby of being a Soviet spy, and he proposes to justify what he has written at trial. He cannot do so without adducing evidence which shows that Sir James Digby is indeed a Soviet spy, and has been so for a number of years. It will not surprise your Lordship to learn that some parts of that evidence are secrets of State of the highest possible sensitivity. I understand the Home Secretary to take the view that if they were to become public, there would be serious damage to our national security.'

'You *understand* him to take that view?' the judge asked.

'Yes, my Lord. I chose the words with care. I have not seen the evidence as yet. Neither has my client, or any of those representing him. The Home Secretary takes the view that the evidence should be released to the parties only if your Lordship agrees with me that the orders I seek for the conduct of the trial should be made. It may be best if I defer to my learned friend Mr Roberts.'

'It may indeed,' the judge replied.

Roberts stood at once.

'My Lord, now that we are *in camera*, I should tell your Lordship that, while I appear for the Home Secretary, I appear for him not only as a Minister of State, but also in his capacity of the minister having oversight of the Security Services. Professor Hollander's article came to the attention of the Security Services shortly after it was published. I am sure your Lordship will understand at once that the article was of great interest to those Services, one of them in particular.'

'Yes,' the judge said quietly.

'Once it was known that Sir James intended to bring this action against Professor Hollander, the Head of the Service in question decided to monitor its progress. In the course of so doing, he was made aware by his staff that the Service was in possession of certain evidence which might be relevant to the case. He brought that evidence – the general substance of it, not the detail – to the attention of the Home Secretary. They both agreed that, in principle, it should be disclosed to the parties. But they also agreed that this could be done only under strict conditions, conditions designed to make sure that the evidence should not come into the public domain.'

Roberts paused for effect.

'My Lord, without going into detail, the Home Secretary believes it to be no exaggeration to say that if this evidence were to become public, it would not only have a serious effect on national security, but would also endanger the lives of a considerable number of people who are working on behalf of our national interest.'

There was a silence.

'What conditions does the Home Secretary seek to place on the disclosure of the evidence?' the judge asked.

'My Lord, firstly that, as my learned friend has said, the action should be heard *in camera* and should be tried by your Lordship without a jury. Secondly, that the Home Secretary should be given leave to intervene for the purposes of the case generally and should be represented by counsel throughout. Thirdly, that the evidence should be disclosed only to the parties and their legal advisers, who are to be required to sign the appropriate form pursuant to the Official Secrets Act.'

The judge nodded.

'Are you authorised to allow me to look at the evidence privately before making my decision?' he asked.

'If your Lordship would allow me a moment ...'

He turned around to the dark-suited men and there was another animated conversation. It seemed to last for a long time, but the judge showed no sign of impatience. Eventually, Roberts turned back to face the court.

'My Lord, yes. The only difficulty is that a good deal of the evidence is encrypted, and would be useful to your Lordship only with the assistance of an officer of the Service who is able to explain it. I am instructed that such an officer could be made available in about an hour. May I add that the same officer will be made available to the parties if and when the evidence is disclosed.'

'I see,' the judge said slowly. 'Thank you, Mr Roberts. Mr Overton, is there anything you wish to add?'

'No, my Lord,' Overton replied. 'Not at this stage. My learned friend has explained the background to this application. But may I reserve the right to reply once my learned friend Mr Wesley has addressed your Lordship?'

'Mr Wesley, it seems to me that I ought to look at the evidence, so that I can be fully informed before hearing your argument on the application,' the judge said.

Wesley stood.

'Yes, I am sure that would be of great assistance to your Lordship,' he replied. 'It is to be regretted that I will have to address your Lordship without having the advantage of knowing what your Lordship and my learned friend Mr Roberts know. But there it is. I will reserve any further matters until your Lordship is ready to resume the hearing.'

'Very well,' Mr Justice Melrose said. 'I will rise now. When the officer is available, please inform my associate, and I will review the evidence in my room with the officer's help.' He smiled. 'Do you want me to sign the form too, Mr Roberts?'

'We would be grateful, my Lord.'

The judge left court without replying.

29

As the parties dispersed in their different groups on leaving court, Bernard Wesley took Miles Overton aside and walked him some way down the corridor to a quieter space.

'Miles, is that right? They haven't shown you the evidence?'

Overton shook his head.

'Not until we sign the form,' he replied. 'You heard what Roberts said. Even the judge has to account for himself.' He chuckled. 'I don't think Melrose liked that very much, do you?'

'That's not the point,' Wesley insisted. 'The point is that, somehow, you or your solicitor knew that this evidence was on offer. We knew nothing about it at all. Roberts told the judge they had evidence "relevant to the case". If so, why not tell both sides about it? The Home Secretary is not intervening in a neutral sense to protect the public interest, is he? He is joining the fray on Hollander's side, and asking the judge to sit *in camera* to cover his tracks.'

'I hardly think that's fair, Bernard,' Miles replied. 'I will be candid with you. Based on the limited information I have been given, I do expect the evidence to be favourable to Hollander's case. I am sure that is the reason why they approached Julia Cathermole, who then instructed me to make the application that the court should sit *in camera*. But I promise you, Bernard, I have no idea what the evidence is, or how favourable it will be.'

Wesley shook his head.

'Bernard, look,' Overton continued, 'we have to face certain realities. Melrose is going to let the Home Secretary dictate the terms. He has no choice. Neither do we. There is nothing either of us can do until we see the evidence. At that stage, we will both have to decide whether it makes a difference to the case. I would suggest that we bide our time today and see what the Home Secretary has to offer. You can always re-open the question of sitting *in camera* and sitting without a jury if you want to.'

He paused.

'Assuming that we both still feel, having seen the evidence, that the case should go to trial,' he added with a smile.

Wesley made as if to walk away, but Overton extended an arm and stopped him.

'Bernard, wait a moment, if you would,' he said, rather uncertainly. 'There is another matter I want to talk to you about, nothing to do with this case. It is a matter in which we have a common interest, I think.'

Wesley stopped and turned back to face him.

'It concerns the Middle Temple committee looking into allegations of touting for work. I believe young Schroeder has been caught up in it.'

For a moment, Wesley was speechless.

'How do you know about that?' he asked. 'You're not a member of the committee, are you?'

Overton laughed.

'No. Quite the reverse, I assure you. I'm not even sure all the members have been selected yet, though I believe that George Kenney is to be the chairman.'

'Lord Justice Kenney?' Wesley asked. 'Well, that's not a good start, I must say. Miles, all this is supposed to be confidential. If it gets around that Ben is under investigation it could have serious consequences.'

'It is confidential,' Miles replied. 'I only know about it because I am in the same boat as you are – as Head of Chambers, I mean.'

'Oh?'

Overton took a deep breath.

'Virginia Castle is living out of wedlock with a solicitor,' Overton said. 'The Inn notified me that the committee will be looking into her situation also.'

'I see,' Wesley replied slowly, after some moments. 'Well, that's rather a …'

'Coincidence? Having both our juniors being accused of touting for work? Yes, you could say so.'

Overton paused.

'Bernard, I'm mentioning it because I feel an obligation to represent Virginia, to give her whatever support I can, just as I am sure you feel an obligation to help Schroeder. She hasn't done anything wrong. The solicitor concerned was sending her work long before they began a romantic relationship. I am sure that is true in Schroeder's case also. But still, it's a tricky situation, and the consequences could be serious. So, I have a proposition for you. I suggest that we bury the hatchet and work together on their behalf. I suggest that we find a common strategy, and appear before the committee together. I'm sure we can arrange to have the two cases heard on the same occasion.'

Wesley nodded.

'Agreed,' he replied. 'Two heads are better than one, and it may be that two cases are better than one, especially if we can show that there is no question of touting for work going on.'

'My thought exactly,' Overton said.

He paused again.

'There is just one thing I need to tell you, though. It does not make any difference in principle, but I will understand if you prefer to keep your distance.'

Wesley laughed.

'That sounds very mysterious,' he said.

'The solicitor with whom Virginia is living is Michael Smart,' Overton said.

Wesley took two deep breaths.

'I see.'

'He was our instructing solicitor in the *Dougherty* divorce case,' Overton continued. 'He was the solicitor who instructed a private detective to follow a member of your chambers, Kenneth Gaskell, resulting in evidence that Gaskell had been committing adultery with his client while the case was going on.'

'Thank you, Miles,' Bernard replied. 'I remember the case perfectly well, without your reminding me.'

'I am not raising the *Dougherty* case to score any points, Bernard,' Overton said. 'That case is over and done with. I thought it was only fair to mention it, because if you agreed to work with me on this, you would be bound to find out before too long, and I wanted to give you the chance of saying no if it was too unpalatable.'

Wesley was silent for some time. Overton pressed him.

'Bernard, surely we can agree that *Dougherty* is water under the bridge. The case settled. The parties got their divorce. Gaskell escaped the consequences of his foolishness and married his sweetheart. I know we had some cross words in the course of it all, but my son returned to me, he is doing well in your chambers, and we all came out of it with no real harm done.'

Wesley smiled thinly. 'Cross words'. Well, that was one way of putting it. The events at the end of the *Dougherty* case flooded back into his mind. Overton had blackmailed him – there was no other word for it – over lunch at their club. The public revelation that Kenneth Gaskell, Wesley's former pupil, had been sleeping with his client during her divorce case would have meant the end of his career, and might well have brought Wesley's chambers down with him. In return for suppressing the evidence of Gaskell's indiscretion, Overton demanded a demeaning surrender in the divorce case. The few days that followed were the worst of Wesley's life. He had been forced to admit what had happened to the instructing solicitor, Herbert Harper. He had barely slept or eaten as he searched desperately for a solution. In the end, he found one. It was not one he was proud of. He justified it because it was necessary, and because it was a proportionate response to being blackmailed by Miles. But it was an inescapable fact that he had blackmailed Miles in return. Wesley knew that Miles Overton had pulled strings to prevent the prosecution of his son, Clive, following the death of a fellow student as the result of a drunken escapade at Cambridge. In the course of securing his son's release, Miles had compromised himself hopelessly. So Wesley had invited Overton to another lunch at the club, and made him a counter-offer of his own: in return for a far more reasonable settlement of the divorce case, he would assist Clive in returning to England from his exile in America, and in starting his own career at the Bar. It was a shameful story, one which gave Bernard Wesley palpitations even now when he thought about it. His relationship with Miles Overton had never been smooth. Behind the façade of professional civility they were bitter rivals, and the *Dougherty* case had done nothing to improve their relationship. The thought of working with him went against the grain. But the careers of two young barristers he believed to be blameless were on the line. *Dougherty* was, as Miles had said, water under the bridge. It was necessary to let it go.

'I appreciate your mentioning it, Miles,' he replied eventually.

'As you say, that is all over with now. I have no reason to be prejudiced against Mr Smart. He was only representing his client, wasn't he? Let's see if we can put an end to this nonsense for Ben and Virginia.'

30

'I have had the opportunity to look at the evidence, Mr Wesley,' Mr Justice Melrose said. 'Not in the kind of detail I would have to if the case goes to trial, but just enough to understand the basic thrust of it. May I make it clear that, having done so, I have returned the evidence to the officer.'

'I am obliged to your Lordship,' Wesley replied. 'But your Lordship has the advantage of me.'

The judge nodded.

'Yes,' he agreed. 'My impression, Mr Wesley, is that there is a great deal of force in Mr Roberts's submissions. If I understand the evidence correctly, there are compelling reasons to do everything possible to ensure that the information contained in the documents does not become publicly known.'

Wesley inclined his head.

'I am not sure there is anything I can say about that, my Lord,' Wesley replied. 'Your Lordship has seen the evidence and I have not. In those circumstances, may I invite your Lordship to agree to hear me on another occasion, when I have had the opportunity to see the evidence, if I wish to re-open the matter?'

'Certainly, Mr Wesley,' the judge replied at once. 'That would only be fair.'

'I am much obliged. And perhaps I may be permitted a few moments now to outline the concerns I have?'

'Of course.'

'Again, I am obliged. First, my Lord, I would be grateful if your Lordship would make it clear to the Home Secretary that, if he is going to intervene in the public interest, he has a duty to remain neutral between the parties.'

Roberts was on his feet immediately.

'I am not sure what that is supposed to mean,' he said.

'My learned friend knows exactly what that means,' Wesley replied. 'If he has evidence with which he is concerned, the proper course is to inform both parties at the same time, rather than take one side into his confidence but not the other, as happened here. It creates a suspicion about the Home Secretary's impartiality.'

'That is an outrageous suggestion,' Roberts protested.

'No, Mr Roberts,' the judge replied evenly, 'it is not. I will tell you candidly that in my view, the Home Secretary would be well advised to avoid the appearance of taking sides. I am sure that the Home Secretary is quite impartial with respect to this case. But he would be well advised to make that abundantly clear, and one way of doing that, if he decides to communicate with the parties, would be to communicate with both of them in the same manner.'

'I will convey your Lordship's advice to the Home Secretary,' Roberts replied icily.

'The second matter, my Lord, is this,' Wesley continued. 'If the Home Secretary has evidence relevant to the case, he has a duty to produce it to the parties. It is not for the Home Secretary to withhold evidence from the court, or to dictate to the court the terms on which he agrees to produce it.'

Roberts leapt to his feet again.

'That is quite wrong, my Lord,' he insisted. His habitual air of calm seemed to be wearing rather thin. 'My learned friend knows perfectly well that the minister has, not only a right, but a duty to protect evidence which might compromise national security. The House of Lords said so in so many words in *Duncan v Cammell Laird*.'

'*Duncan v Cammell Laird* had to do with the plans for a submarine,' Wesley replied immediately. 'I have not seen the evidence, but I doubt it falls into that category.'

'That's not the point ...'

'And in any case,' Wesley continued, 'the proper procedure is for the minister to put the evidence before the court so that the court can decide whether it is protected by Crown Privilege, not simply to bargain with the parties about the terms on which it is to be disclosed.'

For a moment Roberts seemed poised to come out for the next round. But then he suddenly resumed his seat. Ben Schroeder told Bernard Wesley later that he was sure he had seen Roberts exchange a look with Julia Cathermole.

Wesley paused deliberately to allow calm to be restored.

'My final point, my Lord,' he said, 'is that my learned friend Mr Overton's application is overbroad. Perhaps there may be occasions during the trial when the court would need to sit *in camera* to discuss some of the evidence. But to say that the entire trial must be *in camera*, and that we can have no jury, is going too far.'

The judge nodded.

'I will keep all those points under review, Mr Wesley,' the judge said. 'I take it you have no objection to the Home Secretary intervening, as such.'

'My Lord,' Wesley replied, 'if the Home Secretary chooses to afford himself the advantage of Mr Roberts's presence each day, how could I possibly object?'

Looking across to his right, Wesley saw Miles Overton hastily take the red and black spotted handkerchief he wore in the top pocket of his jacket and hold it to his mouth, turning his head away.

The judge was also smiling. 'Then I will grant the Home Secretary's application to intervene, subject to the filing of a proper pleading within twenty-four hours. I will direct that any future proceedings be held *in camera* until further order.'

'My Lord, as far as the question of the mode of trial is concerned,' Wesley continued, 'I will say no more for now except to remind your Lordship that the Plaintiff has a statutory right to trial by jury in a libel case, under section 6 of the Administration of Justice (Miscellaneous Provisions) Act 1933. The mode of trial in cases such as this is not a simple matter of practice. Your Lordship is bound by that provision, and is not entitled simply to ignore it, as my learned friends apparently suggest he may.'

'There are exceptions to that rule,' Roberts pointed out.

'There are,' Wesley replied, 'but they do not apply to this case.'

The judge interrupted.

'I am not going to decide that point today,' he said. 'We have time before trial. I will decide rather nearer the time.'

'As your Lordship pleases,' Wesley replied. 'May I ask, however, that your Lordship does not delay the decision for too long. We are provisionally set for trial in early October, when term will just have begun. I am sure your Lordship will understand that I intend no disrespect when I say that, if your Lordship were to be against me on this matter, I would wish time to take the matter further.'

The judge nodded.

'Duly noted, Mr Wesley. I think that is all for today.'

* * *

As the judge rose, Evan Roberts rushed out of court without a word, closely followed by the Home Secretary's dark-suited representatives. Ben's party followed them out at a more leisurely pace, by which time they were nowhere to be seen. Ben, Wesley, Harper, and Sir James Digby stood together in the corridor outside court. Miles Overton and his entourage had not yet emerged from the courtroom.

'Well, that's rather rude of Roberts, isn't it,' Wesley smiled, 'to rush off like that without wishing us good morning?'

'Treasury Counsel are not used to being spoken to like that, Bernard,' Harper said. 'I sense that you may have ruffled a few feathers.'

'The judge ruffled a few for me,' Wesley replied. 'That's probably what upset Roberts more than anything else. Now he has to tell the Home Secretary that he may have won his point for today, but he is going to have to behave himself in the future. There will have to be at least the appearance of neutrality.'

'Yes,' Harper agreed. 'But that's all it is – the appearance – isn't it?'

'Yes, that's all it is,' Wesley replied.

He turned to face Digby, then shepherded the group away from the court to the far wall of the corridor, where they huddled behind a gothic pillar.

'James, I have some concerns,' he said. 'It's all very well for us to get indignant at Evan Roberts, and the rather crass way the Home Secretary has handled the matter has bought us some limited sympathy from the judge. But that only goes so far. We have to face the fact that the Home Secretary has, or at least thinks he has, some evidence which hurts your case. Not only that, that evidence is significant enough to cause him to take sides against you. Now, I can deal with that in the courtroom, but that is not where the real battleground is. What are we dealing with? What evidence are we going to be confronted with in one or two days' time?'

Digby was silent for some time.

'I can't think what it could be,' he said. 'Whatever it is, it can't implicate me directly, can it? If it did, I would have heard about it before now.'

'That was the point Barratt made at our first conference,' Ben reminded him. 'But now we know that they are afraid of making the evidence public for reasons of national security. That could be the reason why you haven't heard about it yet. Is there anything at all you can think of?'

Digby shrugged in apparent frustration.

'I don't know. I worked with some pretty shady characters during the War,' he said, 'when I was working with the Security Services doing interrogations.'

'What do you mean by "shady characters"?' Ben asked.

'Informants, people whose names came up during interrogations,' Digby replied. 'I must have met a few Soviet agents during that time. Towards the end of the War, there were lots of Russians in London, most of them doing their best not to be sent back to face whatever fate awaited them at home. They were trying to expose all kinds of people to us as German spies. They were peddling all kinds of information, which they hoped to exchange for the right to stay in this country. Rubbish, mostly, though once in a while we got something useful. We knew the Soviet Embassy was doing its best to infiltrate any groups it saw as a threat. Some of the people I dealt with must have been Soviet agents.'

'I don't see why that would turn the Home Secretary against you,' Wesley said. 'I am sure everyone knew what was going on then.'

Digby looked down and took a deep breath.

'All right,' he said. 'I was occasionally asked to pass information to suspected agents.'

Ben and Wesley exchanged looks. Digby noticed.

'No, no, it's not what you are thinking,' he protested. 'It was nothing of any real value – at least, that's what I was told. It was either to make the agent think we were interested in him, or it was material MI6 wanted to find its way to Moscow. It was all so chaotic then – so many people running in different directions – and the right hand never knew what the left hand was doing. I doubt anyone kept records of it all. Perhaps they have some record of my passing information to those people, and they have put two and two together and made five.'

Wesley removed his wig, and ran his hand through his hair several times before replacing it.

'Perhaps,' he said, 'but if it was information of no real value, why would they go to such lengths to keep it out of the public domain all these years later?'

'I have no idea,' Digby replied.

'Perhaps it is because you knew Burgess and Maclean, and Philby,' Ben suggested. 'It would hardly be surprising if they have been rummaging through the archives for anyone with a connection to those men since Philby disappeared.'

'That would make sense,' Digby agreed.

Wesley nodded.

'Well, there it is,' he said. 'We will know in a day or two. Herbert, I imagine Miles will contact me to make the necessary arrangements for the disclosure of the evidence. I will let you know as soon as that happens.'

They all shook hands. Harper and Digby walked away. Ben and Wesley looked after them for some time.

'Do you believe that?' Ben asked.

'Unfortunately, I'm not at all sure I do,' Wesley replied. 'Come on, let's go back to chambers. There is another matter I want to talk to you about – the Middle Temple committee against touting, and its nefarious activities.'

31

'Ben, that's the door,' Jess called from the kitchen.

'I will get it,' he replied.

He had heard the knock. They had both been waiting for it anxiously. It was their first formal dinner for friends as a couple, and although it had been arranged in some haste, planning it had consumed a lot of time and energy. The cooking was Jess's responsibility. She had spent a great deal of time poring over recipe books and conferring on the phone with her mother. Ben had been in charge of drinks and music. An array of pre- and post-dinner drinks stood on the sideboard and one bottle of red wine stood slightly apart, its cork removed, breathing. The voice of Ella Fitzgerald, smooth and assured, was wafting through the flat from the record-player, a soft, sad melody accompanied by haunting muted trumpets and an elegant walking bass line. His part was done. Now, he wanted to do what he could to help Jess with her last-minute preparations. But he found himself getting in her way more than helping and, with her encouragement, he re-assigned himself to finish the table setting.

On hearing the knock, he had hastily arranged the last of the knives and forks he had just placed on the dining table and, on his way to the front door, took in hand the tea towel he had been carrying on his right shoulder in the hope of finding somewhere to discard it where it would not be noticed. There was no such place unless he diverted into the kitchen. No time. He bowed to the inevitable and resigned himself to greeting their guests with the tea towel in place. He swung it jauntily back over his shoulder and opened the front door.

'Hello, Ben', Ginny said. 'This is Michael.'

'A pleasure,' Ben replied, taking Michael Smart's hand. 'Do come in. I hope you are not too out of breath. We are used to it, but it is a bit of a climb.'

Jess appeared from the kitchen.

'Jess, this is Ginny Castle, and this is Michael Smart,' Ben said. 'Ginny, Michael, this is Jess.'

They shook hands. Ginny was holding a bouquet of mixed flowers, which she gave to Jess. Michael presented Ben with a bottle of red wine.

'I hope this will come in useful,' he said. 'Best Parisian *vin ordinaire* acquired during our latest trip, fresh from the cellars of the nearest fine wine merchant to the Gare du Nord.'

'Michael is one of the last of the big spenders,' Ginny laughed.

'He has excellent taste,' Ben smiled. 'The Gare du Nord is far superior to the Gare St Lazare region.'

Jess laughed. 'The flowers are beautiful too, Ginny. Thank you. Come on in, make yourselves at home.'

'It's really nice of you to invite us,' Ginny said. 'Until Miles told us, we didn't know that anyone else was under threat from the committee.'

'We had no idea either until Bernard told us,' Ben said.

They had walked the few steps along the short corridor between the front door and the large room which served as living and dining room combined. At the far end of the room, the dining table was elegantly set with a lace table cloth, and crystal wine glasses, donated by Ben's mother when he had first set up home away from the East End, some three years before. Jess had contributed two pewter candle holders, surplus to requirements at the house of an aunt. The living room area, nearer to the front door, had two large, light brown, comfortable sofas, each covered by a beige throw.

'Sit wherever you like,' Ben said. 'We are now in the East Wing, added by the Third Earl in 1772.'

'In which many of the house's most famous works of art are on display,' Jess added, 'though we regret that the fine 1964 West Ham Cup Final poster is currently on loan to the National Gallery.'

'I would be happy to make a loan of an equally fine Manchester City poster,' Michael grinned, 'circa 1956.'

'Sadly,' Ben replied, 'we have no room for other exhibits at present.'

'Don't let him get started on football,' Ginny begged. 'We won't talk about anything else all night.'

'Amen to that,' Jess agreed. 'What can Ben get you to drink?'

'What can I get you to drink?' Ben echoed.

'Whisky and soda, with a lot of soda,' Ginny replied.

'I'll just go straight for the red wine,' Michael said.

'The St Lazare? An excellent choice, sir,' Ben smiled. 'Jess?'

'I'm all right for now,' Jess replied. 'If you will excuse me, I have to get back to the kitchen for a few minutes.'

'Why don't I come with you?' Ginny said. 'It will give me the chance to tout for some work from Bourne & Davis, and we will leave Ben to tout for some from Michael.'

Jess laughed. 'Follow me,' she said. 'We will tout in total privacy.'

Jess busied herself around the stove, on which pans of potatoes and green beans were simmering. She briefly opened the door of the oven and peered in anxiously.

'Mmm, it all smells delicious,' Ginny said.

'Beef Wellington,' Jess replied, 'my signature dish, which I am making for someone outside my immediate family for the first time. There is a decent fish and chip shop on Canonbury Road if things go horribly wrong.'

'I'm sure it will be great,' Ginny smiled.

Ben followed them in, bringing her whisky and soda. She thanked him. He realised suddenly how different she looked in her beige cashmere sweater and light grey slacks. He had seen her previously only in her robes or the barrister's formal black suit. She had also allowed her hair to hang loose, shoulder length, instead of being tied up in a severe bun to fit under her wig.

When Ben had withdrawn, Ginny pulled up one of the two high stools by the kitchen bench and sat down.

'This situation is a real drag, isn't it?' Ginny asked.

Jess closed the oven door again. She put the finishing touches to the small plates of asparagus she had on her working surface, adding Hollandaise sauce and a slice of lemon to each. She paused, turned away from Ginny.

'It really is,' she replied.

'Michael is so angry about it that it sometimes frightens me,' Ginny said. 'Fortunately, he knows how to control it. If he didn't there would be all kinds of mayhem. He is not a great fan of the

Bar at the best of times.'

'Why not?'

'He thinks of it as a kind of snobby élite, and it offends him to be thought of as an outsider just because he is a solicitor. He resents the fact that the Bar has a monopoly of all the big work in court. To be honest, some of that is just being self-conscious about his accent, about being from the North – as if anyone cares, these days. And he is a brilliant solicitor; he has no reason to lack confidence at all.'

'He should talk to Ben about that,' Jess said. 'They could compare notes, the North versus the East End.'

Ginny laughed. 'They will probably get around to that,' she replied. 'Actually, Michael had mellowed a lot until all this came up. They made him a partner at Brown & Leigh about six months ago, and that has done wonders for his confidence.'

She sipped her drink.

'But since we have been dealing with this, he has been furious all the time. The thought that the Inn is trying to dictate how we live our lives is driving him mad.'

'How are you coping?' Jess asked.

Ginny laughed. 'It's strange. On the one hand I feel very angry about it, you know, the thought that, here we are, adults living in the twentieth century, and yet this medieval nonsense could actually turn our lives upside down. But then, there are times when I actually find it funny, in a macabre kind of way. And there are other times when I feel almost detached from it, as if it's happening to someone else. I think it's because I don't want to dignify it by giving it the time of day. Then I feel guilty because I'm not angry enough, that I'm not as angry as Michael. I sometimes think I'm in denial. Somehow, I don't quite believe that something so ridiculous can be happening.'

She shook her head and sipped her drink again.

'How is Ben doing?'

Jess leaned back against the work surface and folded her arms.

'I haven't seen him get really angry at all. It amazes me. He is so self-controlled. It drives me mad sometimes, because I don't know what he's thinking, or what he's feeling. He talks about it as if it is one of his cases, and it infuriates me, because they are playing with our lives. Sometimes, I find myself thinking: "Doesn't he care about me? My life is involved here, too. Why doesn't he care about what they are doing to me?" So, then I react ...'

She looked down.

'And I take it out on him when I shouldn't, and I end up being unfair to him,' she added.

'Unfair, how?' Ginny asked.

'He has so much more to lose than I do,' Jess replied. 'He has his career as a barrister, which has started really well. I just have my position with Bourne & Davis while I decide what I want to do with my life – it shouldn't compare to what he has, and I think, perhaps I should just give up my job, and make the whole problem go away. But then I think ...'

'You think, why should you? Why should you let them do that to you?'

'Exactly.'

Ginny put her glass down on the table.

'Jess, I don't know Ben all that well. I know him through work – mostly from the Digby case we have going on now – but you don't always get to know people very well through dealing with them in court. I know what you mean when you say he is self-controlled. But I am sure he cares for you very much. He has told me about you, and I know you mean a very great deal to him. You are very important in his life.'

Jess nodded. 'Thank you.'

She glanced at the oven timer.

'Well, I think we can make a start.'

Ginny leapt down from the stool.

'What can I do?'

Jess threw open the door leading to the dining room.

'If you will take two of those plates of asparagus in, I will bring the others and open some white wine.'

'No problem,' Ginny replied. 'What do you want to bet we will be interrupting a conversation about football?'

'That would not surprise me at all,' Jess smiled.

32

'That was fantastic,' Michael said contentedly, placing his knife and fork carefully on his plate.

'It was a true signature dish,' Ginny agreed.

'See, I told you it would be good,' Ben smiled.

'I'm glad you liked it,' Jess said. 'I feel I can relax a bit now.'

'Let me clear these dishes away,' Ben said. 'Why don't we pause for a few minutes before dessert? Michael, there is another bottle of red on the sideboard begging to be opened. Would you mind doing the honours?'

'My pleasure,' Michael replied.

Ben quickly spirited the dishes from the successful Beef Wellington away to the kitchen, returned to the living room, and replaced Ella with Billie Holiday. They listened in silence for a minute or so. By some unspoken agreement, the conversation over dinner had been light, giving all four the opportunity to get to know each other. But there were more serious things to discuss.

'What are we going to do about this nonsense?' Michael asked eventually.

'At this point, I think we should let Bernard and Miles work their magic with the committee,' Ben said. 'They have agreed to work together. We know how good they are. I'm betting the committee will listen to reason when it comes from two of the leading Silks in the country.'

'But what if the committee doesn't listen to reason?' Michael insisted. 'No disrespect, Ben, but the Middle Temple is a classic Old Boys' Club.'

Ben smiled. 'It is,' he agreed. 'But that is one of the reasons why I back Bernard and Miles. They are members of the club. They know the rules. They know how to get things done in that kind of environment. They know how to talk to these people. The committee will listen to Bernard and Miles where they would not necessarily listen to you and me.'

'I agree with that,' Ginny said. 'But we must have a contingency plan of some kind, in case it goes wrong. We may not have very much time before they take disciplinary action against us if Bernard and Miles can't persuade them.'

Jess brought the palm of her hand down angrily on the table.

'How has it reached this point?' she asked. 'That's what I can't understand. How can these old men think that they can control our lives like this?'

'One or more of the old men have read a rule that makes perfect sense in principle,' Ginny replied, 'and have given it a meaning which no reasonable person could think it was ever intended to have. As to the contingency plan, Michael and I concluded that our relationship must come first, and everything else we do must follow from that. We will take whatever steps we have to take to safeguard our relationship.'

'Such as …?' Ben asked.

'First, I would agree publicly not to accept any further work from Brown & Leigh,' she replied. 'In any sane world, that would be enough. But I am picking up from Miles that even that may not be enough. For us, that would mean a change of job for one of us. The obvious last resort would be for me to leave the Bar and re-qualify as a solicitor, and then either go into practice or go in-house with a company or the Government.'

'That would mean you would have to resign from the Bar before they take proceedings to disbar you,' Ben pointed out.

Ginny nodded. 'Yes.'

'And you love the Bar. I can't see you toiling away in an office.'

'No,' she replied quietly. 'It wouldn't be easy.'

'Obviously, I wouldn't put Ben through that,' Jess said, after a short period of silence. 'I could just leave Bourne & Davis and hopefully, that would be the end of it.'

Ben saw that there were tears in her eyes. He stood up, walked around the table, stood behind her chair and put his arms around her. He kissed her cheek.

'You're missing out an important first step, Jess,' he said gently. 'You are the most important thing to me. I will put you first, whatever happens, and we will work out what to do if and when the time comes.'

She took his hand between both of hers, raised it to her lips and kissed it.

'There is always Australia,' she said. 'We have talked about that.'

'They still have a split profession in New South Wales,' Ben added, 'so they need both barristers and solicitors.'

'Now you're talking,' Ginny smiled. 'Ben, we could share chambers in Sydney, and Michael could send us both work. What do you think?'

'I'm just not sure I could do the accent,' Ben grinned. He kissed Jess again and resumed his seat.

'I'm not ready to concede defeat,' Michael said. 'I don't accept that we have to resign ourselves to changing jobs, even if things do go against us in the committee. Ginny has worked hard to get where she is at the Bar. It's what she loves, and I don't see why she should have to give it up.'

Ginny smiled.

'You are about to hear Michael's pet theory,' she said. 'I can't say I'm convinced yet, but it's an interesting idea…'

'I think if the committee does go against us, we should sue the Middle Temple,' Michael announced grandly.

Ben laughed aloud.

'Well, there's a thought,' he replied. 'Sue them where, and for what?'

'Well, you barristers are the experts on procedure,' he grinned. 'But my idea is to sue in the Chancery Division for a declaration that the Middle Temple is acting unlawfully. Perhaps Sir James Digby QC could act for us. He is a Chancery man, I believe.'

Ben was smiling. He stared at Michael for some time.

'So, what do you think?' Michael asked.

'Well, a declaration might be our remedy. But you have to have a cause of action before a declaration can be granted. What is our cause of action?'

'His first stab at that was conspiracy to defraud,' Ginny said, laughing.

'I submitted that to learned counsel for an opinion,' Michael said, 'but she was not impressed.'

'Neither am I,' Ben said.

'So, then I gave the matter further thought. What do you think about the European Convention on Human Rights?'

'The what?' Ben asked.

'I had to ask as well,' Ginny admitted.

'The Convention for the Protection of Human Rights and Freedoms, to give it its full title,' Michael replied, 'signed by all the members of the Council of Europe, of which the United Kingdom is one, in 1950. It came into effect in 1953. It has some interesting provisions. Article 8 guarantees the right to respect for the citizen's private and family life, his home and his correspondence.'

Ben nodded. 'Fair enough. But is that part of our law?'

'Not directly,' Ginny replied. 'But Michael thinks we may be able to rely on it.'

'My theory,' Michael said, 'is that the Government has a duty to respect the provisions of treaties it ratifies, even if there is no corresponding provision in our own law. I'm still checking to see whether the UK registered any reservations when it ratified the treaty.'

'But it's not the Government doing this to us,' Ben objected. 'It's the Middle Temple we have a problem with.'

'We could argue that the Middle Temple controls admission to a profession necessary to uphold the rule of law,' Ginny said, 'which is an important function of government.'

'Which is where I get out of my depth,' Michael admitted.

'So do we,' Ginny grinned.

'The person to ask in my chambers,' Ben said, 'would be Harriet Fisk. She has a background in international law. Her father was a diplomat before he became Master of his college at Cambridge. I will mention it to her next week in confidence, obviously.'

'Can't do any harm,' Michael agreed. 'Brown & Leigh would act as solicitors, I am sure, which would save on costs.'

'I am sure Barratt would help too,' Jess added.

'The more, the merrier,' Michael said. 'Let's hope we don't have to put the plan to the test. Let's hope Bernard and Miles are successful.' He raised his glass. 'But in any case, a toast: to Jess, a wonderful cook; and to two couples who love each other and who are not going to be driven apart by a group of miserable old men.'

33

Sir James Digby

My father died in June 1937. He died suddenly, and yet not suddenly. My mother found him in an armchair in his study, apparently asleep, early in the evening when he failed to appear for dinner. The official cause of death was hypertension, resulting in a sudden death, and I have no doubt that, medically, that is true. But in broader terms his death occurred gradually, over a period of time. It began with the King's death in January 1936; it included Edward VIII's abdication in December in what, to my father, were profoundly shocking circumstances; and, of course, the most devastating blow – the report of Roger's death in November, followed by George Watson's confirmation of it just three months before his death. In that sense, he died, not at all suddenly, of a broken heart. As for me, I was now *Sir* James Masefield Digby, and the duties I had promised Roger I would undertake as baronet and head of the family, for which I felt utterly unprepared, had become a reality.

After my father's death my mother began to sink into a deep melancholy, from which she never truly recovered. Bridget and I visited her at the Manor as often as we could, and decided that we should be married as soon as possible. We held a quiet ceremony at the village church, and a reception for all our local friends, on the lawns, on a beautiful Saturday in August. Bridget was very conscious of the absence of an heir to the Baronetcy, and that very night we began to make love without any precautions. But no heir was conceived. It was only after two years that it occurred to us to consult a doctor, who discovered that she was incapable of bearing children because of a congenital deformity of the womb. Bridget was devastated. She felt that she had failed in her duty as my wife, and although I assured her that I had never felt that she had any such duty, and that her ability to conceive was not, could not possibly be, a question of fault, she was inconsolable. We talked often about adopting a child, and such talk cheered us up briefly, but her heart was not in it, and we never have. Instead, almost as if she were trying to atone for her guilt, Bridget began to spend long periods of time at the Manor, looking after my mother and helping to run the estate, and sometimes putting in a few hours of book-keeping at her father's surgery.

By the end of 1938, my practice was going well, I was making some decent money for the first time, and we had bought our small mews house in Chelsea, which we both genuinely love. It seemed like home when she was there, and seemed very empty when she was not. My professional commitments meant that I could not go to the Manor as often as I should have, and I was grateful to her for lifting a great part of that burden from my shoulders. But I hated the fact that she did it out of a sense of failure and responsibility, and it has always been an unspoken barrier between us.

* * *

Just after Christmas in 1938 I went to Hastings for a day or two to watch some play in the famous annual international chess tournament. I saw a number of people I knew, including Hugh Alexander who, to my surprise, said he was glad to see me because it had saved him a phone call. He asked me to travel to Buenos Aires in August as a member of the British chess team, to compete in the 8th Chess Olympiad. I was obviously very honoured. It was not the first time I had been asked. The Olympiad is a biennial event, but in 1935 I was preoccupied with starting my career at the Bar, and in 1937 I had been preoccupied with my personal and family trauma in the aftermath of losing Roger and my father in quick succession. But I had played in one or two tournaments in 1938 and, despite my lack of practice, I had done rather well. In the British Championship I had almost snatched the title from Hugh when we met in the penultimate round, but after securing an early advantage I made one careless move, let the advantage slip, and drifted into a textbook drawn endgame. I talked the offer over with Bridget. I was very reluctant to leave her for a month, especially as she was still spending so much of her time at the Manor, but she insisted that I should go. I needed cheering up, she said, and she promised to spend more time with me in London when I returned.

I embarked on the SS Asturias II at Southampton on the 5th August with Hugh, Harry Golombek, Stuart Milner-Barry, and Baruch Wood. We had planned to arrive in Buenos Aires in good time to get in some practice and analysis before the tournament began on the 21st. The voyage was a delightful break in itself. The cares of my practice and the estate seemed very far away. One evening, the five of us sat in the dining room late after dinner and talked about ourselves. Like lawyers, chess players are good at talking shop, but often have nothing to say to each other about anything else, particularly intimate details of their lives. But on this evening, for some reason, we talked freely about ourselves, including the part chess played in our lives, and inevitably the conversation turned to the lack of opportunity to play professionally. Hugh and Harry knew many British players for whom it was a dream, but there were too few tournaments and too little money in the game. As a result, no British player could afford to take the risk, and none had ever formally held the rank of grandmaster, even though many would have made the grade given the right opportunities. Hugh and Stuart seemed content with chess as an avocation, but Harry would have gladly been a professional, and had plans to associate himself with the game in other ways, such as journalism, and work as a chess arbiter and referee. Most remarkable of all, Baruch had started his own magazine, *Chess*, about four years earlier, and it was doing well. But all these diversions intruded on the time available for serious study and for playing in tournaments. Fortified by several glasses of red wine, I found myself opening up too, and I told them of my passion for the game, which even a successful career at the Bar would never displace.

Harry mentioned the Soviet Union and, in a striking echo of what Anthony had said about art on the night I learned about Roger's death, he related, without praising it, the Soviet view of chess. The Soviet Union's success in chess was a demonstration of the superiority of Marxist-Leninist thought. The State entered into a pact between Society and the chess player, whereby the player was given the opportunity to show his ability, and if sufficiently talented, would be supported in his profession in return for placing his ability at the service of the State and acknowledging the Soviet State as the creator of, and inspiration for, his success. That night I lay awake in my cabin, watching the dark sea through the porthole, and feeling the rhythmic rocking and swaying of the ship as she made her way through the gentle waves. I tried to imagine my life as it would be if I could live in

an England which took the Marxist-Leninist approach to chess. As I
fell asleep I was conversing in my mind with Anthony about the artist's
responsibility to the Proletariat, and the conversation turned into a
dream.

34

The tournament was scheduled to last from the 21st August to the 19th September. It was an extraordinary event. Twenty-seven nations competed, more than in any previous tournament, and there was great excitement about the participation of Cuba, led by the legendary José Raúl Capablanca whose games I had studied with Mr Armitage. We made a good start, and qualified from our group for the finals. But on the 1st September, when the finals were scheduled to begin, we were awakened in our hotel rooms and asked to dress without delay and report to the British Embassy. A car was waiting for us outside.

When we arrived, the Embassy was in a state of high excitement, with officials running in every direction carrying files and telegraphs. We waited in the lobby for no more than two minutes, before being introduced to the Ambassador, Sir Esmond Ovey. Despite the hour – it was now a little after 3 o'clock – he was immaculately dressed in a beige lightweight suit and his Club tie. Without any formalities, he wished us a brisk good morning and led us up two narrow, creaking, wooden flights of stairs to a quiet corner room. On the door was a notice which warned, in English and Spanish, that unauthorised entry was strictly forbidden. Sir Esmond fumbled with a large set of keys for some time before selecting one which admitted us to the room. It was empty except for a small conference table, six chairs, a sideboard with a jug of water and several glasses, a radio transmitter and a bank of cabinets containing massive tape recorders. A large ceramic ashtray, which had apparently escaped the attention of the cleaners, assuming that cleaners were authorised to enter, occupied the centre of the table. An unobtrusive young man wearing a worn light grey suit and a crumpled red tie followed us into the room, donned headphones, and set about activating the tape recorders. We took seats around the table.

'This room is supposed to be completely secure,' Ovey said, as the young man completed his preparations. 'I hope to God it is, especially given the astronomic amount of money it cost the taxpayer to set it up.'

The young man nodded to indicate that all was ready.

'Gentlemen,' the Ambassador said, 'as from this morning, Great Britain will be at war with Germany.' He looked around the table to gauge our reactions.

The news was not really a surprise. When we had left England, we knew, as did every thoughtful follower of the political situation, that the outbreak of war was more a question of when, rather than if. Personally, I found the news welcome. I was glad that the Government had confronted Hitler and had been forced to abandon Chamberlain's policy of appeasement. I thought that perhaps we had been given a second chance to overthrow fascism after the dreadful defeat in Spain and, of course, I hoped to play some part in taking advantage of that chance, for Roger's sake and my own. Inevitably, the likelihood of war had been a subject of discussion among players from all the competing nations, and the question had arisen of what we would do if war broke out during the tournament. Most players thought that the tournament should continue, despite the diplomatic and political issues which would inevitably arise, and so most teams, including ours, were against an immediate return home. Our Government had different ideas.

'HMG takes the view that you should all return home without delay,' Ovey continued. 'There is a sailing the day after tomorrow for Southampton, calling at Le Havre just for an hour or two, and then home. I don't think you are in any danger here in Buenos Aires, but we will extend you diplomatic protection, just in case. We will have people watching you until you leave and we will make sure you get on board ship without difficulty. There will be someone to meet you when you dock at Southampton.'

There was silence for some time. The reference to protection rather baffled us. We were chess players, not high-ranking state officials or generals. Why would we be in danger in a neutral country? Why would there be any need to spirit us out of Argentina so urgently? Hugh was our captain, and we looked to him to reply.

'Ambassador, we appreciate your concern, of course. But the general feeling at the Olympiad is that the tournament should continue. It will be over in less than three weeks. Surely it would be better to show the flag and not let Hitler send us scurrying home? Do you have any intelligence that suggests we may be in danger?'

Ovey smiled thinly. 'As I said, Mr Alexander, the decision that you should return at once was made by the Government, not by me. I am only the messenger, so to speak. We have a substantial number of British subjects in Argentina at any given time, and this moment is no exception. We shall give assistance to all of them in getting home as, and when, they must, or wish to do so, but I assure you that we do not have the resources to offer all of them protection, or fight for berths for them on every steamer leaving Buenos Aires. This is an arrangement we are making in your case on express instructions from London.'

Hugh nodded slowly. 'May we know why?'

'I have instructions to explain exactly why,' the Ambassador replied at once. 'That is why we are in a hopefully secure room. Before I do, you all need to sign a form for me.'

He gestured to the young man, who took off his headphones and picked up a small pile of papers from the top of the sideboard. He gave us each one form.

'You will get used to signing these before long,' Ovey said. 'You will be doing it quite regularly from now on, I expect. Read it through, please. All it says is that you agree to keep what you are about to hear secret, on pain of being prosecuted. Take it seriously. The consequences of being prosecuted are serious enough in peacetime. I imagine they become considerably more serious in time of war.'

'The Government,' the Ambassador continued, as the young man collected our signed forms, 'is about to set up a centre dedicated to breaking enemy codes. It is believed that the ability to penetrate the enemy's communications without their knowing may be a vital factor in securing a quick victory. This cannot be done without men who have the necessary abilities. The Government has been advised that certain people, including mathematicians and chess players, are more likely to have those abilities than others, and they are keen to recruit men with those abilities without delay. So the Embassy has instructions to deliver Mr Alexander, Mr Golombek and Mr Milner-Barry to England as promptly as possible.'

'Where is the centre to be situated?' Stuart asked.

'Sorry, I can't answer that,' Ovey replied. 'If you have any objections to the Government's plans for you, you will have to take it up with them when you get back, I'm afraid. Not my department. My job is just to get you there safely. Your contact at Southampton will give you further instructions.'

Then Ovey looked at me.

'The Government also has plans for you, Sir James, but they are slightly different. You speak fluent German, I believe?'

'Yes,' I replied.

He nodded. 'I am sure that has something to do with it. Your contact at Southampton will put you in touch with the Special Intelligence Service.'

'MI6?' I asked, surprised.

'The very same,' Ovey replied. 'I don't know exactly what the arrangements are, but you will be meeting a man called Burgess.'

'Burgess?' I fairly gasped. I stared at the Ambassador for several seconds. 'Not Guy Burgess, by any chance?'

I do not know why I should have made that connection. I knew Guy had left the BBC, but it had been some time since I had bumped into him at the Reform, and I did not know what he had been doing since. Guy was an officer of MI6? In so many ways the thought was ridiculous. Yet Donald was in the Foreign Office, so in a strange way everything seemed possible.

'Yes,' Ovey replied. 'Do you know him? Well, anyway, he is in charge of some new group called Section D. God alone knows what they get up to, but I am sure Burgess will tell you all about it himself.'

35

'Sabotage, my dear,' Guy announced cheerfully, as he waved me into a seat opposite him at the small table. 'That's what Section D does – sabotage.'

On arriving at Southampton I said goodbye to my fellow team members with feelings of sadness. The tournament had brought us together and made us friends. But when we would get the chance to play chess again we had no way of knowing. My contact whisked me through customs without their giving me a second glance and, after collecting my luggage, took me to a small café, from where I called Bridget, to make sure she knew I was safe. I asked her to let my clerk know that I was back. My contact, who used the name Dave, and said nothing further about himself at all, instructed me that I was to be at St Ermin's Hotel in Caxton Street SW1 in time for lunch the next day. I would be given further details of my proposed assignment at that time. I signed another form. We shook hands. He asked me to remain in the café for another ten minutes, after which I would be free to make my way to the station and take a train home to London. Bridget was very pleased to see me. We went out for dinner and afterwards made love very affectionately. I told her that it had been thought best that the team should return home immediately, but not why. I suppose that was partly because of the forms I had signed, but I have talked to Bridget about such things many times since, and the main reason was that I still did not know the answer to that question myself. Fortunately, it was the legal vacation, and my clerk had no plans for me the next day, so just after midday I had made my way to St James's Park tube station and around the corner from Broadway into Caxton Street.

'Sabotage?' I asked incredulously. 'You?'

Guy was taking the first drag of a cigarette. He expelled the mouthful of smoke quickly and waved the cigarette in the air, laughing uproariously.

'Yes, I know, I know. It's too outrageous.'

'It certainly is,' I agreed.

'Believe me, I know. The only bad part, my dear, is that the training centre is going to be miles away from London, so God knows how I will meet any beautiful boys. I suppose I will have to sneak away and get on a train when they are not looking. You're not supposed to know that; it's all very hush-hush, so forget I told you. If you tell anyone they will take you to the Tower and have you beheaded.'

'I am sure you have a form ready for me to sign,' I said.

'But of course, my dear.'

Whenever I had seen him at the Reform after he joined the BBC, Guy had looked far more respectable than when I had known him at Cambridge, and he had maintained the improvement now that he worked for MI6; but there was still always something dishevelled about him – the suit or the tie always a bit crumpled, the hair always rather wayward, the shoes always a bit scuffed. Today was no exception, and I suspected that the dry martini he had in front of him was not his first of the day. I ordered coffee. But he had chosen the table well, in a corner of the mezzanine lobby where he commanded a view both of that floor and of the entrance hall on the ground floor below us. And I sensed a new focus, a seriousness and deliberation behind the usual flippancy. Something about Guy was very different.

'What kind of sabotage?' I asked. 'If you're allowed to tell me.'

'Oh, just your common or garden variety, blowing up bridges and pipelines, disrupting supply lines, generally buggering about with the enemy and making his life difficult. This all happens abroad, of course. I don't get involved with any of that. My job is to take charge of people who can do things like that and recruit people who can train them. The armed forces actually find these people, of course. All I do is act as administrator, but it is all quite complicated in terms of supplies and equipment.'

I looked at him for some time, sipping my coffee.

'And how exactly do I fit in with this?' I asked. 'I don't know anything about sabotage.'

'Nor should you, my dear,' he replied, lighting another cigarette. 'Nor should you. We would all be better off if left in ignorance of it, I daresay.'

He suddenly leaned forward and his focus showed itself again.

'Actually, James, you will not be involved with Section D directly. But the SIS does need your services, and Section D may very well be one of the beneficiaries. I was asked to recruit you because we knew each other at Cambridge, but you will be working with a number of people in other Sections as well.'

'Doing what?' I asked, still genuinely puzzled.

'Interrogations and translations,' he replied.

I must have looked blank.

'There will be many occasions when we need to question people who speak German, or have documents translated from German into English,' he continued, 'and when we do, it will always be urgent, and the product will always be extremely sensitive. To take my department, for example, we may have all kinds of ne'er-do-wells and reprobates sent to us by the military because they have an ability to blow things up, or know ten ways to kill a man instantaneously. In many cases, no one will have given much thought to checking into their backgrounds and asking whether we can actually trust them, whether they are actually on our side – basic things like that. There is not likely to be much in the way of records, so it is up to us to gather information by asking the right questions. Many of these people will speak German. That's where you come in.'

I nodded. 'Yes, I see.'

'As the war goes on, there will also be suspected German spies, agents, saboteurs, what have you, from whom we need to obtain information. The Service has used barristers for this kind of thing in the past. It seems an obvious place to find good interrogators. But they are often hampered by having to rely on interpreters, and some of them understand interrogation to mean trying to intimidate people by shouting at them. That doesn't work. The Director feels that we need to take a different tack – find someone with a quiet, low-key, but systematic approach to cross-examination, such as you chaps use in the elegant surroundings of the Chancery Division.'

I laughed. But I was impressed. Guy – or someone – had been thinking about this.

'And unlike those we have used in the past, you have the advantage that you probably won't need the interpreter,' Guy added. 'You will pick up some nuances that someone with only a basic command of German, or none at all, would miss completely; though that will be our secret, and you will always have an interpreter so that you don't have to give away the fact that you understand every word they are saying.'

'Yes, I can see that', I said.

'So we want you to stay in place in your chambers,' he said, 'and continue with your practice. But we expect you to be at our beck and call, twenty-four hours a day, seven days a week. We will give you some leave, of course, and we will compensate you for your time, though not at the rate you would expect for a juicy probate case.'

I nodded. Guy did not rush me.

'What if I'm in court?' I asked. 'I couldn't just …'

'You just need to let us know,' he replied. 'We will send someone to explain the position to the judge. You needn't worry about it.'

Guy ordered another martini and some more coffee for me.

'You will receive details of each assignment from a contact,' he said. 'I am not sure who it will be yet, but he or she will let you know where and when and what sort of character or document you will be dealing with, and so on.'

He lit another cigarette.

'We recommend that you make up some good story about why you will not be called up for active service. Something you can talk about in chambers without looking foolish. Whatever it is, the Service will supply you with any documentation you may need to back it up. And I understand that those barristers who remain in practice will be covering for those who are away on war duty, doing work for them, passing on the fees, that kind of thing. Make sure you do that, won't you? We don't want you to draw attention to yourself.'

'What do I tell Bridget?' I asked. I truly had no desire to lie to her, and I did not see how it would be possible to keep it from her anyway.

'Tell her the truth,' Guy replied immediately. 'We have already vetted her, and she comes up white as snow. Just get her to sign the form.'

'The same one you are about to get me to sign?' I asked.

'You are a prophet, my dear,' Guy replied. 'A veritable prophet.'

36

My wartime duties started slowly. But they seemed to escalate with the onset of the Blitz in September 1940. Several hundred people in London were killed on the first night of the Blitz alone, 7th September, and it soon became clear that my mission of staying in place to be available to MI6 was not a soft option either at work or at home. Chelsea was not a safe area, and the Luftwaffe inflicted heavy damage on the Inns of Court, the worst, which included the almost total destruction of the Temple Church, towards the end of the Blitz in May 1941.

Not long after the Blitz started, I evacuated Bridget to the Manor. She did not want to go, but it was the only thing that made sense. There was no reason for both of us to remain in London and, as travel became more difficult and my work increased, it became obvious that I would not be able to devote any attention to the running of the estate. If there were to be food shortages, as was being predicted, the Manor could play an important part locally in growing fruit and vegetables on a larger scale than before, and there were plans for some of the tenants to introduce livestock. Mr Bevan was getting on in years, and there was a need for someone younger to take over active management of the land. Besides, my mother was slipping further and further into her isolation, and it was only right that someone should be with her, even if she was rarely fully aware of their presence. It seemed only a matter of time before she slipped away altogether, and indeed she did, early in 1942. So we agreed that Bridget would live there for the time being and I would join her whenever I had some leave and travel was possible.

The frequency of interrogations increased rapidly from the autumn of 1940. For the most part the men and women I talked to were wholly innocent, people with German family or connections who seemed threatening to the authorities as more and more bombs rained down on London and the war suddenly became real. After an hour or two it usually became obvious to me that they had no hostile agendas, but rather were genuinely distressed about the position in which they found themselves, and we released them with our thanks for their time. But there were one or two very different cases. One man I interrogated, who had German family on his mother's side, had been found with a wireless transmitter in his room on the top floor of a boarding house in Chiswick. Those old-fashioned radio sets weighed a ton, and the police said it was a miracle he had not brought the ceiling crashing down into the flat below. It turned out that he had no particular feelings for Germany, but was bitter towards the Government because of a long period of unemployment. He had a keen mind, and he had put his free time to good use, learning to operate the radio, becoming fluent in Morse code, and teaching himself the basics of cryptography. Once I had clearly established that history, MI5 took him over, turned him, and put him to work for them under closely supervised conditions. They would not tell me any more than that. He was lucky. Later in the war he might have been tried for high treason and hanged. Another man, whose native language was German, was unmasked as a spy and took little trouble to conceal the fact. He was dealt with accordingly.

From that time on, there was a steady stream of work, both in interrogations and translations of captured documents, but it was not enough to prevent me from maintaining my cover as a practising barrister who spent some time taking on work for those who had gone abroad on war service. There were two other barristers who worked for MI6 in the same way. We were not supposed to know who the others were, but the Bar is a small, close-knit profession. My social life, in the evenings and at weekends when MI6 did not need me, was rather surreal. The Reform was open, but it still reminded me too much of Roger, and I found myself more and more drawn to the house at number 5 Bentinck Street. Bentinck Street is a short distance north of Oxford Street and just east of Portman Square, so it was not too far from my home. Anthony and Guy occupied one floor, and another was occupied by Tess Mayor and Pat Rawdon-Smith, two delightful ladies known for their beauty, charm, and wit, who had been the *Grandes Dames* of Cambridge Society in Anthony's day and were now charming wartime London. I had an open invitation as, it sometimes seemed, did every young man within striking distance. Life at number 5 seemed to be one long party; in retrospect, that was probably mainly because of Guy, for whom life generally was one long party. In fairness, though, we all entered into the spirit. We were loud, drunken and boisterous, and sometimes reckless about black-out regulations; I am sure that, at least subconsciously, it was an act of defiance directed against Hitler, the Luftwaffe, and everyone who threatened our way of life. It was as if we were daring them to do their worst and be damned. They tried; bombs did fall pretty close from time to time, but number 5 Bentinck Street, and its hedonistic occupants, lived to tell the tale.

It was during this period that I lost my naïveté and saw clearly what I should have seen long before. Guy was still with MI6, and I saw him from time to time in connection with work. Donald had been promoted to Second Secretary at the Foreign Office in the wake of his heroic role in the evacuation of the staff of the British Embassy in Paris just before the city fell to the Germans. To my amazement, Anthony had been recruited to MI5. Kim Philby had returned to London after a long period abroad as a war correspondent, during which time he had covered the Spanish war from the Nationalist side; had been awarded the Red Cross of Military Merit by Franco personally; had been based at Arras until the Allied forces had been compelled to evacuate; and had now joined MI6, working under Guy in Section D. Finally, the light dawned. I knew all these men to be committed to socialism on some level or other. But each of them had pursued career paths which gave them solid establishment credentials. They all had the perfect cover. As did I.

* * *

Once I had lost my naïveté, I saw all too clearly that it was only a matter of time. I was waiting for it; and at the end of June 1941 it happened. Anthony and Kim took me aside one evening at number 5. They led me to a quiet room upstairs where we could be well away from the party that was going on at full tilt on the ground floor. Kim had brought a bottle of whisky and three glasses. He closed the door.

'Your reports, and the transcripts of your interrogations have been attracting some attention within the Service, James,' he said, having opened the bottle and dispensed the first round. 'I have spoken to a number of high-ranking officers in various departments. The general feeling is that they are of unusually high quality. Your fluency in German gives you an insight which other interrogators lack. They have been found to be useful right across the Service, and some have been passed to the High Command.'

I felt a flush of pleasure as he spoke. I did take my work very seriously, and my intense involvement with German now had more than made up for my lack of use of the language after coming down from Cambridge. Whoever had thought of using me had been right. I found that I could gain considerable insight from listening, not only to the subject, but also to the often unguarded exchanges between the subject and the interpreter.

'Thank you,' I said. 'I am pleased to hear that.'

There was silence for a few moments.

'Anthony and I would like to make your work available more widely,' Kim said eventually. I sensed that he was feeling his way gingerly. That was unusual for Kim, whose conversation was always brisk and to the point. He was building up to something. I fancied I knew what it was, but I was nervous and felt no inclination to intervene; not just yet, anyway.

'You know, of course, that Hitler has invaded Russia within the last few days?'

'Yes.'

'That makes an enormous difference.'

'Of course.'

'Of course. The Soviet Union is now an ally.'

I nodded. Germany and the Soviet Union had signed a non-aggression treaty, the Molotov-Ribbentrop Pact, in August 1939, to the general dismay and confusion of all of us who had admired the Soviet Union's support of the Republican forces in Spain, and its general opposition to fascism. Coming in the wake of Stalin's purges and the recall of many Soviet agents to Moscow to face show trials and summary executions, the Pact had cost the Soviet Union a good deal of the support it had among left-leaning intellectuals in Great Britain. Many were no longer able to turn a blind eye and assume that the Revolution was just going through a few growing pains. But on 22nd June, in what was widely seen as an act of sheer madness, one which ignored all the lessons of history and summoned up the ghost of Napoleon, Hitler had torn the Pact up and sent his forces hurtling across the tundra towards Moscow. The Pact was dead, and the Soviet Union was indeed an ally; but whether that meant that Stalin could be trusted was a matter which I, along with many others, seriously doubted. I could feel Kim reading my mind.

'I share your reservations about Stalin,' Kim said, with a glance at Anthony, who nodded but said nothing. 'We all do. Even before the Pact, there were the purges, the summary executions, the show trials ...'

'The mass murders,' I added.

'Yes,' Kim agreed. 'There was all of that. But, for better or for worse, we have to live and work with him for the time being. The Revolution is young, and it is being managed by human beings, some of them flawed. I believe very strongly that the Russian people will find their equilibrium in due course, and that they will establish a form of government consistent with the aims of the Revolution, but a government which attaches high importance to the welfare of the people, the cultural life of the State, the propagation of socialism. But at present, they are facing a crisis of life and death, and we have a common enemy, whom we must defeat at all costs.'

He poured more whisky for all of us.

'James, the fact of the matter is this. Your reports and transcripts would be of enormous value to Russia, not only in terms of information, but in terms of insight into the mind of the Nazi regime. I don't want to overstate their importance. You can only report on the people you interrogate, whose knowledge may be limited, and whose insight may be deficient. But this is a war in which information is vital, and you never know what value a particular piece of information may have.'

I took a long drink. Kim refilled my glass immediately.

'If that's the case,' I pointed out, 'surely the Government could send the reports to Moscow directly. That would give them the chance to censor anything they didn't want the Russians to know.'

'In the first place,' Kim replied, 'I doubt that would ever happen. The Government has as little trust in Stalin as most people in the West, and even if they did choose to send some information to Moscow, as you say, it would be censored. It would have to go through so many departments, so many vetting committees, that it would probably be whittled away to almost nothing by the time it arrived.'

I shrugged. 'That may well be so,' I agreed. 'But we have to leave that to the Government to decide, don't we? The longer the war goes on, the more closely we work with Russia, the more contact will open up. The Russians may ask us to share intelligence with them, and I daresay we would, in return for whatever they may have to offer.'

I paused. I knew where we were going now. The time had come to get to the point.

'In any case, I sign the form every time I hand in a report and a transcript. I can't ...'

'I know what we are asking you to do,' Kim said. 'Technically, it is illegal.'

'Technically?' I blurted out. 'There is nothing technical about it, Kim. If I were to be caught doing something like that ...'

'You would land in trouble,' he replied. 'Yes. The fact that you were helping an ally would be some mitigation, but you would still be in serious trouble. Yes, I know that. No one can make you do anything you don't want to. You are free to say no and walk away now. I suppose, ultimately, it's a question of where your real loyalties lie.'

I turned my head away.

'But loyalty is not a simple matter, in my experience,' he said, 'whether it is loyalty to a woman, a cause, or a country. There are so many factors that influence it and, contrary to popular belief, it may change, legitimately in my view, according to circumstances. Loyalty is not an absolute value, James. Isn't that what we learn by living our lives? We may grow up believing in something – religion, King and Country, the British way of life, whatever it may be; and then something happens to make us shift our loyalty. In some ways it is not even a matter of choice. Sometimes, things happen, and we are compelled to change our allegiance. I think you understand that without my telling you, but it may help to know you are not the only one walking along that path. Some of us have been there before you, and many more will follow after. All you can do is be true to your conscience at any given time.'

I stared into my glass. I wondered what Anthony thought about all this. He had said not a word. But I felt his eyes on me, and they were speaking more loudly and conveying a message more clear than any words he could have uttered. We are Apostolic brethren, they were saying; we believe in the Revolution, we believe in socialism; we have seen the evils of fascism and the misery of capitalism; we want to end it; the Russians are the only ones who have lifted a finger to help us; they tried to help in Spain; they tried to come to Roger's aid, they tried to save him; and now the fascists want to destroy them, they are fighting for their lives; surely we owe them something?

So we did. But it was also more personal. We were Apostolic brothers. He had shared the first horror of Roger's death with me; he had held me until the horror melted away into oblivion; he had brought Bridget to care for me; and he had sent a wreath to Roger's memorial service. And that, in the end, was what mattered. It is an ironic truth about human decisions that even those which have the most far-reaching consequences often seem to be made in the blink of an eye, and for reasons that are not altogether logical. The reality may be that the decision-making process has taken years – years of inner change and reflection informed by many events, many ideas, many people – and the emerging decision may have escaped our conscious observation. But by the time the truth finally floods unchecked into the conscious mind, the decision has been made, and there is no turning back. And so, in that moment, with Anthony's eyes on me, I knew my life had changed. I still had a fig leaf: I was not betraying my country, simply helping an ally in a time of desperate need. I did not consider that what I was about to do was spying, and I do not regard it as such today. But the issue of principle had been decided. The only question that remained was ways and means.

'Why can't you copy them within the Service, and send them to whoever you think they should go to?' I asked. Even three months later I would have kicked myself for asking such a naïve question. But Kim showed no impatience. The tension in the room had vanished.

'May I speak completely frankly?' he asked.

I nodded.

'James, things are changing,' he replied. '*Entre nous*, Guy will probably be moved out of the Service later in the year. It's either that, or move him up the chain of command, and there are those higher up who have some question marks about him. They may want to send him back to the BBC for some time. So he may be out of the picture. I will not be staying in Section D. I have put in for the Iberian section, which I'm likely to get because of my history in Spain. There is a lot going on in Spain and Portugal. Both countries may be nominally neutral, but the Wehrmacht is very active there, so there is work to do. It's a bit off the beaten track, but I'm hoping that it will lead me on to Italy and North Africa, where I can have more influence. But the important thing is this. If it works out, I will be reporting to a Major Cowgill, a military bureaucrat of the worst kind – no imagination, a stickler for rules and regulations, a man who loves nothing more than counting paperclips. There would be no way for me to copy documents which have no direct relevance to his department.'

He paused to take a drink.

'No, the only way to do this is to hand the materials directly to someone who can take charge of them and pass them on without delay.'

Kim looked at Anthony. Until this moment he had been nothing more than a spectator, although for me, an influential one.

'Arrangements have to be made,' Anthony said. 'Now that we have your agreement, I will ensure that someone contacts you. He will use the name "Alex"; and he will assign you a work name.'

He smiled.

'We all need to give ourselves something of a new identity from time to time, James, don't we?'

37

I met Alex by arrangement in Green Park about a week later. He spoke immaculate English with the merest trace of an eastern European accent. He was a smartly dressed, pleasant man of average height, in his early fifties, I judged, with thinning, greying black hair and bright blue eyes. He had a wide range of conversation and a good sense of humour – in fact, he was the exact opposite of what I would have expected of a Soviet agent, given my myopic view of humanity at that time. He would call me 'Tom', he said, during our first meeting, as he showed me some basic tradecraft, tricks of the trade such as changing direction unexpectedly, doubling back on myself, choosing the best seat in a bar or restaurant, techniques that would alert me to the danger of someone following me. I was to come to know Alex well over the next few years. Although he seemed to know a great deal about me, he rarely shared personal information with me. But in a strange way we became friends and, despite the inevitable tension, I came to enjoy our many meetings in parks, and the out-of-the-way cafés and pubs he found for us to conduct our business.

The pattern of our work never varied much. After I had handed in my report, my notes of an interrogation, or my translation of a document to my contact at MI6, I would sit down the same evening and reconstruct as much as possible from memory, write it out in longhand, and place it in a plain brown envelope. The signal that I had something to give Alex was a copy of *The Times* from the day before, placed against a plant pot on the window ledge of my front room, from where it could be seen from the street. In reply, an envelope would be pushed through my door, containing a piece of white paper with a time and a single number between 1 and 10 written on it – nothing else. The number identified a list of meeting places which I had memorised, and which Alex would change from time to time. I would meet Alex at the assigned venue, and discreetly hand over my envelope. It worked like clockwork, and it went on until the end of the war. Towards the end there were one or two occasions when Bridget was in London, taking some time off from the Manor. She found one of Alex's messages and questioned me about it, but I was able to deflect her by telling her that it was just a message from my junior clerk about work for the next day. If she doubted that story at all, she probably thought it might have something to do with another woman, but she never pressed me about it.

Once, early in our relationship, Alex raised the question of money. I told him firmly that I would never accept a penny for my work, and I never did. It was just part of my job; and a part of the fig leaf.

* * *

In July 1945, I was asked by the Home Office to spend several weeks in Nuremberg, to serve as an interpreter and translator attached to the British legal team prosecuting the major Axis war criminals. It was meant to be a short-term assignment until a military interpreter became available, but there were crates full of documents to translate, they were desperate for help, and the team liked the fact that I was a lawyer, in addition to speaking and reading German to a very high standard. In the end I covered almost the entire trial, from its beginning in August until the end in October 1946, with short periods of leave with Bridget in Chelsea. My clerk was horrified and tried his best to talk me out of it, but my practice was well-enough established by now, and colleagues covered for me, as I had for them during the War. Nuremberg had been horribly damaged by Allied bombs in the final weeks of the War, and parts of the city were in ruins. Food was in short supply for the population, but the Americans seemed to have ample supplies of both food and drink, and were very generous, not only to our team, but also to the French and the Soviets. They invited us to some rather good parties.

At one of these parties I met a Soviet interpreter who was also a chess player. We spoke mainly in German, although his English was also excellent. We had a very enjoyable conversation, and even played a game in our heads, visualising the board as we exchanged moves. We agreed to a draw after about thirty moves, because we were talking for a suspiciously long time and we needed to circulate. People who don't play chess tend to be amazed when told that you can play in your head, without a board and pieces in front of you. But, of course, that is how you calculate moves during a game, and it is a routine skill for any serious player. I saw him several times after that, in and around the courtroom, and at the occasional reception, and we struck up something of an acquaintance. We had liked each other immediately. His name was Viktor Stepanov.

38

They met in Bernard Wesley's room in chambers. Wesley had asked Sir James Digby to arrive at 10 o'clock, by which time Ben Schroeder, Herbert Harper, and Barratt Davis were already present. Their visitors were expected at 10.30, and there was a sense of nervous tension, of expectation. None of them could escape the thought that this might be their last day of innocence, the day when they discovered whether or not Professor Hollander had a case, whether he had evidence to justify what he had written.

'What little I know about this,' Wesley said, 'I know only because Miles Overton telephoned me yesterday. He said that the release of some documentation kept by the Security Services had been authorised. He would not tell me anything about the documentation, but he confirmed that this is the evidence they had in mind when they made the application to the judge to hold the trial *in camera* and without a jury.'

'So, we are about to see what all the fuss was about,' Herbert Harper observed. 'I do wonder whether this so-called evidence will live up to its billing.'

'It won't,' Digby said firmly.

'I must say,' Barratt Davis said, 'if they have anything worthwhile at all, I am still surprised that James hasn't at least been brought in for questioning before now, if not arrested and charged. What are they being so coy about?'

'Exactly,' Digby said. 'It's all smoke and mirrors, trying to create an illusion of guilt where there is no guilt. It's typical MI6. I had dealings with them during the War, as you know. This is the way they operate. We just have to keep our nerve.'

'Well, we will soon know,' Wesley said, matter-of-factly. 'Ginny

Castle is going to walk copies over from her chambers together with an officer from MI6, who apparently is going to explain it all to us, and then make us sign official secrets forms warning us that we may be transported to Botany Bay for life if we breathe a word about it outside chambers.'

'Explain it to us?' Harper asked. 'Oh, because of the encryption, you mean?'

'Yes,' Wesley replied. 'That is why Ben and Barratt are armed with notebooks and several pens of different colours. They are going to take the most comprehensive notes possible, just in case we are only given the one chance.'

'One lesson we are learning from all this,' Ben added, 'is that we now know that Hollander is not our only opponent.'

'You mean that MI6 are playing for the other side?' Harper asked.

'We have to make that assumption, don't we?' Ben replied. 'It wasn't entirely clear at the time of the hearing before Mr Justice Melrose, because the Home Secretary was separately represented as an intervener. But even then, it was clear that any disclosure of evidence was going to be made to Hollander first, then to us via Hollander. This means that Hollander and the Security Services are working together, at least to some extent.'

'It also means,' Wesley added, 'that the other side have the advantage of us, in that they probably have unlimited access to the officer, whereas we may not see him again until the trial.'

'This is outrageous,' Digby protested. 'What right does MI6 have to take sides against me?'

'If it is of any comfort,' Ben replied, 'the fact that MI6 is working with Hollander doesn't necessarily mean that they care who wins the case. I think the point is that they see you as a suspect. They have a duty to investigate. It may be that the only reason they see you as a suspect is because of Hollander's article. As Barratt said, if they thought they had any kind of case against you, you would have been interrogated ages ago. So, I think they are helping Hollander largely because they think he may be able to help them. If I'm right about that, and it turns out that Hollander has nothing to offer them in return, they will lose interest in him and in the case very quickly.'

'I agree with that completely,' Barratt said.

'That's all very well,' Digby replied. 'But why are they creeping around behind my back? They could have come to me at any time if they had questions, and I would have been glad to answer them. I am not hard to find. After all I did for them during the War, I think the least they could do is to be straight with me. Instead, they are fawning all over this man Hollander just because he has written some total nonsense about me. It's not on.'

Wesley stood.

'Try not to upset yourself, James,' he advised. 'I know it is frustrating, but I also agree with Ben. Once Hollander is shown to be an empty vessel, the tide may turn very quickly, and MI6 may even change sides. We just have to be patient. It may well be that we will have a better sense of that in an hour or two from now.'

He walked to the door of his room.

'I will go and check that Merlin has put out the best china for the tea and coffee,' he smiled. 'It's not every day we have such a glamorous visitor in chambers, is it? We must make a good impression.'

Wesley paused at the door, then turned back suddenly to face Digby.

'James, one further thought, if I may,' he said. 'I think it would be best if you allowed Ben and myself to do the talking during this meeting. It is not going to help for you to make comments at this stage. I don't want to give anything away, and we can be sure that the MI6 officer is trained to remember conversations, even if he is not actually recording the proceedings. If you have any questions you want me to ask, pass me a note, but not a word from you, please. You will have ample time to talk about it later, once our visitors have gone. Agreed?'

'Whatever you say, Bernard,' Digby replied stiffly. 'I will do my best to control myself.'

39

'This is Mr Baxter,' Ginny Castle began. She seemed nervous. 'I am authorised to tell you only that he works for a branch of the Security Services which is the custodian of the documents we are about to show you, and that he is authorised to release to you copies of the relevant documents. This is subject to your signing the appropriate forms under the Official Secrets Act, which he will give you now. I am sure you all understand that under no circumstances may the contents of these documents be disclosed to any other person.'

There was no response. Baxter wished those assembled a cheerful good morning and used one of Bernard Wesley's armchairs as a resting place for the large briefcase he had with him.

'Mr Baxter will remain long enough to explain the documents to you,' Ginny continued, 'and will answer any questions you may have to the extent that he is authorised to do so. After that, he will leave, as will I, so that we do not intrude on any privileged conversations.'

Baxter briskly handed out black file folders, each containing some fifty documents. The file itself and each document was stamped 'top secret'.

They are not leaving us in any doubt about the message, Ben thought, skimming through the files. An Official Secrets Act form lay by itself, loose, at the front of the folder. He read it carefully, and signed as soon as he saw Bernard Wesley do the same. Baxter collected the signed forms and returned them to his briefcase. Digby handed over his form, with his signature deliberately truncated and illegible, at full arm's length, his head turned away from Baxter, who thanked him politely.

Baxter then positioned himself halfway between Wesley's desk and the door, straight in front of the desk, so that he could address all those present without turning. He had a copy of the folder in his hands.

'If I could ask you to open the folders at the first divider,' he began. 'The first few documents do not really require much explanation. They are a record of the trips that Sir James made to Russia, apparently for the purpose of attending the annual Soviet Chess Championship between 1948 and 1960.'

Digby reacted visibly to the word 'apparently', but Wesley extended a restraining arm. Baxter saw.

'When I say "apparently"', he added, 'I don't mean to imply that Sir James did not attend those events. Indeed, you will find, in the file, copies of a number of articles, written by Sir James for various newspapers and chess magazines, which make it clear that he did. If you will follow along with me, you will see that between 1948 and 1952, the championship was held in Moscow, towards the end of the year, almost always in November and December.'

He smiled.

'For some reason, our archivists have added the names of the winners in each year,' he continued. 'They tend to be very thorough, the archivists. They like to err on the side of giving too much detail, rather than too little.'

'They err in other ways also, I see,' Digby blurted out, before Wesley could stop him. 'They have Smyslov down as the winner in 1949. In fact, he tied for first place with Bronstein, so they were joint champions, but there is no mention of Bronstein.'

'I do apologise for that error, Sir James, I'm sure,' Baxter replied blandly. 'I wouldn't know about that myself, of course.'

He paused, and caught the look Wesley flashed at Digby.

'If I may continue, you will see that the system changes after 1952. The tournament is no longer held in Moscow every year. Moscow is the venue in alternate years until 1957, but the competition is also held in a number of different cities. So we have Kiev in 1954, Leningrad in 1956, Riga in 1958, and so on. And after that, Moscow is not even every other year. After 1957, it returns to Moscow only in 1961, which is outside our period of interest. The timing also changes. The tournament is held at the start of the year, in January and February, instead of at the end; and, to accommodate that change, it seems that there was no tournament in 1953 – we go from December 1952 straight to January 1954. That new system continues until 1961, after which there is more variation in the dates, but again, that is outside the period we are concerned with.'

Baxter turned over a number of pages.

'We do not have copies of Sir James's travel documents for each year,' he continued, 'just for some of the more recent ones, though again, I would suggest that does not matter very much, as his trips are well documented in other respects.'

Wesley jumped in before Digby could react again.

'Well, all of this is a matter of public record, isn't it?' he asked. 'I can't see anything top secret about it.'

Baxter laughed.

'I quite agree, Mr Wesley,' he said. 'As you say, this is information any member of the public with the time and inclination could discover for himself. It's the archivists again, I'm afraid. They are trained to use the "top secret" stamp on almost any piece of paper that comes their way, so you can't blame them. However, this information is a necessary background to the second part of the record, which is undoubtedly top secret. May I ask you to turn to divider two, please?'

Everyone in the room turned the pages in unison.

'We now come to the part of the record which does require explanation,' Baxter continued. 'What you have before you in these thirty or so pages is a record of certain events involving western agents behind the Iron Curtain.'

As a hush fell over the room, Ben looked across at Digby. He was staring down at a page of his file. His eyes did not move.

'Their identities cannot be revealed, obviously, so all the information about them, as well as the information about the events in which they were caught up, is encrypted. Some of these agents, the majority, were local people we recruited, people living and working in cities in Russia or cities within the Soviet Bloc – East Berlin, Prague, Budapest, and so on – but a few were people we had infiltrated. That is all I can tell you about that. Each agent is represented in the documents by a five-digit number, a unique number assigned to that agent, and never used to refer to anyone else. You will also see some strange words, such as "Wallflower" and "Aubergine". These refer to networks of agents, and if you match the number with the name, it tells you which agents are members of which networks. There is also a numerical code for the cities in which the agents were based.'

Baxter paused for effect.

'You will notice another numerical code,' he added, 'next to a date, or more usually, a range of dates. This code is used to refer to an event in which an agent was involved. The number 1 refers to information that the agent is confirmed dead. The number 2 refers to a forced relocation. The number 3 refers to information that the agent has disappeared, whereabouts unknown. The number 4 means that the agent is no longer in contact, is no longer transmitting, or our people on the ground have been unable to find him, or her, but no further information is available. The number 5 applies to networks only, and indicates that the network has been obliged to disband temporarily for the safety of its members, in which case, information about the individual agents is recorded as it comes in. Code 6 indicates that the network has been completely rolled up and is no longer viable.'

He selected a page.

'If I may give you one example?' he said. 'Please turn to page 24. Here you see a reference to Network Iris, which was based in East Germany, and consisted of about ten men and women – their numbers are given. This network was one of our best. It had been very productive for several years, but it suddenly went silent in April 1956. So Network Iris was then given a code 4. Our local resident would have done his best to investigate in difficult circumstances, and you see that he received intelligence from agent 78475, not a member of Iris, that agents 58376 and 29735, who were members of Iris, were listed as code 3. In the case of agent 29735, this information was revised to code 1 in June, in the light of further intelligence that he had been taken to Moscow and summarily executed in Lubyanka Prison. On receipt of this intelligence, Network Iris was then revised to code 6.'

Baxter closed his file and held it facing down to the ground.

'And so it goes on,' he said. 'You can work your way through it on your own. I need hardly add that this record has a very limited circulation. It is made available only to senior officers who have a clear need for the information it contains.'

'I take it you are not suggesting that it was made available to Sir James Digby?' Wesley asked.

'I am not suggesting anything,' Baxter replied. 'I am not authorised to discuss with you any significance that this record has, or does not have. My remit is only to explain it. But I do feel free to direct your attention, as a purely factual observation, to the dates on which information about the agents was received, and to invite you to correlate it with the dates of Sir James's trips to Russia. You will find that there is not an exact correlation, but a reasonably close one.'

'Then, you are suggesting something, aren't you?' Ben said. 'You are suggesting a correlation between Sir James's presence in Russia and whatever fate is believed to have befallen your agents.'

'Again, Mr Schroeder, I am not drawing any conclusions myself. It will be for others to draw conclusions.'

Digby was gripping the arms of his chair as if he intended to crush them. His face was bright red.

'On a purely factual basis,' Bernard Wesley asked calmly, 'and without attributing responsibility to anyone, how many agents are believed to have died, or are unaccounted for, during the period between 1948 and 1960?'

Baxter looked down and pursed his lips.

'Approximately five hundred,' he replied, 'not to mention a significant number of innocent individuals who got caught up with them. But you will forgive me if I add that I do not think of these men and women only as numbers.'

Wesley nodded. 'No, of course. I asked simply for information purposes.'

He paused.

'And the information recorded in these documents – and I am not asking for any details at all – is derived from intelligence which officers of your Service received, evaluated, and presumably rated reliable enough to include in the record?'

'That is exactly correct, sir,' Baxter replied.

Wesley exhaled deeply.

'Yes, well, thank you, Mr Baxter. Does anyone have any further questions?' Wesley asked. There was no response.

'Ben, Barratt, do you have an adequate note?' Both nodded.

'If there should be any further questions, Mr Wesley,' Baxter said, 'Miss Cathermole knows how to contact me. I would be glad to help, as long as they are factual questions about the record.'

After Baxter and Ginny Castle had left, Wesley stood and stretched his arms and legs.

'Well,' he said. 'Ben, why don't you go to the clerks' room and tell them we need more coffee, and ask them to send out for sandwiches? We need to go through this material in detail. Now.'

40

'Ben', Wesley said, 'let's summarise what we have, or what we think we have. Applying Baxter's code, do the figures for losses of agents during the period correspond with the estimate he gave us?'

They had worked all afternoon, until almost six o'clock. Bernard Wesley's room was strewn with screwed up pieces of paper, coffee cups, sandwich wrappings and other debris. They had all removed their jackets and, with the exception of Bernard Wesley and Ben Schroeder, who wore stiff collars, ties hung loosely around necks. Ben and Barratt had made a full note of the discussions and the analysis of the documents, and their work almost filled both notebooks. Ben flicked through his notes, and did some quick arithmetic in his head, pointing to figures with his pencil. Barratt had made his own separate note, and was checking Ben's addition.

'It's very close,' Ben confirmed. 'Baxter said about five hundred. If we are reading the code correctly, I make the total number of agents subject to the code 485.'

'487,' Barratt smiled.

'Fine, let's say 485 to 490,' Ben said. 'The majority are codes 3 and 4, with about 80 code 1.'

'Spot on,' Barratt confirmed.

'That's a considerable number,' Wesley said quietly. 'We didn't ask Baxter what it would represent in terms of the percentage of all western agents active behind the Iron Curtain at the relevant times, and I am sure he wouldn't tell us if we did ask him.'

'I will leave it in as a possible follow-up question,' Ben offered. 'You never know.'

'It's all nonsense,' Digby said suddenly. He had been silent for most of the afternoon, watching absently, as if uninterested, as his legal team analysed the evidence. His intervention now took everyone slightly by surprise. He threw his hands in the air.

'What?' he asked. 'You told me to keep quiet while Baxter was here, and I did. I presume I am allowed to say something now.'

Ben and Barratt exchanged glances.

'You can say whatever you wish, James,' Wesley replied.

'Thank you. Look… this kind of stuff is completely unreliable. I was given raw intelligence like this all the time when I was interrogating suspects during the War. It was all we had, so we had to use it. There wasn't anything else. When you have agents working in the kind of conditions we are talking about, you get all kinds of reports. Often they are totally unfounded. At best they are unreliable. Nobody really knows what is going on, but agents feel they have to keep feeding information to whoever is running them. It makes them feel useful. Most of it is bound to be suspect. You can't draw any conclusions from this material at all, and I don't see how any judge could properly admit it in evidence. We do have rules of evidence, after all. It is all hearsay and speculation.'

Wesley thought for some time.

'I am sure that some of the intelligence they received was wide of the mark,' he replied. 'But it can't all be wrong, can it? I mean, whoever in London was running these agents behind the Iron Curtain would find out eventually that an agent had been arrested, or a network had been blown, simply because there were no further communications, wouldn't he? The only thing the intelligence would tell him in addition is how bad things were – whether he was dealing with a code 3 or a code 1, for example. But it would be pretty clear that he had lost an agent, or lost a network.'

Digby was shaking his head, but he did not reply.

'And actually,' Wesley said, 'you could discount a lot of this material, and still have an appalling attrition rate. The losses would still be horrendous.'

There was silence for some time.

'We still have the point about the dates, though, don't we?' Herbert Harper suggested. 'Even Baxter conceded that there was no consistent correlation between the supposed dates when agents disappeared and the dates when James is known to have been in Russia.'

Wesley nodded. 'Yes, but I am not sure what degree of correlation you would expect to see. Let's go with Baxter's apparent theory for a moment – even though he was careful to insist that he was not offering us a theory. Let's assume that James's visits to Russia coincide with the supply of information about agents or networks to a person or persons unknown in the Soviet Intelligence Service. So, now the Russians know who or what they are looking for. But still, you wouldn't expect an instantaneous reaction, would you? Especially if the network was not in Russia but, say, in Poland. They would need time to investigate, and they would need to make a plan to take the network down, which might not be an easy thing to do, at least without giving the game away and allowing the agents the opportunity to run for cover.'

'Or they might risk compromising a counter-intelligence agent of their own,' Barratt suggested. 'In any case, it would take some time. I think you are right, Bernard. We can't take much comfort from the dates.'

Ben stood, turned his chair around, and leaned against it.

'I think we are approaching this in the wrong way,' he said.

Wesley smiled. 'Pray continue.'

'Let's allow Hollander these documents,' Ben said. 'Let's concede that they are a completely accurate record. Let's concede that almost 500 western agents were betrayed and came to grief behind the Iron Curtain between 1948 and 1960 as a result of someone's treachery in passing information to the Russians. What evidence is there that James was that person?'

'Well, we know Baxter's theory about that,' Barratt replied.

'The evidence Baxter has provided us with,' Ben rejoined, 'shows that James made annual trips to Russia to cover the Soviet Chess Championship as a journalist. That's all. There was nothing secret about what he was doing, nothing clandestine. He had a visa to visit the Soviet Union. It was all out in the open, all documented. What Baxter has not given us is one shred of evidence that James had any access to information about western agents behind the Iron Curtain. He had not worked for the Security Services since the War. If he was a courier of information, who was supplying him with the information, and to whom was he delivering that information?'

'Thank you, Ben,' Digby said.

'If we start with the concession that the information was passed to Moscow, and they acted on it in due course,' Ben continued, 'that still leaves open the question of who was passing it. It seems to me that if you were to compile a list of suspects, the name of James

Digby would be nowhere near the top of the list. It is much more likely to be the work of Burgess, Maclean, Philby – all known Soviet agents, and all far more likely to have access to this information than James.'

'That is true during certain periods,' Herbert Harper pointed out, 'but not all the time. For example, Burgess and Maclean are gone after May 1951.'

'Yes,' Ben countered, 'but almost everybody accepts that they were not the only ones involved in espionage during that period. All you have to do is assume that there was at least one other active Soviet agent within MI6 during the relevant period – which many people today believe to be true – and the name of James Digby hardly registers on the list of suspects at all. In legal terms, it doesn't come close to proof of the truth of what Hollander wrote in his article.'

'You make a good point, Ben,' Wesley agreed. 'But Herbert's concern remains valid if we put it in a slightly different way. Your point is that we can offer more plausible suspects for the passing of information during the period 1948 to 1960. I agree. It seems that we probably can, and that tends to let James off the hook. But I am concerned about a slightly different question: what was happening before 1948; and what has been happening since 1960?'

Ben nodded. 'Yes,' he said quietly.

'It would disturb me greatly,' Wesley said, 'to find out that this pattern, or scale of losses, of western agents began in about 1948 and ended in about 1960; that it was far lower before 1948 and was far lower again after 1960. A consistently higher rate of attrition over a particular period of twelve years would be hard to dismiss as a coincidence, wouldn't it? That would give Baxter every reason to suspect a link with James's trips to Russia. It would not necessarily rule out other suspects, but it would push him up several places in the list.'

'But if Baxter had that evidence,' Ben said, 'why didn't he provide us with it? He has given us nothing except 1948 to 1960.'

'That is the one question we need to ask him,' Wesley said. 'We can't ignore it. If the other side hit us with that at trial, we are in a lot of trouble. If there is any such evidence, we need to know exactly what it is. I can't see why Baxter would want to keep it from us. Let's ask him for the data from the end of the War until the end of 1963.'

Ben nodded.

'I will get in touch with Ginny tomorrow.'

'Good,' Wesley said. 'Now, before we call it a day, I want to get your sense of where we are in the light of the evidence – subject to the question I have just raised, of course. Subject to that, how do you feel about the state of our case? Do we press on? Is there any reason to explore the possibility of a settlement? Where do we stand? James, I suppose I should start with you.'

'Yes, I would hope so,' Digby replied. There was some sympathetic laughter. He allowed it to die down before replying. 'We go on, of course. This evidence provides no justification for Hollander's article at all, certainly insofar as it refers to me.'

'I agree that we should go ahead,' Harper said. 'Unless any further evidence comes to light, there is no reason to think we would not win at trial.'

'I agree,' Wesley replied. 'But I must add one thing. I'm afraid Hollander has achieved the first of his objectives. Our hope of striking out Hollander's Defence is now gone. This evidence may not see him home once we get to trial, but in my view it does entitle him to go to trial. It may not be a strong case, but James does have a case to answer.'

'Agreed,' Barratt said.

'Agreed,' Ben confirmed.

Wesley nodded.

'Good. Well, it seems that we are unanimous. Ben will let us know if any further evidence is forthcoming. Subject to that, we will start to make our preparations for trial.'

41

Sir James Digby

When I returned from Nuremberg towards the end of 1946, my war
was over, and I returned to full-time practice. All of us at the Bar had
feared that, with the economy once again in ruins, it would take a long
time for a flow of work to build up. But ironically, wartime conditions
played a part in ensuring that my chambers had more than enough
work to tide us over. There was a sudden flurry of activity in the world
of probate litigation. Many wills had been made in haste during the
war, some by soldiers about to be deployed to the front line, some
by relatives left at home. They were often hand-written, scribbled
on whatever scrap of paper had been close at hand at the time; and
formalities such as dating the will and having signatures witnessed
tended to be overlooked. It was not only a question of formality; the
language of a will written by someone with limited education might be
hopelessly vague or ambiguous. Some were written faintly in pencil and
some by people with illegible handwriting. There was usually a way to
give formal effect to the will if someone was still alive who remembered
it being made; and the judges were charitably inclined even to fairly
outrageous interpretations of the language if it would benefit a war
widow and her children. All of us in chambers gave a lot of free advice,
and appeared in court free of charge, for families of servicemen if the
estate was not unduly large. There were also some cases where the
estate was larger and the will was contested, and solicitors who were
grateful for the work we did for their less well-off clients remembered
us and steered such cases in our direction. Life was returning to some
semblance of normality. Bridget and I were able to travel up to the
Manor more frequently. I began to play chess again.

I truly believed that my connections with the Security Services were
at an end. Indeed, within a day or two of my return from Nuremberg I

had a short interview with a senior person in the Foreign Office, who told me as much in so many words. He thanked me for my service and indicated that it would not be forgotten – when the time came for me to take Silk, he said, I would find the door open for me. And there it ended. Until I went to the Reform Club for dinner a few days after the New Year in January 1948.

* * *

I had gone to the Reform with every intention of having a quiet dinner on my own. We had spent Christmas in London, but Bridget had gone up to the Manor to check that it was surviving a spell of freezing weather, and to see her parents for the New Year, and was not due back for several days. Not much was happening in chambers; it would be another week before solicitors and the courts resumed their normal pace of work as they reluctantly bade farewell to the Festive Period.

As I was finishing the remains of my Club claret, Anthony and Guy walked into the dining room, looked around, and walked casually over to my table. I had enough experience by now to sense that their arrival was no coincidence. Anthony had become a much-respected figure in the art world, and was more than two years into his prestigious appointment as Surveyor of the King's Pictures. But his increasingly socialist view of the role of art in Society was no secret, and I had every reason to believe that he was still active behind the scenes in recruiting others to the socialist cause, particularly at Cambridge, where there were dark rumours that he was talent-spotting among the undergraduate population in the Soviet interest. Guy had left the BBC and had joined the Foreign Office, where he continued to lead a charmed life, and had been acting as personal assistant to a Minister of State. For the benefit of the other diners we went though the motions of wishing each other a Happy New Year, before Anthony suggested that we adjourn upstairs for a glass or two of port. I paid my bill and followed them upstairs to the library floor where the magnificent balcony offers a commanding view over the foyer on the ground floor. We sat at a table on the side of the square farthest from the staircase, outside the main library, where we would see anyone approaching before there was any danger of being overheard. A waiter brought a bottle of the Club port and three glasses.

As ever, Anthony showed no sign of haste. He began by asking with his usual formal politeness about Bridget, and my practice. Guy said hardly a word. I had the distinct impression that Anthony had instructed him to keep quiet. In retaliation, he slumped in his chair and launched into the port with a vengeance.

'I understand you are playing chess again?' Anthony asked.

'Yes, when I have time.'

'Your practice still gets in the way, of course?'

'Yes.'

He sipped his port.

'Tell me about this big tournament they are going to hold in Holland. It's to decide the World Championship, isn't it?'

The question took me completely by surprise. I could not imagine why Anthony would be interested in the World Chess Championship, but at the same time I somehow sensed that he knew all about it without having to ask me.

'The last world champion, the Soviet grandmaster Alexander Alekhin, died in 1946,' I replied. 'It was impossible to hold a tournament until conditions returned to something like normal after the War; so there has been an interregnum. When the War ended, the International Chess Federation decided to invite the six best players in the world to compete for the title: three Soviet grandmasters, Mikhail Botvinnik, Paul Keres and Salo Flohr; a Dutch player, Max Euwe, who is a former world champion; and two Americans, Reuben Fine and Samuel Reshevsky. Late in the day, the Soviets replaced Flohr with a younger man called Vasily Smyslov who they think is a future world champion.'

Anthony smiled as he refilled our glasses.

'But from what I read in the papers, there are only five grandmasters competing?'

I nodded.

'That is true. Fine decided not to play.'

'For what reason?'

I drank deeply from my glass.

'He is a research student in psychology. He said that he is too busy working on his dissertation.'

Anthony allowed some time to pass.

'So work got in the way in his case also?'

'So it would seem,' I replied. 'But he also referred to a theory popular in some circles: that the Soviets intend to fix the tournament to ensure that Botvinnik wins.'

Anthony smiled.

'How exactly does one fix a chess tournament?' he asked. 'I can imagine it in cricket – you know, a batsman might deliberately get himself run out for a duck, or a fielder might drop a catch. But chess?'

'The Soviet grandmasters might agree short, friendly draws among themselves,' I said, 'so that the western players are playing longer, more competitive games, and getting tired. That makes a difference in a long tournament. If that's not enough, they might instruct Keres and Smyslov to lose to Botvinnik. It would not be done in an obvious way. It would attract some suspicion, but it would be almost impossible to prove. And even if it could be proved, the Soviets are so dominant that they can afford to shrug it off.' I paused. 'I don't believe it, anyway.'

'Why not?' Anthony asked.

'For one thing, it is not necessary. Botvinnik is the strongest player in the world now by some margin. You would have to fancy him over a long haul like this.'

I sipped my drink.

'It would be ironic if Fine did pull out for that reason,' I added. 'On current form, he is probably the strongest player outside the Soviet Union. He might have been the only western player with a decent chance of stopping Botvinnik.'

'You don't think either of the others could do it?'

I shook my head. 'Euwe has been playing very badly recently. He seems to have lost his touch. Reshevsky can be brilliant. On his day he can beat anyone, but he is inconsistent and he doesn't keep up with opening theory, which is essential at this level. He will be more or less on his own, whereas the Soviets will have a team of seconds and other experts available to support their players. There was talk of replacing Fine with Najdorf, an Argentinian grandmaster, but for some reason it hasn't happened. Even if it did, I can't see him beating Botvinnik in a long tournament.'

Anthony allowed some time to pass.

'So you rule out the conspiracy theory and you prefer to see Fine as another western chess player denied his destiny by the capitalist system?'

I did not reply.

'Shall we get to the point, my dear?' Guy said, rather petulantly.

'Patience, my dear boy, patience,' Anthony said. 'Order us some more port, if you would be so kind, since you seem to have made quite an impression on this bottle.'

Guy reached over languidly and pressed the call button on the wall by his chair. A waiter appeared almost at once, and Guy held the bottle aloft in his hand. The waiter nodded and returned with a new bottle in what felt like a matter of seconds.

'I understand,' Anthony continued, once our glasses were again full, 'that the match is to be split between Holland and Russia?'

'It starts in March in The Hague, where the first ten rounds are to be played,' I confirmed. 'Then in April it moves to Moscow for the final fourteen rounds. It will all be over by the middle of May.'

Anthony nodded.

'How would you like to be there – for the whole thing?' he asked suddenly.

I was speechless, taken completely aback. I had no idea how to respond. It was something that I had never even considered. Anthony did not rush me. He seemed content to sip his port and gaze up at Sir Charles Barry's wonderful cupola which presides in all its glory, from a great height, over the Reform Club's saloon. I allowed my eyes to follow his.

'Well, obviously, I would love to go,' I admitted eventually. 'It is the most important chess event in living memory, perhaps ever. But it is out of the question. I have too much work. My clerk would kill me – if Bridget didn't beat him to it.'

'What if we could arrange some remuneration for you?' he asked.

'Remuneration?'

'Yes, what if we could arrange for you to cover it professionally, as a journalist? A chess journalist, covering the tournament for a variety of western newspapers and magazines?'

'But there will be journalists all over the place,' I protested. 'Press coverage will have been arranged long ago. Harry Golombek has plans to write a book about the tournament.'

Anthony nodded.

'I understand that, James. But your duties as a journalist would not be unduly onerous, I assure you.'

And in that moment, I knew exactly what he wanted of me.

42

'We are finally in a position to make a difference,' Anthony said simply. 'Guy is in the higher reaches of the Foreign Office. Donald is Acting First Secretary in Washington, and is secretary to the British Delegation on the Combined Committee dealing with nuclear development. Kim has been head of Section IX within the Service – the section in charge of operations against communism and the Soviet Union – and is now Head of Station in Istanbul.'

'And Anthony is surveying the King's pictures,' Guy added, his speech now rather slurred.

Anthony smiled. 'A more than adequate cover, we can all agree,' he said. 'And MI5 still consults me from time to time.' He paused for a sip of port. 'Altogether a most impressive array of talent in a most impressive array of positions of power. We need to take advantage of our hard work and good fortune, James. We need to strike while the iron is hot.'

'What has that to do with the World Chess Championship?' I asked.

'It is not about the tournament as such,' Anthony replied. 'It is more about the opportunities it affords us. There is information we need to send, and which we need to have sent to us. We have access to so much information now, both British and American information, and it is of such high quality, that we need a regular channel of communication. That channel has to be secure and sophisticated. Meeting people like Alex in some café in Hounslow, or wherever, is no longer an option. Kim and I have given quite a bit of thought to the problem, James, and we have finally realised that the solution was right there, under our very noses.'

I looked away.

'Chess is the Soviet Union's window on the world,' he continued. 'It is where they meet the rest of the world. It is one of the few opportunities for Soviet citizens to travel abroad relatively freely, and one of the few opportunities for foreigners to visit the Soviet Union with some degree of freedom. The world championship would simply be your introduction to that world. You have the credentials. No one would question you.'

No one spoke for what seemed like an eternity. Eventually, I gathered my thoughts and spoke up.

'I did some of that during the War, as you know,' I said. 'Even then I was uneasy about it. What I did was illegal. But we were at war, and I persuaded myself that the usual rules didn't apply. I justified it in my own mind because then the Soviet Union was our ally. We were fighting side by side against fascism. That is not the case now. It would amount to spying. I would be betraying my country.'

'Would you?' Anthony asked.

'You don't think so?'

'It all depends,' he replied. 'It all depends on what sort of Britain you see as your country.'

He leaned forward confidentially, his arms on the table in front of him.

'James, listen to me. I know you quite well, I think, and I knew Roger also. You both came from a privileged background in terms of money and property and social position. But neither of you found any satisfaction in that. You saw the suffering. You saw what capitalism was doing to the people around you, and you saw that our Government didn't give a damn about it. You saw Europe given over to fascism, and you saw that the Government didn't give a damn about that either, until it was too late. It was Roger and others like him who saw what was going on and tried to do something about it.'

I suddenly saw myself at dinner with Roger, here at the Reform Club, the last time I had seen him. I remembered his telling me how his experiences in South America had changed him, how they had turned him into a man willing to die in Spain for socialism and for the right of people everywhere to be treated properly and fairly.

I felt for those people, and there is no doubt that I had become an intellectual socialist by then. But South America is so far away, and information about what is really going on is hard to come by. I was spending almost all my time on the estate, learning how to run the place, meeting all kinds of important people Father felt I ought to know. I couldn't even get down to London very often any more. And I suddenly realised that if I went on like this for another couple of years, I was going to forget every principle I had ever learned; I was going to become a country conservative, a loyal son of King and Empire.

I wondered if that was becoming true for me also. I was becoming a successful barrister, and I was in charge of the estate. I was *Sir* James Digby. Was I, too, in danger of forgetting the principles I had learned?

'The Soviet Union is still our ally,' Anthony was saying, 'but in a slightly different context. The battle against fascism has made some progress, but the battle for socialism is just beginning. Think, James, just think, what a truly socialist Britain would be like, a Britain with social and economic justice for all.'

'A Britain in which art would be at the service of the State?' I asked. 'Poussin painting propagandist scenes of industrial realism and parades with endless lines of missiles and marching soldiers?'

He laughed heartily.

'Nicely said, James. But yes, a Britain where art would be at the service of – well the People, that's how I would prefer to put it. Chess too, of course. But don't forget that it works both ways. The chess player is at the service of the People, but the People are also at the service of the chess player. They support him in pursuing his art. In my Britain, Reuben Fine would not have to turn down an invitation to play for the championship of the world.'

And Paul Morphy would not have to go insane and walk the streets talking nonsense to himself until he died a lonely, premature death, I added quietly to myself.

'I don't ask you to do this out of considerations of self-interest,' he added quickly. 'You are not a venal man, James, I know that. I ask you because I believe you know that it is the right thing to do, for the People and for your country; and because I believe you want to continue what Roger started; and because you are loyal to your Apostolic Brethren.'

From his semi-comatose position slumped in his chair, Guy raised his right arm and drunkenly held his glass aloft in a mute, self-mocking toast.

And there it was. There was no moment of epiphany, no vision on the road to Damascus, just the sense that my life had been heading in this direction for almost all my adult life, and that the moment which had now arrived was no more than the mature expression of my own deeply-held values. I could no longer pretend, of course, that I was doing anything other than spying on behalf of a country my Government and its allies regarded as a hostile power. There was no fig leaf any more. But in that moment, I no longer needed one. I was finally committed.

43

I arrived in The Hague on 27th February, a Friday. The World Chess Championship was scheduled to begin with a reception on Monday 1st March for the players, the officials from FIDE, the large Soviet delegation of seconds, reporters and assorted minders, and various Dutch dignitaries. The Mayor of The Hague, Meneer Visser, who on the following morning would make the ceremonial first move for Euwe in his first-round game against Keres, made a gracious speech welcoming all the guests to his city. The sense of relief and optimism, the feeling of civic pride which this quintessentially peacetime event engendered was palpable. At last the Dutch people were again doing what they have always done so well, bringing people together, in peaceful causes, in a spirit of celebration.

A room had been booked for me at the Hotel des Indes in the city centre, which I took to be Anthony's private joke – the hotel had been notorious as the favourite haunt of the First World War spy Mata Hari. Having been much favoured by German officers during the occupation, it had survived the second War in prime condition, and I was very comfortably accommodated. The tournament was held in a magnificent structure called *Het Moors Paleis*, or *Het Dierentuingebouw*, which was the centrepiece of the former Royal Zoological and Botanical Gardens. The gardens no longer had any active role in zoology – that had ended in 1943 because of wartime conditions. But the *Moors Paleis* remained and was used for functions of every kind, from exhibitions to concerts to dog shows. It was a fantastic building with a wonderful stone exterior, and elaborate, elegant internal halls, a perfect venue for a chess tournament. In many ways it reminded me of Alexandra Palace, but smaller, and capable of being accessed without trudging up a steep hill.

It had not been easy to persuade either Bridget or my clerk that covering the world chess tournament as a journalist was a sound career move. In fact I had something of a scene with both though, mercifully, both were brief and did no lasting damage. Bridget did understand how important chess was in my life and, after some resistance, she gave her blessing, and agreed to look after the house as well as the estate while I was away. My clerk too, after the mandatory dire warning about how easily absence from London could mark the beginning of the end of any barrister's hopes of success, took a pragmatic view and gave me a firm date towards the end of May, by which I was to be back in chambers for a trial in the Chancery Division. What exactly my duties were as a journalist was not made clear to me at first. Anthony had provided me with a press pass which gave me access to the playing hall and the press room, where I could mingle freely with other journalists, and the Soviet seconds who, I soon discovered, doubled as shameless propagandists not only for their grandmasters but also for Soviet chess and Marxism-Leninism in general. In due course I learned that I was to write a report on each round, giving the moves of each game, with a few comments of my own, and send it by airmail to an address in London, from where it was to be distributed – mainly, as I was to discover later, to a number of publications which had little connection with, or interest in, chess – though some of my pieces did make an appearance in the newspapers and chess magazines. In the case of a particularly dramatic development – and I could not imagine what that might be – I was to telephone a number in London to make an urgent report. And I was to expect contact from my new case officer.

On the evening of Friday 5th March, a week after my arrival in The Hague, I returned to the Hotel des Indes for dinner and decided on a nightcap in the bar before going up to my room to work on my report. The third round was under way and some interesting chess was being played. I was able to collect the moves of each game from the press office, and I found that I was becoming engrossed in the chess, in analysing and writing explanatory notes for my readers. My passion was being re-kindled. In addition to my writing, I gave a short interview to a local newspaper about why Euwe's run of bad form was continuing, and whether he could recover from his bad start. I could easily have forgotten all about Anthony, and socialism, and my Apostolic Brethren, and immersed myself in the excitement of the event going on all around me.

But as I sat at the bar nursing a whisky and soda and playing in my mind through Reshevsky's accomplished third-round victory over Keres, I was conscious of someone sitting down on the stool next to me, to my left, in the corner of the bar. He ordered a vodka. The accent was unmistakable. I turned to look at him. The face registered immediately, but for a few moments I could not connect it to a name. Smiling, he rescued me from my predicament.

'James, how nice to see you. I thought I saw you at the reception the other night, but I was with my own crowd and couldn't get away. I have not been able to see much of the tournament yet, because of work I have at the Embassy.'

He held out his hand. 'Viktor Stepanov. We met in Nuremberg in less happy circumstances.'

I took his hand. 'Of course. We played to a draw in our heads.'

'Generous on your part,' he smiled again. 'You were about to do me serious damage with knight to d5. You had a clear advantage. Perhaps you will allow me an opportunity to give you more of a game?'

I looked around anxiously. My very basic war-time training in tradecraft had not quite deserted me. He laughed, extended a hand, and placed it briefly on my shoulder.

'Please don't be concerned, James,' he said. 'I don't have a minder, I assure you. I am an official member of the Soviet delegation. Not that I am entirely exempt, you understand, but I am in a responsible position and my superiors understand that I need a certain freedom of movement to do my job. They won't be fretting about me. In any case, I am familiar with how the minders work, and it's not hard to give them the slip if it should be necessary. I do it just to annoy them, sometimes.'

He finished his vodka in one gulp, and ordered another, asking the barman to give me another of whatever I was drinking. I began to feel as though our conversation in Nuremberg, some three years ago, was continuing as if it had never been interrupted. I remembered why I liked Stepanov – the easy, open manner, the effortless conversational English, so unlike the Soviet stereotype.

'So, how do you like The Hague? Are you enjoying working as a journalist?'

'I am, actually,' I replied. 'It makes a welcome change from what I usually do.'

'Of course. Arguing cases in the law courts is important, but not as enjoyable as chess, I think. You are playing well, even with so little time to devote to the game. I think, if you were not a lawyer, you would have been British champion by now.'

I raised my eyebrows. 'You keep up with my progress?'

'I read the British chess magazines, of course,' he replied. 'It helps my English reading as well as telling me what is going on in your country. I have studied your games. Alexander is good, very creative, but I think you could be better, and certainly better than Golombek and the rest.'

'What have you been doing since Nuremberg?' I countered quickly.

'Playing chess,' he replied. 'I have the title of grandmaster now.'

'Congratulations,' I said at once.

We shook hands again. He paused to take a drink.

'Thank you. But I know my limits, James. I am no Botvinnik. I am not even a Smyslov. I will never play in such a tournament as this. I will probably never even win my country's championship. So I pursue other activities also.'

'Such as?'

'Teaching the next generation. I teach at the chess academy in Moscow, give simultaneous exhibitions in schools, you know the kind of thing. We have so many talented young players, James. It is frightening. I see children of twelve who will beat me in two or three years' time.' He laughed. 'This is sometimes depressing, of course. But this is also good, because it means the game continues to thrive, and the children can study chess at the same time as they pursue their general education. Those who are good enough can go on to play professionally.'

I ordered us another drink.

'I also work with the Government,' he continued. 'Ever since Nuremberg, they know I can interpret in English and German. I even picked up some French while I was there but not yet to the required standard. In any case they use me, particularly in connection with chess events. It is very sensitive for them, because they have grandmasters going abroad, and they must be involved in negotiations with the International Federation. I played a small part in the negotiations for this tournament. My God, James, you would not believe how hard-headed both sides were.'

'I hear that there was some pretty hard bargaining,' I said.

'You would not have believed it. Where is the tournament to be? Who shall play? How many rounds? What shall be the official language? It went on and on. To tell you the truth, I am amazed that the tournament is being held at all.'

I stared into my drink for some time.

'Viktor, can I ask you something?'

'Of course.'

'Is there any truth in the rumour that ...'

He suddenly roared with laughter.

'That we will fix the tournament to let Botvinnik win? You ask me about this? You think I would answer this to an English journalist? You think I want to see my name in *The Times* of London, saying that the Soviet Union fixes chess tournaments? James, my dear friend, I will have to defect also. You must give me political asylum for this, I think.'

I had to laugh.

'I'm not asking as a journalist,' I said. 'I'm not asking for anything I can write. I'm asking as a friend, for very personal reasons. Off the record.'

He stared at me for some time. He eventually nodded.

'Then I will tell you the truth. No, there is no fix, James. Botvinnik will win, but he will win because he is the best player. As for Smyslov, his time will come, I think, but not yet. Keres – Keres I like very much, James, I like him personally. He is such a nice man, so modest, and he plays many brilliant games; but he does not have the depth of Botvinnik and, over the course of a long tournament, I do not believe he can prevail.'

'Thank you,' I said.

* * *

'You know why I am here, of course,' he said, after a lengthy silence.

'Yes,' I replied.

He turned around to survey the bar. It was getting late and we were almost alone. The bartender looked as though he wanted to close up for the night as soon as he could, and go home. Viktor ordered one last drink for us, and paid the bill. We left our stools to move to a corner table.

'Before I left Moscow,' he continued quietly, 'I was summoned to appear before the chief of a directorate of Moscow Centre. The Comrade Director told me that he had important contacts within the Security Services in Great Britain and also in the United States. There was an urgent need to exchange information. I was to be useful in making arrangements for this. He told me that it had been arranged with someone in London or Washington that, while in The Hague, I would meet a contact.'

'Me?' I asked.

'Yes.' He smiled. 'I had no idea who it was until I arrived here. I learned of your identity through a top-secret communication yesterday from Moscow Centre to our Embassy, where I am based during the tournament. When I saw your name, I was pleased, of course.'

'And surprised?'

He shrugged. 'No, not surprised. It makes sense that they choose you, as we already know each other. But I am very pleased. James, listen, this is what I have been told. The Comrade Director wishes us to devise a system, whereby you can bring information to be conveyed to Moscow, and Moscow can send information back to London and Washington. I do not suggest that we discuss this yet. When the tournament moves to Moscow, they will make arrangements for us to talk in more secure surroundings. But the Comrade Director wishes me to know that he will do all in his power to help.'

I looked questioningly at him.

'By this, he means that I can provide you with money to defray any necessary expenses while you are abroad, if your own people do not give you enough. He will also ensure that you always have a visa to enter the Soviet Union, and you will be given a press pass in connection with any chess tournament you wish to observe or report on as a journalist. While in the Soviet Union you will not be harassed or troubled by minders. And eventually ...'

'Yes?'

'If, after some period of time, you wish to come over to us, or if it becomes necessary for you to do so, you would be given employment in connection with chess. What this would be, I cannot say, but it can be negotiated.'

I felt overwhelmed. In my head I was hearing Anthony's voice again, and then Roger's. I closed my eyes, and I saw Bridget, and my clerk, and the Manor, and they all seemed unreal, as if they belonged to another world. Was this happening? Who was I, and what world did I live in? I was no longer sure. I had to get out of there and clear my head. I stood.

'Look, Viktor, I'm really tired, and I have a report to file. Can we talk again, another time?'

He showed not the slightest irritation.

'But of course, James. Perhaps tomorrow evening?'

'Yes, tomorrow evening,' I agreed. 'Here, after dinner?'

I had spoken too quickly. I was not sure I would be ready to talk in such a short space of time. It was not good tradecraft to repeat the venue, and I was momentarily embarrassed by that alone; we should have gone somewhere different. I was about to offer an alternative, but he seemed perfectly relaxed, and agreed immediately.

'I will come here for dinner,' he replied. 'I understand the food is excellent. I will see you here in the bar afterwards.'

* * *

When we met the next evening, we drank for some time, and then he took me for a long walk, how long I could not say. But I remember that we passed the Binnenhof and the Buitenhof and the Mauritshuis at least twice, and walked through many nameless little streets full of tall, narrow houses and, in the cold night air of The Hague, I talked to him; talked, with barely a pause to draw breath, until I had bared my soul for him to see.

* * *

In the middle weeks of April, in a comfortable safe house in Moscow, with limitless supplies of vodka, black bread, and caviar to sustain us, Viktor and I met nightly after the tournament had ended for the day; and worked out a system for conveying information securely back and forth between London, Washington, and Moscow. It was simplicity itself.

44

I do not know what I had expected life as a spy to be like. It was not a life I had ever planned for myself. For some years, all went smoothly. I duly received an invitation to attend the Soviet Chess Championship in Moscow in November 1948, and I was invited to the championship each year thereafter up to, and including, 1960. I was invited to send my passport to the Soviet Embassy for my visa to be renewed; in fact it was upgraded to a five-year visa with almost no restrictions. The Soviet championship is an event like no other. No other national championship can boast anything like the number of grandmasters competing. Previous form is no guarantee of success, and even world champions cannot assume that they will win their country's title. The 1948 championship was won jointly by David Bronstein and Alexander Kotov. It was not until 1952 that Botvinnik took the title again, and by that time both Smyslov and Keres had put their names on it. Each year I was provided with a press pass and afforded every facility to prepare my reports, including personal interviews with the leading contenders. And when I returned to London, I picked up my practice where I had left off, and visited the Manor with Bridget whenever we could. It was during this period that I made my only trip to the United States, where I saw New York and Boston, and Paul Morphy's house in Rue des Ursulines in New Orleans.

Viktor also arranged for me to give simultaneous exhibitions at the Moscow Chess Academy, during which I played against some thirty ten- to fourteen-year-olds, some of whom were terrifyingly good. The first time I did this, I had thirty-two opponents, and lost to two thirteen-year-olds. Needless to say, their victories were loudly hailed as a triumph of the Marxist-Leninist method over capitalism and the bourgeois life-style – disregarding the overall result of the match, which was that out of thirty-two games, I won twenty-eight and drew two, a statistic which should have suggested that the bourgeois cause was not entirely hopeless. I did not mind in the least. I was quite ready to put up with a little joshing. The truth was that I was overwhelmed by my first experience of the Academy. I was lost in admiration of the scale and excellence of its teaching régime, and envious of the opportunities which would open up for these gifted young players. I could only imagine, with an ache in my heart, what might have happened if such an academy had been available in England for players such as Hugh Alexander and myself.

Whenever I was in Moscow, they put me up at the Peking Hotel, an absurdly grandiose neo-classical building on Ulitsa Bolshoya Sadovaya. It was pretentious and decidedly mediocre by western standards; not even its most enthusiastic patron could describe it as luxurious. It had all the usual failings of the Soviet hotel. There were periodic power failures and the phones never worked properly when you needed them to. But by Moscow standards it was well above average. The accommodation and food were acceptable and the hotel has a pleasant view over Triumfalnaya Ploschchad, one of the city's better squares. I must admit that once I got used to it, I felt very comfortable there. The staff never seemed to change and, after several stays when I was welcomed by the same familiar faces, it became something of a home from home. I actually began to fall in love with it in a strange kind of way. I was also acutely aware of its convenience from the point of view of my hosts. The Peking was a favourite haunt of KGB officers, and at times the entire place resembled one gigantic safe house. Viktor and I never had any difficulty in finding a secure venue for our meetings. When the Soviet championship was held away from Moscow, I always spent time in the capital once it had ended. I always assumed, without even troubling to verify the fact, that the KGB had bugged every phone in the hotel and kept me under constant surveillance. Once or twice I actually caught them at it, to my pleasure, but I would never have dreamed of complaining.

Initially, work was brisk. With Kim in Turkey, with Guy and Donald in the United States, I brought a good deal of information with me which I had encrypted, and which Viktor and I decrypted together when I arrived. Towards the end of my stay we would encrypt information destined for London and Washington, which I would decrypt for my contact at the Embassy when I returned home. The method Viktor and I had devised was virtually risk-free; as long as the final meeting in London went smoothly – and my contact and I were obsessively careful about our tradecraft – my work was undetectable.

But there were already clouds on the horizon. They were clouds I could do nothing about, but they made me anxious. I saw Anthony every so often at Apostolic meetings – I had taken my wings after the War and so was no longer obliged to attend meetings, but I still went up to Cambridge occasionally, simply because I love the place, and attended meetings whenever I could. I never failed to attend the annual dinner in London. Anthony hinted that both Guy and Donald were drinking far too much and there had been a number of unpleasant public incidents which were causing ripples, if not yet waves, within the Foreign Office. In Guy's case that hardly came as a surprise, but the same could not be said for Donald. Anthony surmised that his marriage was not going well. Sure enough, before the end of 1948, Guy had been transferred to the Far East section; while Donald was posted to Cairo as First Secretary. Neither move caused the work to dry up, but my contact told me that the information was harder to come by and, in some instances, of inferior quality. Things improved again in 1949 when Kim was appointed Washington representative of the Security Services, and so began to have access to much of the same kind of information as Guy and Donald had previously. And in 1950 Guy returned to the United States as Second Secretary at the British Embassy. But in the same year, Donald was ordered back to England after a particularly bad episode of binge drinking turned violent and a colleague was seriously injured in his own home. I took Donald for dinner at the Reform once or twice after his return. He had been ordered to undergo intensive counselling, but he seemed distant and withdrawn. I did my best to reach out to him, but other than confirming Anthony's speculation about his marriage, he gave me no real clue about what had happened to him. Then, on 25th May 1951, disaster struck.

* * *

For weeks after Guy and Donald disappeared, having ostensibly left for a short leisure break on the Continent, the press and Parliament had a field day, speculating about what might have happened to them, and whether they were truly Soviet spies. I could have answered both questions for them immediately. But for some reason, the authorities never quite put all the pieces together; it was not until February 1956 that Guy and Donald gave a press conference in Moscow and removed all doubt on the subject.

Donald had resumed work in November of the previous year, having apparently convinced the Foreign Office that he had recovered from whatever was ailing him and was no longer liable to engage in embarrassing public acts of drunkenness and violence. In all likelihood, he was allowed to resume work mainly to ensure that the authorities could keep an eye on him and tighten the noose which had already been placed around his neck. It seems likely now that he and Guy had finally attracted too much attention. Despite mounting evidence, the CIA's anglophile James Jesus Angleton, who had trained under Kim in England as his relatively new agency was still in the throes of being established, had steadfastly refused to believe that officers of the Secret Intelligence Service or the Foreign Office were capable of the treachery of betraying their country. Ironically, it was a state of mind that exactly mirrored that of the Service itself. The FBI, on the other hand, had no such illusions and no such loyalty. J Edgar Hoover had kept up a steady barrage of pressure against both Angleton and the White House, demanding a full inquiry into the possibility that British officers were giving away American secrets to the Soviets. He was winning the argument.

Guy had gone from bad to worse. His public conduct grew so egregious, culminating in an attempt to claim diplomatic immunity for several speeding offences in a single day, that Ambassador Franks was left with no alternative but to remove him from his post and return him to England. Worse, when Guy had arrived in the United States in September 1950, he had stayed with Kim at his house on Nebraska Avenue, on what Kim assured his reluctant wife would be a temporary basis. In fact it turned into a lasting arrangement and, as a result, Kim was implicated in some of Guy's drunken escapades and, eventually, in the suspicion that had grown up about him in Washington. He was too close to the target. Shortly after Guy and Donald disappeared, Kim was recalled to London. During 1952, he was closely interrogated in a so-called 'secret trial' in a frantic effort to incriminate him. I heard from Anthony that the interrogation had been conducted by a Silk, Helenus Milmo, and I realised with horror that there would have been nothing illogical if the Service had asked me to do it, given my wartime experience. Miraculously, the case against Kim for being the 'Third Man' was never quite proved. In 1955 a Government White Paper conceded as much. Kim was dismissed from the Service, notwithstanding, but almost immediately started work as a foreign correspondent for *The*

Observer, based in Beirut, and there were persistent rumours that he continued to work for the Service using that cover. For me, these were terrible times.

* * *

There is no way to describe the terror of waiting, day by day, for the knock on the door which will bring your life, as you know it, to an end. Everything seemed so clear to me that I could not easily imagine how the trail could fail to lead the authorities to me. In my mind, my links to Guy, Donald and Kim were obvious and compelling, and at first I did not comprehend why the police were not on my doorstep within hours of their disappearance. As I understand it now, even the Americans, for all Hoover's bluster, were not fully convinced of the treachery until April 1954, when Vladimir Petrov, a Third Secretary at the Soviet Embassy in Canberra, defected and identified Guy and Donald as important Soviet agents. Apparently, he made no reference to me. But at the time, I was expecting to be exposed on a daily basis. I felt helpless.

The feeling of imminent exposure is one which has never left me, and it is one almost too terrible to describe. The instant fluctuations in body temperature from sweltering to freezing; the knot in the pit of the stomach so tight that it is hardly possible to hold yourself upright; the nausea; the shaking hands; the insomnia; the waning of all enthusiasm for life; the distraction and inability to concentrate for more than a second or two on the most routine task. There are moments when you feel you have to end it, even if it means going to the police yourself and making a full confession.

For me, exposure would mean, not only the possibility of a long term of imprisonment, but also the most profound and public humiliation before my peers: the Bar; the members of the Reform; the Service; those in the world of chess. Beyond that, it meant that I would have to face up to the possibility that I had betrayed Roger, not only in the material sense of disgracing the family and forfeiting the Baronetcy, but also in the sense that I might have behaved dishonourably, a vice of which I thought him incapable. It was only now, with the threat of exposure hanging over my head, that I asked myself what Roger would have thought, what he would have said, about what I had done. I had convinced myself that I was doing it, at least in part, for him; that I was serving the country which had stood alone to combat fascism in

Spain and had tried to provide support to the forces for which he had fought and died. But Roger had fought fascism on the front line, openly and heroically. If he had killed, he had killed a known enemy by direct action in battle. I had, I assumed, killed also: but indirectly; by betrayal and subterfuge; by the transfer of information. I had killed others about whom I knew nothing at all; all without ever setting foot on a front line or seeing the consequences of my betrayal with my own eyes. In many ways, this was the most terrible of the nightmares which haunted me. Roger's life had been about truth. My life as a spy has required me to lie routinely, and although I convinced myself early on that it was necessary to lie for a good cause, I have never quite been able to reconcile my life with Roger's.

I know that Bridget sensed that something was very wrong. On the face of it, we were a well-to-do couple leading a varied and interesting life. Practice had gone well. In 1955, I took Silk. As the man at the Ministry had promised, my application sailed through at the first time of asking, and I began to be instructed in more serious and complex cases. We could have moved to a bigger house, but our home in Chelsea remained all we wanted. We spent time at the Manor, particularly during the summers, and as the economy gradually recovered after the War, the estate regained much of what had been lost, and started to prosper. With each visit I paid to the Soviet championships, my stock in the chess world continued to grow. I was invited to contribute articles to the major chess magazines. I continued to do well in the British championship, though I have never won it, and I was invited to play in various tournaments in this country, and abroad. But even before the disappearance, I have to think that she sensed the stress I experienced each year when the time grew near for me to leave for the Soviet Union. Once Guy and Donald disappeared, she must have sensed my near panic, though she would not have known, or even suspected the reason for it. I have never spoken to her about my work for the Soviets.

This was partly because of my desire to protect her. But there was a deeper reason. Despite our social ease, with each other and with others, and despite our easy sexual intimacy, which has never dissipated, there is between us an inexplicable barrier to a deeper level of emotional intimacy. I do not know why I have never been able to open up to her with full honesty about my support for socialism; about my feelings for Roger; or about my passion for chess. She is aware of all those things on an intellectual level, of course, but I have never allowed her to see into my soul, to know how much they really mean to me. I think it is connected to our inability to talk about the subject of children. Our lack of children had driven a wedge between us which neither of us wanted. I do not understand why we could not have spoken of it once the worst of the emotional distress had subsided. It was important to both of us, but it had become a taboo subject, and in due course the wedge blocked off other areas of ourselves also. Perhaps I feared that she might reject me, but I do not truly believe that to be true. I believe that, even if she knew everything I have done, Bridget would continue to support me as my partner and as my friend. That has always been the nature of our relationship. Yet I never found the courage to tell her. Instead I have allowed her to suffer, as I know she must have, knowing that something was terribly wrong with me, but unable to fathom what it could be. In many ways it might have been easier for both of us if the police had knocked on the door one morning; for then there would have been no further need for any pretence.

45

For obvious reasons of safety, once Guy and Donald had gone, I made no attempt to contact Anthony or Kim. But they sought me out one evening early in 1952, with elaborate security precautions, for the briefest of meetings. They tried, largely in vain, to reassure me that there was no immediate threat; that my security had not been compromised, and they were insistent that I should continue to travel to the Soviet Union each year for the championship. I had already made that decision. I knew that it could only look suspicious if I stopped my visits as soon as Guy and Donald vanished. They told me that information for me to pass on to Viktor would continue to be provided; by whom they did not say and I did not ask. I did not see them again, but I did assure them that I would continue for as long as I could.

* * *

And so I did. When 1960 arrived and I had still not been unmasked, I was finally beginning to relax to some extent. I was invited as usual to the Soviet championship in January; it was returning to Moscow for the first time in five years, and was won by Tigran Petrosian. But as soon as I saw Viktor at the Peking, just after I arrived, I knew that something was wrong. He seemed tense, and wanted to get our business meetings over with as quickly as possible. He said he was sorry that there was no time this year for me to give my usual simultaneous exhibition at the Academy. We had dinner regularly, but he seemed distracted and I could not draw him into any general conversation. One morning, as we were having coffee and waiting for a round of the championship to start, I could stand it no longer and I asked him directly what was wrong. After a prolonged silence, he told me, quietly and speaking very rapidly, that he was afraid for his safety. The chief of the Directorate who had engineered our partnership had been accused of pro-western sympathies and was now living quietly in a city a long way from Moscow. His successor felt under an obligation to put everything he had done under a microscope, and Viktor had already been interrogated twice, politely but intensely, about his activities during his many trips abroad. The new Comrade Director questioned the quality of the information he was receiving from me, and even suspected that London might be using me to plant disinformation. He had been told not to deal with me again, and he believed that my visa would be cancelled and that there would be no further invitations to the championship. He hoped that the Directorate would honour the promises which had been made to me. He was optimistic about that. Whatever its other failings, he said, Moscow Centre believed strongly in loyalty to its agents. As for himself, he was not so sure. He did not know whether they suspected him of disloyalty; whether he would be allowed to travel abroad again; whether his fate, too, might soon be enforced residence in a city a long way from Moscow, or worse.

We said our goodbyes as the prizes were being presented at the end of the tournament. I never saw Viktor again. In February 1963 I read that he was dead; a heart attack, they said; his body found by a friend, unnamed, in his flat in Moscow.

I had returned to London extremely disturbed, but also, I must admit, relieved that I would no longer have to engage in espionage. I had had enough. I felt that I had done my part, though what exactly I had achieved by it all, I could not have said. I wondered whether anything any of us did – Anthony, Guy, Donald, Kim, Viktor, I myself – actually produced any tangible results at all. There was no obvious sign of a new awareness for social justice, or support for the arts in Britain. Life seemed to go on as ever, for all the espionage that went on. At that point, a quiet life at the Bar and on the estate, playing chess as much as I could, seemed an attractive prospect. But the anxiety never left me. In 1961 and 1962 there were further revelations. Gordon Lonsdale, a Canadian who had been working as a Soviet agent, was arrested and convicted of espionage. John Vassall was caught, more or less red-handed, passing Admiralty secrets to the Russians. And, most frightening of all, George Blake, an MI6 officer, was convicted of spying for the Soviets since the 1950s and sentenced to a term of forty-two years in prison. Every fear I had ever had relating to exposure returned with a vengeance. In January 1963, Kim vanished from Beirut after being interrogated by Nicholas Elliott, a former colleague in MI6. There were rumours that he had made a full confession. In due course he surfaced in Moscow, and the circumstances strongly suggested that someone had made the decision to give him ample time to escape. Apparently the Government had no stomach for another spy trial, or was afraid of what might be revealed as a result. The thought gave me a glimmer of hope. Anthony's career seemed to be progressing unaffected. He became the Slade Professor of Art History at Oxford and was awarded an honorary doctorate at Durham. But there were rumours that he was being interrogated and, in 1964, that he had confessed. If so, nothing was said publicly, but he avoided all contact with me, and I did not pursue any contact with him.

* * *

And now here I am, faced with exposure by an American academic called Francis R Hollander. I have been obliged to sue him to defend what I tell my solicitors and counsel is my good name. The trial is about to start. If it goes wrong, it will be the end. Bridget says she is horrified and will stand by me through it all. She has never asked me whether there is any truth in what Hollander says. Whether that is because she assumes it to be false, or quietly knows it to be true, I do not know. I have met Hollander. I know nothing of his academic abilities, except that he speaks respectable Russian and writes competently enough about political science. He is a mediocre chess player who has insinuated himself into the chess establishment as a fixer for the Americans, and now, apparently, he wants to be a fixer on a larger stage. He has set out to destroy me. He is represented by prestigious counsel and solicitors. But he cannot justify his article. He has no real evidence.

I am a QC. I know about evidence and about the lack of evidence. I fully expect to win my case. That will bring me relief, but it will not leave me with any feeling of satisfaction, much less pride. I do not believe it will even bring peace of mind. I may have forfeited any hope of that many years ago. But first things first. First I must win my case, and then, who knows?

46

Miles Overton had volunteered his chambers for the late morning meeting. In two days' time they would be appearing on opposite sides before Mr Justice Melrose to discuss the arrangements for the trial of the case now known as *Digby v Hollander, the Secretary of State for the Home Department Intervening.* But today, the case was not on the agenda. Any professional rivalry was forgotten for the time being. Today, they were on the same side, with a common goal. After lunch, Overton and Bernard Wesley had an appointment with the Committee formed by the Benchers of Middle Temple to consider the cases of Ben Schroeder and Jess Farrar, and Ginny Castle and Michael Smart. The timing of the Committee's hearing, as their preparations for the trial were entering their most intense phase, was not ideal. But they had not even considered asking for an adjournment. They were all agreed: the problem had to be confronted and dealt with now.

Seated next to Wesley in front of Overton's massive desk, Ben was aware of feelings he had confronted many times: that the Bar was not for men like him; that he was out of step with the legal establishment; that he was standing on the edge of an abyss, looking down, waiting for everything he had worked for to come crashing down about him and carry him with it into whatever horrors lay in the depths of the abyss. But, familiar as those feelings were, this situation was different. This time it was not about his origins as a Jewish boy from the East End of London. It was not about his insecurity at being part of a profession dominated by white, Anglo-Saxon, Oxbridge-educated males. He had proved himself at the Bar, and he knew that he no longer had any logical reason for doubting himself as a barrister. But now, it seemed, he faced an impossible choice between the profession he loved and the woman he loved. There had to be a way out. He had tried to reassure Jess, and himself, over dinner and in bed the evening before, but she seemed withdrawn and reluctant to talk about it. This worried him almost as much as the prospect of the Committee meeting. For Jess, engaging him and prodding him into talking about every conceivable aspect of their lives was as natural as breathing, and her silence filled him with dread. He had not slept, and he was beginning to wonder how much longer he could go on. When his eyes met Ginny's he knew instantly that she was in the same place. He tried desperately to put his fears to one side.

'The composition of the Committee could be better,' Wesley began. As ever, he sounded calm and assured, as if, Ben thought, he was completely confident that nothing could go wrong while he was at the helm. 'But, on the other hand, it could be a great deal worse.'

He took his notebook from the edge of Miles Overton's desk, where he had set it down.

'The Committee consists of a chairman and four members. The chairman is Lord Justice Kenney, affectionately known to us all as the Eagle, because of his remarkable beak-like nose and sharp talons.'

'And because of his natural predatory instincts,' Overton added.

'Yes, indeed. More to the point, he is what one might call a traditionalist when it comes to the Bar.'

'He is what one might call narrow-minded and humourless,' Overton muttered. 'Incurably so, in my view.'

Wesley nodded.

'We could have hoped for better, I agree,' he replied. 'On the bench, he likes to be seen as very much in charge. So we can expect him to throw his weight around. But it does get better. The next two members are Silks, both of whom Miles and I know quite well, Andrew Figg and Raymond Stanislas, both quite reasonable fellows who should at least be open to argument. The fourth member is very interesting – Mr Justice Lancaster, who I don't know all that well, but who you certainly know, Ben.'

'He was the trial judge in my capital murder last year,' Ben said. 'I liked him. He seemed very fair-minded.'

'More importantly,' Wesley replied, 'he watched you cross-examine the victim when your leader had drunk himself into too much of a stupor to drag himself to court. And you did it well. Judges don't forget that kind of thing. I think we may get some sympathy from Lancaster if we play our cards right.'

'But then,' Miles Overton said, 'we have to reckon with number five, the formidable Mary Faulks. I'm not sure we will get too much sympathy there.'

Wesley sat back in his chair.

'No,' he said pensively. 'I am sure they thought they had to have one woman on the Committee, to achieve some balance and ensure fair play.'

Overton snorted. 'To make it look like fair play, I think you mean.'

Wesley smiled.

'A woman ought to help us, in theory, surely?' Ginny ventured, but her voice lacked confidence.

'There are women who might help us,' Overton replied. 'I don't think Mary Faulks is one of them.'

'Why not?' Ben asked.

Overton shrugged. 'It's not malice,' he replied. 'I don't think Mary has a malicious bone in her body. It's just that, as a woman in the generation before Virginia, she has had to fight every inch of the way just to build a decent practice. She is very able. If she were a man she would have a very good practice, and would be in Silk by now. But she's a woman, and she has a decent junior practice, and that's as far as it will go.'

'And to get that far,' Wesley added, 'she had to make her practice her sole mission in life. She feels that she has to look and act like a man as far as possible, black suits and no jewellery every day, and a haircut that Oliver Cromwell would have admired.'

'I've been accused of that look myself,' Ginny smiled, 'though I do try to remain recognisably female.'

Wesley shook his head. 'You're not even close to Mary Faulks's standards,' he replied. 'You know what I mean, Ginny, you've seen it. I am sure that, as a woman at the Bar, you couldn't help but notice her generation.'

'Harriet Fisk and I talk about it all the time,' Ginny said. 'Harriet joined your chambers two or three years after I joined Miles, didn't she? But we still find ourselves talking about our appearance. It is almost as if it is more important than our ability.'

'For Mary Faulks, it was,' Wesley replied. 'She has had to cope with that throughout her career. She has never married, never had children. She may look at you and Harriet and see a new generation changing the rules, a generation of female barristers with a sense of entitlement, who don't feel they have to impersonate men and infiltrate the Old Boys' Club in order to succeed. I am worried that she may resent others having what was denied to her. All she has is the Bar. She may feel she must protect it at all costs, and she may feel that touting for work is not to be tolerated.'

'What Bernard means,' Overton said, 'but is being too delicate to say directly, is that she would probably take a very dim view of a woman using her sexuality, however indirectly, as a means of attracting work.' Seeing Ginny about to react, he added quickly: 'I know that is not what you are doing, Ginny. I am talking of her perception. I think the whole taboo about attractive feminine appearance comes down to that in the end, and it is something she may be sensitive about.'

Ginny sat back in her chair, deflated.

Wesley laid the notebook back down on the desk.

'So, that's what we are up against,' he said. 'As to strategy, I think Miles and I are agreed that we need to isolate Kenney as far as possible. We need to appeal to Figg, Stanislas, and Lancaster to take a more enlightened approach. If we succeed in that, we have a majority of three to two, and if we can isolate Kenney entirely, I have a feeling that Mary might go with the majority view. As Miles says, there is nothing malicious about her. We just have to make her look at the situation through different eyes. I can't believe she would want the next generation of women to have to live as she has, and by now, I think she must realise on some level that the next generation has already decided to make its own rules.'

'It's not too late for her to join with us,' Ginny said.

'No, indeed,' Wesley replied. 'It's not too late. It's just a matter of whether she can bring herself to do it.'

'Will you be asking Ginny and me to speak to the Committee?' Ben enquired.

'Only if they ask,' Wesley replied. 'You have given them written statements which cover everything they could reasonably want to know, and you will be there if they have any questions. I'm hoping it won't be necessary.'

'What is your strategy for isolating Kenney?' Ginny asked.

Wesley smiled broadly. 'I am going to make him nail his colours to the mast as a die-hard traditionalist,' he replied. 'Then I am going to make his colours look ridiculous, in the hope of making him angry.'

Overton joined in the smile. 'Don't ask him any more,' he suggested. 'He won't tell you until it's over.'

'If he looks ridiculous and becomes angry,' Wesley said, 'he will be less convincing to the other members of the Committee, and they will feel less reluctant to disagree with him.'

'That sounds like a potentially risky strategy,' Ben said.

'Potentially,' Wesley replied, 'it is disastrous. But only if it goes wrong.'

47

Bernard Wesley and Miles Overton walked briskly up the short flight of stone steps which led into Middle Temple Hall, Ben and Ginny following closely behind them. Wesley and Overton were Benchers of the Inn, and were therefore on equal terms with the members of the Committee. In any normal circumstances, the thought of addressing an Inn committee, especially together and on the same side of the case, would have removed any feelings of anxiety. But in this case, the lives and welfare of two young barristers in their chambers, and those of their partners, hung in the balance. In reality, this was a trial, or at least a preliminary disciplinary hearing. Both men felt a strong sense of obligation and a strong determination to succeed. They had prepared as thoroughly as they could; they had analysed every argument and counter-argument; but despite the reassurance they had offered to Ben and Ginny they knew that success was far from certain. The issue was a delicate one, and the Bar was still the most conservative of professions.

They made their way to the Parliament Chamber, an elegant, ornately panelled room in the heart of the Bencher's quarters, in which meetings of the Inn's governing body were held. They found the five members of the Committee taking their seats at the top table, by the window which looked out over the Middle Temple garden and led the eye naturally down to the Embankment and the River. The Committee's chairman, Lord Justice Kenney, sat in the middle, his colleagues flanking him on both sides. To his right sat Andrew Figg and Raymond Stanislas; to his left Mr Justice Lancaster and Mary Faulks – clad in heavy, dour, unbroken black with no suggestion of ornamentation. Wesley and Overton duly noted her appearance and exchanged a brief glance. Each member of the Committee had been provided with a file in which the written statements made by Ben and Ginny, and the written submissions made by the two heads of chambers on their behalf were included. Wesley and Overton sat down in front of the top table, with Ben and Ginny behind them.

Lord Justice Kenney welcomed Wesley and Overton politely. He turned over the pages of the submissions without undue haste. He removed his reading glasses and placed them on the table in front of him.

'Bernard, Miles, I am sure you understand the Committee's concern. Both Schroeder and Miss Castle are openly involved in an intimate relationship with a solicitor, or someone employed by a solicitor. If the Bar permits associations between barristers and those employed by firms of solicitors, it is effectively condoning touting for work. Touting has always been against our code of conduct. It brings the Bar into disrepute, and both Miss Castle and Schroeder, as members of the Bar, must be fully aware of that.'

Overton gave the slightest of nods towards Wesley, confirming that, as they had agreed, Wesley would begin, and he would make additional points as needed.

'Yes, George, thank you. I do understand the concern you have expressed,' Wesley began. His stomach felt taut, but his voice was smooth and confident; it betrayed no nervousness, but on the contrary exuded a quiet confidence.

'I would like to deal, not so much with the traditional view of things, but with the reality of contemporary life – not just life at the Bar, but life in the more general sense, life in the England of today in which the Bar works. I ask your indulgence if I approach what I have to say in what may perhaps seem an unusual way. Please allow me to tell you a story, and then ask you a question. Once upon a time, there was a barrister. Let's call him Kenney.'

Lord Justice Kenney looked none too pleased about being required to lend his name to the hero of Wesley's story, but Wesley was a senior Silk, and in the privileged inner sanctum of the Inn, every bit his equal. It would have seemed arrogant, even churlish to protest.

'Kenney has been in practice for almost twenty-five years,' Wesley continued. 'He has a good practice and an unblemished reputation. He is married and has a daughter, aged twenty-one. She is an actress; let's call her Jane. Jane has an admirer; let's call him Walter. Walter saw Jane playing Ophelia at the Old Vic a year or so ago, and was instantly smitten. He had never seen a more beautiful girl, or a more compelling actress. He sent flowers and champagne to her dressing-room. He wrote her letters expressing his admiration. He came to see the show at least twice a week until it closed, and when it closed, he came to see her playing Cecily Cardew at the Theatre Royal.'

He looked across the table.

'*The Importance of Being Earnest*,' he added confidentially, for the benefit of Figg and Stanislas, who were looking blank. 'Oscar Wilde.'

Lord Justice Kenney looked briefly up at the ceiling.

'After some time,' Wesley continued, ignoring the gesture, 'Walter realised that sending compliments and flowers was not enough, and that he was no longer satisfied to see Jane only on the stage from the front row of the stalls. With the aid of a door attendant who was not averse to being slipped the odd ten bob note, Walter inveigled his way backstage on the pretence of being an important theatrical agent, and implored a few moments of her time to declare his love for her – for he knew now that this was no mere passing fancy, no mere illusion induced by the magic of the stage lights.'

Out of the corner of his eye, Wesley saw Miles Overton smiling behind a page of his file.

'To Walter's everlasting joy, Jane gladly accepted his protestations of ardour and, within a short space of time, she took him home to meet her parents, Kenney and Mrs Kenney. They were charmed by Walter, and they were delighted that Jane had found a young man who doted on her so completely. A date was set for their wedding.'

Wesley paused for some seconds.

'The only problem,' he said, 'is that Walter is a partner in a firm of solicitors which regularly instructs members of the Bar.'

Mr Justice Kenney exhaled with some show of frustration. Figg and Stanislas looked at each other with raised eyebrows. Mr Justice Lancaster was already smiling broadly.

'Kenney now comes before this Committee and asks for your opinion on this question: whether he may attend the wedding and thereafter maintain normal social relations with his son-in-law without being disbarred; and whether, in the event of Walter and Jane having children in a few years' time, he may have some access to his grandchildren; and if so, on what conditions.'

There was a long silence. Andrew Figg tapped his pencil thoughtfully on the table.

'Does Walter's firm already instruct Kenney?' he asked.

'Let us assume not,' Wesley replied. 'But, of course, he has it in his power to do so.'

'Even so, there is no suggestion that any actual touting is involved?'

'There is not,' Wesley confirmed.

'The rule is surely not designed to interfere with normal family relationships?' Raymond Stanislas asked.

There was no immediate reply.

'I would hardly describe what Miss Castle and Schroeder are involved in as normal family relationships,' Kenney said.

'I am not sure we can make that kind of distinction in this day and age,' Stanislas replied. 'We are not here to sit in judgment on their moral behaviour.'

'Be that as it may, the question is ridiculous,' Kenney interjected. His voice was raised, not quite to the level of shouting, but enough to indicate that something had annoyed him, whether the use of his name, or the story, or something less obvious. Only Bernard Wesley and Miles Overton knew that it was the reaction Wesley had done his best to provoke.

'I quite agree, George,' Wesley replied blandly. 'But it is ridiculous because the rule that requires the question to be asked is ridiculous.'

Kenney banged a fist down on the table.

'No. The rule is not ridiculous,' he insisted. 'The Bar is right to come down hard on barristers who tout for work. Work should come to a barrister as a result of merit, not as a result of his social connections. Any relationship which gives rise to the appearance of touting should be carefully avoided.'

'Just a minute, though,' Mr Justice Lancaster intervened. 'If you take that to its logical conclusion, it would mean that a man whose father is a solicitor could not come to the Bar. I can personally recall several cases in which men in that position became barristers, and no one ever accused them of touting for work.'

'There have been many such cases,' Stanislas agreed, 'and the same might be said of barristers whose fathers are judges. It might be said that solicitors might send them work to curry favour with the judge.'

'It would mean that a member of the Bar could not join a golf club without inquiring whether the club had members who were solicitors,' Figg added. 'I am not sure I ought to say anything else in case I incriminate myself.'

Kenney shook his head, but said nothing.

Miles Overton suddenly sat up in his chair.

'If I may, George,' he said, 'I would like to address what I see as the fundamental point which Bernard's story compels us to consider. That point is, surely, that having a social relationship with a solicitor is not necessarily the same thing as touting for work.'

'Bernard's story is quite different from the situations in which Miss Castle and Schroeder find themselves,' Kenney replied. 'In Bernard's story the relationship is at one remove. It is not directly between the barrister and the solicitor.'

Overton looked up sharply.

'I have a daughter-in-law,' he said. 'I certainly regard myself as having a direct relationship with her. What if she were a solicitor? I fail to see the distinction. Is your advice to Kenney that he may not attend the wedding, and may see his grandchildren only in Walter's absence?'

'That is patent rubbish!' Kenney shouted. 'I didn't say that at all. I am offended to be asked the question.'

Overton appeared completely unperturbed.

'I will tell you what offends me, George,' he said quietly. 'What offends me is the implication that Bernard and I, as heads of chambers, cannot be relied on to recognise a case of touting for work if we see it, and to take appropriate action where necessary. Virginia came to me of her own volition and told me that a relationship had developed between herself and Michael Smart. That was long before they began to live together. Smart had already been instructing her for a considerable time in a variety of serious cases, and it was obvious that he did so because he recognised her abilities as an advocate, not because of any feelings they might have for each other. She told me she was quite willing to decline further instructions from him if I thought that would be the thing to do. I told her that I saw no need for that at all. And I was confident to say so because I know Virginia. She has the highest professional standards. She would not dream of touting for work, and she has not done so.'

'Ben Schroeder's case is very similar,' Bernard Wesley added. 'There are differences, of course. Ben and Jess are not living together, though their relationship is an intimate and very close one. Jess is not a solicitor; she is a clerk working for a solicitor, and I can assure you that her employer, Barratt Davis, is not a man to look to his clerks to advise him about which barristers he should brief. He was already instructing Ben Schroeder. That is how Ben and Jess met. But those details seem to me to be differences without a distinction. Like Miles, I can assure you that I would not condone touting for work in my chambers under any circumstances. But that is not what is going on here.'

The members of the Committee looked at each other. For some moments Lord Justice Kenney seemed to be at a loss for words.

'What you say may well be true,' he said eventually. 'But it seems to me that the approach you are proposing may encourage others to think that social relations between barristers and solicitors can take place without any restriction. That is bound to lead to abuses. It may have the effect of dragging the Bar down to the level of the street trader.'

'I'm not trying to drag the Bar down, George,' Wesley replied. 'I am merely trying to drag it, however unwillingly, into the twentieth century.'

Wesley turned to face Mary Faulks. He had been observing her, using his peripheral vision, throughout the meeting. She seemed pale and tense, and Wesley had an instinct that she was fighting to suppress some emotion; what it was, he could not tell.

'I suppose what I'm trying to say is this,' he concluded. 'Barristers and solicitors see more of each other than they used to. Perhaps in the old days, they tended to move in different social circles. There may even have been some class distinction, or at least, perhaps we liked to think there was. That is less true today. I am quite in favour of having a rule against touting for work. But I would like to see the rule prohibit conduct in which touting actually occurs, and not apply to cases in which someone imagines that it might occur. We trust barristers a great deal to behave ethically in all kinds of situations, and quite rightly. Let's trust them in this situation also.'

He looked directly at Mary for some time. Eventually, she turned slowly towards Lord Justice Kenney.

'It seems to me,' she said quietly, 'that being a barrister – as a man or a woman, but especially as a woman – is difficult enough as it is, without having to endure the threat of being punished for something one hasn't done.'

Mr Justice Lancaster smiled again.

'Mr Chairman,' he said, 'may I suggest that Bernard and Miles withdraw with Miss Castle and Schroeder, and give us a few moments to consider their cases?'

Lord Justice Kenney nodded his assent.

* * *

When they returned, some ten minutes later, Lord Justice Kenney seemed subdued. He made a pretence of finding his place in his notes.

'We have listened carefully to what you have had to say,' he said slowly. 'The view of the Committee is that all such cases must continue to be dealt with on their merits. But in this case, we find that no criticism can be levelled against either Miss Castle or Schroeder, and we see no reason why they should not continue to receive instructions from the solicitors concerned.'

'And one member of the Committee,' Mr Justice Lancaster added, 'if he may be permitted a short concurring judgment, would like to wish them well.'

'Two members,' Mary Faulks said. 'Two members would like to wish them well.'

'Thank you,' Bernard Wesley said, as they rose to leave.

'If I might just add one thought, George,' Miles Overton said. 'The approach of dealing with each case on its merits may lead the Committee to make some very fine distinctions. If I might offer a modest word of caution, Bernard and I are by no means sure that the present rule could survive a properly framed legal challenge.'

'Legal challenge?' Kenney spluttered. 'No barrister is going to sue his Inn of Court, and no member of the Bar would act for him if he did.'

Overton shrugged.

'You might be surprised, George,' he replied. 'Times are changing.'

* * *

'A quick cup of tea?' Overton suggested, after they had left the Parliament Chamber, and Ben and Ginny had thanked them at some length before departing to give their partners the good news.

'By all means,' Wesley agreed.

They walked slowly to the Queen's room and sat by the window, looking out into the Garden past the top end of the Parliament Chamber.

A waiter brought tea and fruit cake. Wesley raised his cup in the air.

'Well, here's to Walter and Jane.'

Overton raised his own cup in response.

'May they live long, happy lives, and have lots of children.'

'And may Kenney see them whenever he wishes.'

Overton put his cup down and leaned forward confidentially.

'Bernard, while I've got you here … I don't suppose there has been any movement on Digby's part, has there? The case is about to come on; we have the pre-trial hearing on Wednesday, and we go to trial a week from tomorrow.'

'Digby has not moved at all,' Wesley replied. 'He is adamant that Hollander has destroyed his good name, and he wants his day in court.'

Overton nodded slowly.

'Just between the two of us,' he said, 'I can't really say I blame him. The so-called evidence our friends at MI6 produced is not going to persuade Mr Justice Melrose that he has justified his article.'

'That is our view also,' Wesley replied.

They drank tea in silence for some time.

'I don't understand Hollander,' Wesley said. 'Of course, you know him and I don't, but he must surely be a bright enough man. Doesn't he realise the position he is in, or doesn't he care?'

'He realises the position he is in,' Overton replied. 'The difficulty is that he is suffering from the delusion that MI6 are going to bail him out before he goes down for the third time.'

'How exactly are they going to do that?'

'God only knows,' Overton said.

'Well, whatever they are planning to do,' Wesley commented, 'they had better get a move on, hadn't they?'

48

Wednesday, 6 October

'May it please your Lordship,' Bernard Wesley began, 'as your Lordship knows, I appear with my learned friend Mr Schroeder on behalf of the Plaintiff, Sir James Masefield Digby QC. My learned friends Mr Overton and Miss Castle appear for the Defendant, Professor Francis R Hollander. My learned friend Mr Roberts appears on behalf of the Home Secretary.'

'Yes, Mr Wesley,' Mr Justice Melrose said.

'My Lord, the parties come before you today in chambers, as your Lordship ordered at the last hearing. The trial is fixed for next Tuesday, the 12th October. The purpose of the hearing today is for the parties to address your Lordship about their readiness for trial, and to enable your Lordship to give whatever directions he may feel necessary for the trial of the action.'

He opened a heavy dark grey file folder on the desk in front of him, loosened the metal clasp which held the thick pile of documents in place, and turned to the first page, which was a table of contents.

'My Lord, the Plaintiff stands ready for trial. If I might draw your Lordship's attention to the trial bundle we have submitted which, of course, has been served on the Defendant and on the Home Secretary ...'

He allowed the judge time to reach for the file and open it.

'At the beginning, your Lordship will find the table of contents. The first three dividers contain the pleadings. Your Lordship has the Plaintiff's Statement of Claim; the Defence served by Professor Hollander; Requests by both parties for further and better particulars, with the particulars supplied; and a brief Reply by the Plaintiff. Beneath the next divider are all the orders made by your

Lordship in the course of the case. I would like to return to that a little later, if I may.'

Wesley turned over a number of pages.

'The issues which your Lordship is to try are quite straightforward. I am not aware of any matters of law on which we need your Lordship's ruling before the trial begins. The Plaintiff contends that the article published by the Defendant is a libel of an extraordinarily serious nature. The attack on the Plaintiff's reputation is explicit and as damaging as could possibly be imagined. The Defendant admits publication and seeks to justify the libel. In other words, he continues to assert that what he says is true – that Sir James Digby is, and has for many years been, a Soviet spy. It is hard to imagine a more deliberate exercise in character assassination.'

Seeing that Miles Overton was about to object, Wesley quickly moved on.

'Behind dividers five to twenty-one are brief summaries of evidence of the Plaintiff's good reputation, to be given by a number of witnesses who are well qualified to do so: among them a Bishop; three other members of the House of Lords; a member of the Cabinet; two Queen's Counsel; and two of the country's leading chess experts – in addition to various men who knew him at school, at university, and so on. We anticipate that this evidence will show the Plaintiff to be a man of excellent and blameless reputation.'

This time, Miles Overton rose to his feet. 'Perhaps my learned friend would be kind enough to defer his opening speech until the proper time, at the start of the trial.'

'I am drawing your Lordship's attention to the evidence,' Wesley replied, 'because of a submission I wish to make to your Lordship in a few moments.'

'We have been given no notice of any submission to be made,' Overton objected.

'If my learned friend will bear with me,' Wesley replied, 'he will see that I refer to an obvious submission which must be made at this time.'

'Well, let's continue with your trial readiness, Mr Wesley,' the judge suggested, 'and talk about submissions later, shall we?'

'Certainly, my Lord. Divider twenty-two contains evidence disclosed to the Plaintiff on behalf of the Defendant some time ago. I will return to that in a moment also.'

Wesley flicked through the remainder of the bundle.

'My Lord, I think the rest of the bundle is self-explanatory. The Plaintiff is ready for trial.'

He paused, very briefly.

'My Lord, before I defer to my learned friend, it may be convenient for me to outline the submissions I propose to make to your Lordship, so that both my learned friends, for the Defendant and the Home Secretary, can reply to everything I have to say.'

Overton and Roberts both nodded their assent.

'I am much obliged,' Wesley began. 'My Lord, I submit that it is your Lordship's duty, on the present state of the evidence, to strike out the Defence and to give judgment in favour of the Plaintiff on the issue of liability. A hearing to determine the appropriate measure of damages can then be held in due course.'

Wesley did his best to suppress a smile as he saw Overton's indignant reaction out of the corner of his eye.

'And if your Lordship is against me on that,' he continued, 'I submit that your Lordship should now reverse his previous rulings, namely that the trial should be held *in camera* and that the action should be determined by your Lordship sitting alone without a jury.'

Overton leapt to his feet, followed a second later by Roberts.

'Really, my Lord, I must object; and I see that my learned friend Mr Roberts is also concerned. We have not been given notice of these applications, and it is quite improper of my learned friend to make them now, without any advance warning at all.'

The judge looked inquiringly at Wesley, who feigned surprise.

'My Lord, they are such obvious applications that I cannot imagine that my learned friends, with their great experience of these matters, have not anticipated them. The matter is not at all complicated, and I am sure that my learned friends will be able to respond – if indeed, there is any response to make. May I suggest that I outline my argument for your Lordship, and if my learned friends need further time to respond, it can be taken up on another day?'

Mr Justice Melrose nodded.

'Yes, very well, Mr Wesley. Let us proceed on that basis.'

'I am much obliged. My Lord, my first submission is very simple. In the absence of any evidence of bad character or bad reputation attaching to the Plaintiff from any other source, the Defendant has, in effect, the burden of proving that what he said in the article is true, or at least substantially true. We are a week away from trial. The Defendant has disclosed no evidence capable of justifying the article which rises to the level of proof on the balance of probabilities. If the position remains unchanged in ten days from now, your Lordship would be obliged to direct the jury to find for the Plaintiff.'

'There is the evidence disclosed by the Defendant, behind divider twenty-two,' the judge pointed out.

'Yes, my Lord. Let me return to that,' Wesley said, opening his file at divider twenty-two. 'I have spent some time, with the assistance of my learned junior and those instructing me, trying to understand in what way this evidence tends to justify the libel. I have been unable to do so, and I anticipate that your Lordship and the jury will encounter the same difficulty.'

He turned over a number of pages rapidly.

'The evidence falls into two parts,' Wesley continued. 'The first part is simply a record of Sir James Digby's annual visits to Russia, to attend the Soviet Chess Championship between 1948 and 1960 in his capacity as an occasional journalist writing articles and reports for chess magazines. That evidence need not be adduced. Sir James admits that he attended the Soviet championship each year. Indeed, there are so many witnesses to the fact, so much evidence of it, that it would not be possible for him to deny it, even if he wished to. He does not wish to. He has never made any secret of it at all, and he invites your Lordship and the jury to find that he did so.'

The judge nodded and made a note of what Wesley had said.

'The second part consists of a large number of pages of coded information, which is *said*' – Wesley carefully emphasised the word – 'to show that at various times between 1948 and 1960, persons *said* to be western agents behind the Iron Curtain were arrested, tortured, killed, or banished to inhospitable parts of Russia. Your Lordship will not find any express statement to that effect in the documents, because the entire text consists of letters, numbers and symbols of different kinds, which are *said* to represent those events taking place between certain dates. So the documents themselves have no meaning, except that which may be assigned to them by an officer of the Security Services.'

'But if such an explanation were to be given ...' the judge began.

'It would consist of hearsay upon hearsay, speculation upon speculation,' Wesley replied at once. 'It could only be the result of intelligence gathered in the field, so the officer giving evidence would have no personal knowledge of the matters he is dealing with at all.'

The judge was nodding.

'But, my Lord, let me assume, for the purposes of this application, that the information contained in these documents is true. I do not concede it for one moment, but let us assume it to be true. What, I ask rhetorically, has that to do with Sir James Digby? Apparently, the Defendant believes that the fate suffered by the agents is in some way related to Digby's visits to the Soviet Union. To put it bluntly, it is claimed that Digby in some way betrayed these agents. What evidence is there to support that belief? None at all. It is the purest speculation. It is the oldest logical fallacy known to man: *post hoc, propter hoc*. There is no basis for the inference the Defendant invites your Lordship and the jury to draw from the evidence.'

The judge nodded again.

'If I may turn to my second application?'

'By all means, Mr Wesley.'

'My Lord, if your Lordship is against me on my application for judgment, I nonetheless submit that there is no justification for departing from the usual practice in libel cases: namely that the action should be heard in open court, and should be tried by a jury. The Defendant and the Home Secretary persuaded your Lordship on an earlier occasion that it was necessary to sit *in camera* and to dispense with a jury, on the basis that there would be such a volume of sensitive evidence that national security might be compromised if your Lordship allowed the usual practice to be followed. It is now clear that there was no basis for any such concern. The only evidence provided is the evidence behind divider twenty-two to which I have already referred. My Lord, every page of that evidence could be published in *The Times* tomorrow without having any adverse effect on national security at all. It is incomprehensible in your Lordship's file and it would be incomprehensible in the columns of *The Times*.'

He paused for effect.

'My Lord, the principle that actions should be tried in open court is an important one in a democratic society. The administration of justice should not take place behind closed doors. In a case of libel, that principle is even more important than in other cases. The Defendant has made a very public attack on the Plaintiff's reputation.

The Plaintiff must be allowed to reclaim his reputation in an equally public forum.'

'But if the contents of the documents were to be explained by an officer, as you have suggested,' the judge pointed out, 'there would be bound to be some sensitive information, wouldn't there?'

'Perhaps, my Lord,' Wesley replied. 'But there would be no need for names. No personal details of the agents would be given, and the Plaintiff would undertake not to ask any questions calculated to identify them. Even if some sensitive information had to be given, the court could easily sit *in camera* for a short time for that limited purpose, and then go back into open court.'

'What about the jury?' Mr Justice Melrose asked.

'They would be directed not to divulge any details of what was said during the proceedings *in camera*,' Wesley replied. 'If necessary, they could be asked to sign the Official Secrets Act form. I have done so, as has my learned junior, and my instructing solicitors. Why not the jurors, too? If the law trusts jurors to try a case of this kind, as it does, there is no reason not to trust them with important information.'

He paused.

'May I respectfully remind your Lordship also that the Plaintiff has a statutory right to trial by jury in a libel case, under section 6 of the Administration of Justice (Miscellaneous Provisions) Act 1933. Your Lordship cannot simply dispense with a jury for reasons of practice. I must add, my Lord, that if your Lordship were to be against me on that point, I would be obliged to ask for an adjournment of the trial for the purposes of an interlocutory appeal to the Court of Appeal.'

Roberts sprang to his feet.

'The section to which my learned friend refers has two exceptions,' he insisted, 'in cases in which there would have to be a prolonged examination of documents, or where a scientific or local investigation has to be made which could not conveniently be made with a jury.'

'Neither of which has any application to this case,' Wesley rejoined at once.

'I disagree with my learned friend,' Roberts said. 'Your Lordship would be quite entitled to find that there would be a prolonged examination of documents.'

'Your Lordship has the documents in front of him,' Wesley

replied, 'and I am sure your Lordship can easily see how long it would take the jury to examine them. Even with the necessary assistance in decrypting them, it could surely not take more than half a day of trial time.'

He turned towards Roberts.

'And, as far as any question of risk is concerned, I am sure that the Security Services would be quite capable of vetting the jury panel in case it contained anyone who posed an unacceptable security risk.'

Roberts pretended horror.

'Really, my Lord,' he said, 'that is an extraordinary suggestion.'

The judge was smiling.

'No, it's not,' he said. 'Mr Overton, Mr Roberts, I need not trouble you on the Plaintiff's application for judgment. On the procedural applications, if you wish to add anything to your earlier arguments, I will hear you, of course. But there is no need to repeat them.'

'In that case, my Lord, I have nothing to add,' Overton replied.

'Nor do I,' Roberts said.

'Then, let me give my views on the applications,' the judge said. 'Firstly, I am not prepared to give judgment in the Plaintiff's favour today. Despite what Mr Wesley has said, it seems to me that there is an issue to be tried. The Defendant, as well as the Plaintiff, is entitled to his day in court.

'Secondly, having seen the evidence, I am no longer satisfied that the entire action should be tried *in camera*, but I will sit *in camera* for the purpose of dealing with the encrypted evidence, whenever reference is made to it during the trial.'

He paused to consult his notes.

'As far as the question of the jury is concerned, I am persuaded by Mr Wesley's submissions that, whatever my own views may be, I have no power to dispense with a jury. The Plaintiff has a statutory right to trial by jury, and I am not persuaded that the volume of documents is such that a jury could not deal with it. Indeed, I am quite sure that they could do so without difficulty. The jurors will complete and sign the necessary forms under the Official Secrets Act, and I will direct them carefully about their obligations. Lastly, as I have said before, my judgment, with any necessary redactions, will be delivered publicly in open court, and may be reported. If Sir James prevails, his reputation will be fully vindicated in public. Mr Overton…'

Overton stood.

'Mr Overton, I do not wish to be misunderstood. I have not given judgment for the Plaintiff today. But Mr Wesley's submissions about the state of the evidence have a good deal of merit. If the state of the evidence remains the same when the trial begins, my decision is likely to be different. You have a week.'

Roberts got to his feet.

'My Lord,' Roberts said, 'may I make one thing clear on behalf of the Home Secretary? Your Lordship has the Home Secretary's certificate about the evidence. He is prepared to make the evidence available for trial only if the conditions he specified are in place. Your Lordship's rulings mean that those conditions are not in place.'

'My Lord, I may need to go to the Court of Appeal,' Overton said. 'Obviously, if the Home Secretary withdraws his permission for the evidence to be used, the Defendant's case is hopelessly compromised.'

The judge nodded.

'You may have leave to appeal against my rulings, if you need it,' he said. 'I give the same leave to the Home Secretary, should he wish to take the same course. But may I suggest to you both that you do so on an emergency basis? I see no reason to adjourn the trial.'

49

'I spoke with the Minister this morning,' Dick White said, once Baxter had installed himself in a chair in front of his desk. 'He reminded me, in that rather direct way he has, that the trial in the case of *Digby v Hollander* is due to begin next Tuesday, before Mr Justice Melrose and a jury.'

'And his mind is still troubled?' Baxter asked.

'That would be putting it mildly,' White replied. 'He wanted to know what we were doing about it. I had to tell him, of course, that the evidence we have provided to the parties thus far has failed to bring about a settlement; or even to persuade Mr Justice Melrose to sit without a jury. The Minister thinks that we need to do more.'

'We only have five days, sir. I can't see the case settling in that time, whatever we do. In any case, what does he mean by more? What does he want us to do?'

'He wants us to give them more evidence.'

Baxter shifted uncomfortably in his chair.

'Sir, as far as I know, the only other evidence we could give them is "Gawain",' Baxter said. 'Is the Minister aware of what that would involve?'

'No, at least, not in any detail. I told him that there might be some further information we could supply, but that I would be reluctant to do so unless it is really necessary. He asked why. I told him that it might compromise an important source. He didn't press me for details and I didn't offer any.'

Baxter nodded.

'Does he even know anything at all about Gawain – the details, I mean?'

'Good God, no. The Minister knows we have one or two assets in this area of course, but he doesn't know any details, and he wouldn't want to.'

'I am sorry if I seem unduly nervous about this, sir,' Baxter said. 'But Gawain is an asset we can't afford to compromise, as you know; not least because the Americans think they have as much right to him as we do – and they are probably correct.'

'There is no doubt about that,' White agreed. 'Gawain's security is of the highest importance. But at the same time, the Minister is adamant that we must do all we can to prevent the trial from taking place.'

'I am not sure that is possible, sir,' Baxter said. 'Unless the Minister agrees to allow Hollander to use the evidence we have already given him, he has no case. Digby has no reason to settle. I thought Miles Overton was appealing against the judge's rulings?'

'He is, but they can't convene a panel in the Court of Appeal to hear it until Monday. Evan Roberts will support the appeal on the Minister's behalf, but Julia tells me they don't hold out much hope. The judge has seen the evidence, and if he doesn't agree that he needs to try the entire case *in camera*, the Court of Appeal is unlikely to interfere. Julia thinks that they are especially weak on the jury question. Digby has a legal right to a jury.'

Baxter shook his head in frustration.

'Why is the Minister so adamant that the case should be settled?' he asked. 'Why not let nature take its course? If Digby wins the trial by default, there is no real security risk.'

'The Minister doesn't agree,' White replied. 'As he sees it, it is not just a question of the trial itself. He feels that it would be difficult, if not impossible, to keep a lid on it after the trial. If Hollander loses the case – which seems almost inevitable unless we come to his rescue – it would be impossible to shut him up. There is no telling what he might come out with once he gets back to the States.'

'That's true whether Hollander wins or loses,' Baxter pointed out. 'Actually, if he were to win, it might be even harder to control him.'

'Precisely. That is why the Minister insists that there must be no trial. We need the case to settle. Gawain should be enough to accomplish that – even in five days. Don't you think so, really?'

Baxter nodded slowly. 'In any rational world, you would think so. Yes. But the question is: how to disclose Gawain to the parties without compromising him.'

White smiled disarmingly.

'That will be your job, Baxter.'

Baxter returned the smile. 'Thank you, sir.'

'Any thoughts?'

Baxter considered this for some time.

'Well, I would begin with the ground rule that under no circumstances will Gawain give evidence for either side in court, and no information he provides may be used or referred to in court in any way. We can't allow Gawain to become evidence, given the judge's rulings.'

'I agree,' White said with a smile. 'But perhaps there is no need to tell the parties that at this stage? Perhaps that could be left slightly ambiguous, shall we say?'

'I agree, sir. It's likely to be more effective if we leave the threat hanging over their heads.'

'Good. What else?'

'I am against asking Gawain to travel to this country.'

'I agree again,' White said. 'Too risky by far.'

'Which means,' Baxter continued, 'that we have to take the parties to Gawain. I don't think they would be satisfied with a written statement, and I wouldn't want to give them one – too much risk of a leak. If Gawain is going to be as effective as we need him to be, he has to make a personal appearance.'

White nodded thoughtfully.

'How would you arrange that?'

'I am inclined to ask our friends in Gawain's neighbourhood to make a safe house available to us for a meeting urgently, over the weekend. Lawyers only – there is no question of letting either Hollander or Digby anywhere near Gawain, and even as far as the lawyers are concerned, the fewer the better. I would prefer to restrict the meeting to one legal representative from either side, unless you think that would not have enough impact. I only want to do this once, so we have to make sure that Gawain makes a big enough impression on both legal teams.'

White turned in his chair, and stared out of the window of his office for some time.

'I think one per side would be enough,' he replied at length. 'But if so, it should be a barrister rather than a solicitor. Barristers can be rather funny about accepting advice from solicitors. They see it as their role in life to give advice, rather than receive it. In any case, much as I love and adore Julia Cathermole, as we all do, I'm not sure I would want her too close to Gawain.'

He paused.

'Hollander's junior counsel, what was her name, Castle …?'

'Yes.'

'She leans rather to the left, I seem to remember.'

'Yes, sir. But we did a thorough check. She came up white as snow.'

'In that case,' White said, 'I would take both junior counsel and leave the Silks at home. The Silks will have the last word, and I want to offer them the protection of having to rely on the reports they get from their juniors. With any luck, Gawain will persuade the juniors that there is only one recommendation they can make.'

He turned back to face Baxter and leaned forward in his chair.

'What other ground rules do you suggest?'

'Nothing will be provided in writing,' Baxter replied, 'and no notes will be taken during the meeting. Questions will be permitted only for clarification, and Gawain will be instructed not to answer until I have approved the question. Once the meeting is over, that's it. Gawain is gone.'

White nodded.

'Very well,' he said. 'Let's go ahead. This is your responsibility now, Baxter. I want you to take personal charge of this. Don't delegate. Understood?'

'Understood, sir.'

'Make sure that our sister service explains the situation fully to Gawain. It is vital that we have his willing cooperation. He must be made to feel that we are not pressuring him, or putting him at risk in any way. Does he have any direct contact with the Americans?'

'Not that I know of. He's not supposed to. But then again, you never know with the Americans.'

'He must be made to understand that he must not discuss this with anyone else, whoever they may be. It could be dangerous for him.'

'Yes, sir.'

'Presumably you want to keep the nature and purpose of the meeting secret until it takes place? Have you thought of how you will approach the barristers, what you will tell them?'

Baxter smiled.

'That's a tricky one, sir. I will have to give that some further thought.'

'Well, don't take too long about it,' White commented. 'We are running out of time.'

50

The Devereux, a favourite haunt of the Bar just outside the Middle Temple's famous Little Gate, is always busy at 6 o'clock on Friday evenings. On this particular evening, a throng of barristers of all ages, the vast majority men, still formally dressed in dark suits and stiff collars, had gathered for their weekly ritual. It was time to let off steam at the end of a hard week; time to boast of their victories and bemoan their defeats in court; time to praise or complain about the judges who had understood the points they were trying to make – or not; time to raise their spirits for the weekend ahead. They were loud, and there was a constant stream of movement throughout the pub – which was exactly what Baxter had been hoping for.

Ben Schroeder pushed and jostled his way through the crowd until he saw the person he was looking for. Virginia Castle had found a relatively quiet space at the far end of the bar, and was maintaining possession of it against all comers, nursing a glass of white wine. Ben forced his way through an unyielding group of four young barristers arguing over the merits of a judge's decision to grant summary judgment, and purposefully inserted himself next to her.

'Sorry to take so long, Ginny,' he said, almost shouting to be heard above the din. 'I was in conference. I came as soon as the clerks gave me your message.'

She stared at him blankly.

'What message?' she asked.

'You sent me a message,' he said uncertainly, 'saying that you needed to see me urgently about the *Hollander* case, and asking me to meet you here as soon as possible.' She continued to stare. 'Didn't you?'

'No,' she replied. Her voice betrayed some irritation. 'What are you talking about? It was the other way round. I got a message that *you* wanted to see *me* urgently. I've been waiting for almost half an hour. I was nearly ready to give up and go home. What's going on?'

'I have absolutely no idea,' Ben replied.

Baxter had timed his entry to perfection. With a bland apology, he strode right through the middle of the exponents of summary judgment and approached.

'I am very sorry,' he said. 'This is all my fault. I would like to explain, if I may. But can we go outside so that I can hear myself think?'

For a moment they were both taken aback. Then, with a glance at Ben, Ginny left her glass on the bar and followed Baxter as he genially pushed and negotiated his way through several groups of drinkers and cleared a path to the front entrance of the pub. Ben followed. Baxter led the way through the Little Gate into the peace and quiet of the Middle Temple. The long bench by the fountain was unoccupied, and he ushered them to it, gesturing to them to sit with him.

Ginny stared at Baxter. 'Is this your doing?' she asked. 'Are you responsible for bringing us here like this?'

Baxter smiled sheepishly.

'I'm sorry, Miss Castle. Yes, I did send messages to you both via your clerks. It was a bit presumptuous of me, I admit, but I didn't know what else to do. I needed to get you both together at the same time to talk about the case, and I didn't know how else to go about it. The important thing is that you are both here.'

Ginny felt her temperature rising.

'Well, we may be here now,' she said. 'But we are not going to stay here to discuss a case with you outside chambers on a Friday evening in the absence of our clients and our instructing solicitors. If you have something to say, and assuming we are allowed to hear it, you need to contact our instructing solicitors and arrange for a joint conference of some kind in chambers. You obviously don't understand how things are done at the Bar.'

Baxter was nodding.

'As a matter of fact, Miss Castle,' he replied, 'I do understand how things are done. I understand only too well. That's why I had to engage in this silly charade. I need to speak to you, and I'm afraid I don't have time to play by the rules. It's an urgent matter, and if we don't talk about it now it will be too late.'

Ginny shrugged and pushed herself to her feet.

'Well, that's your problem,' she said.

Baxter stood and faced her.

'Actually, it's your problem as well,' he replied. 'And if you will listen to me for five minutes, I think I can make that clear to you. If you won't, then, of course, there is nothing I can do; you are free to leave whenever you wish. But I strongly advise that you give me a few minutes of your time.'

Ginny shook her head, and was about to walk away, but Ben took her arm.

'Wait a minute, Ginny,' he said. 'We both know who Mr Baxter works for, and we both know that the people he works for have already made some material available to us.'

'Which has made no difference at all,' Ginny observed, 'particularly as the Home Secretary won't let us use it in court.'

'Perhaps not,' he replied. 'But I don't think we can ignore the fact that Mr Baxter has gone to great lengths to speak to us. You have nothing to lose by listening to what he has to say.'

He turned to Baxter. 'I assume this is all off the record?'

'It is completely off the record, believe me.'

After several seconds Ginny allowed Ben to guide her back to her seat. He sat down alongside her. Baxter took his seat no more than two feet away from them. He took a deep breath.

'My superiors authorised the release of the evidence regarding Digby's travel to the Soviet Union, and the damage sustained by our agents behind the Iron Curtain as a result …'

'Supposedly as a result,' Ben said. 'It hardly merits the term "evidence". It is pure speculation.'

Baxter nodded.

'Fair enough,' he said. 'Let's say "allegedly as a result". That doesn't matter. The point is this. We released that information because we hoped it might result in a resolution of the case without trial. That didn't work. So be it. My superiors have, therefore, decided to release some further information to both sides.'

He looked pointedly at Ben and Ginny in turn.

'This new information,' he added authoritatively, 'is almost certain to have the desired effect.'

Ben sensed that Ginny was about to snap at Baxter again. He took her hand and squeezed it gently before releasing it.

'Can you tell us why you think that?' he asked.

'No,' Baxter replied. 'The information can be released only under very specific circumstances. When it is released, the answer to your question will be obvious immediately. But I can't jump the gun.'

'But why not go to our instructing solicitors?' Ben asked. 'It's their job to gather evidence. We are not allowed to go digging on our own. Miss Castle is right about that. There are rules.'

Baxter leaned forward.

'The information in question,' he replied, 'is extremely sensitive. Actually, that is something of an understatement. You must understand that there is more involved in this than the lawsuit, however important the lawsuit may be to the parties. The national interest is involved, and the life of at least one person may be in danger. I know you may be sceptical about what I'm saying, but I must ask you to give me the benefit of the doubt. My superiors are not fooling around. They have better things to do, believe me. They are not involving themselves in a piece of private litigation for fun. They need this case to end, and they want to work with you to make that happen.'

He sat back up again.

'To answer your question frankly,' he said, 'we decided to approach you as members of the Bar, because we believe that you are less of a security risk than your instructing solicitors. The need for security far outweighs professional rules in this instance. We will see to it that you are protected against any criticism.'

Ben looked at Ginny for some seconds.

'Give us a moment,' he said.

They stood and walked slowly together for a few yards towards Fountain Court, stopping at the entrance to the building.

'This is complete nonsense,' Ginny protested. 'We don't know who he is, or what he wants. We could get disbarred for this, Ben. I say we walk away now, report the matter to our instructing solicitors and our leaders, and call his bluff.'

Ben shook his head.

'I'm not so sure,' he replied. 'They are going to an awful lot of trouble to make this case go away. Look, Hollander is losing as things stand now. Let's be honest. With the evidence as it is now,

Digby will win, no contest. The judge has already told us that.'

'Which means that you have no obvious interest in any further evidence he may be interested in peddling,' Ginny said. 'So why are you so keen to listen to him?'

'Because I can't afford not to,' he replied. 'I can't afford to be blindsided, and risk Digby being taken by surprise at trial. We can't afford to take chances with this, Ginny. The stakes are too high.'

'But how do we know any of this is genuine?'

'We don't, for sure,' Ben conceded. 'But I don't think Baxter would be so protective of his evidence if he wasn't genuinely worried about the security implications. I think we ought to give him the benefit of the doubt, as he put it. I think I can justify what we are doing, as long as we are doing it together.'

Ginny reflected for a long time.

'All right,' she said eventually. 'I will go along with it for now. But if there is any sign that we are being set up in some way ...'

'We cut and run,' he said. 'Agreed.'

They walked back to the seat by the fountain.

'Assuming that we accept what you tell us,' Ben said, 'how would you propose to make this information available to us?'

Baxter smiled.

'I was waiting for you to ask me that,' he replied. 'I'm afraid it is not altogether simple. I hope you didn't have plans for the weekend.'

51

Ben returned to their table, walking gingerly from the bar with two bottles of Heineken and glasses, which he set down carefully. Just as carefully, he resumed his seat and placed a hand on each side of the table. As they looked at each other across the table, rocking rhythmically back and forth with the motion of the ship, they first smiled, and within a minute broke into loud laughter.

'What in God's name are we doing here?' he asked, as their laughter subsided.

'Trying to get ourselves disbarred?' Ginny suggested.

'I hope not,' he replied.

'When they haul me up in front of the disciplinary committee, I intend to tell them it's all your fault,' she said, pointing a finger at him.

'It probably is. I more or less talked you into it.'

'Not really. I can't claim to have put up much resistance.'

'I think we are doing the right thing, Ginny,' he said, more seriously. 'Quite why, I can't really say. But I think this is right.'

She nodded. 'So do I.'

Before parting from them earlier in the evening, Baxter had given precise, but frustratingly uninformative instructions. They were to go home, pack for two days, and tell their partners that they had been called away urgently to look at evidence in connection with a forthcoming trial, not to be identified. No one else was to be told of their absence. They would be away until Sunday evening. They would need their passports; and if they were prone to sea-sickness they should bring some remedy for it. All expenses would be met, and they would be provided with spending money, as required. Dress would be casual throughout; warm dress was advised for the ship. They were to return to the Temple with their bags, and rendezvous with Baxter on Victoria Embankment at the gate leading into the

Temple, at 9 pm precisely. Baxter did not tell them where they were going, or what to expect.

At exactly 9 pm, a black Humber Hawk pulled up quietly. The driver, a short man smartly dressed in a dark blue suit and a tie, jumped from the car, walked around the front of the vehicle, and greeted them.

'Miss Castle? Mr Schroeder? Good evening to you. Let me take your bags.'

Ben and Ginny had brought one medium size bag each. Baxter's instructions had not provided them with much guidance, and both had erred on the side of bringing a few things more than they were likely to need. It was a fine evening, but there was an autumnal chill in the air, and they each wore a light sweater under a coat. Ginny also wore a dark brown silk scarf. The driver whisked the bags away, and moments later had them safely stowed in the boot. He opened the rear door, and they both climbed in. Baxter turned around to greet them from the front passenger seat. He had abandoned his habitual dark suit and tie in favour of a dark grey sports jacket, light grey slacks, and a blue shirt open at the neck.

'Thank you for being so punctual,' he said. 'I don't think we will have any problem with traffic.' He glanced over at the driver, who shook his head as he signalled and pulled away from the kerb. 'But you never know.'

He rummaged for a moment or two in the inside pocket of his jacket and took out two long envelopes.

'Here are your tickets for the ferry,' he said, handing the envelopes to them. He noted the questioning looks they exchanged, and smiled.

'Well, I did give you a clue,' he said. 'I warned you about seasickness.' He smiled again as he watched them open the envelopes gingerly, as if they were not quite sure what they might find.

'So now you know where we are going – well, in general terms, anyway. We are taking the overnight ferry from Harwich to Hoek van Holland, sailing at 11.30, arriving about 6.30 tomorrow morning. We will get to Harwich a bit on the early side, but there is no harm in that. It's a bit of an obsession of mine, I'm afraid, arriving early for travel. We are sailing on the *Koningin Emma*. She's an elderly lady, requisitioned for service as a troop carrier during the War, but she has been completely refurbished since, and I'm told she is quite comfortable.'

'Mr Baxter, where are we going eventually, in less general terms?' Ben asked.

'You will find out when we arrive,' Baxter replied. 'Sit back and relax.'

Baxter had booked small cabins for each of them, and once the *Koningin Emma* was under way he wished them a good night and disappeared to his own with a sandwich and a cup of soup. Neither Ben nor Ginny was keen to spend any more time in the close confines of a cabin than was necessary. They had a late supper in the restaurant and adjourned to the adjoining bar which, as they were on the high seas, would remain open throughout the journey. It was getting late, but they were in no mood to sleep. It was not a rough crossing, but the sea had a good swell, and it was not easy to walk through the ship without holding on to something.

'What did you tell Jess?' she asked, raising her glass in a toast.

'I told her you and I were eloping,' he replied, raising his own glass, 'running away together to Paris in search of the Bohemian life.'

She laughed. 'I don't think Jess would quite believe in you as a Bohemian,' she said.

'No,' he conceded, 'I am sure you are right. Actually, I followed Baxter's instructions. I said something urgent had come up, and I had to go away for a couple of nights to look at some evidence.'

'Didn't she ask where you were going?'

'Yes, of course. I told her I didn't know, but that I was taking my passport, and she wasn't to worry.'

Ginny laughed again. 'I'm sure that put her mind at ease.'

'I'm sure it didn't, but she accepted it. Jess is very calm; she is one of those people who doesn't get upset unless there's a good reason. What did you tell Michael?'

'About the same. He was anything but calm. I was cross-examined for a good ten minutes. Who was the man I was going with? What did I know about him? What kind of evidence could there be that would need me to take my passport to go to see it? Of course, there was nothing I could say. He realised that I didn't know anything, but he kept on and on about it. How did I know I could trust this man? What if I knew too much about something? What if this was all a ghastly plot to kidnap me? How could he be sure I would be safe? At one point he was talking about turning up on the Embankment at 9 o'clock, and either confronting the man or following us to see where we went. I eventually talked him out of it, but he was serious.'

'Well, he is bound to be concerned about your safety.'

'Michael tends to see conspiracy in everything,' she said. 'It's part of what makes him such a good solicitor. But it's hard for him to let go of it sometimes.'

'I am sure he was happy to hear about the result Miles and Bernard got in front of the Committee,' Ben said. 'Jess certainly was. Things were a bit strained while that was hanging over our heads, to say the least. We have both heaved a big sigh of relief. I am glad it's over.'

'Me too,' Ginny replied. 'Well, you heard Michael when we had dinner at your flat. He was beside himself when we first found out about it. I wouldn't have been entirely surprised if he had taken a can of petrol and burned the Middle Temple to the ground. I tried my best to keep things calm, but it wasn't easy, mainly because I didn't feel calm myself. Still, here's to Miles and Bernard. I think they have definite promise as advocates. They may make it at the Bar yet. What do you think?'

'I think they have every chance,' Ben smiled, raising his glass. 'We will always be in their debt.'

They were silent for some time, as the ship gently eased her way forward, rocking up and down with the swell, which had grown more noticeable as she headed into the open sea.

'Miles and Bernard worked together on our behalf in the Inn but, as I'm sure you know, they have not always been very close,' Ginny said. 'And I am not sure the *Digby* case is going to help, whatever we find out or don't find out, on this trip.'

'They have been against each other in some big cases,' Ben observed.

'Yes,' she replied. She paused for a moment. 'Were you aware of the *Dougherty* divorce case?'

'Not at the time,' Ben replied. 'I knew that it was going on because I met Simon Dougherty one day in chambers. He was waiting for his mother to come out of a conference with Kenneth Gaskell. I saw he was wearing a West Ham scarf, which meant we were co-religionists and I ended up taking him to Upton Park from time to time. I still do. He was living with his mother in Surrey. Your client didn't get access to him until after the divorce settlement, so I took him whenever I could. Now I make arrangements with Dougherty. If his father can't take him to a game, I take him when I'm free.'

'That's really nice of you,' she said.

'He is a great boy,' Ben replied. 'He has been through a lot, but he seems to be doing well now. I didn't know anything else about the case – about the scandal – until after I was taken on in chambers.'

He picked up their empty glasses, made his way back to the bar in a far from straight line, and returned with two more Heinekens.

'I know Bernard blamed Miles for what came out about Kenneth Gaskell,' she said. 'But it was Michael who turned that case around, with his nose for conspiracy, for things being out of place. The wife was killing us. Our man was drinking too much and knocking her around, and we didn't really have a defence. But Michael suspected that Kenneth was having an affair with Anne even while he was representing her in the divorce case. He put a private detective on their trail, and he came back with the evidence.'

'Including the infamous photographs?' Ben asked.

She laughed. 'Infamous, but not particularly interesting,' she replied. 'You couldn't see much detail. But they put Kenneth and Anne together in hopelessly compromising circumstances, and together with the evidence of car registration numbers and what have you, the case was watertight. They had a little love nest going in Hastings.'

She shook her head.

'It was all so bloody stupid,' she said. 'He could have brought down his whole chambers. If anyone was to blame, Kenneth was. I can't imagine Herbert Harper sending work to a man who behaves like that.'

She leaned forward smiling.

'I don't suppose you would like to tell me how Bernard extracted Kenneth, and his chambers, from a mess like that?'

'I can't think what you mean,' he replied, returning the smile. 'Why don't you ask Miles?'

'Perhaps I will,' she said. She sat back happily in her chair, nursing her Heineken. 'That was when Michael and I got together,' she said, 'during that case.'

* * *

The siren announcing the arrival of the *Koningin Emma* at Hoek van Holland woke her passengers from whatever short periods of sleep they had been able to snatch during the crossing. Baxter met Ben and Ginny as they emerged from their cabins, and took them for a quick coffee before it was time to disembark and make their way through the Dutch immigration and customs controls. As they left the customs shed, a uniformed driver met them and took possession of their bags. He led them to a black Mercedes parked a few yards away by the quayside. Baxter exchanged a few words with the man in Dutch before climbing into the front passenger seat. The driver smiled broadly as he opened the rear door for Ginny and Ben. It was a cold morning, the sky was grey and overcast and a light rain was falling. Ginny pulled her scarf tightly around her.

'*Goeden morgen, Mevrouw, Meneer. Welkom in Nederland,*' he said cheerfully. 'Please, make yourselves comfortable. The drive will not be a long one.'

52

Baxter did not suggest that there was anything classified about the route they were taking, and Ben concentrated hard on the unfamiliar Dutch road signs, which told him that the Mercedes was apparently taking the most direct route into The Hague. There was little traffic at that time of the morning and, as the driver had promised, the journey was accomplished quickly. But as they were entering the city, the driver left the main road and took them along a number of residential streets into the heart of a suburb. Ben had no way even of guessing where they were going, or where they were. All the streets looked much the same, rows of elegant, well-painted houses, tall and narrow, and at that hour, quiet. The driver stopped outside one such house, left the car, and had the bags on the front doorstep of the house in a matter of seconds. He waited until Baxter had rung the bell and the door had been opened by a woman, and then drove quickly away.

The woman was in her thirties, tall and slim, with black hair and brown eyes. She wore a simple beige cotton shirt, a brown skirt just below the knee, and brown flat shoes. She extended her hand to Ben and Ginny in turn as they entered the house.

'My name is Paula van Harten,' she said. 'Welcome to The Hague. I am sure you must be tired after your journey. Let me show you to your rooms. If you will follow me…'

Her English was fluent and betrayed only the merest trace of an accent. She began to make her way up a narrow spiral staircase which ran, dizzyingly, the full height of the house like a huge wooden spinal column. Ben made to pick up his case, but Paula gestured to him to leave it.

'I will bring your luggage in a few minutes,' she smiled. 'I am used to these Dutch staircases. They can be hazardous for foreigners. I run up and down them all day.'

Ginny had been assigned the only room on the fourth floor, the top floor of the house. Ben and Baxter had rooms on the third, with the bathroom and toilet between them. The rooms were small, furnished simply but comfortably with single beds, wardrobes, a chair and a writing table with a reading lamp. The windows looked down from a great height; Ben's on to the small garden at the rear of the house and the backs of the identical row of houses in the next street; Baxter's on to the street at the front of the house. Ginny's room was long and thin, spread over the whole of the fourth floor, with two small windows, offering her both views.

'I have arranged lunch for one o'clock, as you asked, Mr Baxter,' Paula said as she left his room. 'I am sure our guests would like to rest, but if they would like coffee or tea with some biscuits, they can come down to the kitchen. Will you explain the arrangements to them?'

'I will,' Baxter replied. *'Dank U wel, Mevrouw.'*

'Als U blieft, Meneer.'

He heard her flat shoes making their way briskly and confidently down the treacherous stairs to bring the luggage. He knocked on both doors to pass on the invitation to visit the kitchen. Ginny gave him a tired smile. Ben was already asleep.

* * *

Lunch was served in the living room, a large room which occupied most of the ground floor. It ran the whole length of the house, on the left-hand side, from the front door to the garden at the rear, access to which was afforded by French windows. On the right-hand side, the staircase began more or less opposite the door of the living room, with a storage space and ground floor toilet underneath. The hallway led down the middle to the kitchen, which also gave access to the garden. The living room consisted of two parts, separated by sliding doors which looked rather flimsy, and in need of a coat of paint. The front part of the room was furnished in the style of a meeting room: most of the space was occupied by a large, square, wooden table which looked heavy and solid; a number of chairs; and a functional long, narrow sideboard. The rear part had two armchairs and a sofa, none looking particularly inviting; and two bookcases with a variety of books in Dutch and English, and back issues of one or two popular magazines. Lunch was eaten at the heavy table. It consisted of *erwtensoep*, a delicious thick pea soup, served with thick chunks of fresh crusty bread smothered with butter; followed by plates of fruit and Gouda cheese. A pot of strong black coffee rounded it off.

As lunch ended Paula van Harten quickly cleared away the dishes and wiped down the table with a damp cloth. After asking whether they wanted more coffee, she withdrew silently. Ben and Ginny sat at the table, finishing their coffee. They had both slept well for about three hours in the quiet of their rooms high above the street, and had been refreshed by a shower and a change of clothes. Baxter sat across from them on the other side of the table.

'We will use this room for our meeting,' he announced. 'Our guest is expected at about four o'clock.'

Ben and Ginny exchanged glances. Ben's watch indicated 2.15. This was the first hint of any kind they had received about the promised evidence. It was not a particularly informative hint. Who the guest was to be, what evidence he or she had, and why they had been brought all the way to The Hague to see or hear it, remained a mystery – and one which Baxter appeared to have no intention of resolving.

'Before he comes,' Baxter continued. 'I want to acquaint you with the ground rules under which the evidence is being provided. The circumstances may be less than ideal from a lawyer's point of view; I do understand that. But, as I tried to explain on Friday evening, there are issues of security and personal safety involved. I believe that will be abundantly clear to you by this evening. As a consequence, my hands are tied. I hope you will feel able to accept the rules. In any case, please don't blame me. I assure you that there is nothing I can do about it.'

He had left a brown, soft leather briefcase on top of the sideboard. He stood, walked over to retrieve it, and extracted two forms, which he pushed across the table.

'Please read these and sign,' he said. 'You are promising that you will reveal nothing of this weekend's activities, including the evidence which will be presented to you later, except to your clients and the other lawyers involved in the case. They will be asked to sign a similar form before the evidence is disclosed to them. I am sure I do not need to emphasise the possible consequences of failing to comply with the obligation you are undertaking by signing.'

Ginny signed almost at once. Ben read through the document slowly and scribbled a signature with a show of reluctance.

'You might at least tell us where we are,' he said.

'I think you know you are in The Hague,' Baxter pointed out. 'The house we are in is a safe house operated by our Dutch sister service, which has placed it at our disposal for the weekend. I am afraid we will not be able to leave the house until it is time to return to Hoek van Holland for our ferry home tomorrow. That's a Dutch guideline, as well as one of ours, and, believe me, Mevrouw van Harten is more than capable of enforcing it.'

'I don't doubt that,' Ginny smiled.

Baxter returned the smile. 'We will have dinner here this evening, with a bottle or two of wine, after the meeting, and tomorrow you will be safely back home. It's not the kind of weather you would want to venture out in, anyway; quite cold and miserable, very Dutch.'

He took possession of the forms they had signed and returned them to his briefcase.

'The guidelines are quite simple, really,' he continued. 'First, our guest will give you an account of certain events. When he has finished, you will be free to ask questions, but there will be a slight delay before he replies in case there is anything I have to censor. No documents will be provided, and no notes will be taken, or recordings made, during the meeting.' He smiled. 'Except, naturally, for whatever recording Mevrouw van Harten is making for her superiors, something we have tried to discourage, but over which we ultimately have no control.'

'No notes?' Ben asked. 'I understand that there may be things you don't want to put in an official document, but if we can't take notes there may be things we miss. If we can't give our clients and colleagues the full picture, the evidence may not have the desired effect.'

'Don't worry, Mr Schroeder,' Baxter replied. 'The story you are going to hear is not particularly complicated, and I have a feeling that you are going to remember almost every word he says, without any trouble at all.'

***

They had all returned and were seated around the solid table at a few minutes before 4 o'clock, Baxter at the side nearer to the door, Ben and Ginny facing him on the far side. A jug of water and four glasses stood on the table, and two large glass ashtrays had been put in place. A packet of Lucky Strike cigarettes and a box of matches lay on the table in front of the fourth chair, to Baxter's right and directly across from Ginny. They sat and waited, tense and silent. At almost exactly 4 o'clock they heard the front door bell ring. They heard Paula van Harten walk swiftly to open the door; they heard a male voice, and a brief conversation in English, during which she was taking his coat and asking him to put his umbrella in the large plant pot by the side of the door. Paula knocked on the door and ushered the man inside. All three stood.

The man appeared to be about fifty. He was not tall, and he was carrying a little too much weight, but he moved easily enough. His face was rugged and he sported a short silver moustache and beard, which matched his thinning hair. His eyes were grey, but not at all unfriendly. He wore a brown pilot's leather jacket and beige trousers. He had a large shoulder bag, which he placed on the floor next to Baxter's briefcase.

'Kurt, come in, please,' Baxter said, as Paula left the room, closing the door unobtrusively behind her. 'I am Baxter. You remember me, of course; we have met before.'

'Yes,' Kurt replied, shaking Baxter's hand.

'And may I introduce Miss Virginia Castle and Mr Ben Schroeder, two of the lawyers in the case our Dutch colleagues have briefed you about. Miss Castle, Mr Schroeder, this is Kurt Weber.'

They shook hands. Ben and Ginny resumed their seats. Baxter asked Weber to sit in the seat to his right. Then he walked to the sideboard and turned to them all with a relaxed smile.

'Now, before we get down to business,' he said, 'may I offer anyone some refreshment?'

He picked up a tall thin, bottle, one of two standing on the sideboard. Next to the bottles were two plates, one with slices of a rough, black bread, the other a plate of what Ben thought must be caviar. He had noticed it when he entered the room.

'If this place was one of ours,' Baxter said, 'we would have some proper gin and tonic, with ice; perhaps some vodka, or even a decent scotch. But as we are guests of the Dutch, we have jenever. It's a kind of gin, I believe, and you can have it either *jong* or *oud*, young or old. The aficionados swear by one or the other, but personally I've never been able to tell the difference. It's something of an acquired taste, but not bad once you get used to it. What would you like?'

'*Jong*,' Weber replied. Baxter filled a small glass and handed it to him, then poured the same for himself. He brought the bottle and two more glasses to the table and took his seat.

Ginny was looking intently at Weber. She shook her head.

'This is not a social occasion, Mr Baxter,' Ben said. 'We are here to work.'

Baxter smiled again. 'I am very conscious of that, Mr Schroeder. As you wish. It's just that, in a minute or less from now, you may need a drink.'

He turned to Weber. 'The floor is yours, Kurt. You may begin.'

Weber turned towards Baxter.

'The rules that were agreed …?'

'Are in effect, yes,' Baxter confirmed.

Weber nodded.

'Thank you.' He coughed, then drank the contents of his glass. Baxter refilled it instantly.

'In that case, I should begin with a proper introduction. My name is not Kurt Weber. It is Viktor Stepanov.'

53

Ben found himself utterly speechless. Neither Baxter nor Stepanov broke the silence. Baxter seemed to be finding the scene slightly amusing.

'We understood that you were dead,' Ben said helplessly, after some time. As soon as he had said it, he realised how ridiculous it sounded.

Stepanov smiled. 'Yes,' he replied. 'In the Soviet Union, it is often advisable to be dead. In some cases it is the only way of staying alive.'

'The face,' Ginny said quietly. 'I recognise you from the photograph in your obituary.'

'Then you are a most perceptive woman,' Stepanov said, smiling again. 'That picture was taken when I was somewhat younger, and before I adopted this disguise.' He fingered his beard.

Ben was leaning forward on the table, both hands over his mouth, trying to recover his composure. Baxter had picked up the bottle and was holding it up invitingly. Ben picked up one of the empty glasses and nodded. Ginny also nodded, and Baxter filled both glasses. He poured water for everyone from the jug.

'I will return to Kurt Weber later,' Stepanov said. 'I should start at the beginning. I was born in Leningrad in 1914. My father loved chess, but we were a poor family, and he grew up before the Revolution, so he had no opportunity to play seriously. But when it became clear that I had some talent he encouraged me to play in local tournaments, and at the age of sixteen I was sent to Moscow to a special school where chess was part of the curriculum. I developed quickly, and started to play in tournaments both at home and abroad. The authorities gave me permission to travel, because of my abilities, and eventually I attained the rank of grandmaster.'

He paused for a drink, jenever first, then water.

'After I had played in a number of tournaments abroad, it became clear that I was not in the first rank of grandmasters. I was good, but in the Soviet Union, good is commonplace. I was not to be one of those who would take the world by storm, and that was what they were looking for: players who would take the world by storm, players like Mikhail Botvinnik and Vasily Smyslov, who would show the world how superior Soviet society was, compared to the degenerate capitalist West with its degenerate, bourgeois approach to chess. Others were coming up through the ranks who were stronger players; who would be, therefore, more useful than I would.'

Baxter was listening carefully, refilling glasses as needed. Ben was now feeling a little more composed. Ginny seemed totally absorbed. She had hardly taken her eyes off Stepanov.

'But fortunately for me,' he continued, 'I had another talent which was developed in the school in Moscow. I was a good linguist. I was asked to specialise in German and English, which were considered to be the most important languages from the point of view of the Soviet State. Later, Chinese became important also, but at that time, German and English. It was not long before I came to the notice of the Government. When Hitler invaded our country I was seconded to a department in Moscow to translate captured German documents and to try to decipher German military codes. After the War, I accompanied the Soviet legal team to Nuremberg as a translator and interpreter. It was there that I first met James Digby. He was working in a similar capacity for the British team. We spoke a few times. His name was vaguely familiar. In those days we did not receive very much information about what was going on in British chess, but the name registered with me. We got on well but, as I say, we had little opportunity to talk. The Soviet team kept itself to itself at that time. We attended receptions, but too much fraternisation was discouraged.'

* * *

'After Nuremberg I was not sure whether the authorities would permit me to travel very much. But once again, my command of languages proved useful. The Soviet Chess Federation had endless arguments with FIDE – the International Chess Federation. In particular, a serious dispute developed about arrangements for the tournament to decide the world chess championship in 1948. The world champion, Alexander Alekhin, died in 1946, and the title was vacant just after the war. It had been proposed to hold a tournament in which a number of the strongest players in the world would compete for the title as soon as arrangements could be made. Unfortunately, the Soviet Chess Federation took a very strong position, assuming that it could dictate the terms. They tried to dictate to the world who should be invited to compete, and where the tournament should be held. Although FIDE represented the entire chess community worldwide, the Soviets refused to agree to their proposals. They justified this by drawing attention to the Soviet dominance in world chess, which had to be conceded. All the same,' he shrugged and smiled, 'the way in which the negotiations were being conducted on our side did us little credit.'

Baxter had walked to the sideboard and carried over the bread and caviar, which he placed on the table, with four small plates. Stepanov paused to help himself to some of each, and washed it down with a mouthful of jenever. For the first time, he took a cigarette from the packet in front of him and lit it. Belatedly, he thought to pick the packet up and offer it around, but he was the only smoker in the room.

'Our Government, of course, wanted the tournament to go ahead, so they asked me to step in and take over the negotiations before the Soviet Federation torpedoed the proposal for the tournament altogether. The situation cried out for some basic diplomacy, and as I spoke languages other than Russian, this helped a great deal to smooth things over. Everyone became a little more relaxed and, in due course, we reached an agreement. I need not go through the whole thing. Suffice it to say that it was agreed to start the tournament off here in The Hague, and move to Moscow for the second half. The Government seemed pleased with my work, and invited me to attend the tournament in The Hague. I was to be based in the Soviet Embassy, for reasons which were not at all clear – until just before I was due to leave Moscow.'

He paused for a drink of water.

'Two days before my departure I was summoned to attend the office of the head of one the Directorates of Moscow Centre,' he said.

'The Soviet Foreign Intelligence Service,' Baxter interjected.

'Yes. The Comrade Director said that my work as an interpreter

and negotiator had come to his attention, and that there was a role
I could play which would be of the greatest service to the Soviet
people in the struggle against the West and the capitalist system. He
asked whether I was prepared to accept this role.' He smiled. 'In the
Soviet Union, when the head of a Directorate of Moscow Centre
makes such an invitation, the correct answer is "yes".'

Ben and Ginny instinctively smiled with him.

'The Comrade Director explained to me that agents working
under his command had cultivated a number of high-ranking
western diplomats and intelligence officials both in London and
Washington, who had been Soviet agents for some years, and had
finally attained positions of some power. These persons now had
access to information of the highest quality, information vital to the
Soviet High Command, and also to those State agencies responsible
for protecting the Soviet people against sabotage and infiltration by
counter-revolutionary elements at home. It was necessary to find a
means of conveying this information to the Directorate, and also
of conveying information from the Directorate to the contacts in
London and Washington. Moscow Centre regarded it as essential that
its contacts should not be compromised, and they wanted a method
of communication which would not involve sending documents,
film and the like, which are too easily discovered and are too easy
to trace back to the source. A British agent known to the contacts
had been identified, and I was to work with this agent in devising
an appropriate system and putting it in place. I was instructed to
approach him during the tournament and, if he was agreeable, to
propose that we should work together once the tournament had
moved to Moscow, where it was easier for the Directorate to arrange
a secure meeting place.'

Stepanov paused again to drink jenever and water.

'The Comrade Director did not tell me the identity of the British
agent before my departure, but after I had arrived in the Netherlands,
a top secret coded message was sent to the Embassy for my attention.
The agent was named as Sir James Masefield Digby.'

54

Stepanov lit another cigarette.

'Of course, the Directorate was aware that Digby and I had known each other in Nuremberg. On returning to the Soviet Union from Nuremberg, we were all required to submit a complete list of all foreigners we had spoken with during our time there. It was, of course, a long list. But nothing escapes the attention of the authorities, and for them it was a fortunate coincidence. I was asked to re-introduce myself to Digby, gain his trust, and then reveal myself as his contact, making sure first that he was indeed ready to work with us, looking for any signs that he might be a double agent. They are always suspicious of everyone. I was told that I would be free to take him to whatever location – bars, cafés, and so on – might be best suited to our conversations. I was told that the minders would leave us alone, and as far as I know they did, though you can never be sure of that. Digby was staying at the Hotel des Indes. I found him in the bar there one evening and we renewed our acquaintance.'

He paused.

'I wish to make it clear to you that I liked Digby,' he said. 'I never thought of myself as exploiting him. Everything he did, he did willingly. Whether this was for purely ideological reasons, or whether he also hoped for some benefit from the Soviet Union at some later time, I do not really know. Perhaps it was both in some measure. But I will say this: Digby never asked for money and, as far as I know, never accepted money from us – certainly not from me. And whatever he did, it was not out of any hatred for his country. It may sound strange, but I had the impression that he loved his country very deeply, and that he believed that what he was doing was in his country's best interests.'

He took a sip of jenever.

'I must admit that I was nervous – after all, I was a linguist and a chess player, not a professional intelligence agent. But I should not have been concerned at all. Recruiting James was easy; there was no resistance at all. On the second occasion that we spoke, he asked if we might leave the hotel and walk. We walked for three or four hours – and it was a cold Netherlands night in March, believe me.'

He smiled.

'But this did not deter him. We seemed to walk endlessly, randomly, around the city centre, in no particular direction, sometimes into areas where we were in danger of getting lost. He did not stop talking during the entire walk. I do not recall having any opportunity to ask a question. He talked very fast, obsessively, moving from one subject to another without warning, stopping in the middle of a story and returning to it ten minutes later, almost like – how you would say, the wave of …'

'A stream of consciousness?' Baxter suggested.

'Yes, exactly, a stream of consciousness. He did not always make sense, but something seemed to possess him and made him say all these things to me.'

'What kinds of things did he talk about?' Ben asked. He glanced at Baxter. 'If I may?'

Baxter nodded.

Stepanov took the last drag of his cigarette and stubbed it out firmly in the ash tray. He shook his head.

'Everything,' he replied simply. 'It was as if he were trying to tell me his whole life story, not just in a historical sense, but his intellectual life story, his emotional life story. But it was somehow all mixed up together, almost as if he could no longer separate historical incidents in his life from the ideas in his head, and as if he could no longer make sense of his motivations. In some ways it felt as though he was justifying himself to me. He talked about his early life at home; the values he was taught; his school; how he discovered chess and how it became a passion for him; his resentment at not being able to play chess as a profession; his time as a student at Cambridge University; the sympathy he had always had for the poorer classes; his wife, and her inability to conceive a child to inherit his title; his introduction to socialism, and how socialism seemed at first to provide the answer to everything; how he doubted socialism many times; his disillusionment with the British Labour Party, and even with the Soviet Union at times because of Stalin; how his faith would somehow be renewed; and ...'

He drained his glass and lit another cigarette.

'And about his brother Roger, who was killed in the war in Spain. He spoke of Roger constantly, almost as a form of punctuation between stories or parts of stories: Roger at home when they were young; Roger at university; as Lord of the Manor in waiting; at his Club in London; involved in every aspect of James's life, even when they were apart. It was pure hero-worship. His recollections of Roger's death were very painful to listen to.' He smiled. 'They had a strange way of writing letters to each other. He tried to explain it to me, but I did not take it all in.'

'And at the end of it all,' Stepanov said, as Baxter refilled his glass, 'he agreed to work with me. When the world championship moved to Moscow in April, we worked together in a safe house provided by the Directorate. We came up with the system that was required. It was simplicity itself.'

He suddenly laughed out loud.

'Shall I show you?'

He looked at Baxter, who nodded.

'Yes, I think I must show it to you.'

55

Stepanov sprang to his feet and retrieved his shoulder bag from where it had been lying by the sideboard. He reached inside and took out a folding chess board and a yellow cloth bag fastened at the top by a string pull. This contained a set of plastic chess pieces. He unfolded the board and laid it out on the table in front of him. He opened the bag and turned it upside down, allowing the pieces to fall on to the board. In a matter of seconds he had the pieces set up as if for a game, so that he was playing white.

'The problem set for us by the Comrade Director,' he began, 'was to devise a system for passing information in both directions without the need to carry copies of documents, film, and the like. So we needed a method of encrypting that information at source, and decrypting it on arrival in a way which would allow the information to be conveyed accurately.'

He allowed his hand to run along the top of the white pieces.

'The chess board has sixty-four squares, alternately black and white. The squares are identified by a letter and a number. The files run up and down and are designated by the lower case letters "a" to "h", with "a" being the file on the left hand side of the board, as White sees it. The ranks, going across the board, are designated by the numbers 1 to 8, again seen from White's point of view. So the black square in the corner by my left hand is a1, the square above that a2, and so on until we come to a8. Then the second file begins with the square next to a1, which is b1, and then we go to b2 and so on until we reach b8. Is everyone with me?

Ben and Ginny nodded.

'In addition, each player has eight pieces: a king, a queen, two rooks, two bishops, two knights; and he has eight pawns. The pawns are technically not referred to as pieces, though this does not matter for our purposes. You see here the positions in which the pieces start the game, lined up on the first rank for White, the eighth rank for Black; the pawns in front of them on the second and seventh ranks. The order of the pieces is more or less symmetrical, the rooks in the corners, then the knights, then the bishops, and finally the king and queen occupying the two remaining squares, with the queen on the square of her own colour.'

Stepanov moved the pawn in front of the white king two squares forward on the board.

'Obviously, a game consists of movements of the pieces from one square to another. Each piece may move only in the manner prescribed by the rules. The moves played in any competitive game are recorded by the players. There is a notation for this. White has the first move. You see that I have begun the game by advancing this pawn by two squares. I record this simply as e4, indicating the square to which the pawn has been moved. We could say e2-e4, but the simpler the better as long as the notation is not ambiguous. Let us assume that Black responds by advancing the pawn in front of his king by two squares.'

He made the move.

'We would record this as e5. Next, White moves the knight on his king's side from g1 to f3, attacking the black pawn. When the pieces move, they are represented by a letter: in this case, in English notation, the letter N is used for the knight because K is reserved for the king. So the move is recorded as Nf3. In other languages, of course, the appropriate letters are used. So, in German we would say Sf3, because the knight is *der Springer*; in French we would say Cf3, because the knight is *le chevalier*. Then, if Black responds by moving his queen's knight from b8 to c6, defending his king's pawn, we would record it as Nc6.' He made the move. 'Then White moves his king's bishop from f1 to b5, threatening to capture the black knight, and so indirectly renewing the threat to the black pawn by attacking its defender.' He made the move. 'We would record this as Bb5. Yes?'

Ben and Ginny nodded again, enthralled.

'For any system of encryption designed to convey complex information,' Stepanov continued, 'there must be a sufficient number of permutations of the symbols. Chess moves consist of symbols. Please take my word for it, that with sixty-four squares, sixteen pieces, and sixteen pawns, the number of possible permutations is very large, far greater than would be required to express the kind of information that needed to be conveyed.'

'But the number of permutations is limited by the way in which the pieces and pawns are permitted to move under the rules,' Ben pointed out.

'Yes,' Stepanov agreed. 'But the number still remains large. Actually what is far more significant is that there are very many moves that are simply bad moves, moves which no serious player would even consider making. That is a far greater limitation. But still there are enough permutations; and we can increase them, because we can use not only the moves players actually make in a game, but as commentators, we can suggest alternatives, and analyse what might have happened if those alternatives had been played. This gives us many more potential moves.'

'So, the information is encrypted in the form of the moves of a game played in a tournament, or moves which would have been reasonable but were not in fact played?' Ben asked. Baxter remained silent, and indicated no objection.

'Excellent,' Stepanov replied. 'You see it exactly. So, all that was required was for James to travel to an important chess tournament, in which a sufficiently large number of games would be played. The Directorate ensured that he received an invitation each year to the Soviet championship, and that he was granted the appropriate visa. The Soviet championship was, naturally, more secure than any event abroad. It is held in different cities, but James and I always met at the Hotel Peking in Moscow at the end of the tournament, wherever it was held. It was particularly convenient at this hotel, for various reasons.'

He lit another cigarette.

'Let me give you one example of how it worked,' he said. 'Let us suppose that a contact in London or Washington has information of a diplomatic nature to pass on to Moscow Centre.' He smiled. 'This brings us back to the fact that notation in different languages can be used. For diplomatic information we would choose French, because French is the language of diplomacy; for military information, German; for technical information of other kinds, English; or if the information was specific to a particular country, we would sometimes simply use the language of that country.'

Baxter had walked to the sideboard to open a new bottle of

jenever. 'Only the *oud* left, I'm afraid,' he observed. 'I hope that's all right.'

'Let us assume that London wishes to advise Moscow that western agents are being infiltrated into city A from city B,' Stepanov continued. 'James has a contact at the Embassy in London, who meets with him and describes generally the information to be conveyed. James would first designate two squares on the board to represent cities A and B.'

He suddenly laughed aloud again.

'This was very funny. James insisted that the western cities should be represented by white squares, and cities behind the Iron Curtain by black squares, as if the Eastern Bloc were the bad guys. This was perhaps rather ironic in view of what we were doing, but nothing I could say induced him to change his mind. The Comrade Director was put out, and he was insisting it should be the other way around. So I had to intervene to try to reach a solution. After much difficulty, I was able to persuade the Comrade Director that this was a small concession to make in return for such great service to the Soviet people, and so James had his way; it was ordained that the white squares were reserved for western cities.'

Involuntarily, Ben and Ginny joined in his laughter, and even Baxter was unable to suppress a broad smile.

'Then, of course, there had to be a code for the agents. We could have used a crude method, a combination of letters to spell out names, but the Comrade Director considered that this would be insecure, and also unnecessary. In most cases, Moscow would be able to identify the persons referred to, given sufficient information about their movements and their importance. This is where the pieces came in. In some cases you could identify the agent quite well by assigning a piece. For example, an exceptionally important agent would be represented by the king or the queen; but the queen could also mean a female agent; everything was a matter of context; sometimes a person acting out of religious conviction would be represented by a bishop; a military attaché or the like by a knight; a low-level agent by a pawn, and so on. Moscow was always represented by the square d8, the square of the black queen. Washington was d1, the square of the white queen, and London was e2. So the easiest way to represent the movement of a high-ranking diplomat suspected of involvement in espionage from Washington to Moscow would be the move Dd1 to Dd8, using the French notation, provided that the Queen could legally move to d8 in the circumstances of the game – her path was not blocked, and so on. In other cases, where the move would not be legal, more than one move might be required. But the move can always be suggested.'

'So,' Ginny asked, 'once Digby had encrypted the information by assigning squares and pieces, he would use moves made in the Soviet championship to convey the information to you?'

'Yes; or moves which might plausibly have been made during a game. That gives a very wide selection of moves.'

Ginny glanced at Baxter, but Baxter seemed to have no inclination to rein in their questions.

'And this was all in reports Digby made of the tournament – I take it he was officially there as a journalist?'

'Yes, he was an accredited journalist. But he might send me a version of his report which differed to some extent from those he sent to the newspapers and magazines, simply to draw my attention to some particular moves, perhaps by underlining or some such device.'

'And as long as he gave you the details of the encryption, you had access to the information immediately.'

'I myself did not,' Stepanov said, 'but I had an encryption from which the Comrade Director could draw the necessary conclusions, once I explained the encryption to him.'

'All right,' Ben said. 'I understand that. But the Soviet championship takes place once a year. What if information had to be conveyed at other times?'

'Yes, of course,' Stepanov replied. 'There is an important chess tournament going on somewhere in the world at any given time of year, so we could have arranged other meetings. But it would have been insecure, suspicious, for us to be meeting regularly, and there might be no way to arrange secure accommodation for our meetings abroad. So we had another way of using the system. Postal chess is very popular throughout the world for people who cannot go to tournaments.'

'The moves are sent by post?' Ben asked. 'That must mean that games go on for a long time?'

Stepanov smiled. 'Sometimes for years,' he agreed. 'But we did not need to conduct an actual game. We could simply exchange postcards, appearing to be part of a game, or notes for an analysis. This is how beautiful this is. You don't even need to use an envelope. Postal games are played using postcards. So James might send me a card using German notation, saying for example: "Sd6; White threatens to follow up with Tg7, with a considerable advantage."'

'Which could mean?'

'Which could mean: "an agent with military ties has arrived in Prague, and will link with a more senior colleague in Riga in the near future; the situation is dangerous; we need to watch it carefully". Perhaps this refers to a suspected western operation with some military aspect in which these agents are implicated.'

'But we had other symbols which could be used also. The notation for castling, a protective move, is 0-0 or 0-0-0, depending on whether you castle king's side or queen's side. We used this to suggest that evasive action was being taken, or should be taken. To indicate danger, we often used the + symbol, which is used to indicate that the king is in check. In case of the gravest danger, a life and death matter, we would use ++, the symbol for the king being checkmated – which brings the game to its end. We would sometimes indicate the wisdom of certain action by the use of ! – which in chess notation indicates a good move, or ? which indicates a bad move. There were so many variations.'

Ben nodded thoughtfully. 'Extraordinary,' he said.

'This system was useful also to clarify information which was not completely clear to the Comrade Director as it was originally provided,' Stepanov added. 'For example, the reference to the agent might be ambiguous. In this case, I would send James a card saying, perhaps: "Your last card got wet while in transit. Please clarify whether your move was Qf8 or Rf8." He would clarify, and this would solve the problem.'

Ginny suddenly sat up in her chair, and turned to Baxter.

'This explains the evidence you provided to us before, doesn't it? It explains how you were able to relate what happened to the agents to Digby's annual visits to the Soviet championship?'

Baxter nodded. 'We were puzzled at first by the timings in some cases, but once Viktor explained about the postal chess system, all became clear. There was an obvious correlation.'

'It worked for information passing in the other direction also,' Stepanov added. 'If the Comrade Director had intelligence that a particular Soviet agent or network in Paris might be threatened, I would encrypt this intelligence, using French notation and referring to f1 as the square for Paris; give the encryption to James if he was in Moscow, or send him a postcard if he was in London; and he would pass it on to his contact at the Embassy.'

He sat back and surveyed the room with satisfaction, a craftsman proudly demonstrating his work.

'The most beautiful thing of all,' he concluded, 'is how secure the system was. There was nothing anybody could suspect, no suspicious documents or photographs; and even if they suspected, there was nothing that could be proved, unless James was caught meeting with his contact in London. Even then, neither he nor I knew the information in any real detail.'

He drained his glass of *oud* with a flourish.

'And so it continued,' he said, 'from 1948 to 1960.'

56

Stepanov had asked for a comfort break. Ben and Ginny were also anxious to stretch their legs for a while. Ginny stepped into the hallway where she could walk up and down. Ben stood quietly by the window, and looked out over the dark street in front of the house. The street looked exactly the same as it had when they arrived, but in the intervening period the world had changed. He had still not fully recovered from the shock of learning the identity of the man who had arrived at the house as Kurt Weber. He was already imagining the conversation he would have to have with Bernard Wesley and Herbert Harper, and then with Sir James Digby. It was one he was not looking forward to. He sensed that what he had learned was important enough to justify the massive departure from protocol involved in his presence at this house in The Hague. He doubted that anyone would be in the mood to question what he had done. But the case had been turned inside out. Digby and his legal team would now have to take decisions which would decide the fate, not only of Digby's reputation, but of his future life; and the omens were not promising. He was intrigued by Ginny's reaction. She could have been forgiven if she had shown some kind of pleasure or satisfaction about the change in her client's fortunes; but she had remained completely impassive, apparently focused intently on every word that Stepanov was saying, without any overt display of emotion. Probably just good manners, he concluded. She must be waiting until Stepanov had gone and Baxter left them alone before dinner. They could talk then.

Paula van Harten had entered the room quietly with a small trolley, from which she unloaded a fresh jug of water, fresh glasses, a new bottle of *jong*, a pot of coffee with cream, and sugar, a plate of *speculaa* biscuits, and a clean ashtray. Having placed them on the table, she withdrew as softly as she had entered.

'Things began to change in the middle years of the 1950s,' Stepanov continued, when they had re-assembled. 'Moscow Centre was always fuelled by paranoia, but never like this. Everyone was under suspicion. Officers were being recalled from abroad, and either subjected to torture and show trials, or simply summary execution. The lucky ones were sent into exile to some God-forsaken city in the middle of nowhere with snow on the ground for most of the year. And these were, as far as anyone knew, loyal and competent people. The future of the Service was uncertain. It was not possible to continue indefinitely under these circumstances. But because of the paranoia, no one seemed to care.'

Baxter had opened the new bottle of *jong*, and was filling the fresh glasses.

'No one outside the top echelons even understood what was going on,' Stepanov said. 'Morale was at rock bottom and we had a lot of defections, but of course, that only increased the paranoia. In 1959, the Comrade Director told me that my relationship with Digby was being called into question. It was thought that the information we were providing was not sufficiently important, and they were worried about the information we were giving to Digby. They had endless questions. Who is he? Why should we trust him? What if he is a double agent? From an intelligence point of view, James had impeccable credentials, but the professionals were not being listened to any more. The professionals employed reason to make their calculations, but paranoia has no time for reason.'

He lit a cigarette and inhaled deeply.

'At the end of 1959, the Comrade Director was removed and sent to live in one of those cities in the middle of nowhere with snow on the ground. A new man was installed as Director, a major from a tank regiment, suddenly promoted to full colonel in the KGB, probably because his wife's uncle was a big noise in the Communist Party, or he was in favour with the Politburo for a few days for betraying one of his colleagues. This man knew nothing of intelligence work and seemed to think that the use of force was the solution to every problem. But so it went at that time.'

He drank deeply of his water, then a shot of jenever.

'James came to the 1960 championship in Leningrad,' he continued, 'and we met as usual at the Hotel Peking. But I had to tell him that our work was now finished, at least until times changed again and Moscow Centre was once more ruled by reason. I advised him against returning to the Soviet Union until then. It would not have been safe for him. It was not safe for me, but I had no choice. After that I lay low. I did not apply for permission to travel to any tournaments abroad in 1961. I continued to teach at the Academy in Moscow, and generally made myself useful to the Soviet Chess Federation. I translated one or two chess books into German for the Soviet Foreign Languages Publishing House. Every day I waited for the knock on the door which would indicate that the Directorate considered me to be a traitor.'

He lowered his head down on to the table and covered it with his hands for some time. Ginny looked at Baxter, but he shook his head. Eventually, Stepanov lifted his head again.

'The knock never actually came,' he said. 'Apparently, the good major-turned-colonel had a limited attention span, and it took him most of his time just to keep up with developments in his Directorate. But it was just a matter of time. I had not been forgotten altogether, and some good friends advised me that my safety could not be guaranteed for long. So, in 1962, I applied for permission to travel to Varna, Bulgaria, for the Chess Olympiad to assist the Soviet team as a translator and interpreter. As often happens in the Soviet Union, the left hand had no idea what the right hand was doing, and whatever suspicion may have attached to me within the Directorate, no one thought that my application to travel to Varna posed any problem. I had a good record for being useful at international tournaments.'

He paused for some time.

'We sometimes take decisions without being in possession of all the facts, or knowing what the consequences will be. Sometimes we are just in the right place at the right time. By now, I was sure that they would come for me eventually, and I was desperate. If I had been in the West, I would have made a run for it. I would have tried to defect immediately – I would have gone to the local police or some friendly embassy, asked for political asylum, whatever I could do – and without proper planning, the result would probably have been catastrophic.'

Baxter refilled his glass.

'As it was,' he said, 'I found myself importuning an American. He was a college professor of political science who spoke good Russian, and he did for the American teams at these events what I did for the Soviets. So we had met during negotiations from time to time, and he was the only American I felt able to approach. Certainly, I could not approach any member of their team. His name is Francis Hollander.'

He smiled wryly.

'I acted completely recklessly, irresponsibly. I threw whatever tradecraft I had to the winds. I almost dragged him out of the tournament hall during a quiet moment, with no warning at all, to some bar in a backstreet somewhere. It was madness. There were minders everywhere, as always. But somehow, we got away with it. Perhaps it was because we were so direct about it. Perhaps it was so blatant that they assumed it was just tournament business. In any case, we sat at a corner table, and I begged him to speak to the American authorities about allowing me to defect. I knew that I had to offer him something of value if there was to be any chance that he would take me seriously; and so I told him the whole story about what had been going on between Digby and myself – well, actually, *almost* the whole story. Desperate as I was, I realised that I must keep something back, so I refused to divulge the details of what our work had accomplished in terms of the loss of western agents. I said that I would reveal that only to the CIA once I was safely out of the Soviet Union. He listened to what I had to say in complete silence. For some time I thought I had failed to persuade him. But then, he promised that he would speak to the CIA when he returned to the United States. I gave him my address and telephone number. We invented a cover story to explain our visit to the bar, something to do with the order of the matches to be played, and we avoided each other for the rest of the tournament.'

Baxter leaned forward with his arms on the table.

'And there,' he said, 'I am afraid I must draw the line. All I will tell you is that the CIA were considerably more interested in Viktor than they led Professor Hollander to believe. They contacted my department. There was then a joint operation between the CIA and our Service, to extract him from the Soviet Union. The details of that operation are, and will remain, secret. Suffice it to say that, fortunately, it was successful.'

'But the Soviets would have realised eventually that the bird had flown the coop,' Ginny said. 'They would have waited a while before declaring that he died in respectable circumstances; but in the meantime he had been given asylum in the Netherlands, with a new identity. And here we are today.'

'I didn't say that he had been granted asylum in the Netherlands,' Baxter pointed out. 'The Hague is easily accessible by train from a variety of countries in western Europe.'

Ginny smiled. 'Of course.'

'Are there any more questions?' Baxter asked.

Ben shook his head.

'No. Thank you,' Ginny added.

They stood and shook hands all round.

'I must ask one thing,' Stepanov said, as he was about to leave the living room. 'It sounds rather strange, no doubt. But I would like to pass on my best wishes to both parties in this case. I owe my life, everything, to Francis, of course. It is a debt I can never repay. But to James also I owe much. I always liked James. I hope very much that nothing bad will happen to him. If you have any influence at all, I hope you will intercede for him in some way. He has done some things which it is difficult for those in his country to forgive. I know that. But he is an honest man, and you don't meet so many honest men any more.'

* * *

'Would I be right in thinking that Kurt Weber is not the actual name he is using?' Ben asked.

'He is using it today,' Baxter replied blandly.

Ben laughed.

'All right. But you have given us a lot of information. Miss Castle and I have to go back and help our clients make some major decisions. Is there any evidence of identification I can take back to them? That's the first question they are going to ask – how do we know it was Stepanov we met?'

Baxter picked up his briefcase from the floor and took out a passport.

'Soviet passport in the name of Viktor Stepanov issued in 1958,' he announced, handing it to Ben open at the page bearing the photograph. 'It is genuine. You can believe me, or not, as you choose, Mr Schroeder, but it was the first thing we checked when we took him out of Russia. You can count on that. We had to satisfy ourselves that he was who he said he was. Our experts went over it with a fine tooth comb. It is the real thing.'

He waited for Ben and Ginny to examine it as thoroughly as they wished.

'Besides,' he said, 'you know the man you met today is Viktor Stepanov. You know that without my having to tell you.'

He took the passport back.

'Well, we have some time before dinner,' he said. 'Why don't I leave you two alone until then? I'm sure you have a few things to talk about. After all, I've done all I can now. The rest is up to you.'

* * *

Ben stood slowly and walked back to the window, looking out into the street. Ginny watched him for some time, then pushed her chair back, stood and walked quietly over to join him.

'I'm sorry, Ben.'

He turned to look at her.

'I'm not. We did the right thing.'

'Yes.'

'If we had not heard this evidence, Digby would have won his case next week, and Hollander would have been ruined, just for speaking the truth.'

They were silent for some time. She put her hand on his shoulder.

'But I am sorry for you, Ben. Digby betrayed you, didn't he? You, Bernard, Herbert Harper, all of you.'

'We are the least of his betrayals,' Ben replied quietly.

57

Once Baxter had left with the signed forms, it took Ben Schroeder slightly more than forty minutes to relate the details of his trip to The Hague, and summarise the evidence provided by the man who had been introduced as Viktor Stepanov. He was not interrupted once. When he finished, a tense, shocked silence permeated Bernard Wesley's room. Wesley had turned his chair almost half way around, partly so that he could look out of his window over the Middle Temple Garden, and partly so that he could avoid looking at James Digby. Digby sat in front of Wesley's desk, leaning forward, his hands on his knees, his head hanging down. His face was white, and he was breathing heavily. Herbert Harper sat next to Digby. Ben was sitting beside Barratt Davis to the side of Wesley's desk. Wesley slowly returned his chair to its original position.

'Extraordinary,' Herbert Harper said. Another period of silence followed.

'Well, I think we can all agree that this changes the landscape,' Wesley said eventually. 'Is there anything you want to say about this, James?'

It took Digby almost a minute to reply.

'It's impossible,' he replied, trying unsuccessfully to control the tremor in his voice, 'quite impossible. Viktor Stepanov is dead. You've seen his obituary. Even Hollander says he is dead.'

'It appears that Hollander may have been misinformed,' Wesley said.

'It appears,' Ben said, 'that Stepanov's alleged death from heart failure was a story put out by the Russians after a decent interval, to cover their embarrassment.'

'Says who?' Digby protested. 'MI6?'

Ben nodded. 'Losing a grandmaster through defection to the West is one of their worst nightmares under any circumstances. But it was even worse in Stepanov's case. Stepanov knew too much. He had a lot of very sensitive information. They had to assume he would blow their entire network in England and the United States wide open.'

'Of course, someone in MI6 or the CIA was bound to realise his potential,' Wesley said.

'Yes,' Ben replied. 'Baxter wouldn't give me any details, of course. But he told me that MI6 engaged in a joint extraction operation with the CIA. As soon as Hollander returned from the Varna Olympiad, he went to the CIA and told them that Stepanov wanted to defect, just as he wrote in his article. The CIA was grateful to Hollander for the information, but they kept him in the dark about their plans, for obvious reasons. Viktor Stepanov was dead to Hollander anyway, and to the world of chess, as soon as he left Moscow. He would become Kurt Weber, or whoever he is now. But the CIA saw immediately that Stepanov might have a lot to tell them about the leakage of information to Moscow which had been going on for several years, so they proposed to MI6 that they cooperate in getting him safely out of Moscow, re-settling him somewhere in the West, and debriefing him at leisure when he was safe. They thought that justified what must have been a very risky operation. I don't see any reason not to believe Baxter about that.'

There was another silence.

'Mr Schroeder, did Baxter show you any evidence of identification of Stepanov?' Herbert Harper asked.

Ben nodded. 'A Soviet passport in Stepanov's name, with his photograph and signature.'

'All of which can easily be forged,' Digby snorted, still struggling to breathe evenly. 'I saw many documents of that kind during the War, which were plausible at first glance, but which turned out to be false on closer examination. Any security service could fabricate such a document.'

Ben exhaled deeply.

'Baxter said that they went to great lengths to authenticate it,' he replied. 'That makes sense to me. They would have to make sure they knew who they were dealing with.'

He looked directly at Bernard Wesley.

'Bernard, I suppose I can't rule out entirely the possibility that MI6 involved myself and Ginny Castle in an elaborate charade: taking us all the way to The Hague to meet a man who is falsely claiming to be Viktor Stepanov; producing a false passport to support his claim; allowing the man to tell us a pack of lies about recruiting James to be a spy, and then collaborating with him to exchange stolen information over a number of years. But I can't think of a good reason why they would do so.'

'Neither can I,' Bernard Wesley said.

Digby affected a look of anger, but remained silent.

'Well,' Herbert Harper began slowly, 'I suppose MI6 might have their own reasons for wanting to build a case against James, if they suspect him of carrying information to Russia during all those chess tournaments.'

Barratt Davis sat up in his chair.

'In that case, why not just arrest him?' he asked. 'If they think this evidence from Stepanov, or whoever he is, will stand up, why haven't they at least brought James in to be interrogated? It doesn't make sense.'

'In addition to that,' Ben added, 'there are two good reasons to assume that the man we met is Stepanov. First, his story explains the documentary evidence we were given previously. Those documents suggested a link between James's visits to Moscow every year, and the pattern of bad things happening to western agents behind the Iron Curtain. Until now, we were able to write that off as a coincidence. We can't do that any more. Stepanov provides the link, doesn't he? In fact, Stepanov would be the most likely source of the evidence, wouldn't he? MI6 gave us the documents, hoping that they would result in some settlement of the case. It didn't work, so now they are filling in the gaps for us. I think the message they are sending is rather clear.'

'They are pulling the wool over your eyes,' Digby replied. He was almost shouting. 'Can't you see that?'

Ben did not reply.

'You said there was a second reason, Ben,' Wesley said.

Ben nodded.

'We recognised him from his photograph, even before we saw the passport,' Ben replied. 'Ginny recognised him the moment he walked through the door, even though he has grown a beard and a moustache.'

Wesley smiled.

'I don't doubt that you were both convinced,' he said, 'but we all know how dangerous evidence of visual identification can be.'

Ben shook his head vigorously.

'Both Ginny and I know that, Bernard,' he replied, 'and yet we are both sure of what we saw. And think about this for a moment: the odds of finding someone who looked so exactly like Stepanov, and who would be willing to live the life he is living would be unbelievably small. Whoever this man is, he is exposing himself to all kinds of danger.'

'From whom?' Digby objected. 'The Russians know that Stepanov is dead, whether he died from a heart attack, or whether they killed him themselves. Whoever this man is, he poses no threat to them.'

'On the contrary,' Ben replied. 'I believe the Russians know perfectly well that Stepanov is alive, and that he poses a great danger to them'.

'If Stepanov is in fact dead, James,' Wesley said, 'we have to explain why MI6 is spending so much effort, not to mention a considerable amount of money, on this elaborate charade.'

'There was something else, too,' Ben said quietly.

'Go on.'

He turned to Digby.

'Well, I have already told you what he said about recruiting you in The Hague. What I didn't tell you was how detailed his account was; the detail he gave about your meetings in the Hotel des Indes; about a long walk you took together late at night in The Hague; about what you told him during that walk.'

'Indeed?' Digby sounded almost indignant. 'And what exactly did he say about that?'

'He said that you talked about your bitterness about not being free to play chess professionally; your concerns about the lack of social justice in Britain; and about the death of your brother Roger in Spain; that these were all reasons you gave him for being willing to work for the Soviets.'

'Anyone could have told him about those things,' Digby insisted. 'I have never made any secret of any of that.' But he had taken a little too long to reply; his moment had passed. A long silence ensued. Herbert Harper eventually broke it.

'Bernard, I suppose there is no reason why we couldn't ask for the Soviet passport to be examined by an independent expert?' he suggested. 'I know Customs and Excise have experts who examine passports all the time. They must see Soviet passports regularly enough.'

Wesley nodded, as if to indicate that he did not disagree with what Harper had said, but he did not reply.

'Or we could ask that they allow James to be confronted with this man,' Harper added.

'I think it was fairly clear from what Baxter told us,' Ben said, 'that they would not allow that.'

'They will have to allow it if Hollander calls him as a witness,' Harper replied.

Wesley shook his head.

'I think not' he said. 'They have already persuaded Mr Justice Melrose that he has a duty to conduct the trial *in camera* while any sensitive evidence is given. This afternoon, Miles may persuade the Court of Appeal that he ought to hold the whole trial *in camera*. In any case, I assume that the judge would have no difficulty in allowing sensitive witnesses to give evidence from behind a screen of some kind.'

'That would not preclude having him properly identified,' Harper pointed out. 'Perhaps we should apply yet again to re-open that question.'

'Perhaps,' Wesley said. 'What do you think about that idea, James?'

The question was asked sharply, abruptly. Harper looked expectantly at his client. But Digby bowed his head again and did not reply.

'Well, would you at least care to deny what this man, whoever he was, told Ben?'

Digby sat up in his chair, raised his head, and looked away, in an apparent attempt to suggest that denying such allegations was beneath his dignity.

* * *

'I see,' Bernard Wesley said quietly.

For a considerable time, no one spoke.

Barratt Davis stood and walked slowly to the window to the left of Wesley's desk.

'I would like to put forward a suggestion about where we should go from here,' he said. 'I don't think it goes too far outside my role of keeping an eye on things from a criminal point of view.'

Wesley spread his arms out in front of him above his desk.

'By all means,' he said.

'I think Ben is correct in saying that Baxter is trying to send us a message – on behalf of those he works for, of course,' Barratt began. 'What we have to do is to make sure we interpret that message correctly. I don't believe that they have any interest in the outcome of the case as such, in terms of whether there is a settlement or not. I believe that what they are agonising over is whether they want to try to prosecute James. They may be less assured about their ability to keep it all quiet in a criminal court, and they may be uncertain about whether they have enough evidence. There may even be questions from on high about whether this kind of prosecution is desirable at all. It seems to me, from the way they are dealing with this, that they are balanced on a knife edge, and are waiting to see how the civil case ends before they make a decision.'

Wesley nodded. 'Go on.'

'If we look at what has happened recently,' Barratt continued, 'it would be possible to argue that the policy of prosecuting everyone ruthlessly, as in the cases of Lonsdale, Blake and Vassall, has been counter-productive, except for the satisfaction of putting them behind bars. We know that those prosecutions have led to a further loss of confidence in the intelligence services. The Government may well be feeling that the satisfaction of putting spies behind bars is not worth the price of falling confidence.'

'Are you suggesting,' Herbert Harper asked, 'that if we were to abandon the case, it might influence the Government not to prosecute?'

'It might,' Barratt replied. 'In any case, I don't see that we have anything left to lose. I agree with Ben; it is very unlikely that this new evidence is all a huge fraud by MI6; that they have spent all this money and gone to all this trouble for the sole purpose of sowing the seeds of doubt and confusion in our camp. I think we flatter ourselves if we believe that. The strong probability is that Viktor Stepanov is alive and well and that he has told them all about it.'

He paused.

'Hollander has his evidence. This case has slipped away,

gentlemen. It is time to accept that it is no longer a case we can win. The only remaining question is how badly we are going to lose. It is time to focus on a way of limiting the damage, a way of salvaging whatever we can from the wreckage.'

'I agree that we must do all we can to prevent James from being prosecuted,' Bernard Wesley said, after a long pause. 'But I am reluctant to commit myself to throwing our hand in without knowing more. Unfortunately, I don't see any way of testing the waters except by opening up a direct line of communication with someone very high up in the Home Office. That would be a very dangerous thing to do, because if they are minded to prosecute, we would be playing into their hands, and there would be no way back.'

'I agree,' Barratt said. 'But I think there may be another approach.'

Every eye in the room turned to him.

'Consider the case of Kim Philby,' he said.

Digby looked away into space.

'Details are hard to come by,' Barratt continued, 'but over the years, they had their eye on Philby. We all know that. Yet, all the signs are that he was allowed to disappear from Beirut rather than being taken into custody. It may be that the information he provided satisfied them; or it may be that they didn't have the stomach for another trial. I come back again to the fact that James has not been arrested, despite the evidence we know they have, whether that evidence came from Stepanov or from anyone else.'

Wesley stared down at his desk for some time.

'So, you are proposing that we abandon the case in an effort to deflect a prosecution? I take it you are not suggesting that James should offer to talk to the authorities?'

'I do wish you would stop talking about me as if I am not here,' Digby protested, but without conviction. The others in the room ignored him.

'No,' Barratt replied. 'Without knowing what the Government's intentions are, that would be far too risky. I am proposing that we throw our hand in, but in very specific circumstances. I take it that the trial is still listed to begin tomorrow morning at 10.30?'

'Yes.'

'Then,' Barratt said, 'I suggest that we abandon ship at 10.30 tomorrow morning, and not a moment before.'

'I don't understand,' Herbert Harper said. 'If we are ready to concede, surely it would be better for me to call Julia Cathermole without delay. Why …?'

Barratt did not reply. He smiled grimly in the direction of James Digby, who met his gaze for some seconds before turning away abruptly.

'Am I mistaken, Barratt?' Digby asked slowly, deliberately avoiding Barratt's eyes. 'Or am I hearing the gentle strains of the *Nunc Dimittis*?'

'I have said as much as I want to say, James,' Barratt replied. 'What you hear is a matter entirely for you.'

58

'I regret to say, My Lord, that I am unable to answer your Lordship's question.'

Bernard Wesley was standing before Mr Justice Melrose in the Silks' row in his courtroom at the Royal Courts of Justice. A notice attached to the outside door of the court informed the reader that the trial in the case of *Digby v Hollander, the Secretary of State for the Home Department Intervening* was taking place within, but that the trial was closed to the public, and that no one who was not involved in the case was permitted to enter. Despite the private setting, Mr Justice Melrose had ordered that robes be worn as usual. He was brightly arrayed in the red robes and white ermine of a judge of the Queen's Bench Division of the High Court. Ben Schroeder sat behind Wesley in the row reserved for junior counsel. Behind Ben sat Herbert Harper and Barratt Davis, wearing dark suits. To Wesley's left, Miles Overton sat, with Ginny Castle behind him and, behind Ginny, Julia Cathermole and Professor Hollander, wearing his usual academic uniform, a brown suit with a polka-dot bow tie. Between Ben and Ginny sat Evan Roberts, and behind him two dark-suited men, with official black briefcases bearing the Royal Coat of Arms on the floor at their feet. No one else was present except the Judge's associate, who acted as court clerk, and a court reporter.

Mr Justice Melrose had just asked Bernard Wesley why his client, Sir James Masefield Digby QC, was not present for the scheduled start of the trial at 10.30. It was a question to which Wesley had no answer of his own personal knowledge, and about which he was not prepared to speculate for the benefit of the court.

'There is no reason known why Sir James is not present?'

'There is no known reason, my Lord. I last saw Sir James

yesterday morning, when we had our final consultation before trial. My learned junior and my instructing solicitors were present also. Sir James was, of course, well aware of the date and time fixed for the trial. My instructing solicitors have been in contact with the clerk at his chambers, and with his home address, but with no success.'

'Are you applying for an adjournment for a short time to permit further inquiries to be made?'

'No, my Lord.'

Mr Justice Melrose was visibly perplexed. Litigants and witnesses often ran late for a variety of reasons – they might be held up in traffic, they might have problems with public transport, occasionally they might be taken ill; the delays that resulted were frustrating but were an inevitable part of the life of any court, and the court would accommodate them to a reasonable extent. If, on the other hand, a party or witness deliberately absented himself from a trial, the court's attitude was necessarily very different, and the results were likely to be unpleasant. The judge had expected Bernard Wesley to ask for an adjournment, at least until later in the morning and, if further information came to light, perhaps until later in the day, or even the following day. The fact that Wesley made no such application could only mean that he did not expect Digby to attend, or had no reason to think that he would. But that did not make sense. It was an extraordinary situation. Hollander's article had made the gravest of allegations against Digby. Digby's action for libel had been his only possible remedy, and today was to be his day in court. The judge had the uncomfortable feeling that he was not being told the whole story. For a judge, that was a feeling which was not exactly unknown; indeed, it came with the territory. But this was an extraordinary case by any standards. He felt he had to make at least one more attempt.

'Are you quite sure you do not want to make any application, Mr Wesley?' he asked, trying his best, not altogether convincingly, to sound menacing.

'Quite sure, my Lord.'

Wesley sat down. The judge looked towards Miles Overton, who stood immediately.

'Mr Overton, do you have any application?'

'I do, my Lord,' he replied immediately. 'As the Plaintiff has failed to appear to pursue his case at the time appointed for trial, and as your Lordship has been offered no prospect that he is likely to appear, I ask that the Statement of Claim be struck out and judgment given for the Defendant.'

Wesley stood.

'I do not oppose the application, my Lord.'

To his own amazement, Mr Justice Melrose heard himself make an order in the terms Overton had proposed.

'I further ask that the Plaintiff be ordered to pay the Defendant's costs,' Overton added.

'I cannot resist that application,' Wesley replied.

The judge bowed to counsel and retired to his chambers to contemplate how odd life on the bench could sometimes be, and to reflect on the far less interesting case the list office would doubtless find for him now that the exotic case of *Digby v Hollander, the Secretary of State for the Home Department Intervening* had ended.

* * *

'Thank you, Mr Overton, thank you, Miss Castle,' Hollander said, offering his hand to each in turn. 'I will always be in your debt.'

They were standing, with Julia Cathermole, next to a large Gothic pillar in the hallway outside the courtroom.

'Well, I'm not sure we really did very much,' Overton smiled. 'You seem to have had – what is it you say in America? – all the bases covered.'

Hollander laughed. Julia thought he already looked five years younger, now that the weight of the case had dropped from his shoulders.

'That was Julia,' he said, 'and her friends in the intelligence services. Nothing to do with me. I came here with no evidence at all.'

'But you always believed the evidence would come, didn't you?' Ginny asked. 'Why was that? What gave you that confidence?'

Hollander shrugged.

'I believed implicitly what Stepanov had told me. Look, I don't really know anything about intelligence work. But I have spent some time behind the Iron Curtain in connection with chess, and behind the Iron Curtain you just get a feeling for certain things. Stepanov was desperate to defect. I have had hints dropped on other occasions. It's not unusual when you are around Russians. So many of them want out. But it's always by innuendo – how beautiful they have heard America is; do you consider yourself fortunate to have been born in America? – that kind of thing; always indirect, nothing that could come back to haunt them.'

He leaned back against the pillar.

'But not this guy. This guy drags me out of the tournament to some crummy bar, in God only knows what district of Varna – it reminded me of some joint on the South Side in Chicago, but without the glamour. That in itself was crazy. The Soviets had minders everywhere, as they do at every international event. Just talking to foreigners can get you into trouble unless there is a clear reason related to chess. Stepanov didn't care about any of that. Maybe he took steps to shake the minders off – I guess he must have done – but he got me on my own in a bar, and there was nothing indirect about it. This guy was not dealing in hints or innuendos.'

He paused for a moment, shaking his head.

'He came right out and told me that his life was in danger and he wanted to defect. He explained why. He told me the whole story of his involvement with Digby, from day one, when he recruited him in The Hague. You didn't have to be an intelligence officer to know that he was deadly serious. He had not only come out and asked me whether I could help him to defect. He had entrusted me with almost everything he had to bargain with. I have to think that was because he knew the CIA would be interested and, in all honesty, I think he believed it was the only chance he had.'

'And when Francis had duly delivered the message, the CIA didn't even have the decency to tell him that Stepanov was alive and free,' Julia added in disgust.

'Baxter said there were security reasons for that,' Ginny said. 'It does make sense.'

'Until the operation had been carried out, absolutely,' Julia replied. 'Of course, you wouldn't breathe a word until then. But once Stepanov was free, they could have told him. They wouldn't tell him where he was or what name he was using, obviously. There would be no question of Francis meeting Stepanov again. But to keep him in the dark – especially after Stepanov's death had been reported – there was no call for that.'

'You assumed that the Russians had done him in, of course?'

Overton asked. 'You didn't believe the heart attack story for a moment, I imagine?'

Hollander shook his head.

'It was one coincidence too many,' he replied. 'That's what made me feel so badly about it and, I suppose, what put the idea for the article in my head.'

'You felt the world should know?'

'I was angry that Digby had got so many people killed, and now, for all I knew, he had added Stepanov to his list of victims. So I decided to put it out there.'

'You always believed that the truth would come out, didn't you,' Julia asked, 'despite everything?'

'Yes. I knew you had contacts with the British intelligence services, and I had to believe that my article could not go unnoticed on both sides of the Atlantic. I didn't go into all the detail, of course. I didn't want to tip Digby off that I knew about the code with the chess board and pieces. I figured that might be a useful detail to come up with later.'

'How right you were,' Overton smiled. 'But apparently Viktor Stepanov beat you to it.'

'Knowing he is alive is even better than winning the case,' Hollander said.

He looked at Julia for a few moments.

'I suppose there really is no chance that I could ...?'

She was shaking her head vigorously.

'No. I guess not. I knew that. Well, I am glad it worked out for him.'

'You knew that Digby wasn't going to appear this morning, didn't you?' Miles Overton asked suddenly.

'Let's say I had a shrewd idea,' Hollander grinned.

'He was never going to come to court,' Ginny said. 'Not once he heard from Stepanov from beyond the grave.'

'I told you,' Hollander said. 'It was Oscar Wilde all over again. The only difference is that Digby saw what was coming and bailed out before it hit him. If it wasn't for that he would be playing chess in Reading Gaol pretty soon.'

'As it is,' Ginny observed, 'we will probably be hearing about his new life in Moscow after a decent interval.'

'You can count on it,' Hollander said. 'They will be running pictures of his press conference in the *Daily Mirror* in a few months from now.'

They stood in silence together for some time, and then shook hands again. Miles Overton and Ginny Castle turned to leave for the robing room. But Miles suddenly turned back.

'What are your future plans, Professor Hollander?' he asked. 'Do you intend to continue in academia, or have you set your sights on something more in the public eye, now that you have had a taste of the limelight? Your passion for the truth is unusual in this day and age. The American public would benefit from it.'

Hollander laughed.

'Now that you mention it, Mr Overton,' he replied, 'I have given some thought to politics. I have a few contacts in the Democratic Party. It has occurred to me that I might have a shot at running for Congress in a year or two. And I really think I would enjoy being Governor of my State somewhere down the road. I'm not sure whether I could make it, but ...'

'I wouldn't bet against you,' Ginny said.

59

When Ben arrived back in chambers, he dutifully reported to the clerks' room.

'Thank you for coming back, Mr Schroeder,' Merlin said cheerfully. 'But if I were you, sir, I would have yourself a nice long weekend, starting now. You have worked hard on this case, and I am sure the outcome has been a bit of a shock. You have earned it.'

'Are you sure you don't need me?'

'No, sir. If anything urgent comes up, I've got Mr Weston available. You can take that set of papers in your pigeon-hole with you in case you get bored. It's for next Monday morning, Inner London Sessions, three counts of burglary. Hopeless case by the look of it, but the solicitors say he is determined to fight it. Oh, and there's a letter for you in the pigeon-hole too, from Middle Temple. Enjoy your weekend, sir. I will see you next week.'

Ben gratefully accepted his senior clerk's advice. He collected his letter and brief and walked to the door.

'Thank you, Merlin,' he said, turning to leave. On opening the door of the clerks' room, he almost collided with two men wearing uniforms bearing the Middle Temple coat of arms, one carrying a tall ladder. They were walking quickly towards the main door to chambers. One of them muttered an apology, but did not slow down at all. Ben turned back towards Merlin.

'Who are they?' he asked.

Merlin shrugged. 'They're from the Inn, sir, a Mr Whitehead, and I forget the other fellow's name. Something to do with pest control. Apparently they left some equipment here before when there was an infestation, and they just called to take it away.'

***

Ben made his way back to his flat in Canonbury. He opened the door and went into the living room, where Jess sat at the dining table. To her right were two glasses and a bottle of Chablis in an ice bucket. She leapt to her feet to hug and kiss him.

He smiled.

'You seem to have been expecting me,' he said. 'Obviously the news got through.'

'Barratt called me to tell me what happened,' she replied. 'He didn't have any plans for me, and I didn't think you would be doing any more work today, so I thought I would pick up a bottle of something nice and be here to welcome you. In the circumstances, it's not exactly a celebration, I suppose, but ...'

He kissed her.

'Thank you,' he said. He poured a glass for each of them, and they toasted each other.

He put his glass down on the table.

'Actually, we do have something to celebrate.'

'Oh?'

'It's official.'

He had put his briefcase down by the door when he came in. He walked over to retrieve it, sat down at the table balancing it on his knee, opened it, and removed a letter with an envelope which had already been torn open. He handed it to Jess without a word. She sat next to him and read the letter. It was dated two days earlier and bore the distinctive crest of the Middle Temple, the *Agnus Dei*.

Dear Schroeder,

The Committee appointed to consider the circumstances of your relationship with Miss Jess Farrar has concluded that there is no evidence to suggest that any conduct is involved which would in any way constitute a breach of the Code of Conduct for the Bar. Nor does the Committee consider that any criticism can be made either of you or Miss Farrar. Accordingly, you may consider this matter closed.

Yours sincerely,
Master George Kenney
Committee Chairman

She shook her head. 'Those arrogant …' she allowed her voice to trail away. 'I don't want to consider the matter closed. I want to …'

He took her hand.

'I know,' he said. 'But we need to let it go.'

She nodded. 'Yes,' she said.

'I am sure Ginny has the same letter,' Ben said.

'I'm glad for her, and for Michael,' Jess said.

She released his hand and looked down at the table.

'Ben, I need to apologise to you,' she said quietly.

'For what?'

'For the way I've been treating you while this whole thing has been going on. I've been treating you as if this were all your fault. It's not, and it never has been. It's the fault of all those stupid old men who are still living in the eighteenth century. I made you feel bad because I tried to put you on the spot about what you would do if it went the wrong way. I shouldn't have done that. I'm really sorry.'

He took her hand again and leaned across to kiss her on the cheek.

'It's all right,' he replied. 'If anyone is to blame, I am. I know it sounded as if I expected you to give up your job with Barratt, and there is no reason why you should.'

'There was every reason,' she replied. 'The job with Bourne & Davis was never meant to be more than a break while I decided what to do with my life. I was wrong to compare it with your career at the Bar.'

'But you took to it. You are even thinking of becoming a solicitor,' Ben pointed out.

She shook her head.

'Not any more,' she said.

'Oh?'

She refilled their glasses.

'Yes, I've realised that's not what I want to do with my life. If this business with the Middle Temple had gone the wrong way, I would have left Bourne & Davis. Actually, I'm going to, anyway; not immediately, so don't say anything to Barratt, but it won't be too long.'

'Really? Does that mean you have decided on a career?' he asked.

'Yes,' she replied. 'I'm going to read for the Bar.'

She watched Ben's utterly blank face for several seconds before clapping her hands together and laughing uproariously.

'You should see your face,' she said affectionately. 'It's a real picture.'

He was staring at her, expecting her to protest that she had been joking. She did not.

'Are you serious?' he asked eventually.

'Perfectly,' she replied. 'I've spent quite a while following Barratt Davis around now and watching barristers in action, and I have concluded that, present company honourably excepted, I could do the job at least as well.'

She laughed again.

'What's the matter? Afraid of the competition?'

'No …,' he protested, joining in her laughter.

'Well, you needn't worry. I wouldn't want to do crime. I want to do family law, or perhaps personal injury – something that allows me to help people in a crisis.'

He raised his glass.

'I'll drink to that,' he said.

Her laughter suddenly drained away.

'Ben, do you think I'm mad?' she asked. 'Am I getting ideas above my station?'

'No,' he replied firmly. He kissed her. 'I think it's a wonderful idea. You must join Middle Temple, of course, even if it is populated by stupid old men from the eighteenth century.'

'It will give us an excuse for having dinner together,' she pointed out.

They drank their wine companionably for some time.

'Jess, there's something else I wanted to talk to you about,' he said.

She looked up inquiringly.

'All this going to and fro from my place to yours, you going to and fro from yours to mine – it's starting to get a bit much.'

'Yes, I know,' she replied.

'So, what I was thinking was …' he hesitated, 'if you are ready, we should look for a place together, somewhere bigger, where we will be comfortable. We could avoid all the travelling, we could spend more time together, and …'

She kissed him.

'I am ready,' she replied simply.

They held each other without speaking for a long time.

'Then, of course, we will have to face our next challenge,' she said.

He nodded.

'Yes.'

'Your family.'

'Yes.' He paused. 'Jess, I am sure they like you.'

'They have met me twice,' she replied, 'the first time during an emergency situation, when your grandfather had his heart attack and I drove you home from Huntingdon; the second time when I came home with you for a party. On those two occasions, it didn't matter that I'm not Jewish. But it will from now on.'

He kissed her again.

'I promise you, Jess, I will not allow that to come between us.'

'I know,' she replied. 'But I don't want to be the cause of strife in your family, and I don't want to live on bad terms with them.'

'You won't,' he promised. 'I really don't think it will come to that.'

He paused and smiled.

'We've dealt with the eighteenth-century old men at Middle Temple,' he replied. 'We will deal with my family if we need to.'

60

Moscow
11 December, 1965

Bernard Wesley Esq, QC
2 Wessex Buildings
Temple
London EC4

My dear Bernard,

I won't apologise for not turning up for the trial. I am sure you
didn't expect me. Perhaps I should have stayed and faced the
music. Perhaps that would have been the right thing to do. But I
couldn't see that any useful purpose would be served by allowing
myself to be locked up for the rest of my life. That is what would
have happened, isn't it? They would have prosecuted me and I
would have rotted away in prison, watching from behind bars as
Britain's privileged élite continue to ignore the inevitable march of
history, and carry on as they always have. I am not naïve enough
to think that I can do much about that from where I am now, but
I certainly couldn't from some cell in Wandsworth.

Please don't think that I am ungrateful to you or Herbert, or
to Ben and Barratt. On the contrary, I appreciate the candour
with which you all dealt with me, which was not always
comfortable at the time, but was in the end the only thing that
saved me. Of course, I particularly appreciate Barratt's subtle
Nunc Dimittis, which confirmed me in a course of action I
already knew was inevitable. I regret that I could not thank you
all in person. That, obviously, was out of the question. Once the
decision had been taken to extract me, I was not allowed to see
anyone, even Bridget. I was whisked away very efficiently, if in a

somewhat roundabout manner. I can't talk about the details, of course, but there was no doubt about my ultimate destination.

They say I can get back in touch with Bridget soon. They may even bring her over to join me in a year or so, when the fuss has died down a bit and it can be done quietly. I don't know whether she will come. I have betrayed her greatly. I have left her with the care of our London house and the estate, without enough money to manage; and we have no child, no heir, to hold us together. She has ties to England which do not involve me; her parents are growing old. In truth, I can think of little reason why she would give up England to come to live with me in these circumstances in Moscow. But I have always loved her, and so I hope against hope that she will.

They have made good on the promises they made when I first agreed to work with them. They are giving me a teaching role in the Chess Academy, teaching not only chess theory, but also English and German; at last, knowledge of foreign languages is beginning to be seen as a valuable skill, rather than evidence of sedition or disaffection. I have picked up a fair amount of Russian over the years, and I have been studying the language intensely since I arrived, so I am confident that I can manage for teaching purposes. Chess, in any case, is an international language by means of which teacher and student can communicate with few words. I will be allowed to play in a number of domestic chess tournaments each year; and so, for the first time, I can properly class myself as a professional chess player. It is too late for me now, I think, to aspire to the title of grandmaster, especially as no foreign travel will be allowed, certainly for many years. In any case, judging by the youngsters I see at the Academy, you have to start young these days if you are to scale the heights, and my liberation has not come in time for that.

When I first came into contact with organised socialism, at Cambridge in the early 1930s, there were many men who proudly told everyone who would listen that they would gladly leave England behind to live in Moscow. They regarded Moscow as their spiritual home. But almost all of the men who were loudest in their fervour had never seen Moscow. Their enthusiasm was based on some idealised image of a proletarian paradise, where Marxist principles governed daily life and from which capitalism and class structure had been forever banished. Hardly anyone had seen the reality, which was that Moscow was by then a second-rate European capital, impoverished more than enriched by the Revolution, its capacity to flourish stunted and curtailed by the elementary flaws inherent in Marxist economics. Hardly anyone pictured a city of shortages and poverty; the grey drudge of everyday Muscovite living; the endless queues for bread; the power outages; the phones without lines; the endless cajoling and bribing of self-important bureaucrats; for which a nominal freedom from class oppression is poor compensation. Those who did visit the city found themselves closely guarded, shepherded everywhere from one approved site to the next, visiting and seeing only what was permitted; lest they see too much, and lest the image of the proletarian paradise be sullied.

I myself visited Moscow many times before I came here to live. But visiting the city, however often, cannot prepare you for living in it, for being part of it, for having your fortune inextricably linked to it. As a visitor, you can overlook a great deal, forgive a great deal. When you know that you are to return to the familiar comforts of England within a few days, you can harbour the illusion that the hardships you see are simply the growing pains of a new socialist society seeking to adapt itself to the complex challenges of twentieth-century life. But as a resident, you see the hardships too often and in too many places. As a resident you notice the faces of the people, you hear their voices; and you begin to see that Marxism is just as powerless to create happiness and contentment in the midst of such surroundings as the religions it has sought to replace. In the face of the reality of Moscow in 1965, illusions vanish into thin air almost as soon as they are born. To many of the people, communism is only serfdom under another name, only another chapter in an endless saga of exploitation and misery, and the course of history moves on indifferently without sweeping those things away, despite Marx's promise that it must and would. The Czar has been reborn as the Communist Party, and his henchmen as its henchmen. And so life goes on.

But despite this, Bernard, I have no complaint about being here. I am quite content to be here in my tenth floor flat in a tower block uncomfortably distant from the city centre: the block with its unkempt, smelly corridors, its flaking paint and its soulless graffiti; the flat with its single small bedroom; its small living room; its kitchen in which the power is not always on; its bathroom in which the hot water does not always flow; the view from its windows looking out on a sea of endless grey which seems to suffocate any thought of individualism or originality. I am content, not because I can ignore the reality of life here; but because I prefer, if you will, communist oppression to capitalist oppression, communist misery to capitalist misery; because I believe that here, it can and will get better.

But I was never one of those who couldn't wait to leave England behind to live in the brave new world of Moscow. I never fell prey to the illusion that I would be leaving misery behind and entering paradise. You see, Bernard, I was brought up to love England and, despite my socialist ideals, I have never ceased to love her. My goal in everything I did was not to harm England, not to bring her under a Soviet yoke; but to sweep away those old relics of the past – the social prejudices, the class system, the economic oppression – which hold England back and deprive her people of the freedom to realise their true potential. That is what I wanted to achieve, or help to achieve. I have never wanted to change England's true essence. I hoped to bring about change from within. I never looked for a life anywhere else. England is my home. So for me, my exile is a painful one, one which I did not willingly seek, and one I embrace only because I must. There are days when the thought of never seeing England again drives me to despair. I will miss her every day for the rest of my life.

What do I miss? I miss the estate, where I played so happily with Roger when we were children on those hot summer days. I miss my house in Chelsea, where I lived with Bridget, and which was the chief source of our happiness together. I miss Lincoln's Inn and my chambers, where I found such an enjoyable way of making enough money to live comfortably. I miss the Reform Club, where I last saw Roger alive, and where I have so often enjoyed the company of many good friends. Most of all, I miss Cambridge.

I miss Cambridge because so much of my life was formed

there. I miss it because of the people who surrounded me daily – those bright vibrant people, so full of ideas and so full of life, steeped in academia but also firmly planted in the world. It was there that I grew into my maturity as a chess player and learned the extent and limitations of my talent for the game. It was there that I learned to see chess as, not merely a game, but an art form which in the right hands could help to transform Society; and from this I gained a broader picture of the importance of art and culture in any Society which places the welfare of its people first. It was in Cambridge that I embraced socialism and accepted it as the antidote to fascism and to the injustices I saw in Society. It was where I formed my vision for a new, changed England. It was where I was accepted into the Brotherhood of the Apostles, and learned from them about the freedom to think and to speak out; about friendship and loyalty to one's brothers; about placing that loyalty above all loyalties except that of being true to oneself.

I miss Cambridge, not only for its symbolism in my life, but also for its timeless beauty. I miss the colleges; the simple dignity of the Senate House; the magnificence of King's Chapel; the elegance of the Great Court at Trinity. I miss the river at Grantchester, where at the dawning of a beautiful day I made love to Bridget for the first time, and where we briefly wished we could stay for the rest of our lives. When I look out over the grey concrete of Moscow from the small windows of my flat as the light is fading on a winter afternoon, and realise that I shall never see Cambridge again, it is all I can do to carry on. At those times, some lines come back to me, lines written by Rupert Brooke – a brother Apostle, by the way, in case you didn't know – three years before his death on foreign soil; expressing his yearning for a time that had passed and the city he would never see again.

Say, is there Beauty yet to find?
And Certainty? And Quiet kind?
Deep meadows yet, for to forget
The lies, and truths, and pain?… oh! yet
Stands the Church clock at ten to three?
And is there honey still for tea?

That's all I have to say, really, Bernard. I don't seek any forgiveness or absolution. I don't even ask for understanding. I don't think that will be possible before significant time has elapsed. In a generation or two, the history of our time will have been written, and the world may look rather different by then. At least feelings will have subsided to some extent.

Oh, there is one thing you might do for me, if it's not too much trouble. Could you pass on the enclosed sheet of paper to Professor Hollander, by way of his solicitor?

Thank you.

Yours sincerely,

James Digby

Moscow
11 December, 1965

Dear Professor Hollander,

Please don't be concerned. This isn't in code. There is no hidden
message. It's just a reminder of something beautiful we have in
common. A peace offering of a kind, if you will.

London 1912
White: Edward Lasker
Black: Sir George Thomas

1.	d4	f5		11.	Qxh7+!	Kxh7
2.	e4	fe		12.	Nxf6+	Kh6
3.	Nc3	Nf6		13.	Neg4+	Kg5
4.	Bg5	e6		14.	h4+	Kf4
5.	Nxe4	Be7		15.	g3+	Kf3
6.	Bxf6	Bxf6		16.	Be2+	Kg2
7.	Nf3	0-0		17.	Rh2+	Kg1
8.	Bd3	b6		18.	Kd2++	
9.	Ne5	Bb7				
10.	Qh5	Qe7				

Isn't it wonderful?

Yours sincerely,
James Digby

Author's Acknowledgements

This is a novel. Sir James Digby QC and Professor Francis R Hollander are fictitious characters. But for the purposes of the story, they had to blend into the periods of history and the institutions with which the book is concerned; to participate in certain well-documented events; and to encounter certain well-known historical figures. This inevitably results in some historical anomalies, for which I make no apology. But I have done my best to do justice to those historical institutions, events and figures which feature in the novel – including my Club, the Reform, membership of which I have in common with one or two important figures in my story. To do that required a good deal of research, both about the Cambridge Spies and the world in which they grew up and lived; and about the world of chess, whose fringes I inhabited for a while much earlier in my life. I gratefully acknowledge my debt to the following sources in particular.

Miranda Carter, *Anthony Blunt: His Lives*, Macmillan (London, 2001)

John Fisher, *Burgess and Maclean: A New Look at the Foreign Office Spies*, Robert Hale Limited (London, 1977)

Kim Philby, *My Silent War: The Autobiography of a Spy*, Modern Library, Random House Inc (New York, 1968)

Ben Macintyre, *A Spy among Friends: Kim Philby and the Great Betrayal*, Bloomsbury Publishing PLC (London, 2014)

Richard Deacon, *The Cambridge Apostles: A History of Cambridge University's Elite Intellectual Secret Society*, Robert Royce Limited (London, 1985)

Russell Burlingham and Roger Billis, *Reformed Characters: The Reform Club in History and Literature*, Reform Club (London, 2005)

Antony Beevor, *The Battle for Spain: The Spanish Civil War 1936-1939*, Weidenfeld & Nicolson (London, 2006)

Dr Max Euwe, *Wereld Kampioenschap Schaken 1948*, De Tijdstroom, Lochem (The Netherlands, 1948)

Alexander Kotov and Mikhail Yudovich, *The Soviet School of Chess*, Foreign Languages Publishing House (Moscow, 1958)

Irving Chernev, *1000 Best Short Games of Chess*, Hodder & Stoughton (London, 1957)

It is from Chernev's book that I took the text of Edward Lasker v Sir George Thomas, London 1912. Other sources give a slightly different order for the first few moves. But there is no doubt about the position after 10 ... Qe7, or the magnificent devastation wrought by Lasker beginning with 11. Qxh7+!

About Us

In addition to No Exit Press, Oldcastle Books has a number of other imprints, including Kamera Books, Creative Essentials, Pulp! The Classics, Pocket Essentials and High Stakes Publishing > oldcastlebooks.co.uk

For more information about Crime Books go to > crimetime.co.uk

Check out the kamera film salon for independent, arthouse and world cinema > kamera.co.uk

For more information, media enquiries and review copies please contact Frances > frances@oldcastlebooks.com